焦點英語 閱讀 3

三版 作者 Owain Mckimm / Zachary Fillingham / Laura Phelps / Richard Luhrs　譯者 黃詩韻 / 林育珊 / 邱佳皇

全英文學習訓練英文思維及語感
可調整語速／播放／複誦模式訓練聽力

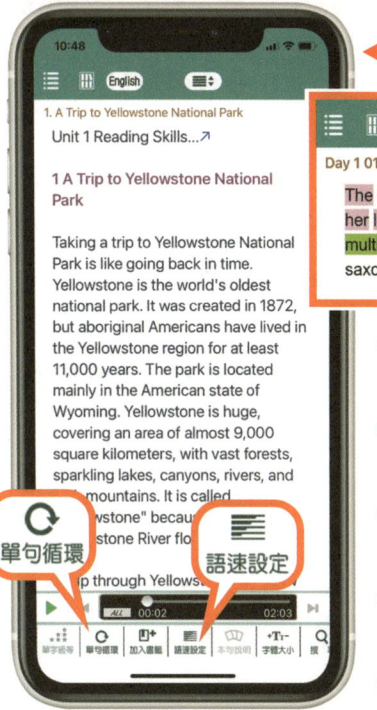

◀ 全文閱讀

◀ 單句閱讀色底表示單字級數

◀ 單句閱讀

單句循環　語速設定

- 標示高中字彙、全民英檢、多益字級，掌握難度，立即理解文章
- 設定自動／循環／範圍播放，訓練聽力超有感
- 設定 7 段語速、複誦間距及次數，扎實訓練聽力
- 設定克漏字比率學習，提高理解力、詞彙量及文法
- 睡眠學習，複習文章幫助記憶

快速查詢字義 理解文章內容

課後閱讀測驗檢驗理解力

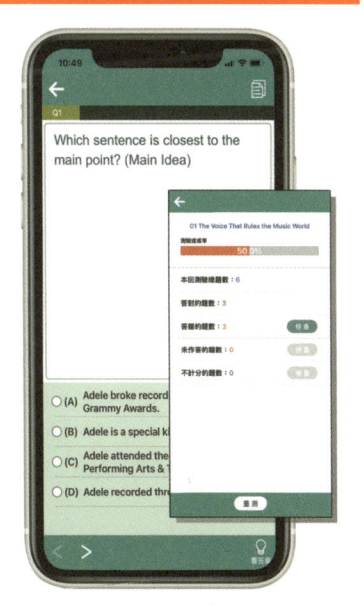

強力口說練習

錄下發音和原音比對辨識，精進口語能力。

單字分析掌握單字力

提供全書總單字量及單字表，掌握單字難易度，針對不熟單字加強學習。

Contents

Introduction 本書簡介……6
How to Use This Book 使用導覽……7

Week 1

Day 1
Animals — 01 The Sweetest Poison 10

Day 2
Business — 02 The Barons Who Built America 12

Day 3
Culture — 03 Growing Up Around the World 14

Day 4
Business — 04 Cradle to Cradle 16

Day 5
Entertainment — 05 Where Giants Walk the Earth 18

Day 6
Arts & Literature — 06 The World of Criminal Graffiti 20

Week 2

Day 1
Animals — 07 Mini Mind Control 24

Day 2
Arts & Literature — 08 Struggle and Genius 26

Day 3
Culture — 09 When the Streets Turn Red 28

Day 4
People — 10 Making His Mark 30

Day 5
Technology — 11 The Magic Mirror 32

Day 6
Animals — 12 The Animal That's Also an Environment 34

Week 3

Day 1
Entertainment — 13 And the Worst Actor Goes To 38

Day 2
Geography — 14 A River of Fire in the Sky 40

Day 3
Animals — 15 The Soft Glow of the Natural World 42

Day 4
History — 16 The Realm of the Khans 44

Day 5
Mystery — 17 The City Lost Under the Sea 46

Day 6
Culture — 18 Celebrating in Color 48

Week 4

Day 1
Geography — 19 Windows Into the Underworld 52

Day 2
Animals — 20 Small but Deadly 54

Day 3
Business — 21 The Bigger They Are the Harder They Fall 56

Day 4
Entertainment — 22 Dancing in the Moonlight 58

Day 5
Geography — 23 A White Ocean 60

Day 6
Health & Body — 24 Hearty French Feasting 62

Week 5

Day 1
Science — 25 Not the Only You? 66

Day 2
Language — 26 Permanent Tongue Twisters 68

Day 3
People — 27 The Electric Henry Ford 70

Day 4
Health & Body — 28 Facing the Future 72

Day 5
Science — 29 The Dark Mystery of Deep Space 74

Day 6
Arts & Literature — 30 Cows, Sharks, and Spots 76

Week 6

Day 1
Animals — 31 Forever Young 80

Day 2
History — 32 The War That Never Ends 82

Day 3
Environment — 33 The Next Atlantis? 84

Day 4
Arts & Literature — 34 Japan's Literary Superstar 86

Day 5
Business — 35 Rare Earth Elements 88

Day 6
Sports — 36 The Artful Imparting of Enthusiasm 90

Week 7

Day 1
Culture — 37 A New You? 94

Day 2
Arts & Literature — 38 Becoming the Sculpture 96

Day 3
Business — 39 Money-Making Mimicry 98

Day 4
Technology — 40 The Adventure of Books 100

Day 5
Environment — 41 The End of Ink? 102

Day 6
Arts & Literature — 42 A Method in the Madness 104

Week 8

Day 1
Geography — 43 Walking on the Moon 108

Day 2
Culture — 44 Say It With Your Fingers—Carefully! 110

Day 3
Business — 45 Profit for a Cause 112

Day 4
Nature — 46 A Beautiful Menace Under the Ice 114

Day 5
Technology — 47 The Eyes Have It! 116

Day 6
Sports — 48 Learn to Fight Like an Israeli 118

3

Week 9

Day	Category	No.	Title	Page
Day 1	Health & Body	49	An Oil to Go Nuts For	122
Day 2	Geography	50	Towering Beauties	124
Day 3	Culture	51	A Mystical, Magical Soup	126
Day 4	History	52	Gold Fever	128
Day 5	Environment	53	Building a Greener Future	130
Day 6	Health & Body	54	Hidden Dangers	132

Week 10

Day	Category	No.	Title	Page
Day 1	Environment	55	Is It Getting Darker in Here?	136
Day 2	Technology	56	Building the Future	138
Day 3	Language	57	The Great Absorber	140
Day 4	Environment	58	A Floating Landfill	142
Day 5	Technology	59	Water for Everyone	144
Day 6	Health & Body	60	Old Ways, New World	146

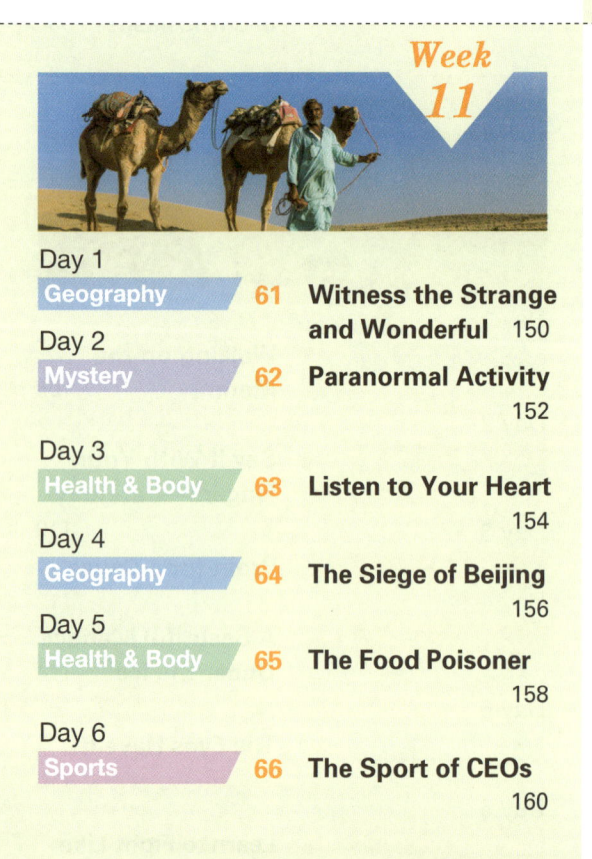

Week 11

Day	Category	No.	Title	Page
Day 1	Geography	61	Witness the Strange and Wonderful	150
Day 2	Mystery	62	Paranormal Activity	152
Day 3	Health & Body	63	Listen to Your Heart	154
Day 4	Geography	64	The Siege of Beijing	156
Day 5	Health & Body	65	The Food Poisoner	158
Day 6	Sports	66	The Sport of CEOs	160

Week 12

Day	Category	No.	Title	Page
Day 1	Language	67	In Danger of Falling Silent	164
Day 2	Health & Body	68	Doctor, Doctor!	166
Day 3	Mystery	69	Gone and Back Again	168
Day 4	People	70	An African Hero	170
Day 5	Entertainment	71	Come Watch Me Play	172
Day 6	People	72	Dancing Queen	174

Week 13

- Day 1 **Technology** 73 People Power 178
- Day 2 **Language** 74 Communication Breakdown 180
- Day 3 **Mystery** 75 The Skull and Bones Society 182
- Day 4 **Nature** 76 The Cold-Blooded Collapse 184
- Day 5 **Arts & Literature** 77 Writing the Unexpected 186
- Day 6 **Geography** 78 Something in the Wind 188
- Day 7 **Culture** 79 Tears for Hire 190

Week 14

- Day 1 **Health & Body** 80 A Challenging Diagnosis 194
- Day 2 **Nature** 81 Synthetic Signal Blockers 196
- Day 3 **Mystery** 82 Can the Future Really be Known? 198
- Day 4 **Social Behavior** 83 Breaking the Habit 200
- Day 5 **Environment** 84 The Stolen Hour 202
- Day 6 **People** 85 The Heroes Who Heal 204
- Day 7 **Sports** 86 En Garde! 206

Week 15

- Day 1 **Mystery** 87 Speaking Spooks 210
- Day 2 **Social Behavior** 88 The Magic Social Number 212
- Day 3 **People** 89 Education Where It's Needed Most 214
- Day 4 **Sports** 90 Korean Combat! 216
- Day 5 **Animals** 91 A Tale of Two Chimps 218
- Day 6 **Social Behavior** 92 Trapped in a Small Space 220
- Day 7 **Science** 93 Journey to the Center of the Earth 222

Week 16

- Day 1 **Language** 94 Humanity's First Words 226
- Day 2 **Nature** 95 Troubled Waters 228
- Day 3 **Social Behavior** 96 Part of the Herd 230
- Day 4 **Science** 97 The Hobbit 232
- Day 5 **Social Behavior** 98 On Human Kindness 234
- Day 6 **Sports** 99 Loose Your Arrows! 236
- Day 7 **Science** 100 Cracking the Case 238

Translation 課文中譯……240
Answers 習題解答……285

Introduction

This book is the third volume of a series of books concentrating on training reading skills. Each article is accompanied by six essential questions to help readers understand the article. These questions are within the framework of the following categories:

◆**Main Idea**◆ Readers will have to ask themselves, "What point is the writer trying to make?" By asking this question, they will be aware of looking for an answer during the reading process.

◆**Subject Matter**◆ The subject matter question can help readers focus on the articles they are reading. After reading the first few lines of the article, readers should ask themselves, "What is the subject matter of this article?" They will start concentrating instantly.

◆**Supporting Details**◆ The article is made up of details that support the main idea. Supporting details come in various forms, such as examples, explanations, descriptions, definitions, comparisons, contrasts, and metaphors.

◆**Inference**◆ Inference questions ask the readers to find the inferences and assumptions made in the article. The main goal of the question is to train readers' abilities of critical and logical thinking.

◆**Words in Context**◆ Words in Context are important in understanding an article. Mistaking the meanings of some Key Words or phrases can lead to a gross misunderstanding of the author's message.

◆**Others**◆ Other reading skills include:

Clarifying Devices The author might use similes and metaphors to capture readers' attention and spark their imaginations. The most widely used clarifying devices are signal words (*first, second, next, last, finally*), and transitional words or phrases (*in brief, in conclusion, above all, therefore*). Organizational patterns are also clarifying devices, including the chronological pattern, in which events are ordered by the time at which they occurred.

Text Form A text form refers to a type of writing such as fantasy, autobiography, or newspaper article. Knowing the text form can help readers achieve a better understanding of the purpose of the article and determine how to interpret the article.

Cause and Effect Cause and effect questions are concerned with why things happen (causes) and what happens as a result (effects). Understanding cause and effect relationships can guide readers to understand how one event or action caused another to occur. Words like *so, because,* and *as a result,* are good clues that help readers recognize a cause-and-effect relationship.

Fact or Opinion A fact is something that is true and is supported by evidence. An opinion is something you believe or feel. Being able to identify facts and opinions can help readers differentiate between what is real and what is someone's point of view or thought, and explore their knowledge or opinions on a topic.

Author's Tone An author's tone is the attitude the author takes on the subject he or she is writing about. It gives readers clues as to how the author feels about his or her subject. This type of question is usually described using an emotion word such as *serious, humorous,* or *hopeful*.

How to Use This Book

In our reading plan, the 100 articles are divided into 16 weeks. Readers should read 6–7 articles each week. By following the plan, the readers will make steady progress in mastering English reading skills.

The articles are written about various kinds of topics: culture, mystery, business, people, arts & literature, and more. Readers will learn English as they explore their world.

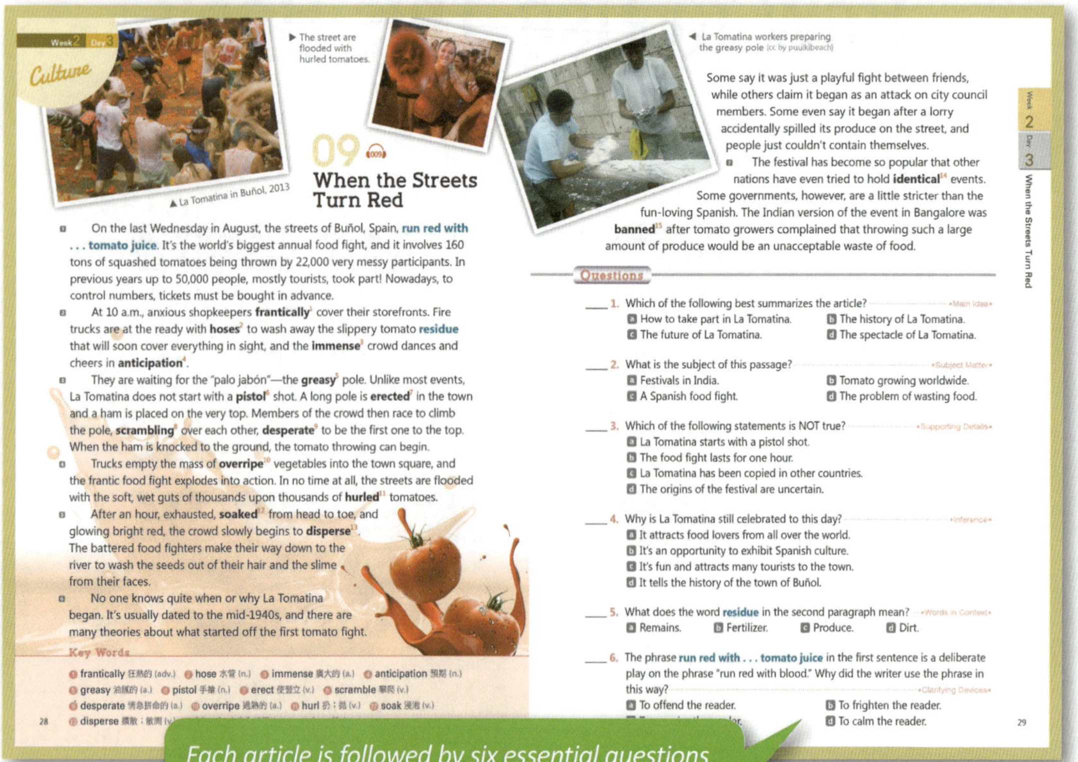

Each article is followed by six essential questions to help readers understand the content.

Bountiful pictures that provide additional information related to the articles will enhance readers' pleasure in reading.

Week 1

Day 1 Animals	01 **The Sweetest Poison**	10
Day 2 Business	02 **The Barons Who Built America**	12
Day 3 Culture	03 **Growing Up Around the World**	14
Day 4 Business	04 **Cradle to Cradle**	16
Day 5 Entertainment	05 **Where Giants Walk the Earth**	18
Day 6 Arts & Literature	06 **The World of Criminal Graffiti**	20

Week 1　Day 1

Animals

01

The Sweetest Poison

① When it comes to chocolate **addictions**[1], dogs are no different from humans. They love the sweet and delicious taste. But did you know that chocolate can be a death sentence for man's best friend?

▲ Dogs can have serious reactions to chocolate.

② Chocolate contains **caffeine**[2] and **theobromine**[3]. These two ingredients are why it's almost impossible to fall asleep if you eat a candy bar before bedtime. Although they can make our hearts race, they aren't particularly harmful to us. A person would have to eat a lot of chocolate before he or she got seriously sick.

③ Dogs on the other hand are a completely different story. Their bodies cannot **metabolize**[4] theobromine as quickly as we can. This means that it stays in their system for a very long time. While our chocolate **buzz**[5] lasts for about 20 to 40 minutes, theobromine can remain in a dog's system for days.

④ The **symptoms** of chocolate poisoning are very serious. Early symptoms include **vomiting**[6], **excessive**[7] **urination**[8], and the inability to sit still. As the theobromine continues to **be absorbed into**[9] the dog's bloodstream, more serious symptoms begin to appear. These include **dizziness**[10], muscle **twitching**[11], and **seizures**[12]. If the dog doesn't get to a **veterinarian**[13] quickly, it could fall into a **coma**[14] and eventually die.

⑤ Obviously, all chocolate is toxic to dogs. However, some types of chocolate are more dangerous than others. White chocolate has very low levels of theobromine. A 20-pound dog would have to eat 55 pounds of it to cause serious symptoms. Baking chocolate on the other hand is far more **toxic**[15]. It only takes two ounces of baking chocolate to cause serious symptoms

▲ Caffeine and theobromine can create a chocolate buzz.

Key Words

❶ addiction 成癮 (n.)　❷ caffeine 咖啡因 (n.)　❸ theobromine 可可鹼 (n.)　❹ metabolize 代謝 (v.)
❺ buzz 興奮 (n.)　❻ vomit 嘔吐 (v.)　❼ excessive 過度的 (a.)　❽ urination 排尿 (n.)
❾ be absorbed into 被……吸收　❿ dizziness 暈眩 (n.)　⓫ twitch 抽搐 (v.)　⓬ seizure 癲癇 (n.)
⓭ veterinarian 獸醫 (n.)　⓮ coma 昏迷（狀態）(n.)　⓯ toxic 有毒的 (a.)　⓰ suffering 受苦 (n.)

▶ White chocolate is relatively less toxic for dogs to eat.

in a 20-pound dog. Generally speaking, the darker the chocolate, the more dangerous it is for dogs to eat.

6   You would think that dogs would stay away from something so harmful, but that is not the case. Dogs love eating chocolate as much as we do. They don't seem to care too much about the pain and **suffering**[16] that come afterward. That's why it's extremely important to make sure that your dog never eats even the smallest amount of chocolate. It doesn't take much for it to develop a taste for chocolate.

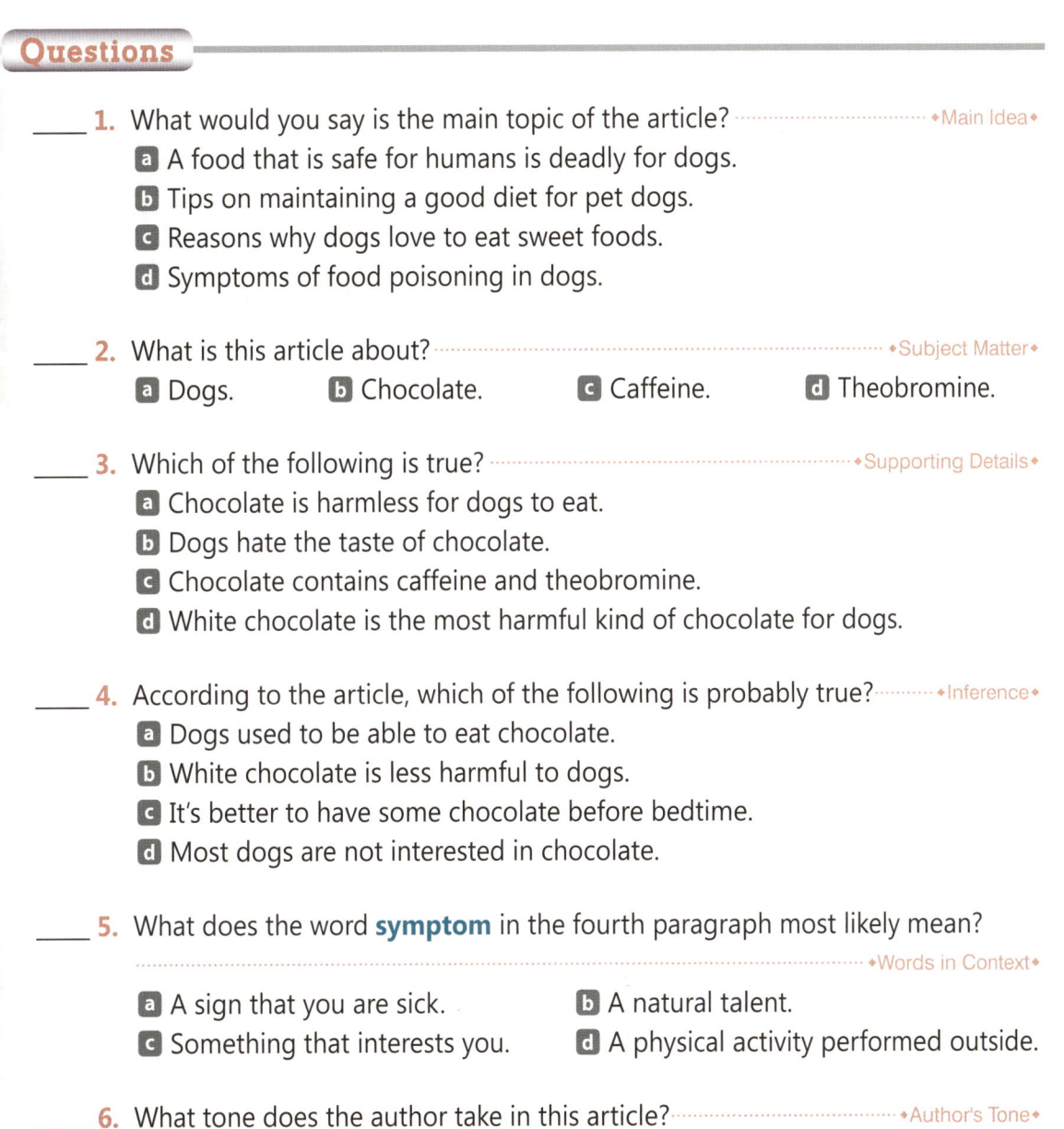

Questions

____ 1. What would you say is the main topic of the article? ◆Main Idea◆
   a A food that is safe for humans is deadly for dogs.
   b Tips on maintaining a good diet for pet dogs.
   c Reasons why dogs love to eat sweet foods.
   d Symptoms of food poisoning in dogs.

____ 2. What is this article about? ◆Subject Matter◆
   a Dogs.   b Chocolate.   c Caffeine.   d Theobromine.

____ 3. Which of the following is true? ◆Supporting Details◆
   a Chocolate is harmless for dogs to eat.
   b Dogs hate the taste of chocolate.
   c Chocolate contains caffeine and theobromine.
   d White chocolate is the most harmful kind of chocolate for dogs.

____ 4. According to the article, which of the following is probably true? ◆Inference◆
   a Dogs used to be able to eat chocolate.
   b White chocolate is less harmful to dogs.
   c It's better to have some chocolate before bedtime.
   d Most dogs are not interested in chocolate.

____ 5. What does the word **symptom** in the fourth paragraph most likely mean?
◆Words in Context◆
   a A sign that you are sick.   b A natural talent.
   c Something that interests you.   d A physical activity performed outside.

____ 6. What tone does the author take in this article? ◆Author's Tone◆
   a A mocking tone.   b A concerned tone.
   c A tragic tone.   d An indifferent tone.

Week 1 Day 2
Business

◀ Jay Gould (1836–1892)

02
The Barons[1] Who Built America

① Imagine an era when people went from **rags**[2] to riches and then back to rags in mere weeks. Imagine politicians that could be bought and sold like **stock**[3]. This was America's **Gilded**[4] Age of the 1870s and 1880s. It was the age of the robber barons.

② Robber barons were American businessmen who became incredibly wealthy in the period following the American Civil War. They made their fortunes building the railroads, oil fields, banks, steel mills and ports that eventually helped America become a global economic power. As the "robber" in their name suggests, some of them were willing to **bribe**[5], steal, and cheat in order to **squash**[6] all of their **competitors**[7] and establish **monopolies**[8].

oil fields

③ Jay Gould is one of the more **notorious**[9] examples of a robber baron. He was born in 1836 and worked as a small-time businessman until his father-in-law **appointed**[10] him manager of a struggling railroad. This opportunity marked the beginning of a career that was **characterized** by buying and selling railroad companies, often at the expense of the public. Mr. Gould was known to bribe public officials whenever his companies needed certain **legislation**[11] passed. In 1869, he and his notorious partner, Jim Fisk, **triggered**[12] a market panic by attempting to establish a monopoly on American gold. He was even involved in a **conspiracy**[13] to **kidnap**[14] a **shady**[15] investor who had once accepted a bribe from him and then fled to Canada. According to a 2009 list on a popular American business Web site, Jay Gould is the eighth worst CEO in American history.

Key Words

❶ baron 大亨；巨頭 (n.) ❷ rag 破布 (n.) ❸ stock 股票 (n.) ❹ gilded 鍍金的 (a.) ❺ bribe 行賄 (v.)
❻ squash 壓扁 (v.) ❼ competitor 競爭者 (n.) ❽ monopoly 壟斷 (n.) ❾ notorious 惡名昭彰的 (a.)
❿ appoint 任命 (v.) ⓫ legislation 立法 (n.) ⓬ trigger 引起 (v.) ⓭ conspiracy 陰謀 (n.)
⓮ kidnap 綁架 (v.) ⓯ shady 不正當的；非法的 (a.) ⓰ disgrace 丟臉 (v.) ⓱ donate 捐獻 (v.)

▶ Andrew Carnegie
(1835–1919)

④   Not all of the robber barons were as shady as Jay Gould. In fact, some of them used their fortunes to improve society. Andrew Carnegie made a fortune in the steel industry and came to be regarded as the second-richest man in history. However, Mr. Carnegie believed that "a man who dies rich dies **disgraced**[16]." This philosophy led him to **donate**[17] most of his money to social causes before his death. Mr. Carnegie built public libraries in not just the United States, but Canada, Ireland, and Australia as well. He also donated large sums to schools and universities throughout America.

Questions

____ 1. Which of the following can summarize this article? ◆Main Idea◆
   a America's Gilded Age was characterized by the robber barons.
   b America's Gilded Age was an era of construction and discovery.
   c Robber barons built railroads, oil fields, banks, and steel mills.
   d All of America's robber barons were generous.

____ 2. What is this article mainly about? ◆Subject Matter◆
   a Rich people.   b Railroads.   c Criminals.   d Monopolies.

____ 3. Which of the following statements is NOT true? ◆Supporting Details◆
   a The robber barons built railroads, steel mills, and oil fields.
   b Jay Gould gave his fortune to the needy before he died.
   c Robber barons wanted to establish monopolies to make money.
   d Andrew Carnegie made his fortune in the steel industry.

____ 4. What can we infer from this article? ◆Inference◆
   a The robber barons and their associates were all eventually arrested.
   b Andrew Carnegie and Jay Gould were friends.
   c It was extremely difficult to make money during the Gilded Age.
   d The American economy grew rapidly during the Gilded Age.

____ 5. What does the word **characterized** in the third paragraph most likely mean?
   ◆Words in Context◆
   a Hated.   b Loved.   c Distinguished.   d Extremely prosperous.

____ 6. What caused the marketing panic in 1869? ◆Cause and Effect◆
   a Too many robber barons bribing public officials.
   b Jay Gould attempting to establish a monopoly on American gold.
   c Andrew Carnegie using his fortune to build public libraries.
   d Jay Gould kidnapping an investor who had betrayed him.

Week 1　Day 3

Culture

03
Growing Up Around the World

▶ In the United States, many girls celebrate sweet 16.

❶　　The **transition**[1] from childhood to **adulthood**[2] is a long, difficult process for anyone. It is also very important socially, and every culture has its own way of celebrating it. Depending on where you live, your coming-of-age **ceremony**[3] may be one of the happiest or unhappiest **occasions**[4] of your life!

❷　　Just *when* one stops being a child is itself a question of culture. In Malaysia, some girls celebrate their 11th birthdays by **reciting**[5] the final chapter of the Koran, Islam's holy text, from memory. This proves that they are now full members of the **community**[6]. In the United States, "sweet 16" is the special birthday for many girls, whose families throw large parties for them. Americans can drive at 16, so some lucky girls get cars, too!

❸　　The Japanese celebrate adulthood even later—at age 20—for both girls and boys. Known as *Seijin No Hi*, the occasion includes traditional clothes, a ceremony at the local government office, gifts, and of course a big party. Twenty **currently**[7] being the legal drinking age in Japan, it no doubt also includes quite a **hangover**!

❹　　While most coming-of-age traditions last only a short time, some go on for years. The Amish of North America are known for living as their **ancestors**[8] did nearly two centuries ago. They reject electricity, cars, fashion, and sometimes even hot running water. At age 16, however, they are given freedom to do as they like on weekends. For many, this means dressing in modern styles, using modern **conveniences**[9], and so forth. Some young Amish people **wind up**[10] spending years away from their communities. Some stay away forever. Those who wish to return to the Amish way of life, however, must do so by age 26.

▼ Amish family

❺　　Not all **rites**[11] of **passage**[12] are happy events, at least not for their **participants**[13]. In the Amazon rain forest, 13-year-old boys of

Key Words

❶ transition 過渡 (n.)　❷ adulthood 成年 (n.)　❸ ceremony 典禮；儀式 (n.)　❹ occasion 場合 (n.)
❺ recite 背誦；朗讀 (v.)　❻ community 社群 (n.)　❼ currently 現在地 (adv.)　❽ ancestor 祖先 (n.)
❾ convenience 便利 (n.)　❿ wind up（使）結束　⓫ rite 儀式；慣例 (n.)　⓬ passage 過程 (n.)
⓭ participant 參與者 (n.)　⓮ tribe 部落 (n.)　⓯ weave 快速穿行 (v.)

▶ Many Japanese girls celebrate *Seijin No Hi* by wearing *furisode*, a style of kimono with long sleeves that hang down.

the Sateré-Mawé **tribe**[14] must spend 10 minutes wearing a pair of gloves with stinging ants **woven**[15] into them. Other tribes mark adulthood by tattooing young people's skin or filing down their teeth. Ouch!

6   Everyone grows up, no matter how or where. That means coming-of-age ceremonies will always be a part of life, including yours!

Questions

____ 1. Which of these statements is closest to being the main idea of the passage? ◆Main Idea◆
   a Sixteen-year-olds are allowed to drive in the United States.
   b Growing up is difficult, and society makes it even worse.
   c Coming-of-age celebrations vary greatly from culture to culture.
   d Young Japanese people really shouldn't drink so much.

____ 2. What does this passage deal with for the most part? ◆Subject Matter◆
   a Rituals and ceremonies.
   b Different ways of dressing.
   c The Islamic holy book.
   d Great birthday presents.

____ 3. Which of the following is true about the Amish? ◆Supporting Details◆
   a Their society died out nearly 200 years ago.
   b They enjoy using electronic appliances and driving.
   c They have to get married by the age of 26.
   d Their young people choose their own way of life.

____ 4. From the passage, what can we assume about tribal coming-of-age ceremonies? ◆Inference◆
   a They're often very painful.
   b They're only for boys.
   c They always involve insects.
   d Everyone really enjoys them.

____ 5. What is a **hangover**? ◆Words in Context◆
   a A party for someone's 20th birthday.
   b A sick feeling caused by drinking too much.
   c A traditional item of Japanese clothing.
   d An official in a local government.

____ 6. Which of the following statements is an opinion? ◆Fact or Opinion◆
   a People in different countries are considered adults at different ages.
   b It's more fun to come of age in the United States than in Malaysia.
   c Coming-of-age ceremonies in some cultures would be crimes in others.
   d Some rites of passage are for girls, some for boys, and some for both.

Week 1 Day 4

Business

▶ circular economy

04
Cradle to Cradle

1   Imagine flying into Amsterdam's Schiphol Airport. After getting your passport stamped, you **retrieve**[1] your **suitcase**[2] from a luggage **conveyor belt** made of 99-percent recyclable **materials**[3]. Once outside, you hop into a non-polluting electric taxi and ride to your hotel in the nearby Park 2020 complex. It looks like any other hotel, but it's not. The materials used to build it don't belong to its owners. They are simply being rented for as long as the hotel stays in business. If it ever closes, they will be **reclaimed**[4] by their owners and used to **construct**[5] new buildings. Any repairs to the hotel will be handled the same way.

2   These are just a few examples of a **circular**[6] economy, in which use replaces **consumption**[7], and **maximum**[8] effectiveness with **minimal**[9] damage is the rule. The Netherlands is a world leader in this new way of doing business, but other countries are starting to catch up.

3   In a circular economy, resources are used for as long as possible and waste, if any, is minimized. That may just sound like recycling on a grand scale, but it goes a lot farther. Traditional recycling reduces the quality of materials, but circular practices maintain or even improve it. And they often do so by changing those materials completely.

4   Take the Shih An Farm in Kaohsiung, for example. It is home to 700,000 chickens, which produce a lot of eggs and an **enormous**[10] amount of **manure**[11]. While the eggs go to shops and restaurants, the manure goes straight to Taiwan's largest biogas power plant, located right on the farm. There it is mixed with wastewater, which has been used to wash eggs. The resulting gas is stored in huge tanks and used to provide electricity for over 1,000 homes. If you live in that area, your television, refrigerator, and smartphone may **literally**[12] be powered by poop!

5   By reusing the toxic wastes **generated**[13] by **manufacturing**[14] and reducing the need for fresh resources, circular economies offer a

Key Words

❶ retrieve 取回 (v.)   ❷ suitcase 行李箱 (n.)   ❸ material 材料 (n.)   ❹ reclaim 拿回 (v.)
❺ construct 建築 (v.)   ❻ circular 循環的 (a.)   ❼ consumption 消耗 (n.)   ❽ maximum 最大的 (a.)
❾ minimal 最小的 (a.)   ❿ enormous 巨大的 (a.)   ⓫ manure 糞便 (n.)   ⓬ literally 確實 (adv.)
⓭ generate 產生 (v.)   ⓮ manufacture 製造 (v.)   ⓯ mentality 心態 (n.)   ⓰ corporation 公司；企業 (n.

▶ biogas power plant

double benefit. By focusing on repair rather than replacement, they also challenge the grabbing consumer **mentality**[15] of many people and **corporations**[16]. Impressive advances have been made in technology; will the same be true of our attitudes?

Questions

____ 1. What is the main idea of this passage? ••• •Main Idea•
   a People who live in the Netherlands are really smart.
   b Chicken manure can be used to power televisions.
   c Traditional recycling is a waste of time and energy.
   d A new style of manufacturing is becoming popular.

____ 2. What would be another good title for this passage? ••••••••••••••••••••••••••••••••••• •Subject Matter•
   a The Nightmare of Toxic Waste.
   b A High-Tech Visit to Amsterdam.
   c Creating More by Consuming Less.
   d Change Your Stupid Attitudes, People!

____ 3. Which of these is an example of a circular economic practice? ••Supporting Details•
   a Flying into Schiphol Airport in Amsterdam.
   b Recycling plastic bottles so they can be reused.
   c Turning used acid and wastewater into cleaning fluid.
   d Buying eggs from the Shih An Farm in Kaohsiung.

____ 4. What is probably true of companies in the circular economy? •••••••••••••••••• •Inference•
   a They're concerned about their impact on the environment.
   b They don't make as much money as traditional companies.
   c They only exist in the Netherlands and Taiwan.
   d They all have power plants located right on their property.

____ 5. What is a **conveyor belt**? ••• •Words in Context•
   a A special belt worn by people with back problems.
   b A place to keep your luggage while you're flying.
   c The person who stamps your passport at an airport.
   d A long moving surface that carries items over a distance.

____ 6. What is one likely result of having a circular economy? •••••••••••••••••• •Cause and Effect•
   a The chickens at the Shih An Farm will produce a lot of eggs.
   b Resources will be used as long as possible and waste will be minimized.
   c The Netherlands will be the world leader in this way of doing business.
   d Traditional recycling will reduce the quality of materials.

05 Where Giants Walk the Earth

1　　He doesn't look a day over 35 (and never has), but Superman will soon be 80 years old. He first appeared in the pages of *Action Comics* number 1 in June 1938. That comic book cost 10 cents when it was published, but in 2014 a copy sold on eBay for an **eye-popping** US$3,207,852. The Man of Steel, apparently, is also the Man of Gold!

2　　The world's most expensive comic book, of course, is a story in itself. But it's just one of many stories involving *Action Comics*' **publisher**[1], DC Comics. Within a year of Superman's **debut**[2], DC introduced Batman in **issue**[3] 27 of its ***Detective***[4] *Comics* title. The fastest man alive, the Flash, followed very quickly indeed in 1940, and the first major female superhero, Wonder Woman, in 1941. All were highly successful, and came to define what is called the Golden Age of Comics.

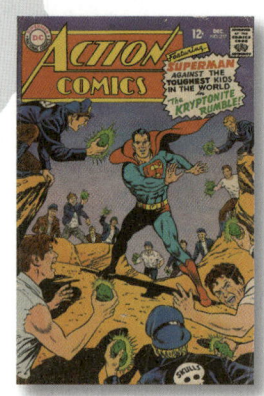

▲ *Action Comics*
(cc by HART)

3　　By the late 1940s, however, superheroes were losing their **popularity**[5]. Superman, Batman, and Wonder Woman survived, but many other DC characters did not. The company's comedy, horror, science fiction, and romance comics helped it hold on to fans. Still, the 1950s were a difficult decade for most comic book publishers, including DC. One **highlight**[6] occurred in 1956, when the Flash was reintroduced with a new origin, costume, and secret identity. This was the beginning of the *Silver* Age of Comics, though no one knew it at the time.

▲ *Detective Comics*
(cc by Jeremy Tarling)

4　　Ironically, the new age DC had started would cause it to lose the top **spot**[7] among American comic book publishers. The company's **fiercest**[8] **rival**[9], Marvel Comics, **dominated**[10] the industry for the next 30 years. Even Superman and Batman couldn't **compete with**[11] Spider-Man, the X-Men, the Hulk, and Marvel's many other hugely popular characters. DC still got plenty of respect, but it was a **distant**[12] second in terms of sales.

Key Words

① **publisher** 出版社 (n.)　② **debut** 初次登場 (n.)　③ **issue**（報刊）期號 (n.)　④ **detective** 偵探 (n.)
⑤ **popularity** 流行 (n.)　⑥ **highlight** 最精采的部分 (n.)　⑦ **spot** 點 (n.)　⑧ **fierce** 兇猛的 (a.)
⑨ **rival** 競爭對手 (n.)　⑩ **dominate** 支配 (v.)　⑪ **compete with** 與……競爭　⑫ **distant** 遙遠的 (a.)
⑬ **series** 系列 (n.)　⑭ **renew** 更新；重新開始 (v.)　⑮ **imitate** 模仿 (v.)

[5] That started changing in the late 1980s. The success of the Batman film **series**[13] **renewed**[14] people's interest in DC's characters. Superman and Wonder Woman later found new fans through movies as well. DC and Marvel now battle year after year for sales just as their superheroes battle supervillains for the safety of mankind. Who says life can't **imitate**[15] art?

(cc by Rob Thurman)

Questions

____ 1. What is the main idea of this article? ◆Main Idea◆
   a Superman has been around for a very long time.
   b DC Comics has given us many famous characters.
   c DC comic books are better than Marvel comic books.
   d Marvel comic books are better than DC comic books.

____ 2. What does this article mainly focus on? ◆Subject Matter◆
   a A superhero.   b A supervillain.   c A comic book.   d A company.

____ 3. Which of the following is one of DC Comics' accomplishments? ◆Supporting Details◆
   a Starting the Silver Age of Comics in the 1950s.
   b Selling more comics than Marvel Comics in the Silver Age.
   c Selling the most expensive comic book ever in 2014.
   d Introducing Wonder Woman as a movie character in 1941.

____ 4. From the article, what can we assume about DC Comics? ◆Inference◆
   a It has always been America's most successful comic book company.
   b It has never been America's most successful comic book company.
   c It has sometimes been America's most successful comic book company.
   d It is not an American comic book company.

____ 5. What does **eye-popping** mean? ◆Words in Context◆
   a Ordinary.   b Interesting.   c Remarkable.   d Logical.

____ 6. Which of the following statements is an opinion? ◆Fact or Opinion◆
   a Wonder Woman was the first major female superhero.
   b Batman first appeared after Superman.
   c Spider-Man became popular during the Silver Age of Comics.
   d DC comics is a really amazing and creative company.

Week 1 Day 6

Arts & Literature

◀ *Shop Until You Drop* by Banksy

06

The World of Criminal Graffiti[1]

[1] Banksy, the **anonymous** graffiti artist, first became active in Bristol, United Kingdom, in the early 1990s. His **distinctive**[2] style of black-and-white **stenciling**[3] is the consequence of having to paint quickly to avoid being arrested. **Legend has it that**[4] while he was hiding from the police, the idea of stenciling originally came to him when he saw a stenciled serial number on the bottom of a garbage truck. Banksy's **preference**[5] for painting on walls in public places makes some people view him more as a criminal than an artist.

[2] Banksy's works can be found on the streets of Bristol, New York, London, and New Orleans. In 2005, he even did a series of **thought-provoking**[6] paintings on the West Bank **barrier**[7]. To many, he is regarded as an artistic **genius**[8]. This belief creates a difficult question: If Banksy is an artist, does that mean that all graffiti is art as well? Banksy often makes fun of traditional **notions**[9] of what art is. He has been known to walk into major museums and hang his own pieces on the wall. The Mona Lisa has also been a **recurring**[10] character in his paintings.

[3] Banksy's art raises another **critical**[11] question: Is the artist even important? Nobody knows who Banksy really is. The mystery surrounding his identity has caused the media to **speculate**[12] openly. In 2016, scientists from Queen Mary University claimed to have found the identity of Banksy. Using a method known as "geographic **profiling**[13]," researchers believe the artist is Bristol local Robin Gunningham. Gunningham has neither confirmed nor denied

▶ stencil on the waterline of the Thekla by Banksy

Key Words

[1] graffiti 塗鴉 (n.)　　[2] distinctive 特殊的 (a.)　　[3] stencil 模板印刷 (v.)
[4] legend has it that . . . 據傳說……　　[5] preference 偏好 (n.)　　[6] thought-provoking 發人深省的 (a.)
[7] barrier 屏障 (n.)　　[8] genius 天才 (n.)　　[9] notion 概念 (n.)　　[10] recur 再發生；再現 (v.)
[11] critical 關鍵的 (a.)　　[12] speculate 推測 (v.)　　[13] profiling（罪犯）特徵分析 (n.)
[14] antiauthority 反權威的 (a.)　　[15] antiwar 反戰的 (a.)

the findings. Others speculate that Banksy is actually a group of graffiti artists who all operate under the same anonymous title. Whatever the truth is, Banksy doesn't want to be discovered.

▲ *Naked Man* by Banksy

▲ *Knife Hoodies* by Banksy

[4] Whoever Banksy really is, his art is clearly **antiauthority**[14] and has an **antiwar**[15] message. Banksy's being anonymous is perhaps his most important message of all. If the artist is unknown, we can observe the art for itself without drawing unnecessary conclusions about its meaning.

Questions

____ 1. Which of the following statements best summarize this article? ◆Main Idea◆
   a Graffiti artists are real artists.
   b Banksy challenges conventional views.
   c Graffiti artists cause damage to society.
   d Banksy's life story is the stuff of legends.

____ 2. What is this article about? ◆Subject Matter◆
   a Graffiti.   **b** An anonymous artist.   **c** Major museums.   **d** Criminals.

____ 3. Which of the following statements is true? ◆Supporting Details◆
   a Banksy went to Queen Mary University.
   b Banksy's works have appeared in major museums.
   c Banksy's works first appeared in New York City.
   d Banksy chose stenciling in order to save money on paint.

____ 4. Which of the following can we infer from the article? ◆Inference◆
   a Graffiti is illegal in the United Kingdom.
   b This artist comes from a very rich family.
   c People can see Banksy's work in every country of the world.
   d Banksy has been arrested before.

____ 5. The first paragraph mentions Banksy is an anonymous graffiti artist. What does **anonymous** mean? ◆Words in Context◆
   a You don't have a license.   **b** Nobody knows your identity.
   c Everybody knows your identity. **d** You are a beginner.

____ 6. What can this article best be described as? ◆Clarifying Devices◆
   a An expository essay.   **b** A personal story.
   c A timeline.   **d** A biography.

Banksy's Work Around the World

IN BRISTOL

▲ *Police Sniper* in Upper Maudlin Street in Bristol

▲ *Mild Mild West* on a brick wall in the city center in Bristol, UK

IN LONDON

▲ Banksy's CCTV graffiti in London

▲ Banksy's graffiti in Pollard Street, London

IN BETHLEHEM

▲ Banksy's graffiti on a wall in the occupied territory of Bethlehem

IN SAN FRANCISCO

▲ stencil graffiti piece by Banksy in San Francisco

Week 2

Day 1 Animals	07	Mini Mind Control	24
Day 2 Arts & Literature	08	Struggle and Genius	26
Day 3 Culture	09	When the Streets Turn Red	28
Day 4 People	10	Making His Mark	30
Day 5 Technology	11	The Magic Mirror	32
Day 6 Animals	12	The Animal That's Also an Environment	34

Week 2 Day 1 Animals

▼ an ant victim of *Ophiocordyceps*
(cc by Katja Schulz)

07
Mini Mind Control

1. Deep in the tropical rain forests of Thailand, ant society is facing a terrible crisis. Workers aren't coming home. Queens are locking themselves in their chambers. They're all terrified of the same thing—**zombie**[1] ants!

2. The panic is being caused by a particularly **sneaky**[2] **fungus**[3] called *Ophiocordyceps*. This fungus can literally **take over**[4] an ant's mind and make it do things that it doesn't want to do.

3. Imagine an **innocent**[5] ant out for a **stroll**[6] on a sunny day. It comes across a strange **corpse**[7] covered in *Ophiocordyceps* fungus but pays it no **heed**[8]. Over the next couple of days, this ant continues its normal routine like nothing is wrong. Three days pass and it starts to experience physical effects. This is the fungus slowly destroying muscle tissue as it takes over the ant's nervous system. In a few more days, the ant starts to **convulse**[9] and loses control of itself.

4. This is when the fungus really takes over. It forces the ant to climb up a leaf and bite it. Perhaps strangest of all, zombie ants always perform this final death bite at noon, when the sun is highest in the sky.

5. Now comes the **gross**[10] part. After the ant is dead, the fungus starts to grow out of its head like a mushroom. Over the course of two weeks, the fungus **converts**[11] the ant's insides into sugars, so it has food to grow. When it's ready, it will **release**[12] new **spores**[13] that can **doom** any nearby ants.

6. *Ophiocordyceps* is extremely powerful, and it has been known to destroy entire colonies of ants. But ants have gotten used to the threat and do their best to keep themselves safe. If a healthy ant sees another ant displaying zombie **tendencies**[14], it will drag the **infected**[15] ant as far away from all of the other

Key Words

1. **zombie** 殭屍 (n.) 2. **sneaky** 鬼鬼祟祟的 (a.) 3. **fungus** 真菌 (n.) 4. **take over** 接管
5. **innocent** 純真的 (a.) 6. **stroll** 散步；溜達 (n.) 7. **corpse** 屍體；殘骸 (n.) 8. **heed** 注意 (n.)
9. **convulse** 痙攣 (v.) 10. **gross** 噁心的 (a.) 11. **convert** 轉換 (v.) 12. **release** 釋出 (v.)
13. **spore** 孢子 (n.) 14. **tendency** 傾向 (n.) 15. **infect** 感染 (v.) 16. **moth** 蛾 (n.) 17. **mantis** 螳螂 (n.)

◀ *Ophiocordyceps* can kill spiders as well.
(cc by Mushroom Observer)

ants as possible. Better to abandon that one infected ant than risk zombie spores being released all over the colony!

7 It's not just ants that have to live in fear of this zombie fungus. There are lots of different species of *Ophiocordyceps*. Each of them targets a particular insect, such as **moths**[16], **mantises**[17], and even spiders.

Week 2 Day 1 Mini Mind Control

Questions

____ 1. Which of the following is the main topic of this article? ◆Main Idea◆
   a Ant species in Thailand.
   b Fungus, the enemy of ants.
   c Social habits of ants.
   d Eating habits of ants.

____ 2. What is the main topic of this article? ◆Subject Matter◆
   a Thailand.   b Ants.   c A fungus.   d Mushrooms.

____ 3. Which of the following statements is true? ◆Supporting Details◆
   a Zombie ants can bite other ants to infect them.
   b Zombie ants eat other ants for food.
   c Zombie ants always die at noon.
   d *Ophiocordyceps* is only found in Thailand.

____ 4. What can we infer from this article? ◆Inference◆
   a *Ophiocordyceps* is not a new threat to ants.
   b Zombie ants occasionally fight zombie spiders.
   c Ant species in Thailand will be destroyed by *Ophiocordyceps*.
   d *Ophiocordyceps* will one day be able to infect humans.

____ 5. In the fifth paragraph, the writer mentions that spores doom any ants that are near. What does **doom** mean? ◆Words in Context◆
   a To make someone or something happy.
   b To make someone or something longer.
   c To make someone or something fall asleep.
   d To make someone or something die soon.

____ 6. How does the author create interest in the subject in the first paragraph? ◆Clarifying Devices◆
   a By using a suspenseful description.
   b By using precise arguments.
   c By using a biased opinion.
   d By using contrasts of time.

25

Week 2 Day 2
Arts & Literature

▶ Fyodor Dostoyevsky
(1821–1881)

08

Struggle and Genius

[1] "Nothing in this world is harder than speaking the truth, nothing easier than flattery," or so says Fyodor Dostoyevsky in his 1866 classic *Crime and Punishment*. These words reflect an **intimate**[1] knowledge of what it is to be human, and they came from the pen of a literary genius on the **verge**[2] of financial **ruin**[3].

[2] Fyodor Dostoyevsky, one of the giants of Russian literature, was born in Moscow on November 11, 1821. His parents had **emigrated**[4] from what is now Ukraine. He was the second of seven children, and he almost immediately began to suffer from temporal lobe **epilepsy**[5]. This was a condition that would **linger**[6] for his entire life. Dostoyevsky went to school for mathematics, a subject he **despised**[7]. He served in the Russian army for three years, from 1841 to 1844. After being **discharged** from the military, he began to write fiction.

[3] Things started to go badly for Fyodor in 1849. This was the year when he was **arrested**[8] and **sentenced**[9] to death along with a group of **intellectuals**[10] in St. Petersburg. Tsar Nicholas I, the leader of Russia at the time, was terrified of **revolution**[11]. Fyodor Dostoyevsky and his fellow intellectuals were brought out into a **courtyard**[12], tied to poles, blindfolded, and told they were going to be shot in the head. But the bullets never came. It was all a trick, a **mock**[13] **execution**[14] meant to teach them a lesson. The experience **shattered**[15] Fyodor's nerves, and he never quite recovered his peace of mind. Afterward, he was sent to Siberia, where he was forced to labor and serve in the army until 1859.

[4] After returning to St. Petersburg, Fyodor continued his writing, but things didn't get any easier. He began to **drown**[16] in debt following the deaths of his wife and brother in 1864.

◀ gravestone of Fyodor Dostoyevsky in St. Petersburg

Key Words

[1] intimate 親密的；熟悉的 (a.)　[2] verge 邊緣 (n.)　[3] ruin 毀滅 (n.)　[4] emigrate 移居 (v.)
[5] epilepsy 癲癇 (n.)　[6] linger 逗留 (v.)　[7] despise 厭惡 (v.)　[8] arrest 逮捕 (v.)
[9] sentence 判刑 (v.)　[10] intellectual 知識份子 (n.)　[11] revolution 革命 (n.)　[12] courtyard 庭院 (n.)
[13] mock 假的 (a.)　[14] execution 處刑 (n.)　[15] shatter 粉碎 (v.)　[16] drown （使）淹沒 (v.)

▶ *The Brothers Karamazov*
(cc by Scott W. Vincent)

He also developed a terrible gambling habit. It is said that he had to rush the last part of *Crime and Punishment* because he had gambled away his last kopek.

5   In the years leading up to his death in 1881, Fyodor wrote some of his most famous novels such as *The Idiot* and *The Brothers Karamazov*. He was survived by his second wife and four children.

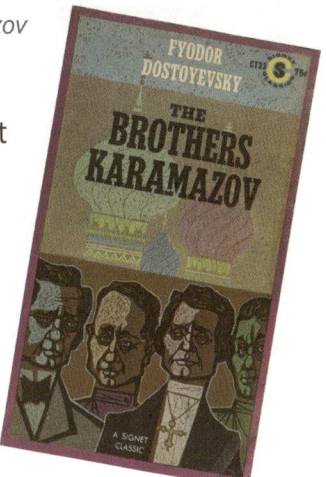

Questions

____ 1. What would you say is the main topic of the article? •Main Idea•
   a Russia has many literary geniuses.
   b One of Russia's literary geniuses had a difficult life.
   c Good writing comes from a difficult life.
   d Russia is a difficult place to grow up in.

____ 2. What is this article about? •Subject Matter•
   a A Russian author.   b Suffering.   c Epilepsy.   d Mock executions.

____ 3. Which of the following statements is NOT true? •Supporting Details•
   a Fyodor Dostoyevsky was born in Moscow.
   b Fyodor Dostoyevsky had a gambling problem.
   c Fyodor Dostoyevsky was arrested and sentenced to death.
   d Fyodor Dostoyevsky's parents were very rich.

____ 4. What can we guess about Fyodor Dostoyevsky from this article? •Inference•
   a He became addicted to gambling.
   b He had been very popular his entire life.
   c He must have known Tsar Nicholas I personally.
   d He enjoyed his time in Siberia.

____ 5. What does the word **discharged** in the second paragraph mean? •Words in Context•
   a To be charged with a crime.
   b To be released from something.
   c To develop a bad reputation with the police.
   d To write a masterpiece.

____ 6. Which of the following is the writer's opinion? •Clarifying Devices•
   a Dostoyevsky was born in Moscow.
   b Dostoyevsky was married with children.
   c Dostoyevsky was a literary genius.
   d Dostoyevsky was a gambler.

Week 2 Day 2 Struggle and Genius

Week 2 Day 3

Culture

▶ The streets are flooded with hurled tomatoes.

▲ La Tomatina in Buñol, 2013

09

When the Streets Turn Red

1. On the last Wednesday in August, the streets of Buñol, Spain, **run red with . . . tomato juice**. It's the world's biggest annual food fight, and it involves 160 tons of squashed tomatoes being thrown by 22,000 very messy participants. In previous years up to 50,000 people, mostly tourists, took part! Nowadays, to control numbers, tickets must be bought in advance.

2. At 10 a.m., anxious shopkeepers **frantically**[1] cover their storefronts. Fire trucks are at the ready with **hoses**[2] to wash away the slippery tomato **residue** that will soon cover everything in sight, and the **immense**[3] crowd dances and cheers in **anticipation**[4].

3. They are waiting for the "palo jabón"—the **greasy**[5] pole. Unlike most events, La Tomatina does not start with a **pistol**[6] shot. A long pole is **erected**[7] in the town and a ham is placed on the very top. Members of the crowd then race to climb the pole, **scrambling**[8] over each other, **desperate**[9] to be the first one to the top. When the ham is knocked to the ground, the tomato throwing can begin.

4. Trucks empty the mass of **overripe**[10] vegetables into the town square, and the frantic food fight explodes into action. In no time at all, the streets are flooded with the soft, wet guts of thousands upon thousands of **hurled**[11] tomatoes.

5. After an hour, exhausted, **soaked**[12] from head to toe, and glowing bright red, the crowd slowly begins to **disperse**[13]. The battered food fighters make their way down to the river to wash the seeds out of their hair and the slime from their faces.

6. No one knows quite when or why La Tomatina began. It's usually dated to the mid-1940s, and there are many theories about what started off the first tomato fight.

Key Words

1. frantically 狂熱的 (adv.)   2. hose 水管 (n.)   3. immense 廣大的 (a.)   4. anticipation 預期 (n.)
5. greasy 油膩的 (a.)   6. pistol 手槍 (n.)   7. erect 使豎立 (v.)   8. scramble 攀爬 (v.)
9. desperate 情急拼命的 (a.)   10. overripe 過熟的 (a.)   11. hurl 扔；拋 (v.)   12. soak 浸泡 (v.)
13. disperse 擴散；散開 (v.)   14. identical 完全相同的 (a.)   15. ban 禁止 (v.)

◀ La Tomatina workers preparing the greasy pole (cc by puuikibeach)

Some say it was just a playful fight between friends, while others claim it began as an attack on city council members. Some even say it began after a lorry accidentally spilled its produce on the street, and people just couldn't contain themselves.

7 The festival has become so popular that other nations have even tried to hold **identical**[14] events. Some governments, however, are a little stricter than the fun-loving Spanish. The Indian version of the event in Bangalore was **banned**[15] after tomato growers complained that throwing such a large amount of produce would be an unacceptable waste of food.

Questions

____ 1. Which of the following best summarizes the article? ◆Main Idea◆
   a How to take part in La Tomatina.
   b The history of La Tomatina.
   c The future of La Tomatina.
   d The spectacle of La Tomatina.

____ 2. What is the subject of this passage? ◆Subject Matter◆
   a Festivals in India.
   b Tomato growing worldwide.
   c A Spanish food fight.
   d The problem of wasting food.

____ 3. Which of the following statements is NOT true? ◆Supporting Details◆
   a La Tomatina starts with a pistol shot.
   b The food fight lasts for one hour.
   c La Tomatina has been copied in other countries.
   d The origins of the festival are uncertain.

____ 4. Why is La Tomatina still celebrated to this day? ◆Inference◆
   a It attracts food lovers from all over the world.
   b It's an opportunity to exhibit Spanish culture.
   c It's fun and attracts many tourists to the town.
   d It tells the history of the town of Buñol.

____ 5. What does the word **residue** in the second paragraph mean? ◆Words in Context◆
   a Remains.   b Fertilizer.   c Produce.   d Dirt.

____ 6. The phrase **run red with . . . tomato juice** in the first sentence is a deliberate play on the phrase "run red with blood." Why did the writer use the phrase in this way? ◆Clarifying Devices◆
   a To offend the reader.
   b To frighten the reader.
   c To surprise the reader.
   d To calm the reader.

Week 2 Day 3 When the Streets Turn Red

29

10 Making His Mark

1   On February 4, 2004, a Harvard student created an Internet phenomenon from his dorm room. The website was Facebook, and it changed the way people all over the world communicate. But Facebook isn't the only impact Mark Zuckerberg had on the world.

2   Computers have been a **constant**[1] **theme**[2] in Mark Zuckerberg's life. He learned the basics of computer programming from his dad. At just 12 years of age, he wrote a simple messaging program, ZuckNet, for his family home. Shortly after that time, messaging programs like AOL Instant Messenger took off **nationwide**[3].

3   Mark then wrote another program called Synapse. Synapse used **artificial**[4] **intelligence**[5] to study the way users listen to music. The program was so impressive that he received job offers from major software companies like Microsoft. Mark **declined**[6] these **offers**[7], having decided that he would rather further his studies instead. Like with ZuckNet, Mark's program Synapse came just before another program called Pandora gained popularity.

4   Mark's **zeal** for programming **flourished**[8] during his time at Harvard. In his second year, he wrote a program that helped students select courses and find study groups. He also created Facemash, a **precursor**[9] to Facebook that asked users to compare people's faces. Of course, after Mark created Facebook, it started to spread quickly. This time, it was Mark's own program that took over and dominated the space.

5   Today, Facebook is still the most-used form of social media, with over 2 billion monthly users. But this is not enough for Mark. He **genuinely**[10] believes that the Internet makes people's lives better. So, he wants to get everyone on the planet connected to the Internet. In 2013, Zuckerberg **launched**[11] a new company called Internet.org.

▶ Facebook is the most-used form of social media today.

Key Words

1. constant 固定的 (a.)　2. theme 主題 (n.)　3. nationwide 全國的 (a.)　4. artificial 人工的 (a.)
5. intelligence 智慧 (n.)　6. decline 拒絕 (v.)　7. offer 工作機會；提議 (n.)　8. flourish 蓬勃發展 (v.)
9. precursor 先驅 (n.)　10. genuinely 真誠地 (adv.)　11. launch 發起 (v.)　12. drone 無人機 (n.)
13. laser 雷射 (n.)　14. access 使用途徑；機會 (n.)　15. initiative 倡議 (n.)

▶ Priscilla Chan and Mark Zuckerberg
(cc by Lukasz Porwol)

The company uses artificial intelligence, **drones**[12], and even **lasers**[13] to increase Internet **access**[14] for everyone.

However, Mark is not only interested in computers. He and his wife, Priscilla Chan, also value education, health, sustainable energy, and human equality. Together, they started another organization called the Chan Zuckerberg **Initiative**[15]. Through this organization, they will donate 99% of their wealth to such causes over their lifetimes. With every new project, Mark Zuckerberg continues to change the world.

Questions

____ 1. What would you say is the main topic of the article? •Main Idea•
   a Mark Zuckerberg leads a busy life as a billionaire.
   b Nobody knew if Facebook would be a success during its early years.
   c Mark Zuckerberg developed many computer programs before Facebook.
   d Mark Zuckerberg has made many contributions to the world.

____ 2. What is this article mainly about? •Subject Matter•
   a Facebook.   b An Internet entrepreneur.   c The Internet Age.   d Harvard.

____ 3. Which of the following statements is true? •Supporting Details•
   a Mark Zuckerberg created Synapse after Facebook.
   b Everyone in the world has access to the Internet.
   c Facebook has the most users of any social media today.
   d Programming is Mark Zuckerberg's only hobby.

____ 4. Which of the following statements is likely true? •Inference•
   a Microsoft knew that Zuckerberg was going to be a great computer programmer.
   b Mark Zuckerberg has always been extremely bad at math.
   c ZuckNet was the precursor to programs like AOL Instant Messenger and MSN Messenger.
   d Mark Zuckerberg thinks people shouldn't spend so much time online.

____ 5. What does the word **zeal** in the fourth paragraph most likely mean?
   •Words in Context•
   a Dislike.   b Enthusiasm.   c Ignorance.   d Fear.

____ 6. What can this piece best be described as? •Clarifying Devices•
   a A descriptive essay.   b A narrative essay.   c A biography.   d A timeline.

Technology

Week 2　Day 5

11 The Magic Mirror

▼ Virtual dressing rooms let people see how clothes look without trying them on. (cc by MHSzymczyk)

① What if customers could try on their favorite clothes in a store without having to enter a **dressing room**¹? Or better yet, without leaving their bedroom? Technological **advances**² are allowing us to do just that. This new shopping experience could be coming to a mall near you sooner than you think.

② This new technology is called a "**virtual**³ dressing room." Imagine standing in front of a full-length mirror that shows your **reflection**⁴ and also lists the clothes **available**⁵ for **purchase**⁶. Customers can **browse**⁷ through clothes with a simple **downward**⁸ **motion**⁹ of their hand. Clothing selected by a customer will appear virtually on top of the customer's reflection. Customers can now see what the **outfit**¹⁰ looks like just as it would in real life. If the customer doesn't like the color, all he or she needs to do is point at a different part of the mirror and select a new one.

③ Though this sounds a lot like science fiction that will be arriving sometime in the distant future, this technology is here today. Virtual dressing rooms are already being put to use in department stores around the world. Topshop, a world-class clothing **chain store**¹¹, has **implemented**¹² virtual dressing rooms that use Microsoft's Kinect technology in its Moscow **branch**¹³. Macy's department store in New York City experimented with the technology in 2010 when it built a "magic mirror." The installation allowed customers to try on anything in the store. If they liked how they looked, they could post an image of their new virtual outfit on their Facebook page. Customers who used these virtual dressing rooms found that it saved them a lot of time. It allowed customers to sort through the items they were interested in by **narrowing**¹⁴ their search to the clothes they like the most.

Key Words

❶ dressing room 化妝間；更衣室 (n.)　❷ advance 進展 (n.)　❸ virtual 虛擬的 (a.)
❹ reflection 倒影 (n.)　❺ available 可得到的 (a.)　❻ purchase 購買 (n.)　❼ browse 瀏覽 (v.)
❽ downward 向下的 (a.)　❾ motion 動作 (n.)　❿ outfit 裝束 (n.)　⓫ chain store 連鎖店 (n.)
⓬ implement 實施 (v.)　⓭ branch 分店 (n.)　⓮ narrow（使）縮窄 (v.)　⓯ unnatural 不自然的 (a.)

▲ Topshop　　　　　　　　　　　　　▲ Macy's in New York City

4　　While it's true that this technology is starting to appear in stores around the world, it's still far from perfect. For one, the clothing's image can look **unnatural**[15] and doesn't always give a good feel for the real thing. Not to mention, the technology has no way of informing the customers of how the clothes will actually feel on them.

Questions

_____ 1. What is the main idea of this article? ••◆Main Idea◆
   a A new store is changing the way that people shop.
   b Virtual dressing rooms are changing the way that people shop.
   c Shopping is becoming extremely popular in Moscow.
   d The evolution of magic mirror technology has changed chain stores.

_____ 2. What is this article about? •••◆Subject Matter◆
   a Shopping.　　**b** A new invention.　　**c** Moscow.　　**d** Shopping malls.

_____ 3. Which of the following statements is NOT true? •••••••••••••••••••••••••••••••◆Supporting Details◆
   a Virtual dressing rooms have already been built.
   b There are still problems with virtual dressing room technology.
   c Some virtual dressing rooms can post directly to Facebook.
   d Every Macy's store has a virtual dressing room.

_____ 4. According to the article, what is likely to happen? ••••••••••••••••••••••••••••••••••••••◆Inference◆
   a Virtual dressing room technology will eventually get popular.
   b Macy's will give up on virtual dressing rooms.
   c Virtual dressing rooms will replace normal dressing rooms one day.
   d Virtual dressing rooms are extremely cheap to build.

_____ 5. What does the word **installation** in the third paragraph mean? ◆Words in Context◆
   a A piece of equipment.　　　　　　　　**b** A theater.
   c A washroom.　　　　　　　　　　　　**d** A bus station.

_____ 6. How does the writer begin the passage? •••◆Clarifying Devices◆
   a With a serious thought.　　　　　　　**b** With a warning.
   c With an imaginary situation.　　　　　**d** With a joke.

Week 2　Day 6

Animals

The Animal That's Also an Environment

❶　　It looks like a plant. It feels like a stone. But **coral**¹, which we consider a colorful setting for television programs about fish and other **marine**² life, is actually an animal. And if we view a coral **reef**³ as a single **organism**⁴, then it is by far the largest and oldest living thing on Earth.

❷　　Distant relatives of jellyfish and **sea anemones**⁵, corals are **invertebrates** despite having a sort of **skeleton**⁶. "Hard" corals' skeletons, known as calicles, are made of **limestone**⁷. "Soft" corals, on the other hand, have wood-like skeletons. Only hard corals can form reefs. They do this by attaching themselves to rocks in shallow areas of tropical seas. A single coral can divide itself thousands of times, creating **clones**⁸ which connect their calicles to form a colony. This colony is in fact one animal, and can connect with other colonies to form a reef. Some reefs are believed to be over 50,000 years old!

❸　　If you've ever watched a TV show about ocean life, you probably think corals are very colorful. In fact they are clear, and get their rainbow tones from the billions of **algae**⁹ (plants) which attach to them. This relationship is highly **beneficial**¹⁰ to both parties. Corals get most of their food from the algae they host, but are also equipped with **poisonous**¹¹, hooked **tentacles**¹². These are used mostly at night, when the algae are asleep, to catch **plankton**¹³ and even small fish. That's right—corals are meat-eaters!

❹　　Since they must live near coastal areas, corals cover less than one percent of the ocean floor. Nevertheless, they support roughly 25 percent of all marine life. This is a problem, because reefs are rapidly falling victim to a variety of natural and man-made threats. Pollution, storms, global warming, boats,

Key Words

❶ coral 珊瑚 (n.)　❷ marine 海洋的；海生的 (a.)　❸ reef 礁 (n.)　❹ organism 生物；有機體 (n.)
❺ sea anemone 海葵 (n.)　❻ skeleton 骨骼 (n.)　❼ limestone 石灰岩 (n.)
❽ clone 複製品；無性繁殖物 (n.)　❾ algae 水藻（複數）(n.)　❿ beneficial 有益處的 (a.)
⓫ poisonous 有毒的 (a.)　⓬ tentacle 觸手 (n.)　⓭ plankton 浮游生物 (n.)
⓮ potentially 潛在；可能地 (adv.)　⓯ fatal 致命的 (a.)　⓰ bleach 白化；漂白 (v.)

and the dumping of soil and sand into the world's oceans are all deadly to corals. Even a slight change in water temperature can cause corals to lose their algae covering, resulting in a **potentially**[14] **fatal**[15] condition known as **bleaching**[16].

[5]   If people cannot protect the world's oldest and largest organisms, what can we do? The time has come to start thinking about our impact on our environment—especially when that environment is itself an animal.

▶ Algae attached to corals give corals their color.

▶ coral bleaching

Questions

____ 1. What is the main idea of this article? ◆Main Idea◆
   a Corals are very beautiful and colorful animals.
   b Pollution is destroying the world's oceans.
   c Some coral reefs may be over 50,000 years old.
   d Corals don't look or feel like animals, but they are.

____ 2. What does this passage deal with for the most part? ◆Subject Matter◆
   a A type of creature.   b People's behavior.
   c The world's oceans.   d Global warming.

____ 3. Which of the following statements is true about corals? ◆Supporting Details◆
   a They can be found in all the oceans of the world.
   b They can be found at all depths of the world's oceans.
   c They catch some of their food by themselves.
   d They rely on the algae they host for all of their food.

____ 4. What can we infer about corals from the passage? ◆Inference◆
   a They all have hard skeletons.   b There are many different varieties.
   c They only eat plants.   d They are doing very well everywhere.

____ 5. What is an **invertebrate**? ◆Words in Context◆
   a An animal which has bones.
   b An animal which has no bones.
   c An animal which eats meat.
   d An animal which has poisonous tentacles.

____ 6. Where would you be most likely to find this article? ◆Text Form◆
   a In a diving instruction manual.   b In a comic book about sharks.
   c In a scientific magazine.   d In a seafood cookbook.

Biodiversity of Coral Reefs

▲ crown-of-thorns starfish

▲ banded sea krait

▲ giant clam

▲ cleaner shrimp

▲ jellyfish

▲ sea horse

▲ dugong

▲ sponge

▲ sea turtle

▲ eel

▲ clownfish

▲ sea urchin

▲ butterfly fish

Week 3

Day 1 Entertainment	13 And the Worst Actor Goes To . . .	38
Day 2 Geography	14 A River of Fire in the Sky	40
Day 3 Animals	15 The Soft Glow of the Natural World	42
Day 4 History	16 The Realm of the Khans	44
Day 5 Mystery	17 The City Lost Under the Sea	46
Day 6 Culture	18 Celebrating in Color	48

Entertainment

Week 3 Day 1

▶ John Wilson (cc by Par Lance)

13
And the Worst Actor Goes To . . .

1 Winning an Oscar is every actor's dream. It is considered the height of **achievement**[1] for anyone **involved**[2] in the movie industry. The Golden Raspberry Awards (or "the Razzies"), **to the contrary**[3], are the opposite of the Oscars and celebrate the very worst in moviemaking.

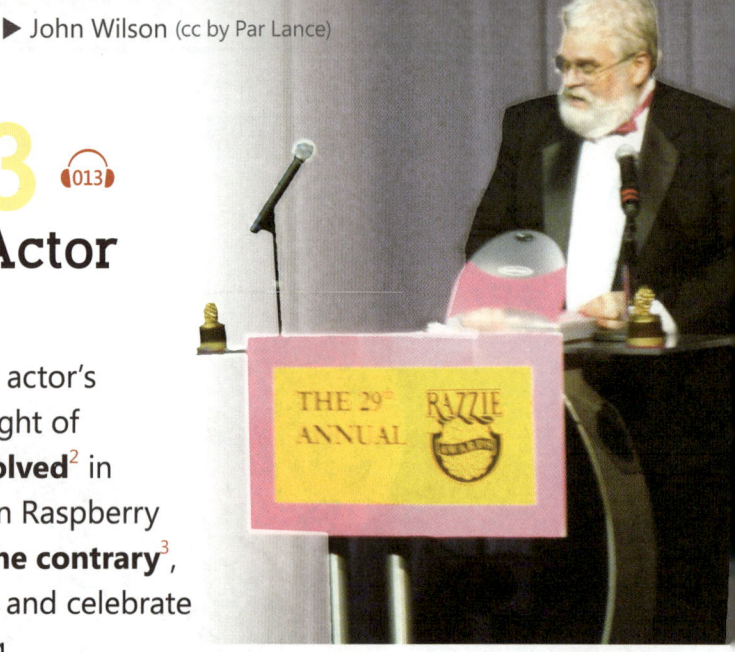

2 Awards are given in **categories**[4] such as Worst Movie, Worst Actor, Worst Screenplay and Worst Director. It goes without saying that most actors dread hearing that they've been **nominated**[5] for a Razzie.

3 The Razzies began in 1981 at the house of John Wilson, a Hollywood-based writer. Every year he would hold a dinner party on the night of the Oscars. He decided it would be fun to hold a fake award **ceremony**[6] which celebrated the year's worst movies. That year, *Can't Stop the Music* won the first Gold Raspberry Award for Worst Picture. Using a broomstick and **foam**[7] ball as a fake microphone, Wilson **hauled**[8] his guests onstage to make some comedic speeches.

4 Everyone agreed that Wilson's fake awards had been so funny that they should happen every year. By 1984, the ceremony had moved from Wilson's house into a school **auditorium**[9] and even managed to attract reporters from CNN.

5 Since then, the Razzies have gained **a cult following**. In order to take advantage of the **surge**[10] in media presence in Hollywood, the Razzies take place the night before the Oscars. Now, the ceremony can get the attention it **deserves**[11] without having to compete with the Oscars.

6 In 2005, actress Halle Berry turned up in person to accept her award for Worst Actress. Holding her 2002 Oscar in one hand, and her Razzie in the other, she gave a **hilarious**[12] speech to the crowd. Interestingly enough, in 2010, actress Sandra Bullock won an Oscar and a Razzie in the same year.

Key Words

1. achievement 成就 (n.) 2. involve 包括；牽涉 (v.) 3. to the contrary 恰恰相反的
4. category 種類 (n.) 5. nominate 提名 (v.) 6. ceremony 典禮；儀式 (n.) 7. foam 泡綿 (n.)
8. haul 拖 (v.) 9. auditorium 禮堂 (n.) 10. surge 激增 (n.) 11. deserve 應該；應得 (v.)
12. hilarious 引人發笑的 (a.) 13. poke fun at sb. 取笑某人 14. peel 果皮 (n.) 15. slap 摑掌 (n.)
16. elite 菁英 (n.)

◀ Sandra Bullock accepted her award for "Worst Actress of 2009" for her performance in *All About Steve*.
(cc by Shari B. Ellis)

The Razzies (cc by Par Lance)

7   Some claim, however, that the Razzies and John Wilson are cruel by **poking fun at**[13] the worst movies. Wilson has responded by saying "a banana **peel**[14] on the floor, not a **slap**[15] in the face," although not everyone in Hollywood agrees with him. Nevertheless, it won't stop the Razzies from making fun of the Hollywood **elite**[16] any time soon.

Questions

_____ 1. What is the main idea of this article? ··· ◆Main Idea◆
    a The Razzies take place in Hollywood.
    b John Wilson is the founder of the Razzies.
    c The Razzies boldly make fun of bad movies.
    d Actors often complain about the Razzies.

_____ 2. What is the subject of this article? ··································· ◆Subject Matter◆
    a An award ceremony.   **b** A famous actress.
    c A historical event.   **d** The worst fruit.

_____ 3. Which of the following statements is true? ······················· ◆Supporting Details◆
    a The Razzies were first held in an auditorium.
    b The Razzies don't care what the Hollywood elite thinks.
    c To get a Razzie, you must have already won an Oscar.
    d Hollywood actors grow up dreaming about winning a Razzie.

_____ 4. What can be inferred from John Wilson's description of the awards as "a banana peel on the floor, not a slap in the face?" ··························· ◆Inference◆
    a The Razzies are meant to be hateful and cruel.
    b The Razzies are both cruel and funny.
    c The Razzies should be thrown in the garbage.
    d The Razzies are a joke, not an attack.

_____ 5. What does **a cult following** in the fifth paragraph mean? ········· ◆Words in Context◆
    a An event with a strangely popular fanbase.   **b** A religious organization.
    c A natural wonder.   **d** An overlooked occasion.

_____ 6. What is the passage mostly about? ······························· ◆Clarifying Devices◆
    a A joke about an event.   **b** A metaphor for an event.
    c A theory about an event.   **d** An account of an event.

Week 3 Day 1 And the Worst Actor Goes To . . .

Week 3 Day 2
Geography

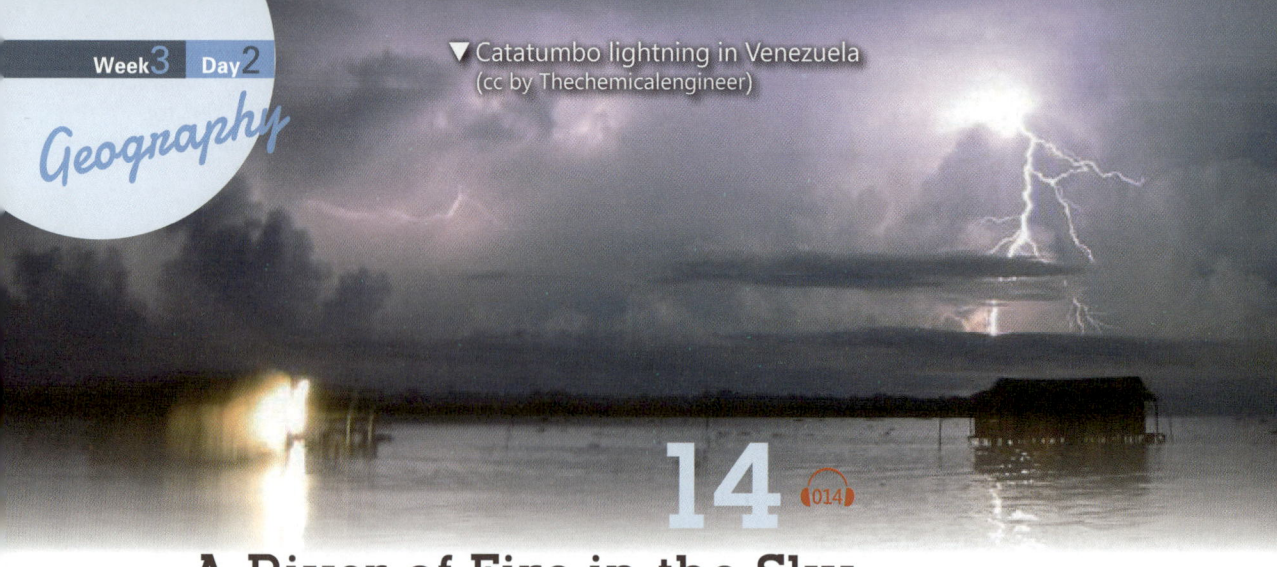

▼ Catatumbo lightning in Venezuela
(cc by Thechemicalengineer)

14

A River of Fire in the Sky

1. In northern Venezuela, where the Catatumbo River flows into Lake Maracaibo, thunder and lightning **rage**[1] on up to 300 nights each year. It's an **eternal**[2] thunderstorm that lights up the sky with over 20,000 flashes of lightning per night and is known to local tribes as "the river of fire in the sky."

2. The first mention of this **extraordinary**[3] natural **phenomenon**[4] is in a 1597 poem, which tells how the ships of English pirate Sir Francis Drake, who was planning to attack the area, were **illuminated**[5] by the recurring flashes of lightning. As a result, Drake's surprise attack was spotted and **prevented**[6].

3. The lightning is so bright that it can be seen 500 km away on the Caribbean island of Aruba, leading to its **alternate**[7] nickname, "The Maracaibo Lighthouse."

4. Though the lightning itself is no different from that in common thunderstorms, a number of factors make the storms truly **spectacular**[8]. Large amounts of natural gas in the area's atmosphere allow the lightning to recharge faster than usual, resulting in more flashes over shorter periods of time. Also, dust **particles**[9] in the atmosphere often give the flashes an unusual red or orange hue, and storms can last for up to 10 hours at a time.

5. The prevailing theory is that the storms are caused by warm winds flowing in from the Caribbean Sea to the north, which mix with cold air blowing from the Andes mountain range to the south.

▶ satellite image of Lake Maracaibo

Key Words

1. rage 肆虐 (v.)　2. eternal 永久的 (a.)　3. extraordinary 非凡的 (a.)　4. phenomenon 現象 (n.)
5. illuminate 照亮 (v.)　6. prevent 避免 (v.)　7. alternate 替代的 (a.)　8. spectacular 壯觀的 (a.)
9. particle 微粒 (n.)　10. concentration 集中 (n.)　11. ozone 臭氧 (n.)　12. rip 撕裂 (v.)
13. molecule 分子 (n.)　14. spectacle 奇觀 (n.)　15. gang（歹徒等的）一幫 (n.)　16. bandit 土匪 (n.)

6   Mountains of almost 5,000 meters in height surround the lake, and this traps the hot and cold winds in a relatively small area, causing an intense **concentration**[10] of conditions perfect for a thunderstorm.

7   The thunderstorm is also one of the greatest individual sources of natural **ozone**[11] in the world. Ozone is created as the lightning **rips**[12] through **molecules**[13] of oxygen, rearranging them into ozone. The new ozone usually stays in the lower levels of the atmosphere, however, never actually reaching and healing the damaged ozone layer.

8   For those eager to see the **spectacle**[14] firsthand, a warning: Tourists should be aware that this area of Venezuela is full of drug **gangs**[15] and armed **bandits**[16], making a visit potentially dangerous as well as awe-inspiring.

▶ statue of Sir Francis Drake

Week 3 Day 2 A River of Fire in the Sky

Questions

_____ 1. Which of the following is the main topic of the article? •Main Idea•
   a The drug gangs of Venezuela.
   b The never-ending storm.
   c Weird weather in South America.
   d Natural lighthouses.

_____ 2. The article mostly focuses on which of the following? •Subject Matter•
   a The dangers of visiting the site.
   b The storm's various nicknames.
   c How ozone is created.
   d The unique nature of the storm.

_____ 3. Which of the following statements is NOT true? •Supporting Details•
   a Catatumbo lightning helps heal the ozone layer.
   b The phenomenon can be seen up to 500 km away.
   c The lightning sometimes looks red or orange.
   d Lake Maracaibo is a dangerous place to visit.

_____ 4. Which group of people is most likely to be interested in the area? •Inference•
   a Historians researching pirate history.
   b Journalists interested in local legends.
   c Environmental researchers.
   d Poets seeking inspiration.

_____ 5. What does the word **hue** in the fourth paragraph mean? •Words in Context•
   a Sound.   b Texture.   c Color.   d Design.

_____ 6. What does the article mostly resemble? •Text Form•
   a An article in a geographic magazine.
   b A scientific paper.
   c A retelling of a legend.
   d A weather report.

Week 3　Day 3

Animals

15
The Soft Glow of the Natural World

firefly

comb jelly

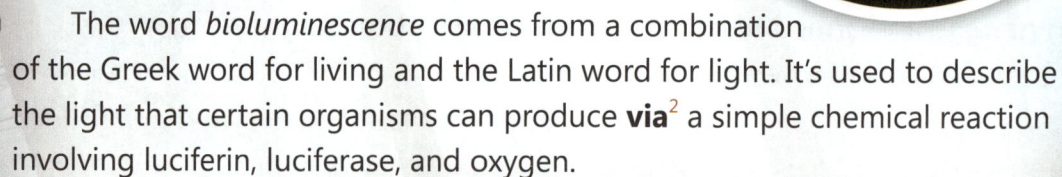

1　Whether it's fireflies glowing in the night sky or an angler fish illuminating the darkest depths of the ocean, bioluminescence shows us just how clever the process of **evolution**[1] can be.

2　The word *bioluminescence* comes from a combination of the Greek word for living and the Latin word for light. It's used to describe the light that certain organisms can produce **via**[2] a simple chemical reaction involving luciferin, luciferase, and oxygen.

3　Most people **assume**[3] that bioluminescence is restricted to fireflies and glowworms, but in reality several organisms can glow in the dark, including fish, whales, squid, bacteria, and even mushrooms. Bioluminescence also comes in a whole **spectrum**[4] of colors, from the black dragonfish's red glow to the way Vibrionaceae bacteria can make the ocean look like milk.

4　So what's the point of all this glowing? The answer has to do with evolution. Each **species**[5] has **evolved**[6] bioluminescence in order to survive in its environment.

5　Take fireflies for example, their bioluminescence serves a few purposes. It helps them attract things they want such as **prey**[7] and **potential**[8] mates. It also helps them avoid potential dangers. Predators think twice about eating fireflies because they know that the chemicals that produce bioluminescence taste awful.

6　Firefly bioluminescence is fairly **straightforward**[9]. Other species can be a lot more **complex**[10]. Mycena lucentipes, a glowing mushroom found in Brazil, is one such example. Insects are a constant threat to these mushrooms, so they rely on bioluminescence to attract animals that like to chow down on insects. This is like evolution's **version**[11] of the old saying "the enemy of my enemy is my friend."

Key Words

① evolution 演化 (n.)　② via 憑藉 (prep.)　③ assume 以為 (v.)　④ spectrum 光譜 (n.)
⑤ species 品種 (n.)　⑥ evolve 演化 (v.)　⑦ prey 獵物 (n.)　⑧ potential 潛在的；有可能的 (a.)
⑨ straightforward 簡單的 (a.)　⑩ complex 複雜的 (a.)　⑪ version 版本 (n.)
⑫ fascinating 迷人的 (a.)　⑬ defense 防衛機制 (n.)　⑭ predator 掠食者 (n.)　⑮ tycoon 商業大亨 (n.)

angler fish

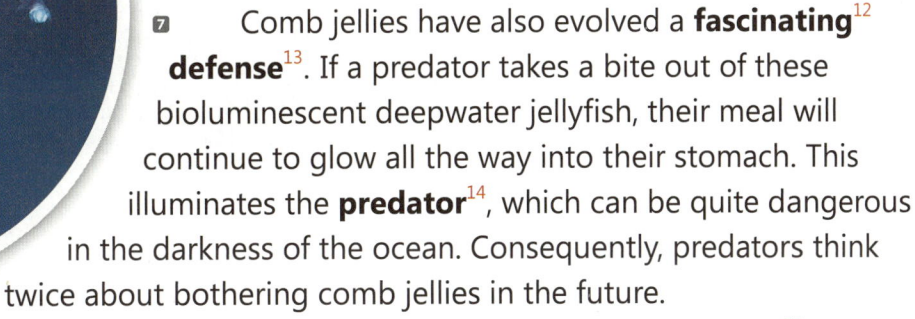

7 Comb jellies have also evolved a **fascinating**[12] **defense**[13]. If a predator takes a bite out of these bioluminescent deepwater jellyfish, their meal will continue to glow all the way into their stomach. This illuminates the **predator**[14], which can be quite dangerous in the darkness of the ocean. Consequently, predators think twice about bothering comb jellies in the future.

8 The process of evolution is truly amazing. It's like nature's **tycoon**[15]— it identifies a gap in the market and uses **innovation** to fill it. What's more, if evolution can find a way to make living organisms create light like a light bulb, what can't it do?

Questions

____ 1. Which of the following best summarizes the topic of the article? ◆Main Idea◆
   a The incredible genius of evolution.
   b The life and times of fireflies.
   c The bioluminescence of marine life.
   d The importance of bioluminescence.

____ 2. What does this article mainly focus on? ◆Subject Matter◆
   a Fireflies.   **b** Predators and prey.   **c** Bioluminescence.   **d** Jellyfish.

____ 3. Which of the following statements is NOT true? ◆Supporting Details◆
   a Bioluminescence comes in different colors.
   b Bioluminescence is caused by a chemical reaction.
   c Fungi can also have bioluminescence.
   d Bioluminescence is caused by poisonous chemicals.

____ 4. Which of the following can we infer from this article? ◆Inference◆
   a Bioluminescence is mainly used to see in the dark.
   b Fireflies are the most common bioluminescent organism.
   c Bioluminescent mushrooms are poisonous.
   d Humans will one day evolve bioluminescence.

____ 5. The last paragraph of this article mentions using innovation to fill gaps in the market. What does **innovation** mean? ◆Words in Context◆
   a Something new and different.   **b** Something old and tested.
   c Something simple and effective.   **d** Something forgotten.

____ 6. What tone does the author take in this article? ◆Author's Tone◆
   a Outraged.   **b** Emotional.   **c** Instructive.   **d** Humorous.

History

Week 3 Day 4 ▶ Mongol Empire

under the reign of Genghis Khan in 1227
under the reign of his heirs at its greatest extent in 1279

16

The Realm[1] of the Khans

[1] The **barren**[2] plains of Mongolia are among the world's most **obscure**[3] places. Eight hundred years ago, though, they were the center of the largest **contiguous** land empire ever created. From 1206 to 1294, the Mongol Khans (leaders) **conquered**[4] an area stretching from Korea to Hungary. At its greatest extent, their empire covered 24 million square kilometers!

[2] It all began with Temujin, a Mongolian **tribal**[5] chief who defeated his many rivals in battle. Uniting their tribes under his **command**[6], he created a legal system for all Mongols. Never heard of him? How about Genghis Khan? He took this title, which means "universal leader," at a **council**[7] in 1206. The Mongol Empire was born.

[3] Over the next 21 years, Genghis Khan's armies moved in all directions. They soon controlled northern China, southern Russia, Central Asia, and areas of the Middle East. When the great khan died in 1227, this **territory**[8] was divided into four kingdoms to be ruled by his **descendants**[9].

[4] Ogedei, Genghis's third son, was elected the new great khan in 1229. Under his **leadership**[10], the empire continued to grow. Eastern Europe, Persia, and northern Korea were soon Mongol territory. Ogedei's death in 1241, however, was the start of a long struggle for power among members of his family.

[5] Under Kublai Khan, one of Genghis's grandsons, the empire reached its height. Focusing on **expansion**[11] in East Asia, Kublai brought all of China and Korea under Mongol control. He also conquered areas of Southeast Asia, but was unsuccessful in his **attempts**[12] to take over Japan and Java. By the time of his death in 1294, the empire had **permanently**[13] divided.

Genghis Khan (1162–1227)
Ogedei Khan (1186–1241)
Kublai Khan (1215–1294)

Key Words

1. **realm** 王國；領域 (n.)　2. **barren** 貧瘠 (a.)　3. **obscure** 偏僻的 (a.)　4. **conquer** 征服 (v.)
5. **tribal** 部落的；種族的 (a.)　6. **command** 指揮；命令 (n.)　7. **council** 議會 (n.)　8. **territory** 領土 (n.)
9. **descendant** 後裔；子孫 (n.)　10. **leadership** 領導 (n.)　11. **expansion** 擴張；擴大 (n.)
12. **attempt** 試圖 (n.)　13. **permanently** 永久地 (adv.)　14. **homeland** 祖國；故鄉 (n.)

▶ Mongolian yurt

It would soon shrink greatly. By the late 1300s, the khans controlled little more than Mongolia itself.

The Mongol Empire united most of Eurasia for the first and only time in history. Although it existed for less than 150 years, it had a major impact. The Mongols encouraged—and often forced—large populations to move far from their **homelands**[14]. This resulted in the beginnings of many modern states such as Russia and Iran. The eastern world has changed a lot since the days of the khans, but it would not be what it is if not for them.

Questions

____ 1. What is the main idea of this article? •Main Idea•
  a The Mongols forced many people to move.
  b Mongolia is a very obscure place.
  c The khans and their armies did remarkable things.
  d Kublai Khan was unable to take over Japan.

____ 2. What does this article primarily deal with? •Subject Matter•
  a A movement.   b An empire.   c A culture.   d A battle.

____ 3. Which of the following was a problem for the khans? •Supporting Details•
  a Finding enough soldiers to control their empire.
  b Conquering a very large part of the world.
  c Creating a legal system for all Mongols.
  d Struggling against their relatives for power.

____ 4. What can we assume about Kublai Khan? •Inference•
  a He didn't really want to be the great khan.
  b He was very angry about not conquering Java.
  c He wasn't interested in taking over more of Europe.
  d He wanted his grandfather to be proud of him.

____ 5. What does **contiguous** mean? •Words in Context•
  a Sharing a border.   b Having mountains.
  c Conquering land.   d Moving in all directions.

____ 6. Where would you be likely to find this article? •Text Form•
  a On a world history website.
  b In a Mongolian travel advertisement.
  c On the front page of a newspaper.
  d In a biography of Genghis Khan.

Week 3 | Day 5

Mystery

17
The City Lost Under the Sea

▼ statue of Plato

1 When Plato wrote in 360 BC about an advanced island society named Atlantis, he probably had no idea that his words would become such a historical mystery. Even today, over 2,000 years after his dialogues were originally written, we are still trying to discover whether Atlantis is fact or fiction.

2 Plato described an island **empire**[1] that was rich in resources and military power. He also mentioned that Atlantis was once **allies**[2] with Athens, the city where Plato is thought to have been born. In the end, Atlantis **betrayed**[3] Athens and launched an **invasion**[4] against its former ally. Its attempt failed, and afterward the island of Atlantis suffered a **series**[5] of natural **catastrophes**[6] that caused it to be "swallowed by the sea."

3 Some people believe that there's no mystery at all. Plato was just using Atlantis as a **metaphor**[7] to teach his readers a **moral**[8] lesson. Their argument is supported by two important pieces of evidence. First, Plato was known to use metaphors frequently in his writing. Secondly, Plato claimed that these events occurred in 9000 BC. Back then, Athens was probably just a **handful**[9] of people sitting around campfires, if it was anything at all.

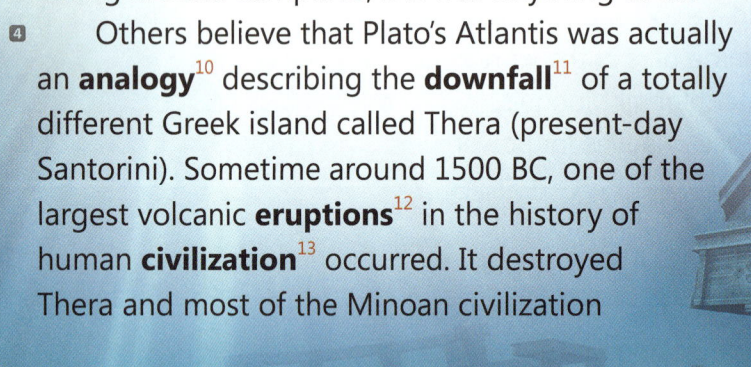

4 Others believe that Plato's Atlantis was actually an **analogy**[10] describing the **downfall**[11] of a totally different Greek island called Thera (present-day Santorini). Sometime around 1500 BC, one of the largest volcanic **eruptions**[12] in the history of human **civilization**[13] occurred. It destroyed Thera and most of the Minoan civilization

Key Words

① empire 帝國 (n.)　② ally 同盟 (n.)　③ betray 背叛 (v.)　④ invasion 入侵 (n.)　⑤ series 系列 (n.)
⑥ catastrophe 大災難 (n.)　⑦ metaphor 隱喻 (n.)　⑧ moral 道德的 (a.)　⑨ handful 少量 (n.)
⑩ analogy 類推 (n.)　⑪ downfall 覆滅 (n.)　⑫ eruption 爆發 (n.)　⑬ civilization 文明 (n.)
⑭ shrug off 不予理會　⑮ account 描述 (n.)　⑯ ruins 廢墟；遺跡（常用複數）(n.)

along with it. Supporters of this theory **shrug off**[14] the 9000 BC date that Plato recorded; maybe he was just tired that day and added an extra zero by mistake.

5 Finally, there's a group of people who believe that Plato's **account**[15] of Atlantis is the literal truth. For them, the **ruins**[16] of this advanced island civilization are somewhere at the bottom of the sea just waiting to be discovered. What's more, finding them won't be easy. While most people who believe in Atlantis place it somewhere in or around the Mediterranean Sea, others claim that it's in the Atlantic Ocean or the North Sea off the coast of Sweden. That's quite a large area to search.

◀ Santorini

Questions

_____ 1. Which of the following is the main topic of this article? ◆Main Idea◆
   a Various interpretations of the economy of Atlantis.
   b Various interpretations of the society of Atlantis.
   c Various interpretations of Plato's writings.
   d Various interpretations of Greek myths.

_____ 2. What does this article focus on? ◆Subject Matter◆
   a Plato.   b A mysterious island.   c Greece.   d Volcanoes.

_____ 3. Which of the following statements is true? ◆Supporting Details◆
   a Atlantis has been found off the coast of Florida.
   b People disagree over the existence of Atlantis.
   c Plato visited Atlantis four times in his life.
   d Atlantis was destroyed by a terrible plague.

_____ 4. What can we infer from this article? ◆Inference◆
   a There is no historical record of Athens from 9000 BC.
   b Atlantis was destroyed by an alien civilization.
   c Atlantis is actually modern-day Hawaii.
   d Plato had visited Atlantis himself.

_____ 5. What does the word **literal** mean in the last paragraph? ◆Words in Context◆
   a Loose.   b Actual.   c Literate.   d False.

_____ 6. What caused Atlantis to be swallowed by the sea? ◆Cause and Effect◆
   a Alien invasion.   b Having a large military.
   c Being allies with Athens.   d Natural disasters.

Culture

Week 3 Day 6

18 Celebrating in Color

[1] Padma opened her eyes, threw off her blanket, and **darted**[1] out of bed. The day that she had been looking forward to for a long time had finally arrived. It was the last full moon of the winter season. It was time to celebrate Holi, the Hindu Festival of Colors.

[2] Padma didn't even have time to finish dressing before Sanjay **beckoned**[2] to her from outside the window. In a flash, she ran downstairs and out the door. Her mother didn't even have enough time to **scold**[3] her for wearing nice clothes on Holi.

[3] Armed with water pistols and red, blue, and yellow *gulal* color **powder**[4], Padma and Sanjay set out. They rode their bikes through the streets searching for people to **ambush**. Whenever they came across someone, they would shout "Holi hai!" and shower them with water and handfuls of *gulal*. Eventually, they ran into a **rival**[5] group of children and an all-out war broke out. When the battle was over, the **warriors**[6] on both sides looked like rainbows.

[4] They went back to Padma's apartment for lunch. Sanjay could eat with Padma's family because normal rules regarding the separation of **castes**[7] aren't followed during Holi. As the two kids chewed on sweets, Padma's mom told them about where Holi came from.

[5] Holi **originated**[8] from the story of a demon king named Hiranyakashyap and his sister Holika. One day, the demon king asked his son Prahalad who the greatest god was. When Prahalad answered "Vishnu," the **Supreme**[9] god, instead of his father, the demon king became **enraged**[10] and **demanded**[11] that his sister Holika kill this **rebellious**[12] son of his. Holika

▲ colorful powder for Holi

Key Words

[1] dart 狂奔 (v.)　[2] beckon 點頭示意 (v.)　[3] scold 責罵 (v.)　[4] powder 粉末 (n.)　[5] rival 競爭者 (n.)
[6] warrior 戰士 (n.)　[7] caste 種姓 (n.)　[8] originate 源自 (v.)　[9] supreme 至高的 (a.)
[10] enrage 使發怒 (v.)　[11] demand 要求 (v.)　[12] rebellious 反叛的 (a.)　[13] crisp 鬆脆物 (n.)
[14] bonfire 營火 (n.)　[15] feast 筵席 (n.)

▶ People celebrate Holi regardless of caste and race.

agreed, but when she tried to drag Prahalad into a pit of fire, the gods protected him and she was burnt to a **crisp**[13].

6 After lunch, Padma and Sanjay headed out to ambush more people with water and *gulal*. That night, there was a huge **bonfire**[14], and all of the locals came out to sing, dance, and enjoy a giant **feast**[15] together. Later that night, back in her bed, Padma was still smiling when she finally closed her eyes. She was already looking forward to next year's Holi celebrations.

Questions

____ 1. Which of the following topics best summarizes the article? ◆Main Idea◆
   a A day in the life of Padma.
   b The origin of the Festival of Colors.
   c Padma and Sanjay's Friendship.
   d How to Celebrate Holi.

____ 2. What does this article focus on? ◆Subject Matter◆
   a A festival.   b A game.   c Paintings.   d An art.

____ 3. Which of the following statements is NOT true? ◆Supporting Details◆
   a Holi is known as the Festival of Colors.
   b People throw colored powder on Holi.
   c People use water pistols on Holi.
   d Holi is celebrated at the end of July.

____ 4. What can we infer from this article? ◆Inference◆
   a Sanjay has a lot of siblings.
   b Sanjay and Padma belong to different social classes.
   c Sanjay lives with Padma's family.
   d Holi is celebrated twice a year.

____ 5. The third paragraph mentions that Padma and Sanjay searched for people to ambush. What does **ambush** mean? ◆Words in Context◆
   a To surprise attack a person.   b To laugh at a person.
   c To shout a person's name.   d To chase a person away.

____ 6. What can this article best be described as? ◆Clarifying Devices◆
   a A timeline.   b A descriptive essay.
   c A narrative essay.   d A biography.

Week 3 Day 6 Celebrating in Color

49

Festivals in India

Elephant Festival

is celebrated every year in March on the occasion of Holi in Jaipur, India.

Holi Festival

is celebrated at the end of the winter season on the last full moon day of the lunar month Phalguna (February/March).

Diwali
(The Festival of Lights)

is on the 15th day of the dark fortnight of the Hindu month of Ashwin (October/November).

Week 4

Day 1 Geography	19 Windows Into the Underworld	52
Day 2 Animals	20 Small but Deadly	54
Day 3 Business	21 The Bigger They Are the Harder They Fall	56
Day 4 Entertainment	22 Dancing in the Moonlight	58
Day 5 Geography	23 A White Ocean	60
Day 6 Health & Body	24 Hearty French Feasting	62

Windows Into the Underworld[1]

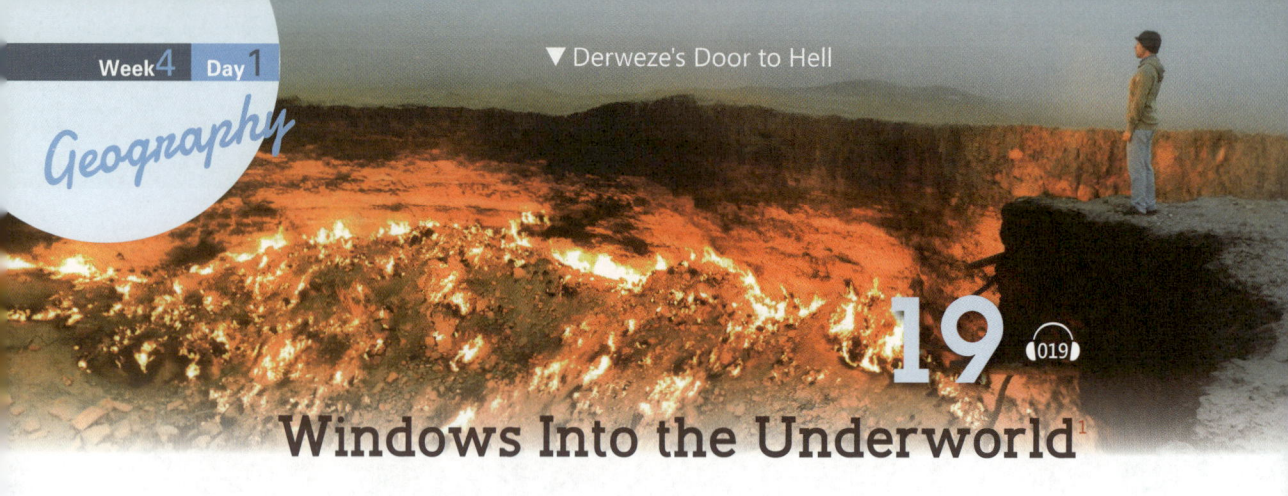

1 Near the small village of Derweze in the deserts of Turkmenistan, a **gaping** hole, 328 feet wide, burns red with a light that can be seen for miles around. It looks like Hell itself has opened up and is pouring its insides into the world above.

2 The ancient Greeks had many stories of heroes **venturing**[2] into Hell to **rescue**[3] lovers or question the dead, and the Italian poet Dante wrote of entering through an **archway**[4] on which the words "ABANDON ALL HOPE, YE WHO ENTER HERE." were **inscribed**[5].

3 This **fascination**[6] with entering the underworld has resulted in many places being labeled "gates of Hell," perhaps because of a strange natural phenomenon (often to do with fire, smoke, or darkness) or because of a legend or **superstition**[7] attached to the place.

4 The most visually **impressive**[8] of these gates is Derweze's Door to Hell in Turkmenistan, which has been burning constantly for over 40 years.

5 The Door to Hell is not an entirely natural phenomenon. Russians **drilling**[9] at the site in 1971 accidentally **pierced**[10] a massive underground **deposit**[11] of natural gas. The ground **collapsed**[12] beneath the drill, and the entire **operation**[13] fell into the pit.

6 In order to prevent the poisonous gas escaping into the atmosphere, the Russians decided to set the deposit on fire. They thought the gas would burn out in a few days, but the fires are still alight to this day.

7 You don't need a giant pit of fire to create a good gates of Hell myth, though. Hellam Township, Pennsylvania, has not only an unusual name, but also a disturbing story attached to it, giving rise to the belief that Hell's gates may be found in the woods near the town.

8 Legend has it that there was once a mental **asylum**[14] in the woods. Fearing the patients would escape, the **residents**[15] built seven gates around the asylum.

Key Words

1. underworld 陰間 (n.) 2. venture 冒險 (v.) 3. rescue 拯救 (v.) 4. archway 拱門 (n.)
5. inscribe 刻 (v.) 6. fascination 魅力 (n.) 7. superstition 迷信 (n.)
8. impressive 予人深刻印象的 (a.) 9. drill 鑽 (v.) 10. pierce 刺穿 (v.) 11. deposit 蘊藏 (n.)
12. collapse 倒塌 (v.) 13. operation 操作機械 (n.) 14. asylum 精神病院 (n.) 15. resident 居民 (n.)

▶ Dante Alighieri (1265–1321)

One day a fire broke out in the asylum, and many of the patients were burned alive, stopped from escaping by the seven gates. The story goes that if someone finds these gates and passes through all seven, they will go directly to Hell itself.

ABANDON ALL HOPE, YE WHO ENTER HERE.

Questions

____ 1. Which of the following best summarizes the main topic of the article? ◆Main Idea◆
   a The gates of Hell in ancient Greece.
   b Modern day gates of Hell.
   c How to visit the Door to Hell in Derweze.
   d US towns with strange names.

____ 2. Which of the following would be suitable as an alternative title for the passage?
   ◆Subject Matter◆
   a Hell on Earth.
   b Doors of Opportunity.
   c Ghost Hunting in the United States.
   d Gas Leak Set Alight.

____ 3. Which of the following statements is NOT true? ◆Supporting Details◆
   a The hole in Derweze was caused by Russian drillers.
   b Hellam was the sight of a gas explosion in 1971.
   c The ancient Greeks had many stories about the underworld.
   d Many gates of Hell sites are natural phenomena.

____ 4. Which of the following can we infer about the story of the Seven Gates of Hell?
   ◆Inference◆
   a It is based on fact and has scientific evidence to prove it.
   b It is just a story which grew popular because of the town's name.
   c It is taken seriously and being investigated by the US government.
   d It is connected to the creation of the Door to Hell at Derweze.

____ 5. What does the word **gaping** in the first paragraph mean? ◆Words in Context◆
   a Wide open.   b Narrow.   c Evil.   d Attractive.

____ 6. Which of the following statements is an opinion? ◆Fact or Opinion◆
   a The Derweze Door to Hell was caused by a drilling accident.
   b There are many places around the world labelled "the gates of Hell."
   c The Derweze Door to Hell is the most visually impressive "gates of Hell."
   d The ancient Greeks had many stories about heroes entering Hell.

Week 4 Day 1 Windows Into the Underworld

Week 4 Day 2
Animals

▶ box jellyfish

20
Small but Deadly

① The world is a dangerous place, especially for a small animal. In the wild it pays to have a deadly weapon, be it for **self-defense**[1] or better hunting. From snakes to snails, some animals have developed a weapon more effective than big teeth or sharp claws, a weapon that can kill no matter how strong the **threat**[2]: **venom**[3].

② Many of the world's deadliest animals live in the sea. The terrifying box jellyfish is about three meters long and its venom can kill in less than three minutes. Some reports claim that this jellyfish has killed more than 5,500 people since 1954. Though **stings**[4] can be treated with **vinegar**[5], the venom acts so quickly that most people die in the water before even reaching the shore. You'd better be careful the next time you decide to take a **dip**[6].

③ Good things also come in small packages, and so, it seems, does venom. The blue-ringed **octopus**[7] is only the size of a golf ball, but it is one of the world's most deadly animals. Its bite has enough venom to kill 26 humans, but you might not even realize you've been bitten as its bite is often tiny and painless. Its venom is so powerful that most people die within minutes and there is no **antivenin**. However, there is still hope. If the **victim's**[8] heart can be kept going long enough, the venom will eventually leave the body with no harmful side effects.

④ While most creatures use their venom in self-defense and won't attack unless **provoked**[9], the Brazilian **wandering**[10] spider is particularly dangerous because of its **aggressive**[11] nature. Several things make this spider an **unpleasant**[12] customer. The first is it likes to move around a lot and lives in heavily **populated**[13] areas, hiding

▶ blue-ringed octopus

Key Words
① **self-defense** 自衛 (n.)　② **threat** 威脅 (n.)　③ **venom** 毒液 (n.)　④ **sting** 螫 (n.)
⑤ **vinegar** 醋 (n.)　⑥ **dip** 游泳 (n.)　⑦ **octopus** 章魚 (n.)　⑧ **victim** 受害者 (n.)　⑨ **provoke** 挑釁 (v.)
⑩ **wander** 漫遊 (v.)　⑪ **aggressive** 侵略性強的 (a.)　⑫ **unpleasant** 令人不悅的 (a.)
⑬ **populate** 居住於 (v.)　⑭ **conserve** 保存 (v.)　⑮ **reassuring** 使人放心的 (a.)

◀ Brazilian wandering spider

in houses, boxes, and cars; the second is it has the most effective venom of all species of spider; the third is that it's huge—sometimes as big as a man's hand! Luckily though, many of its bites contain no venom at all as it prefers to **conserve**[14] its supply for prey. Even more **reassuring**[15] is that no deaths have been reported since the discovery of the antivenin.

Week 4 Day 2 Small but Deadly

Questions

____ 1. Which of the following best summarizes the article? ◆Main Idea◆
   a Some animals use venom to protect themselves, others to hunt.
   b The box jellyfish is the world's deadliest animal, killing in minutes.
   c The Brazilian wandering spider is aggressive and lives in cities.
   d Many kinds of creatures use venom, and they're all very dangerous.

____ 2. What is the subject of this article? ◆Subject Matter◆
   a How rare the box jellyfish is.
   b Different kinds of venomous creatures.
   c Why people should not live in cities.
   d How important self-defense is.

____ 3. Which of the following statements is NOT true? ◆Supporting Details◆
   a The blue-ringed octopus' bite is extremely painful.
   b The box jellyfish is one of the world's deadliest creatures.
   c The Brazilian wandering spider often delivers bites without venom.
   d A box jellyfish's sting can kill in less than five minutes.

____ 4. According to the article, what should you do if you are stung by a jellyfish?
   ◆Inference◆
   a Capture the jellyfish.   b Stay in the water.
   c Apply vinegar to the sting.   d Ignore the sting.

____ 5. What does the word **antivenin** in the third paragraph most likely mean?
   ◆Words in Context◆
   a A book full of information.   b A cure for venom.
   c A piece of advice.   d A creature that lives in the ocean.

____ 6. What form does this article take? ◆Text Form◆
   a A narrative.   b A pros and cons list.
   c A timeline.   d A series of examples.

55

Week 4 Day 3
Business

◀ Lehman Brothers

21
The Bigger They Are the Harder They Fall

1   The investment bank with a 160-year history, Lehman Brothers, **weathered**¹ its fair share of crises. From railroad **bankruptcies**² to the Great Depression and even two world wars, it appeared the Lehman was built to last. That all changed however, on September 15, 2008 when that Lehman Brothers' luck ran out. It became the biggest bankruptcy in American history.

2   Just five years before its collapse, business was **booming**³ for the investment bank. In 2003 and 2004, the firm **acquired**⁴ a series of **subprime**⁵ **mortgage**⁶ lending companies. Subprime refers to high-interest **loans**⁷ that are given to financially risky clients. Most of the people who received subprime loans didn't earn enough money to pay them off. However, this wasn't considered to be a problem as long as property prices kept going up. Lehman Brothers was one of the Wall Street firms that **dove headfirst** into the subprime mortgage market, and from 2005 to 2007 it was rewarded with record profits.

3   In early 2008, however, everything changed. Property prices began to drop, and homeowners across America were suddenly on the **hook**⁸ for loans that were worth more than their houses. In March 2008, Bear Stearns, another large investment firm, nearly collapsed due to its exposure to subprime lending. Lehman Brothers stock gradually started to fall.

4   By September 2008, Lehman stock had fallen off a **cliff**⁹. Global equity markets **plunged**¹⁰ worldwide, and the firm looked for **salvation** elsewhere. In a desperate attempt to stave off bankruptcy, Lehman looked for a partner that could buy it out. It reached out to Barclays PLC, Bank of America, and even the Korean Development Bank, but no deal could be reached in time to save it. The fourth-largest investment bank in the United States went under.

5   Even though the American Government **bailed out**¹¹ other financial **institutions**¹² such as Bear Stearns, Fannie Mae, and Freddie Mac, it did nothing

Key Words
❶ weather 平安渡過（困境）(v.)   ❷ bankruptcy 破產 (n.)   ❸ boom 迅速發展 (v.)
❹ acquire 收購 (v.)   ❺ subprime 次級的 (a.)   ❻ mortgage 房貸 (n.)   ❼ loan 貸款 (n.)
❽ hook 鉤子 (n.)   ❾ cliff 懸崖 (n.)   ❿ plunge 猛跌 (v.)   ⓫ bail out 援助   ⓬ institution 機構 (n.)
⓭ asset 資產 (n.)   ⓮ irony 諷刺 (n.)   ⓯ panic 恐慌 (n.)   ⓰ recession 衰退 (n.)

to stop the collapse of Lehman Brothers. The decision to not help was based on Lehman's lack of valuable **assets**[13]. The **irony**[14] is that so many homeowners went bankrupt during this time for this very reason. After the news of Lehman Brothers' bankruptcy was announced, the Dow Jones Industrial Average dropped 500 points. This triggered a wider **panic**[15] as investors pulled their money out of markets in America and around the world. The Great **Recession**[16] had begun.

▶ the Great Depression

Questions

____ 1. What is the main topic of this article? ◆Main Idea◆
   a. The collapse of one of Wall Street's most powerful banks.
   b. The history of one of Wall Street's most powerful banks.
   c. The rise of one of Wall Street's most powerful banks.
   d. A short history of the Great Recession of 2008.

____ 2. What is this article about? ◆Subject Matter◆
   a. The Great Recession.
   b. An investment bank.
   c. Wall Street.
   d. Subprime loans.

____ 3. Which of the following statements is NOT true? ◆Supporting Details◆
   a. Lehman Brothers collapsed in 2008.
   b. Lehman Brothers was in business for over 150 years.
   c. The US government assisted in other investment banks.
   d. The Great Recession started in 2007.

____ 4. According to the article, which is most likely true? ◆Inference◆
   a. Many homeowners couldn't pay off their loans.
   b. Lehman Brothers caused the Great Recession.
   c. The Great Recession was caused by changing weather patterns.
   d. Wall Street banks didn't take risks before the market crashed.

____ 5. What does the word **salvation** in the fourth paragraph mean? ◆Words in Context◆
   a. Losing all one's money.
   b. Commercial Awareness.
   c. Saved from harm.
   d. Being dismantled.

____ 6. What is the phrase **dove headfirst** in the last sentence of the second paragraph an example of? ◆Clarifying Devices◆
   a. It is a simile.
   b. It is a metaphor.
   c. It is an observation
   d. It is an example.

Week 4 Day 4

Entertainment

▶ flyer of Full Moon Party

22
Dancing in the Moonlight

[1] Every month, the island of Ko Pha Ngan in Thailand plays host to one of South East Asia's most **infamous**[1] parties—The Full Moon Party at Haad Rin Beach. On the night of the moon, partygoers wearing bright **neon**[2] clothing and neon body paint crowd onto the beach. Fire-dancers perform dangerous, **awe-inspiring**[3] **stunts**[4]. DJs play all kinds of head-spinning music. **Vendors**[5]—their **stalls**[6] covered in bright lights—sell giant, sweet cocktails served in beach **pails**[7].

[2] Up to 30,000 people attend the party each month, all looking for an unforgettable experience. And while the party is particularly popular with young backpackers, anyone and everyone is welcome to attend. Indeed, the fun of the Full Moon Party is that you never know who you might meet beneath Ko Pha Ngan's giant full moon, or what friendships or romances you might **kindle**[8] there. Most people don't stop dancing until the sun comes up the next morning.

[3] No one is quite sure how or when these parties began, though there are many stories. Most people think they started sometime in the late 80s, probably as a going away party at one of the beach's holiday **bungalows**[9]. But **regardless**[10] of when or how the parties began, news of them quickly spread by word of mouth. Soon, not only had the parties become a regular **occurrence**[11], but they were increasingly bigger and wilder, too.

[4] Some might say, though, that the parties have now become too popular, with locals complaining about the noise and mess caused by the partygoers. The parties have also become increasingly dangerous, due to the large number of **revelers**[12] and the excessive drinking that goes on. Broken glass causes bare-footed partyers particular problems, and the **numerous**[13] **attractions**[14] and

Key Words

❶ infamous 聲名狼藉的 (a.)　❷ neon 霓虹的 (a.)　❸ awe-inspiring 令人驚嘆的 (a.)　❹ stunt 特技 (n.)
❺ vendor 小販 (n.)　❻ stall 攤位 (n.)　❼ pail 桶 (n.)　❽ kindle 點燃；煽動 (v.)　❾ bungalow 平房 (n.)
❿ regardless 無論如何 (prep.)　⓫ occurrence 發生 (n.)　⓬ reveler 狂歡者 (n.)
⓭ numerous 許多的 (a.)　⓮ attraction 景點；吸引力 (n.)　⓯ bucket list 人生清單；遺願清單 (n.)

◀ partygoers wearing bright neon clothing and neon body paint

activities involving fire leave many with minor burns. In addition, thieves take advantage of the fact that most tourists will be out all night to break into their hotel rooms and steal their valuables.

5   Because of this, it's not clear how long the Thai government will allow the parties to continue. So if attending a Full Moon Party is on your **bucket list**[15], you'd better do it quickly!

◀ fire dancer performance

Questions

____ 1. What is the author's main point in the article? ◆Main Idea◆
  a No one is sure when the Full Moon Party in Thailand began.
  b Attending a Full Moon Party in Thailand is lots of fun, but it has its risks, too.
  c Full moon parties are particularly popular with young backpackers.
  d The Full Moon Party may not be around for much longer.

____ 2. What is the article about? ◆Subject Matter◆
  a A national celebration.
  b A daily TV show.
  c A rare sighting.
  d A regular event.

____ 3. Which of the following is true? ◆Supporting Details◆
  a The Full Moon Party stops at midnight.
  b On average, around 300 people attend each Full Moon Party.
  c The Full Moon Party takes place once a month.
  d No alcohol is served at the Full Moon Party.

____ 4. Which of these would be a good piece of advice for someone going to a Full Moon Party? ◆Inference◆
  a Always wear shoes.
  b Wear plenty of sunscreen.
  c Don't talk to strangers.
  d Go to bed early.

____ 5. In paragraph three, the author writes that news of the parties spread by word of mouth. What does it mean if news is **spread by word of mouth**? ◆Words in Context◆
  a It is broadcast on TV.
  b It is kept quiet for as long as possible.
  c It is passed orally from person to person.
  d It is transmitted in a secret code.

____ 6. How does the writer create interest in the first paragraph? ◆Clarifying Devices◆
  a By providing a vivid description.
  b By making a joke.
  c By quoting a famous person.
  d By referencing a scientific study.

Week 4 Day 5

Geography

▼ Salar de Uyuni (Salt Flat), Bolivia

23 A White Ocean

Salar de Uyuni covered with water

1   One **geophysicist**[1] described it as "a white ocean with no waves." Imagine standing on 10,582 square kilometers of barren white land as flat as a dinner plate, and you have some idea of what it might be like to visit the Salar de Uyuni, the world's largest salt flat in Bolivia, South America.

2   Formed from the gradual drying of a **gigantic**[2] **prehistoric**[3] lake, the Salar is covered with a solid salt **crust**[4] a few meters thick and hides a 20-meter-deep lake of salt water beneath the surface. It looks like a region of Antarctica rather than South America, and visitors find it difficult to convince themselves that it's salt, not snow, that they're **treading**[5] on.

3   The salt flat is dotted occasionally with small islands, which are the tops of ancient volcanoes once **submerged**[6] beneath the lake, but which are now the perfect **habitat**[7] for 1,000-year-old **cacti**[8] growing at a rate of one centimeter per year.

4   The area is astonishingly flat, with elevation varying 80 centimeters at most over an area the size of a small country. This has made it perfect for **satellites**[9] to use to adjust their **altimeters**. Satellites usually use the ocean floor to determine exactly how high they are in space, but the clear weather and uniform nature of the Salar makes it about five times more effective at giving **accurate**[10] readings.

5   The salt flat has also been an **economic**[11] lifesaver for Bolivia, which is South America's poorest country. It is **estimated**[12] that up to 70% of the world's **lithium**[13] supply is contained in the heavily concentrated salt water beneath the Salar's hard surface. Lithium, which is essential for making batteries, is **extracted**[14] from the Salar by creating small ponds on the surface filled with the

Key Words

[1] geophysicist 地科學家 (n.)   [2] gigantic 巨大的 (a.)   [3] prehistoric 史前的 (a.)   [4] crust 外殼 (n.)
[5] tread 踩；踏 (v.)   [6] submerge 淹沒 (v.)   [7] habitat 棲地 (n.)   [8] cactus 仙人掌 (n.)
[9] satellite 人造衛星 (n.)   [10] accurate 精確的 (a.)   [11] economic 經濟的 (a.)   [12] estimate 估計 (v.)
[13] lithium 鋰 (n.)   [14] extract 提煉 (v.)   [15] evaporate 蒸發 (v.)   [16] breed 繁殖 (v.)

◀ Isla Incahuasi, inside the Salar de Uyuni, featuring giant cacti

salty solution from beneath. The lithium and salt are separated as the water **evaporates**[15] in the sun.

6   Visitors to the salt flats will also be able to see pink South American flamingos, which **breed**[16] there in November, and also the famous Palacio de Sal, a hotel made entirely of salt, where the one important rule is "Don't lick the walls!"

Questions

1. Which of the following best summarizes the article? ◆Main Idea◆
   a. The Salar de Uyuni has been good for Bolivia's economy.
   b. The Salar de Uyuni is a natural wonder with many amazing features.
   c. The Salar de Uyuni is a salt flat in Bolivia.
   d. The Salar de Uyuni was formed from a prehistoric lake.

2. What does this article mainly focus on? ◆Subject Matter◆
   a. The appearance and practical uses of the Salar de Uyuni.
   b. The age and formation of the Salar de Uyuni.
   c. The animal and plant life of the Salar de Uyuni.
   d. Hotels and places to stay on the Salar de Uyuni.

3. Which of the following statements is NOT true? ◆Supporting Details◆
   a. The Salar de Uyuni is an important source of lithium.
   b. Flamingos breed on the Salar de Uyuni every November.
   c. There is a hotel made entirely of salt on the Salar de Uyuni.
   d. The Salar de Uyuni is the world's second-largest salt flat.

4. Which of the following can we infer from the article? ◆Inference◆
   a. The Salar de Uyuni is covered with snow in winter.
   b. No life can survive in the Salar de Uyuni.
   c. It's possible to visit the Salar de Uyuni as a tourist.
   d. The Salar de Uyuni was once covered in trees.

5. What does the word **altimeter** in the fourth paragraph mean? ◆Words in Context◆
   a. A device used to measure temperature.
   b. A device used to measure wind speed.
   c. A device used to measure height.
   d. A device used to measure air pressure.

6. What tone does the author take in this article? ◆Author's Tone◆
   a. Argumentative.   b. Descriptive.   c. Intimate.   d. Pessimistic.

Week 4 Day 5 A White Ocean

Week 4 Day 6

Health & Body

▶ Moderate consumption of red wine has a positive effect on health.

24

Hearty French Feasting

1. When you think of French food—the rich creams, the buttery sauces, **heaps**[1] of cheese, **succulent**[2] red meat—do the words "heart attack" **leap**[3] to mind?

2. Well, they shouldn't because despite eating four times as much butter and almost twice as much cheese as Americans, the death rate from heart disease in France is under half of what it is in the United States.

3. It's been called the French **paradox**[4], and scientists have linked it to various factors from the French habit of snacking less to the Mediterranean climate, which encourages more exercise.

4. The phenomenon, which **contradicts**[5] common sense, has largely **baffled**[6] scientists, but the **prevailing**[7] theory about why this **counterintuitive** trend occurs is centered on the French love of red wine.

5. Research has shown that **moderate**[8] consumption of red wine does have a positive effect on health and long life. Scientists originally thought that the chemical **resveratrol**[9] was responsible for this effect, but it seems that resveratrol levels in red wine are too low to create an effect as large as the French paradox.

6. Another chemical has been found in wine that does occur in sufficient quantities to protect the cells in human blood **vessels**[10] effectively. **Oligomeric procyanidins**[11] occur in greater quantities in the wines of those French regions which have the healthiest people. Whatever the science behind the phenomenon, the **revelation**[12] that wine could keep you heart healthy resulted in a huge surge in wine imports in the United States.

7. Other theories that attempt to explain the French paradox suggest that simple French eating habits, such as eating smaller **portions**[13] of food over a longer period of time, have a positive influence on their health. French people tend not to snack between meals, eat less fried food, and take more time between courses to allow their food to digest properly.

Key Words

❶ heap 一堆 (n.)　❷ succulent 多汁的 (a.)　❸ leap 跳躍 (v.)　❹ paradox 悖論 (n.)
❺ contradict 發生矛盾 (v.)　❻ baffle 使困惑 (v.)　❼ prevailing 盛行的；普遍的 (a.)
❽ moderate 適度的 (a.)　❾ resveratrol 白藜蘆醇 (n.)　❿ vessel 血管 (n.)
⓫ oligomeric procyanidins 原花青素 (n.)　⓬ revelation 揭示 (n.)　⓭ portion 一部分；一份 (n.)
⓮ ample 豐富的 (a.)　⓯ artery 動脈 (n.)

▼ French eat smaller portion of food over a longer period of time.

Also, the sunny weather of southern France provides **ample**[14] opportunities for the French to get larger doses of vitamin D from the sun. Vitamin D helps prevent the hardening of **arteries**[15] and reduces the risk of heart attacks.

Theories aside, it seems if you want to enjoy good food and still have a healthy heart, it's simply better to have been born French.

Questions

____ 1. Which of the following is the main topic of the article? ········· ◆Main Idea◆
   a The benefits of living in France.
   b Prevailing theories of preventing heart disease.
   c The health benefits of French wine.
   d The mystery of the healthy French.

____ 2. What is this article about? ············· ◆Subject Matter◆
   a A particular chemical.
   b A medical contradiction.
   c French culture.
   d American eating habits.

____ 3. Which of the following statements is NOT true? ········· ◆Supporting Details◆
   a Death from heart disease in the United States is more common than in France.
   b The French do not snack between meals like Americans tend to do.
   c The French paradox is mostly due to genetic factors.
   d Red wine has been found to be good for your health.

____ 4. Which of the following is probably true? ············· ◆Inference◆
   a Americans who live permanently in France become less healthy.
   b The French paradox is of interest to those studying nutritional science.
   c Doctors are prescribing French foods to overweight Americans.
   d Sunbathing is an effective cure for genetic heart disease.

____ 5. What does the word **counterintuitive** in the fourth paragraph mean?
   ············· ◆Words in Context◆
   a Exactly how something should be.
   b Happening all over the world.
   c Of great interest to everyone.
   d The opposite of what you'd expect.

____ 6. What was the effect of the revelation that red wine is good for your heart?
   ············· ◆Cause and Effect◆
   a Scientists began to study the chemicals in red wine.
   b Americans began importing more red wine.
   c Oligomeric procyanidins were found to protect human cells.
   d The chemical resveratrol was discovered in red wine.

French Food

▲ foie gras

▲ escargot

▲ croissant

▲ baguette

▲ caviar

▲ truffle

▲ French onion soup

◀ coq au vin

▲ ratatouille

▲ soufflé

▲ crème brûlée

Week 5

Day 1 Science	25 Not the Only You?	66
Day 2 Language	26 Permanent Tongue Twisters	68
Day 3 People	27 The Electric Henry Ford	70
Day 4 Health & Body	28 Facing the Future	72
Day 5 Science	29 The Dark Mystery of Deep Space	74
Day 6 Arts & Literature	30 Cows, Sharks, and Spots	76

Science

Week 5 Day 1

25 Not the Only You?

1. You've just sat down and opened your textbook. It's time to improve your English reading ability and learn some new vocabulary. But maybe there's another version of you who decided not to study today. Maybe there's yet another version who gave up on studying because he or she decided to become a **professional**[1] dancer sometime last year. Maybe there's a particularly **vulgar**[2] one who prefers to **rip**[3] the pages out of this textbook and eat them rather than use them to master the English language.

2. While this might sound a little crazy, the **theory**[4] of **parallel**[5] universes has actually become well **established**[6] in certain scientific circles.

3. Think of a **deck**[7] of cards. If you **shuffle**[8] that deck hundreds of thousands of times, you will eventually get every possible **combination**[9]. Some experts in the field of **quantum**[10] physics believe that the same concept applies for our universe. If the universe is **infinite**[11], meaning that it goes on forever without stopping, then every possible combination of particles must exist somewhere.

4. Quantum physicists are also encouraged by evidence that matter can exist in two different states **simultaneously**. In 2010, researchers at the University of California made a tiny piece of metal **vibrate**[12] and stay still at the same time. If their conclusions are correct, then the reality of our universe is based on observing one of those possible states. The one that we don't see is being observed by someone else in a parallel universe. This process of observing one of many possible different states is what causes our reality to **split**[13] into different parallel universes. In the simplest terms, the theory of parallel universes assumes that our actions and decisions can be measured on the quantum level.

Key Words

❶ professional 專業的 (a.)　❷ vulgar 粗俗的 (a.)　❸ rip 撕；扯 (v.)　❹ theory 理論 (n.)
❺ parallel 平行的 (a.)　❻ establish 建立 (v.)　❼ deck 疊 (n.)　❽ shuffle 洗牌 (v.)
❾ combination 組合 (n.)　❿ quantum 量子 (n.)　⓫ infinite 無限的 (a.)　⓬ vibrate 振動 (v.)
⓭ split 分裂 (v.)　⓮ layman 外行人 (n.)　⓯ theoretical 理論的；假設的 (a.)

In **layman's**[14] terms, the decision to eat a hot dog makes particles in the brain react in a certain way.

Many of the scientists who believe in the **theoretical**[15] existence of parallel universes admit that it's probably impossible for us to travel between them. However, 100 years ago, most scientists believed that space travel was impossible. You might just get to meet the version of yourself that became a professional dancer one day after all.

▶ The decision to eat a hot dog makes particles in the brain react in a certain way.

Questions

____ 1. Which of the following best summarizes the article? ·······•Main Idea•
   a Your particles are always in motion.
   b There may be another version of you somewhere out there.
   c Matter can exist in two states simultaneously.
   d The most disputed theory in modern biology is about particles.

____ 2. What is this article about? ·······•Subject Matter•
   a Quantum physics.
   b States of matter.
   c Parallel universes.
   d Studying English.

____ 3. Which of the following statements is true? ·······•Supporting Details•
   a Scientists have traveled between parallel universes.
   b Matter can only exist in one state at one time.
   c The theory of parallel universes is becoming established.
   d The universe is a deck of cards.

____ 4. Which of the following is likely true according to the article? ·······•Inference•
   a There is proof of the theoretical existence of parallel universes.
   b It's possible to travel through time.
   c The universe is not infinite at all; it's finite, but we can't see the end.
   d Scientists are being influenced by Hollywood blockbusters.

____ 5. The fourth paragraph of this article mentions something existing in two different states simultaneously. What does the **simultaneously** mean? ·······•Words in Context•
   a As a gas.
   b At the same time.
   c One after the other.
   d As a liquid.

____ 6. How does the writer create interest in the first paragraph? ·······•Clarifying Devices•
   a By giving an amusing narrative.
   b By giving examples to prove a point.
   c By giving a biased opinion.
   d By giving contrasts of time.

Week 5 Day 2
Language

26 Permanent Tongue Twisters

1 The way that our body hears, understands, and produces speech is extremely complex, and like any other complex process, it can **malfunction**[1] sometimes. This is called a language **disorder**[2], and it can have serious consequences when it comes to communicating with our fellow human beings.

2 Language disorders come in two forms: **developmental**[3] and **acquired**[4]. Developmental language disorders occur naturally in some children when they are growing up. They can affect the growth of speech organs such as the **larynx**[5], **vocal cords**[6], or the parts of the brain that are responsible for communication. Acquired language disorders can happen to anyone, no matter one's age. They are most often caused by head **trauma**[7] or a lack of oxygen to the brain.

3 Some language disorders come in both developmental and acquired forms. Take **stuttering**[8], for example. Stuttering is a disorder where the flow of someone's speech is constantly **interrupted**[9]. The first sound of a word might be repeated ("g-g-g-go"), or lengthened ("mmmmake"). Sometimes, the word cannot leave the mouth at all.

4 Most of the time, stuttering is a developmental language disorder that **emerges**[10] in children, more often boys, around the age of three. Eighty percent of these children eventually stop stuttering before they become adults. However, there are rare instances when stuttering can be an acquired disorder. In these cases, a head trauma, a **stroke**[11], or drug use can cause sudden stuttering in an adult.

5 **Aphasia**[12] is another type of acquired language disorder. Much like acquired stuttering, a person can develop aphasia after suffering a head trauma or a stroke. The **symptoms**[13] of aphasia are extremely diverse. Some of them are simple, such as difficulty pronouncing words or using complete sentences.

▶ speech therapist and patient

Key Words

1. malfunction 故障 (v.) 2. disorder 失調 (n.) 3. developmental 發展的；發育的 (a.)
4. acquire 獲得 (v.) 5. larynx 喉頭 (n.) 6. vocal cords 聲帶 (n.) 7. trauma 創傷 (n.)
8. stutter 口吃 (v.) 9. interrupt 打斷 (v.) 10. emerge 出現 (v.) 11. stroke 中風 (n.)
12. aphasia 失語症 (n.) 13. symptom 症狀 (n.) 14. nonsense 無意義的 (a.)
15. therapist 治療師 (n.) 16. accuracy 正確 (n.) 17. clarity 清楚 (n.)

▶ speech organs

Others are quite serious, such as the inability to read or write. Some other symptoms are just downright strange, such as using **nonsense**[14] words in place of real ones.

6   The good news is that treatment for language disorders is improving all the time. Although most disorders cannot be cured, they can usually be reduced. Speech **therapists**[15] help patients to improve the **accuracy**[16] and **clarity**[17] of their sounds—and, equally importantly, their confidence.

Questions

___ 1. What would you say is the main topic of the article? ◆Main Idea◆
   a An analysis of different forms of stuttering.
   b An analysis of developmental and acquired language disorders.
   c How a head trauma can affect the way that you speak.
   d The complexity of the way that humans comprehend language.

___ 2. What is the article about? ◆Subject Matter◆
   a Head trauma.   b Aphasia.
   c Communication disorders.   d Speech therapists.

___ 3. Which of the following statements is true? ◆Supporting Details◆
   a Language disorders can only be developmental.
   b Language disorders can only be acquired.
   c The symptoms of aphasia are few and simple.
   d Some sufferers of aphasia can't read or write.

___ 4. According to the passage, which of the following could be a problem for people with language disorders? ◆Inference◆
   a Everyday communication.   b Use of illegal drugs.
   c Difficulties with breathing.   d Understanding children.

___ 5. What does the word **diverse** in the fifth paragraph mean? ◆Words in Context◆
   a Similar.   b Risky.   c Various.   d Dangerous.

___ 6. What is the writer's intention in the final paragraph? ◆Clarifying Devices◆
   a To make the reader angry.
   b To end on a positive note.
   c To summarize the content of the passage.
   d To offer an unusual opinion.

Week 5 Day 3

People

▶ Elon Musk
(cc by Steve Jurvetson)

27
🎧 027

The Electric Henry Ford

1. If Elon Musk has his way, you and your friends will soon be driving electric cars. For longer trips, you'll **zip**¹ around in **sealed**² **pods**³ that are faster and cheaper than airplanes. And someday you might even own an apartment on **Mars**⁴! Does that sound **far-fetched**? Well, if you've ever used PayPal to buy something, you're already part of Mr. Musk's rapidly changing world.

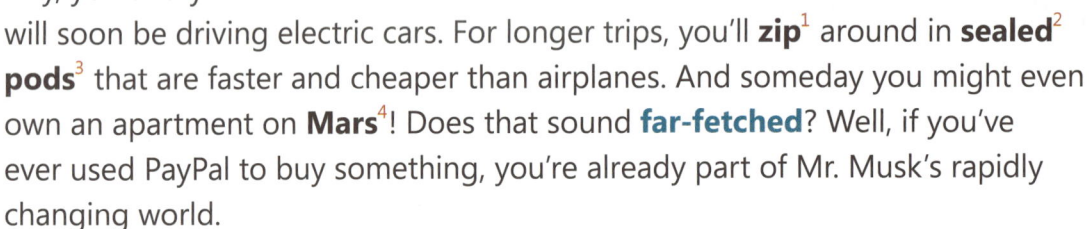

2. Born in South Africa in 1971, Elon Musk studied physics and economics in the United States. His early interests included clean energy, space travel, the Internet, and social change. **Remarkably**⁵, he has had a major impact in all of these areas.

3. After starting—and later selling—a successful software company, Musk helped establish PayPal in 2001. This online money **transfer**⁶ company has changed the way people pay for many things.

4. Most of us would consider that enough of an accomplishment. Just a year later, however, Musk literally launched SpaceX, a rocket manufacturing company. His purpose was to **advance**⁷ space travel technology, and he succeeded. In 2012, SpaceX became the first private company ever to **dock**⁸ a **vehicle**⁹ at the International Space Station! Maybe Musk's dream of building a human colony on Mars by 2040 isn't so crazy after all.

5. Meanwhile, back here on Earth, Musk set up SolarCity in 2006. As you might imagine, this is a **solar**¹⁰ power company, currently the second-largest in America. **Renewable**¹¹ energy was also the main reason Musk took over the Tesla electric car company in 2008.

▼ SolarCity is the second largest provider of solar power systems in the US.

Key Words

1. zip 快速移動 (v.)　2. seal 密封 (v.)　3. pod 吊艙 (n.)　4. Mars 火星 (n.)
5. remarkably 引人注目地 (adv.)　6. transfer 轉移；調動 (n.)　7. advance 發展 (v.)　8. dock（使）靠岸
9. vehicle 車輛 (n.)　10. solar 太陽的 (a.)　11. renewable 可再生的 (a.)　12. transportation 運輸；交通工具
13. envision 設計；想像 (v.)　14. commercial 商業的 (a.)　15. dismiss 摒棄 (v.)

◀ SpaceX Dragon orbiting Earth

Tesla now allows other carmakers to use its technology to develop their own electric vehicles. For Elon Musk, it seems, money isn't everything—though he certainly has plenty of it!

[6] And the ideas just keep on coming. The "hyperloop" **transportation**[12] system Musk **envisions**[13] would have people traveling through tubes in sealed pods at speeds of up to 1,200 kilometers per hour. That's nearly 50 percent faster than the average **commercial**[14] airplane! Musk also wants to make artificial intelligence more widely available and someday connect it directly to the human brain.

[7] From anyone else, that would sound like science fiction. But given all that this remarkable man has already done, we can't **dismiss**[15] anything he might imagine.

▶ Tesla Model S

Questions

____ 1. What is the writer trying to tell us in this article? •Main Idea•
   a Elon Musk cares about renewable energy.
   b People might be living on Mars by 2040.
   c One man can achieve a lot in many different fields.
   d The hyperloop is faster than commercial airplanes.

____ 2. What is this article primarily about? •Subject Matter•
   a Advances in technology.   b The future of mankind.
   c The events of someone's life. d Education in the United States.

____ 3. In which of these areas was Elon Musk first successful? •Supporting Details•
   a Space travel.   b Software.
   c Artificial intelligence.   d Automobiles.

____ 4. What can we assume about Elon Musk from the reading? •Inference•
   a He had a very good childhood.   b He doesn't like to fly on airplanes.
   c He never uses PayPal to buy things. d He cares about the environment.

____ 5. What does **far-fetched** mean? •Words in Context•
   a Hard to believe.   b Extremely fast.
   c On another planet.   d Rapidly changing.

____ 6. How could the author's tone in this passage best be described? •Author's Tone•
   a Insulting.   b Admiring.   c Humorous.   d Disturbing.

Week 5 Day 3 The Electric Henry Ford

71

Week 5　Day 5

Science

▼ The Hubble Space Telescope composite image shows the ring of dark matter in the galaxy cluster CL 0024+17.

29

▶ Fritz Zwicky (1898–1974)

The Dark Mystery of Deep Space

❶　　Question: How many **astronomers**[1] does it take to change a light bulb? Answer: None. Astronomers aren't afraid of the dark! Bad jokes aside, astronomers may not be afraid of the dark, but they certainly lose a lot of sleep over dark matter.

❷　　Dark matter is four times more common in our universe than ordinary matter, but it is impossible to see with a **telescope**[2], and scientists only know of its existence because of the effects it has on **visible**[3] matter.

❸　　Actually, "know" is perhaps too strong a word. Dark matter is an idea, a **hypothesis**, which tries to fill in the gaps between what we can see and what scientific data tells us about the universe. However, experiments have yet to detect the existence of dark matter particles, and this has caused some scientists to doubt the standard model for the structure and **formation**[4] of the universe.

❹　　The existence of dark matter was first suggested by a Swiss physicist named Fritz Zwicky in 1933. Observing a **galaxy**[5] **cluster**[6] called the Coma Cluster—where over 1,000 galaxies, each containing billions of stars, collect together in an unimaginably **vast**[7] **cosmic**[8] group—Zwicky found a puzzling **inconsistency**[9].

❺　　Zwicky made a mass **calculation**[10] based on the amount of visible matter in the cluster and also calculated the speed at which the galaxies in the cluster were moving. He realized that this mass did not provide enough gravity to keep these fast-moving galaxies in **orbit**[11]. The galaxies should have been flying out of the cluster, rather than staying inside it. Zwicky then calculated the mass of the cluster based on the speed of the galaxies and discovered that it was 400

Key Words

❶ astronomer 天文學家 (n.)　❷ telescope 望遠鏡 (n.)　❸ visible 可見的 (a.)　❹ formation 形成 (n.)
❺ galaxy 銀河 (n.)　❻ cluster 群 (n.)　❼ vast 廣闊的 (a.)　❽ cosmic 宇宙的 (a.)
❾ inconsistency 不一致 (n.)　❿ calculation 計算 (n.)　⓫ orbit 天體的運行軌道 (n.)
⓬ assumption 假定 (n.)　⓭ remain 保持 (v.)

74

◀ Coma Cluster

times more than the calculation based on the visible matter. He reasoned that there must be some kind of invisible matter which made up the difference in the calculations.

❻ Due to the extreme difficulties that scientists have in detecting dark matter, new theories about its formation and behavior are seldom conclusive. Scientists have to make **assumptions**[12] based on the indirect influence of dark matter on other cosmic structures, and this means that the secrets of dark matter could, for a long time, **remain**[13] in the dark.

Questions

____ 1. Which of the following is the main topic of the article? ◆Main Idea◆
   a The experiments that try to find dark matter.
   b Why dark matter is invisible.
   c The mysterious nature of dark matter.
   d The man who discovered dark matter.

____ 2. What is the focus of this article? ◆Subject Matter◆
   a Space exploration in the 21st century.
   b Discovering new galaxies.
   c How the universe was created.
   d A theory about the universe's structure.

____ 3. Which of the following statements is NOT true? ◆Supporting Details◆
   a Dark matter cannot be seen with a telescope.
   b Dark matter particles have been created in a laboratory.
   c Scientists detect dark matter via its influence on other bodies.
   d The Coma Cluster contains over 1,000 galaxies.

____ 4. According to the last paragraph, what can we infer about the existence of dark matter particles? ◆Inference◆
   a It will be proved very soon.
   b It will never be proved.
   c It will be replaced by another theory.
   d It will stay a mystery for some time.

____ 5. What does the word **hypothesis** in the third paragraph mean? ◆Words in Context◆
   a A mistake.   b Electricity.   c A theory.   d A machine.

____ 6. How does the writer create interest in the first paragraph? ◆Clarifying Devices◆
   a By asking a serious question.   b By telling a funny riddle.
   c By giving a definition.   d By stating a scientific fact.

Week 5 Day 6

Arts & Literature

▼ *The Physical Impossibility of Death in the Mind of Someone Living*, 1991
(cc by Isabell Schulz)

30
Cows, Sharks, and Spots

▲ Damien Hirst

1   Damien Hirst's **masterpieces**[1] are not the kind you hang on your wall. **Installations**[2] of flies **feasting**[3] on a cow's head, a **calf**[4] cut in two, and a **skull**[5] covered in diamonds are all examples of his thoroughly modern take on art.

2   Hirst almost failed high school art, and he worked on building sites before studying fine art at university. As a student, he spent time working at a **mortuary**[6]—a place where dead people are stored before **burial**[7]. This experience had a clear influence on his work, much of which deals with death. He often makes use of dead animals, preserving them in chemicals and displaying them to the public. An artist who **embraces**[8] the macabre, Hirst is one of the UK's most influential **contemporary**[9] talents, and his works regularly sell for millions of dollars.

3   Hirst's first major work was called *A Thousand Years* and is a **commentary**[10] on life and death. A cow's head is eaten by **maggots**[11], which turn into flies, and are then killed by an electric insect killer. Some flies survive and lay eggs, which continue the cycle. Art **patron**[12] Charles Saatchi was so amazed at the originality of the concept that he bought the installation on the spot.

4   Saatchi then agreed to fund Hirst's future work. Hirst used the money to buy a shark and **suspended**[13] it in formaldehyde (a chemical that preserves dead flesh), calling the work *The Physical Impossibility of Death in the Mind of Someone Living*. The work sold for $12 million in 2004. Although the two men stopped working together after a series of a disagreements, Saatchi still insists that Hirst is a genius.

5   Hirst's art has caused **controversy**[14] because many of his installations are completed by assistants. His famous *Spot Paintings*, of which there are over 300,

Key Words

① masterpiece 傑作 (n.)   ② installation 裝置 (n.)   ③ feast 盡情享用 (v.)   ④ calf 小牛 (n.)
⑤ skull 頭骨；骷髏 (n.)   ⑥ mortuary 太平間 (n.)   ⑦ burial 葬禮 (n.)   ⑧ embrace 擁抱 (v.)
⑨ contemporary 當代的；同時期的 (a.)   ⑩ commentary 評論 (n.)   ⑪ maggot 蛆 (n.)
⑫ patron 贊助者 (n.)   ⑬ suspend 使懸浮 (v.)   ⑭ controversy 爭議 (n.)   ⑮ randomly 隨機地 (adv.)
⑯ sequence 一連串 (n.)   ⑰ retrospective 回顧展 (n.)

consist of **randomly**[15] colored **sequences**[16] of dots, but only five were painted by Hirst.

A 2012 **retrospective**[17] of Hirst's work at the Tate Modern gallery showed how divisive his work really is: it attracted more visitors than any show before it, but also a huge number of complaints. Love him or hate him, Damien Hirst is a record-breaker who won't easily be forgotten.

▼ *A Thousand Years,* 1990
(cc by Gazanfarulla Khan)

Questions

____ 1. Which of the following statements best sums up the article? ◆Main Idea◆
   a Damien Hirst is an unconventional, divisive, but also incredibly successful artist.
   b Hirst's 2012 Tate gallery show attracted more visitors than any show before it.
   c Hirst likes to use the bodies of dead animals in his works of art.
   d Hirst almost failed high-school art, but later went on to study art at university.

____ 2. What is this article about? ◆Subject Matter◆
   a Modern art in Europe.
   b A modern artist.
   c Animals in contemporary art.
   d The themes of life and death.

____ 3. Which of the following statements is NOT true? ◆Supporting Details◆
   a Damien Hirst had no training in art.
   b Damien Hirst's work sells for a high price.
   c Hirst likes to use dead animals in his art.
   d Much of Hirst's work is assembled by assistants.

____ 4. Which statement probably applies to Damien Hirst? ◆Inference◆
   a He is not a well-respected artist.
   b He is an artist without imagination.
   c He is now a very rich man.
   d He is an artist who copies others' work.

____ 5. What does the word **macabre** in the second paragraph most likely mean?
   ◆Words in Context◆
   a Using modern technology.
   b Having a funny subject matter.
   c Using old-fashioned techniques.
   d Having death as a subject.

____ 6. How does the writer describe Hirst's work? ◆Clarifying Devices◆
   a Using exaggerated language.
   b Using similes.
   c In a humorous tone.
   d Briefly and simply.

Damien Hirst and His Works

▲ Damien Hirst presents his new exhibit, Requiem.

▲ The Golden Calf (cc by Jim Linwood)

▲ In the name of the father (cc by Uri Jimenez Carrasco)

▲ Saint Bartholomew, Exquisite Pain at Wallace Collection (cc by Peter Clarke)

▲ The Promise of Money

▲ Temple

Week 6

Day 1 Animals	31	Forever Young	80
Day 2 History	32	The War That Never Ends	82
Day 3 Environment	33	The Next Atlantis?	84
Day 4 Arts & Literature	34	Japan's Literary Superstar	86
Day 5 Business	35	Rare Earth Elements	88
Day 6 Sports	36	The Artful Imparting of Enthusiasm	90

Week 6 Day 1
Animals

▼ *Turritopsis dohrnii*, the immortal jellyfish

31 Forever Young
(031)

1 Have you ever wondered what it would be like to live forever? Most people consider this an impossible dream, but for one species of jellyfish, **immortality**[1] is just another part of life. It's been called "the immortal jellyfish," and it is only about five millimeters long, smaller than your fingernail.

2 What's special about this kind of jellyfish is that it can **reverse**[2] its life cycle by changing its cells in a process called transdifferentiation. After it becomes sexually **mature**[3], it can force its cells to become those of a **progressively**[4] younger version of itself. Its umbrella and **tentacles**[5] are absorbed back into its body, and it sinks to the ocean floor to become an immature **pod**[6], or polyp. This polyp can then produce new jellyfish **identical**[7] to the adult.

3 One of the benefits of reversing its life cycle is that the jellyfish can survive periods when food is scarce or conditions are dangerous. By returning to its immature stage, it can wait out these **harsh**[8] conditions as a polyp and emerge again when conditions are more stable.

4 Though it can still be killed by other sea creatures, this **remarkable**[9] ability to survive against all **odds**[10] has allowed the tiny jellyfish to spread around the world. Scientists **suspect**[11] that these immortal animals are being accidentally ferried around the world by long-distance cargo ships. The jellyfish get **sucked**[12] into the ships and are then transported thousands of miles away from their original habitats. There are now so many in the world's oceans that some are calling it an **invasion**[13].

5 The species was discovered over a century ago, but its amazing ability was not noticed until fairly recently. This power to dramatically **alter**[14] its cells has been of great interest to scientists who are trying to find ways to cure illnesses

Key Words

❶ immortality 永生 (n.)　❷ reverse 倒轉 (v.)　❸ mature 成熟的 (a.)　❹ progressively 逐漸地 (adv.)
❺ tentacle 觸手 (n.)　❻ pod 莢 (n.)　❼ identical 完全相同的 (a.)　❽ harsh 嚴厲的 (a.)
❾ remarkable 卓越的 (a.)　❿ odds 機會；困難 (n.)　⓫ suspect 懷疑 (v.)　⓬ suck 吸吮 (v.)
⓭ invasion 入侵 (n.)　⓮ alter 改變 (v.)　⓯ incurable 無法治癒的 (a.)　⓰ eliminate 消除 (v.)

like cancer and heart disease. These currently **incurable**[15] conditions could be **eliminated**[16] by the discovery of how to change one kind of cell into another.

G   Although it might take a while for scientists to figure out how we humans can permanently avoid dying of old age, there is no doubt that the immortal jellyfish holds the key to immortality.

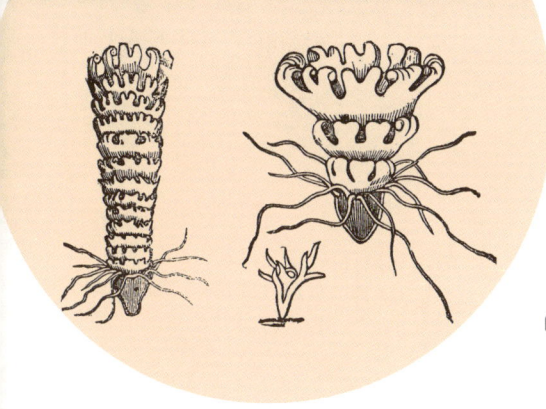

▲ life cycle of a jellyfish showing polypoid stage (bottom), budding stage (left), and medusa stage (right)

Week 6 Day 1 Forever Young

Questions

____ 1. Which of the following is the main idea of this article? ·········· ◆Main Idea◆
   a The immortal jellyfish is found all over the world.
   b The immortal jellyfish was discovered in the 1800s.
   c The immortal jellyfish holds the secret to immortality.
   d The immortal jellyfish fights for survival.

____ 2. What does this article focus on? ·········· ◆Subject Matter◆
   a An interesting creature.   b An impossible dream.
   c Scientific discoveries.   d Ship and boat building.

____ 3. Which of the following statements is NOT true? ·········· ◆Supporting Details◆
   a The immortal jellyfish can theoretically live forever.
   b The immortal jellyfish has spread all over the world.
   c The immortal jellyfish can alter its cells.
   d The immortal jellyfish's ability was known a century ago.

____ 4. Which of the following statements is probably true? ·········· ◆Inference◆
   a Studying the immortal jellyfish will result in a medical breakthrough.
   b The immortal jellyfish population will begin to shrink rapidly.
   c Scientists will not find anything useful by studying the immortal jellyfish.
   d Human beings will become immortal within the next decade.

____ 5. What does the word **ferried** in paragraph four mean? ·········· ◆Words in Context◆
   a Hunted.   b Destroyed.   c Lost.   d Transported.

____ 6. Which of the following could this article also be used as? ·········· ◆Text Form◆
   a A pamphlet advertising skin cream.
   b A script for a short nature documentary.
   c An article in a diving magazine.
   d The preface to a book about sea creatures.

81

Week 6 Day 2

History

32 The War That Never Ends

▶ territory of Palestine

❶ In ancient times, the land known as Israel was the home of the Jewish people. The Romans conquered Judea, as they called it, in the first century BC. For the next 2,000 years, this small piece of desert would be part of many **successive** empires. As time passed, most Jews left for other parts of the world. In their place came Arabs, who called the land Palestine and themselves Palestinians.

❷ After World War II, the United Nations decided to give most of Palestine back to the Jews. This involved removing countless Palestinians from their homes. Fighting **broke out**[1] between the long-time Arab **residents**[2] and the new Jewish arrivals. The Jews **ultimately**[3] won the struggle and Israel was founded in 1948.

❸ Armed conflict **immediately**[4] broke out again, however, this time between Israel and its Arab neighbors. Over the next 25 years, a series of wars would be fought in the region. Some were started by the Jews, and some by the Arabs. Israel won them all, however, and the Palestinians continue to **suffer**[5] under a harsh Israeli **occupation**[6]. As a result, many have turned to **terrorism**[7] in an effort to force the Jews out.

❹ What can be done? Israel insists it has a right to exist and be recognized as a Jewish state. It also says it has the right to keep the **territory**[8] it has captured. Arab countries refuse to recognize Israel until it gives back all of that territory. They also want the **descendants**[9] of Palestinians who lost their homes when Israel was created to be allowed to return there.

❺ The conflict between the Arabs and Israelis has had a major impact on the wider world. Western countries, especially the United States, support Israel politically, **militarily**[10], and financially. This has caused many Arabs and other Muslims to **resent**[11] the West, sometimes violently. Many people throughout the

Key Words

❶ break out 爆發　❷ resident 居民 (n.)　❸ ultimately 最終地 (adv.)
❹ immediately 立刻；馬上 (adv.)　❺ suffer 受苦；受難 (v.)　❻ occupation 佔領；統治 (n.)
❼ terrorism 恐怖主義 (n.)　❽ territory 領土 (n.)　❾ descendant 後裔；子孫 (n.)
❿ militarily 軍事地 (adv.)　⓫ resent 憤怒；怨恨 (v.)　⓬ sympathize 同情 (v.)　⓭ abuse 濫用；虐待 (n.)
⓮ climate 形勢；趨勢 (n.)　⓯ extreme 極端的 (a.)

▶ Old City of Jerusalem

world **sympathize**[12] with the Palestinians. They wonder why the West ignores Israelis **abuses**[13] and calls the Israelis victims.

6   In the current political **climate**[14], attitudes on both sides of the Arab-Israeli conflict are only growing harder and more **extreme**[15]. Whatever else may happen, the war that never ends will continue for a long time to come.

Questions

____ 1. What is the writer trying to tell us in this article? ◆Main Idea◆
   a Israel has been a part of many different empires.
   b People throughout the world sympathize with the Palestinians.
   c Attitudes in the Middle East are getting more extreme these days.
   d The conflict in the Middle East is a very complicated long-term issue.

____ 2. What does this article describe for the most part? ◆Subject Matter◆
   a The military conquests of the Roman Empire.
   b A series of problems which have not been solved.
   c American financial and military support for Israel.
   d A war which was fought sometime around 1948.

____ 3. Which of the following is true of many Palestinians? ◆Supporting Details◆
   a Their ancestors defeated the Israelis in a battle.
   b Their ancestors lost their homes when Israel was created.
   c They are supported by the West in their struggle against the Israelis.
   d They are welcome as refugees in many Arab countries.

____ 4. What can we assume about Palestine at the end of World War II? ◆Inference◆
   a It was controlled by the Palestinians.
   b It was controlled by the Jews.
   c It was controlled by neither the Palestinians nor the Jews.
   d It was controlled by both the Palestinians and the Jews.

____ 5. What does **successive** mean? ◆Words in Context◆
   a Of the ancient world.   b Of the modern world.
   c Coming before one another.   d Coming after one another.

____ 6. Which of the following is a fact? ◆Fact or Opinion◆
   a The Arabs and Israelis fought a series of wars between 1948 and 1973.
   b Israel has a right to exist and be recognized as a Jewish state.
   c Palestinians have a right to return to their ancestors' homes in Israel.
   d The conflict in the Middle East cannot be resolved and will never end.

Week 6 | Day 3

Environment

33 The Next Atlantis?

▼ Chao Phraya River

① Day by day, little by little, Thailand's capital of over eight million people is sinking into the sea. Its **annual**[1] rate of **descent**[2] ranges from 1.5 to five centimeters. That's very **substantial**[3] for a city that was built on swampland only 1.5 meters above sea level.

② There are several factors behind Bangkok's slow descent into the **Gulf**[4] of Thailand. First and foremost is **urbanization**[5]. Every year, Bangkok **expands**[6] to absorb new waves of people arriving from the surrounding countryside. Heavy buildings are built on top of **irrigation**[7] **canals**[8] and natural **flood**[9] defenses, causing coastal **erosion**[10]. More people means more groundwater must be extracted for them to drink, and the more groundwater that's extracted, the faster Bangkok sinks. It is a **vicious**[11] cycle that is difficult to stop.

③ What's more, the sinking process is **irreversible**[12]. Every inch that Bangkok sinks is an inch that it will never get back.

④ Bangkok is going down just as sea levels are coming up. This dangerous combination has led some experts to predict a **catastrophe** in the not-so-distant future. Some believe that parts of Bangkok will be underwater by 2030. Smith Dharmasaroja of Thailand's National Disaster Warning Center goes a step further. According to him, Bangkok will have become the next Atlantis by 2100.

⑤ The government of Thailand must act fast if it wants to avoid this catastrophe. One plan is to construct a system of seawalls in the Gulf of Thailand to protect the city from rising sea levels. However, these walls would cost billions of dollars and several **prominent**[13] members of the scientific community

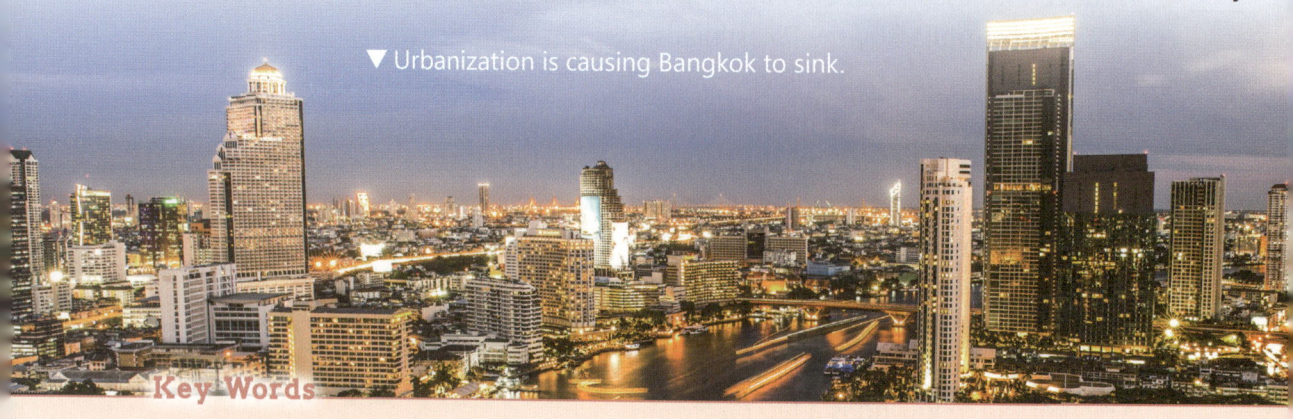

▼ Urbanization is causing Bangkok to sink.

Key Words

① annual 每年的 (a.)　② descent 下降 (n.)　③ substantial 大量的 (a.)　④ gulf 海灣 (n.)
⑤ urbanization 都市化 (n.)　⑥ expand 擴大 (v.)　⑦ irrigation 灌溉 (n.)　⑧ canal 運河 (n.)
⑨ flood 淹水 (n.)　⑩ erosion 侵蝕 (n.)　⑪ vicious 惡性的 (a.)　⑫ irreversible 不可逆轉的 (a.)
⑬ prominent 著名的 (a.)　⑭ option 選擇 (n.)　⑮ assert 主張；維護 (v.)　⑯ sprawl 蔓延 (n.)

◀ Population in Bangkok increases every year.

believe that they might not even help. They point out that the last major floods to threaten Bangkok came from the north, not the south.

6   Another **option**[14] is to **assert**[15] more government control over Bangkok's urban **sprawl**[16]. Buildings need to be moved back from the Chao Phraya River and built on higher ground.

7   Saving Bangkok will take time, money, and effort. If the government of Thailand delays for too long, it might find that it only has one more option left: abandon the Venice of the East and build a new city somewhere else.

Questions

____ 1. Which of the following can summarize this article? ······ ◆Main Idea◆
- **a** Bangkok is the Venice of the East.
- **b** People are fighting to save a sinking city.
- **c** There are dangers to pumping groundwater.
- **d** Urbanization can be dangerous to a city.

____ 2. What is this article mainly about? ······ ◆Subject Matter◆
- **a** Typhoons.   **b** Pollution.   **c** Bangkok.   **d** Water.

____ 3. Which of the following statements is NOT true? ······ ◆Supporting Details◆
- **a** Bangkok is sinking up to five centimeters annually.
- **b** Urbanization is causing Bangkok to sink into the sea.
- **c** The Thai government has asserted control over urban sprawl.
- **d** Some experts believe Bangkok will be fully underwater by 2100.

____ 4. What can we infer from this article? ······ ◆Inference◆
- **a** The Thai government is already solving Bangkok's sinking problem.
- **b** Bangkok has been sinking for over 20 years.
- **c** The experts are wrong, and Bangkok isn't really sinking.
- **d** The Thai government will act quickly and save the city.

____ 5. What does the word **catastrophe** in the fourth paragraph most likely mean?
······ ◆Words in Context◆
- **a** A miracle.   **b** A terrible disaster.
- **c** A sudden change.   **d** A new ice age.

____ 6. Which of these best describes the author's tone in this article? ······ ◆Author's Tone◆
- **a** Humorous and relaxed.   **b** Urgent and concerned.
- **c** Sad and sincere.   **d** Detached and academic.

Week 6 Day 4
Arts & Literature

◀ Haruki Murakami (cc by Galoren.com)

34

Japan's Literary Superstar

[1]   Haruki Murakami's **aptitude**[1] for **blurring**[2] the line between the real and imagined has earned him **fame**[3] on both sides of the **Pacific**[4]. What makes this Japanese writer so popular not only in his home country but also overseas?

[2]   For starters, Murakami has quite a romantic background. Born in 1949 to parents who were Japanese **literature**[5] teachers, he studied drama at a university in Tokyo. After graduating, he worked at a record shop for a while before deciding to open up a jazz bar with his wife in the mid-1970s.

[3]   The **inspiration**[6] to write a novel came to him while watching a baseball game in 1978. After he got home that night, he grabbed a pen and started writing. Months later he sent his work off to a literary **contest**[7] and they agreed to publish it. This was *Hear the Wind Sing*, his first novel. Murakami kept on writing but remained **relatively**[8] unknown in Japan until the publication of *Norwegian Wood* in 1987. A decade later, international audiences fell in love with him upon the release of *The Wind-Up Bird Chronicle*. When his 2013 novel *Colorless Tzukuru Tazaki and His Years of Pilgrimage* was released in Japan, it sold 350,000 copies in the first three days.

[4]   Murakami's books have now been **translated**[9] into over 50 languages worldwide and many people openly **speculate**[10] that he will one day win the Nobel Prize in Literature. That was quite an inspirational game of baseball!

[5]   Readers the world over also love Murakami's **unique**[11] style. It's as if he can see through our world and into the next. This lets him write novels that provide readers with the **purest**[12] form of escape, letting them take a vacation from reality.

[6]   His **prose**[13] flows from a mix of Eastern and Western culture. He had a Japanese **upbringing**[14], yet many of his cultural

▲ *Norwegian Wood* (cc by Heartoftheworld)

Key Words

[1] aptitude 天資 (n.)　[2] blur 使模糊不清 (v.)　[3] fame 名譽 (n.)　[4] Pacific 太平洋 (n.)
[5] literature 文學 (n.)　[6] inspiration 靈感；啟發 (n.)　[7] contest 比賽 (n.)　[8] relatively 相對地 (adv.)
[9] translate 翻譯 (v.)　[10] speculate 推斷；推測 (v.)　[11] unique 獨特的 (a.)　[12] pure 純潔的 (a.)
[13] prose 散文 (n.)　[14] upbringing 教養 (n.)　[15] contradiction 矛盾 (n.)　[16] manifest 顯露 (v.)

influences came from the West. He grew up reading Western authors such as Kurt Vonnegut and F. Scott Fitzgerald and listened to music by Thelonious Monk, Nat King Cole, the Beatles, and Bob Dylan.

7   The end result was an author who was raised on rebels yet lived in a society where everyone **conformed**. This **contradiction**[15] did not **manifest**[16] itself in his novels as a political point of view, but rather as a blurred line between reality and fantasy.

Questions

____ 1. Which of the following is the main topic of this article? •Main Idea•
   a Why Haruki Murakami is so famous worldwide.
   b The next winner of the Nobel Prize for Literature.
   c The life story of Haruki Murakami.
   d An analysis of Haruki Murakami's prose.

____ 2. What is this article about? •Subject Matter•
   a A novel.   b A writer.   c A romance.   d Prose.

____ 3. Which of the following statements is true? •Supporting Details•
   a Haruki Murakami was inspired by a football game.
   b Haruki Murakami opened a hostess bar.
   c Haruki Murakami studied literature at university.
   d Haruki Murakami read many Western books.

____ 4. Which statement most likely applies to Haruki Murakami? •Inference•
   a His first popular novel was *Norwegian Wood*.
   b He will never win the Nobel Prize for Literature.
   c He takes a lot of vacations.
   d He loves to watch movies.

____ 5. The first sentence of the last paragraph of this article mentions that Murakami lived in a society where everyone conformed. What is the meaning of **conform**?
   •Words in Context•
   a Rebel and do things differently from other people.
   b Fit in and do things the same way as other people.
   c Not worry about what people think about you.
   d Only care about working and never relax.

____ 6. How does the author create interest in the fourth paragraph of the article?
   •Clarifying Devices•
   a With a humorous observation.   b With an interesting fact.
   c With an example.   d With logical arguments.

35 Rare Earth Elements

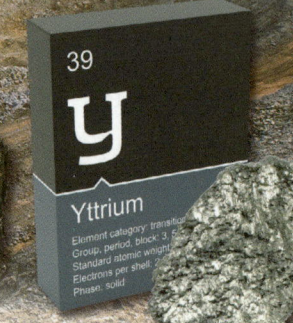

1. Rare earth elements (REEs) such as scandium and yttrium are, in fact, not particularly rare at all. Many of these seventeen **minerals**[1] are as common as **copper**[2], and the rarest are 200 times more **abundant**[3] than gold. Chances are though that you wouldn't recognize their names if you saw them, as they are part of an **obscure**[4] chemical group unknown to most without a chemistry degree. Even so, they are an **essential**[5] aspect of modern technology, from batteries and lamps to jet engines and satellite communication systems.

2. While they are common in the earth's crust, they seldom form **deposits**[6] large enough to mine and usually remain spread out thinly throughout the crust. They are, therefore, very difficult to find in any kind of usable quantity, and so are referred to as rare.

3. Add to this that many of these elements are **indispensable**[7] for making things our society now takes for granted, like smartphones and refrigerators, and you have something that can truly be considered valuable.

4. **Extracting**[8] and exporting these elements is, **understandably**[9], a very **profitable**[10] business. The country that has come to lead this industry over the past 20 years is China, which has gone from producing 27% of the world's REEs in 1990 to producing over 90% now. This has given China a **priceless**[11] monopoly on the world's supply of these incredibly sought-after minerals.

5. This caused controversy in 2009 when the United States, the European Union, and Mexico, all of which are **dependent**[12] on China for their supply of REEs, complained to the World Trade Organization (WTO) that China's export **allowance**[13] for REEs was too low.

6. China progressively cut the amount of REEs that it exported, reducing the amount by 35% in 2011—an act that caused prices to skyrocket. This action was **declared**[14] illegal by the WTO in July 2011. China **protested**[15], saying it

Key Words

1. mineral 礦物 (n.) 2. copper 銅 (n.) 3. abundant 充足的 (a.) 4. obscure 無名的 (a.)
5. essential 必要的 (a.) 6. deposit 儲存 (n.) 7. indispensable 不可或缺的 (a.)
8. extract 提煉 (v.) 9. understandably 可以理解地 (adv.) 10. profitable 獲利的 (a.)
11. priceless 無價的 (a.) 12. dependent 依賴的 (a.) 13. allowance 定量；限額 (n.) 14. declare 宣布 (v.)
15. protest 抗議 (v.) 16. foreseeable 可預見的 (a.)

was limiting its exports in the name of conserving natural resources for future generations. Nevertheless, in 2015 the country was forced to drop its export limits.

7   While it's true that mining and processing REEs are difficult and dangerous jobs, the huge global demand for these vital minerals will continue to dominate global trade for the **foreseeable**[16] future.

▶ cargo ships in China loaded with rare minerals for export

Questions

____ 1. What is the main idea of this article? ◆Main Idea◆
   a Rare earth elements are difficult and dangerous to mine.
   b Rare earth elements play an important part in our world.
   c Rare earth elements are primarily found in China.
   d Rare earth elements are used in refrigerators.

____ 2. What is the main focus of the second half of this passage? ◆Subject Matter◆
   a The process of extracting rare earth elements.
   b The cost of rare earth elements.
   c China's control of the REE industry.
   d The WTO's involvement in the REE industry.

____ 3. Which of the following statements is NOT true? ◆Supporting Details◆
   a China produces most of the world's REEs.
   b The United States depends on China for its supply of REEs.
   c Rare earth elements are actually quite common.
   d Rare earth elements are only found in China.

____ 4. Which is a likely outcome of China's dominance over rare earth element production? ◆Inference◆
   a Businesses will move to China to save on costs.
   b The cost of rare earth element products will drop.
   c China will have no more problems with its trading partners.
   d The earth's REEs will be used up faster than expected.

____ 5. What is the meaning of **monopoly** in paragraph four? ◆Words in Context◆
   a An exclusive control over something.   b A weak grasp of something.
   c A rare sighting of something.   d A careless attitude toward something.

____ 6. How does the writer support his claims about China? ◆Clarifying Devices◆
   a By using a list.   b By comparing two examples.
   c By including an expert's opinion.   d By using statistics.

Week 6 Day 6 ▼ Johnny Campbell

Sports

36 The Artful Imparting of Enthusiasm[1]

🎧 036

[1]   When most of us think of cheerleading, we picture **elaborate**[2] **routines**[3], extremely dangerous **stunts**[4], and short skirts. Did cheerleading always look as **glamorous**[5] as it does in Hollywood movies like *Bring it On*? Where did this **peculiar**[6] sport that is now practiced by over 1.6 million people around the world come from?

[2]   The story of cheerleading begins in late-nineteenth-century America. In 1898, a University of Minnesota student named Johnny Campbell **was stumped**[7] over how he could help his school's football team win a critical game against a rival school. He decided that the best way he could help the team would be to get the crowd more involved. On the day of the big game, he stood in the stands and led cheers of "rah rah rah, Min-e-so-tah!" His enthusiasm was **infectious**[8], and Minnesota won the game. The concept of cheerleading was born.

[3]   In the years following 1898, cheerleading **squads**[9] started to **pop up**[10] in schools across America, yet the sport continued to be completely dominated by men in its early years. This changed in 1923 after the University of Minnesota once again **pioneered**[11] a new trend—this time, the concept of female cheerleading squads. When World War II broke out in the 1940s, women made further advances by filling the gap left by men going overseas to fight. This is how cheerleading became the **primarily**[12] female sport that we know it as today.

[4]   Female cheerleaders meant different kinds of cheerleading routines. The **stationary** and monotonous cheers of old were quickly replaced with arm movements, kicks, and **tumbles**[13]. The sport continued to evolve with every passing year.

[5]   Cheerleading took another step toward its modern form in 1975, when the Universal Cheerleaders Association (UCA) opened a training camp that included

Key Words

❶ enthusiasm 熱情 (n.)　❷ elaborate 精巧的 (a.)　❸ routine（表演）固定動作 (n.)　❹ stunt 特技 (n.)
❺ glamorous 有魅力的 (a.)　❻ peculiar 奇怪的 (a.)　❼ be stumped 語塞；被難倒 (v.)
❽ infectious 有感染力的 (a.)　❾ squad 小隊 (n.)　❿ pop up 突然出現　⓫ pioneer 當先鋒；倡導 (v.)
⓬ primarily 主要地 (adv.)　⓭ tumble 翻觔斗 (n.)　⓮ competitive 競爭的 (a.)　⓯ spotlight 聚光燈 (n.)

◀ tumble

cheerleaders performing routines set to background music. This laid the foundation for **competitive**[14] cheerleading.

In 1982, the sport stepped into the **spotlight**[15] when ESPN broadcasted the 1st Cheerleading National Championship. Since then, competitive cheerleading has grown in popularity in America. It has also become more and more popular overseas. There are an estimated 100,000 cheerleaders competing in countries such as Australia, Canada, Japan, Finland, France, Germany, and Taiwan.

Questions

____ 1. Which of the following is the main topic of this article? ◆Main Idea◆
   a How to become a good cheerleader.
   b Why modern cheerleaders are mostly female.
   c The origins of modern cheerleading.
   d Facts and fiction of modern cheerleading.

____ 2. What is this article about? ◆Subject Matter◆
   a ESPN.
   b A physical activity popular in America.
   c Tumbles.
   d The University of Minnesota.

____ 3. Which of the following is NOT true? ◆Supporting Details◆
   a Cheerleading started out as a sport dominated by men.
   b Cheerleading ended up as a sport dominated by women.
   c Cheerleading was invented in America.
   d Men abandoned cheerleading because it was seen as feminine.

____ 4. What can we infer from this article? ◆Inference◆
   a There are international cheerleading competitions.
   b There are only American cheerleading competitions.
   c Cheerleading will never be an Olympic sport.
   d Cheerleading will stop evolving and changing.

____ 5. The fourth paragraph of this article mentions stationary cheering routines. If something is **stationary**, what is it doing? ◆Words in Context◆
   a Moving incredibly quickly.
   b Standing still and not moving.
   c Moving in a circular motion.
   d Using paper to convey a message.

____ 6. Which of the following statements is given supporting evidence in the article? ◆Clarifying Devices◆
   a Cheerleading is a glamorous sport.
   b Cheerleading is a peculiar sport.
   c Cheerleading is a dangerous sport.
   d Cheerleading is a popular sport.

Cheerleading Poses

▲ jump

▲ split

▲ heel stretch

▲ high V

Cheerleading Stunts

▲ Cupie

▲ liberty (cc by DeusXFlorida)

▲ pyramid

Week 7

Day 1 Culture	37 A New You?	94
Day 2 Arts & Literature	38 Becoming the Sculpture	96
Day 3 Business	39 Money-Making Mimicry	98
Day 4 Technology	40 The Adventure of Books	100
Day 5 Environment	41 The End of Ink?	102
Day 6 Arts & Literature	42 A Method in the Madness	104

Week 7　Day 1

Culture

37　A New You?

1　More and more Asians are discovering that they don't need to keep the face that they were born with or the **bum**[1] made huge by too many late-night bubble teas. The body they've always wanted is just a doctor's visit away!

2　Asia is quickly becoming the plastic surgery capital of the world. Thirty years ago, plastic surgery rates **lagged**[2] behind the West due to low incomes, fewer **qualified**[3] doctors, and a culture that **shunned**[4] **outward**[5] **vanity**[6]. Now, countries like South Korea and Taiwan are the places to go to have your face and body altered. In South Korea, 20 people in every thousand have had plastic surgery. Most of them had their **procedures**[7] done in Gangnam, a wealthy district of Seoul. More and more people from Vietnam, Taiwan, and Japan are also **flocking**[8] to Gangnam, where over 500 clinics offer "a new you."

3　So, what's changed to make Asian people so **keen**[9] to go under the knife? **First and foremost**[10], people have more money in their pockets. A beautiful face has become a symbol of success in Asia, which means plastic surgery can help you display your success to the world. There is also a lot of workplace pressure to get plastic surgery. It's not just the actors and actresses who are looking for **eternal**[11] youth, but regular people as well. Some job seekers get plastic surgery so they don't lose a job to someone who has the same **qualifications** but a prettier face.

4　Asian people tend to want different plastic surgery procedures than their Western **counterparts**[12]. In the West, customers often want to look younger by having **wrinkles**[13] or bags of fat under their eyes removed. Asian customers on the other hand often want to look like

◀ plastic surgery sign in the Seoul

Key Words

1. bum 屁股 (n.)　2. lag 落後 (v.)　3. qualify 符合資格 (v.)　4. shun 迴避 (v.)　5. outward 外在的 (a.)
6. vanity 虛榮 (n.)　7. procedure 手術 (n.)　8. flock 聚集 (v.)　9. keen 渴望的 (a.)
10. first and foremost 首先　11. eternal 永恆的 (a.)　12. counterpart 對應的人或物 (n.)　13. wrinkle 皺紋
14. eyelid 眼皮；眼瞼 (n.)　15. enlargement 放大 (n.)　16. reduction 減少 (n.)　17. chop 劈 (v.)

Westerners. Popular procedures in Asia include double-fold **eyelids**[14], breast **enlargement**[15], and cheek or lip **reduction**[16].

This shouldn't come as too much of a surprise. After all, Asia was the birthplace of some of the first plastic surgery procedures. A fourth century Indian medical textbook called the *Sushruta Samhita* contained a section describing how to reconstruct someone's nose if they happened to have it **chopped**[17] off.

Questions

____ 1. Which of the following is the main topic of the article? •Main Idea•
   a The fall of plastic surgery in Asia.
   b South Koreans' love for plastic surgery.
   c The rise of plastic surgery in Asia.
   d Asia being the birthplace of plastic surgery.

____ 2. Which of the following could be an alternative title for this article? •Subject Matter•
   a How to Find a Job After Graduating.
   b Changing Perceptions of Plastic Surgery in Asia.
   c The Latest Fashion Trends in Asia.
   d An Old Asian Tradition Conquers the Western World.

____ 3. Which of the following statements is true? •Supporting Details•
   a Taiwan is the world's plastic surgery capital.
   b Seoul is home to over 400 plastic surgery clinics.
   c Plastic surgery is only performed in certain Western capitals.
   d People all over the world get the same plastic surgery procedures.

____ 4. Which of the following is likely true, based on the information in the article? •Inference•
   a Asian incomes have risen over the past three decades.
   b Plastic surgery will lose its popularity in the near future.
   c Only old people are interested in plastic surgery.
   d Asian culture hasn't changed in the past 30 years.

____ 5. The third paragraph of this article mentions someone having the same qualifications as you. What are **qualifications**? •Words in Context•
   a Skills or accomplishments that allow you to do something.
   b A family background of people in the same profession.
   c A positive attitude or passion for doing a certain task.
   d The most basic knowledge required to do a certain task.

____ 6. How is this passage best described? •Clarifying Devices•
   a A timeline.   b A narrative essay.   c A descriptive essay.   d A biography.

Week 7 Day 2
Arts & Literature

▶ *What the Birds Know* by Patrick Dougherty

38 Becoming the Sculpture[1]

[1] We use art to **convey**[2] our thoughts, opinions, and experiences. It's something that can help us reach out and form **bonds**[3] with our fellow human beings. But why should art be limited to a **canvas**[4], book, or film **reel**[5]? Why can't it cover four walls and a ceiling, or expand to the size of a building? Well, with installation art, it can.

[2] Installation art was born out of the **conceptual**[6] art movement of the 1970s. Conceptual art is the belief that the ideas **associated with**[7] a piece of art are more important than the **aesthetic**[8] or how it looks. A good piece of conceptual art will make us think. It won't necessarily **stun**[9] us with its beauty.

[3] Think of installation art as taking the concept of sculpture and turning it inside out. Usually, when we examine a sculpture, we are on the outside looking in. However, in the case of installation art, the art piece is all around us. In a sense, we become the sculpture.

[4] Chinese artist Ai Wei Wei's 2010 piece *Sunflower Seeds* is a great example of installation art. It involved the artist spreading millions of **porcelain**[10] sunflower seeds across the floor of London's Tate Modern. Each unique seed was hand-painted in a small **workshop**[11] in China. The **overall**[12] aesthetic contrasts the quaintness of being painted by hand with the harsh industrial environment of the Tate Modern, which was formerly a power station. The installation also **provoked**[13] discussions about Chinese manufacturing and globalization.

[5] Néle Azevedo is another **renowned**[14] installation artist. She travels around the

▲ *Sunflower Seeds* (cc by Ai Wei Wei)

▲ *Minimum Monument* by Néle Azevedo

Key Words

1. sculpture 雕塑 (n.) 2. convey 傳達 (v.) 3. bond 聯結 (n.) 4. canvas 畫布 (n.) 5. reel 膠捲 (n.)
6. conceptual 概念的 (a.) 7. associate with 與……有關 8. aesthetic 美學 (n.)
9. stun 使大吃一驚 (v.) 10. porcelain 瓷器 (n.) 11. workshop 工作室 (n.) 12. overall 全面的 (a.)
13. provoke 煽動 (v.) 14. renowned 有名的 (a.) 15. miniature 小型的 (a.) 16. mold 鑄造；塑造 (v.)

world creating hundreds of **miniature**[15] ice sculptures of people. Of course, it's **inevitable** that her creations will melt as soon as temperatures warm up, but that's exactly the point. Néle **molds**[16] her melting men to raise awareness about the threat of global warming.

[6] There are lots of other installation artists out there trying to pull us into the sculpture. Patrick Dougherty uses sticks and twigs to build huge houses, huts, monuments, and even highways in the open air. In France, Guillaume Reymond creates an impression of massive robots using heaps of used cars and trucks. Anything is possible when the world is your canvas.

Questions

____ 1. What would you say is the main idea of the article? ·········· ◆Main Idea◆
   a The global popularity of installation art.
   b A description and examples of installation art.
   c The history of installation art.
   d An analysis of the concept of sculptures.

____ 2. What is this article about? ·········· ◆Subject Matter◆
   a Sculptures.   b An art form.   c Movements.   d The Tate Modern.

____ 3. Which of the following statements is true? ·········· ◆Supporting Details◆
   a Ai Wei Wei has never created installation art.
   b Installation art was invented in the 1950s.
   c Installation art can be the size of a building.
   d Néle Azevedo builds cars out of twigs.

____ 4. What can we infer about installation art pieces from this article? ·········· ◆Inference◆
   a They are always very cheap and easy to make.
   b They don't tour the world much because they're hard to move.
   c They aren't very popular at all.
   d They are more thought-provoking than other conceptual art.

____ 5. What does the word **inevitable** in the fifth paragraph mean? ·········· ◆Words in Context◆
   a Assured.   b Avoidable.   c Unlikely.   d Doubtful.

____ 6. Which of these was an effect of Ai Wei Wei's piece *Sunflower Seeds*?
   ·········· ◆Cause and Effect◆
   a The Tate Modern was converted from a power station into an art gallery.
   b Ai Wei Wei spread porcelain seeds on the floor of the Tate.
   c Guillaume Reymond created massive robots using old cars.
   d People began to discuss Chinese manufacturing and globalization.

Week 7 Day 2 Becoming the Sculpture

39 Money-Making Mimicry

1. In the world of big business there are two major strategies one can follow: an **emergent**[1] strategy or a **deliberate**[2] strategy. An emergent strategy is what you would expect an up-and-coming business to adopt. It is flexible, experimental, and full of new approaches to find the **optimum**[3] business model. A deliberate strategy, however, is what a company employs after it identifies the most profitable angle of attack. A deliberate strategy is one that expands **aggressively**[4] and pushes its winning strategy forward at breakneck speed.

2. Most Western businesses begin with an emergent strategy and then make the transition to a deliberate one. China, which has experienced **unprecedented**[5] expansion over the last three decades, has been forced to take a shortcut where developmental strategies are concerned. Instead of starting out with an emergent strategy and transitioning to a deliberate one, the **bulk**[6] of Chinese **enterprise**[7] has simply cut out the emergent stage and powered through with a deliberate strategy not always of their own making. This has resulted in China's rapidly expanding economy being **dubbed** a "copycat economy."

3. As a result of this copycat strategy, many foreign investors in China have taken issue over **perceived**[8] **breaches**[9] of their intellectual property rights (IPRs), which **prohibit**[10] people from copying and releasing a product without the permission of its original creator.

4. The US ambassador to China, Garry Locke, has advised that without a better attitude to **enforcing**[11] IPRs, many of China's young business talents will simply go abroad, creating problems for China as a growing economic power. However, Chinese **spokesmen**[12] have dismissed this advice, insisting that China's entrepreneurs would only be hindered by such restrictions.

▶ Shanghai, a rapidly expanding city

Key Words

1. emergent 突現的 (a.)　2. deliberate 深思熟慮的 (a.)　3. optimum 最理想的 (a.)
4. aggressively 積極進取地 (adv.)　5. unprecedented 空前的 (a.)　6. bulk 大規模 (n.)
7. enterprise 企業 (n.)　8. perceive 察覺 (v.)　9. breach 侵害 (n.)(v.)　10. prohibit 禁止 (v.)
11. enforce 實施 (v.)　12. spokesman 發言人 (n.)　13. approximately 大約地 (adv.)　14. surpass 勝過 (v.)
15. copyright 著作權 (n.)　16. perspective 觀點 (n.)

▶ Major car firms have accused some Chinese companies of breaching copyright over the designs of their cars.

[5] Take China's automotive industry for example. The number of cars in China went from one million in 1977 to a current total of **approximately**[13] 85 million, and the number of vehicles produced per year has **surpassed**[14] even the United States. Major car firms such as BMW and Mercedes-Benz have accused some Chinese companies of breaching **copyright**[15] over the designs of their cars. But, to supply such a rapidly rising demand in such a short period of time, it seems that this copycat strategy is necessary if, from a Western **perspective**[16], undesirable.

Questions

____ 1. Which of the following is the main idea of the article? ◆Main Idea◆
   a There are two basic kinds of business strategy, emergent and deliberate.
   b China's rapid growth has made it necessary for it to pursue a controversial economic strategy.
   c Many foreign investors are troubled by China's copycat economy.
   d China produces more vehicles per year than the United States.

____ 2. What is this article about? ◆Subject Matter◆
   a What intellectual property rights are.
   b The BMW corporation in China.
   c China's foreign policy.
   d Enterprise in China.

____ 3. Which of the following statements is NOT true? ◆Supporting Details◆
   a China's economy has been expanding rapidly for around 30 years.
   b There are currently around 85 million cars in China.
   c The American ambassador agrees with China's position on IPRs.
   d Many Chinese businesses employ deliberate strategies without emergent ones.

____ 4. What does this article imply? ◆Inference◆
   a China has had to create an economic strategy to meet its own needs.
   b China's economy would be better if it listened to the advice of the American ambassador.
   c China's automobile industry is slowing down.
   d America follows a similar economic strategy to China's.

____ 5. What does the word **dubbed** in the second paragraph mean? ◆Words in Context◆
   a Awarded.   b Refused.   c Taught.   d Labeled.

____ 6. Which of these does the author do in the first paragraph? ◆Clarifying Devices◆
   a Provide two examples.
   b Provide two definitions.
   c Provide his opinion.
   d Provide facts and figures.

Week 7 Day 4

Technology

▶ A bookworm loves to engage with plots.

40
The Adventure of Books

1 There is nothing a **bookworm** loves more than getting absorbed into the world of an **engaging**[1] novel. In the near future, however, the humble paper-and-ink book is set to take a dive headfirst into the new and exciting **dimension**[2] of **interactive**[3] reading.

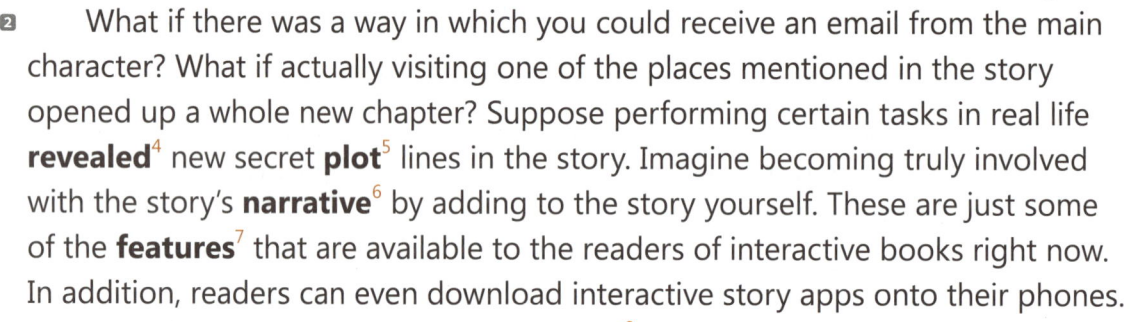

2 What if there was a way in which you could receive an email from the main character? What if actually visiting one of the places mentioned in the story opened up a whole new chapter? Suppose performing certain tasks in real life **revealed**[4] new secret **plot**[5] lines in the story. Imagine becoming truly involved with the story's **narrative**[6] by adding to the story yourself. These are just some of the **features**[7] that are available to the readers of interactive books right now. In addition, readers can even download interactive story apps onto their phones.

3 Even though this sounds **revolutionary**[8], in fact, readers have been getting involved with plot lines for almost half a century. *Choose Your Own Adventure* books began to be published in the 1970s. The reader was given a choice at the end of every few pages. For example, the sentence: "If you would like to question the gardener, turn to page 23" was written to give the reader the **option**[9] of where the story went next. Each choice would **eventually**[10] lead the reader to one of around 40 different endings.

4 Video games have also made use of interactive fiction. Text adventure games were some of the first computer games ever made. Players simply had to **input**[11] commands such as "open the mailbox" or "leave the house" in order to advance the plot.

5 A **variation**[12] on text adventure games that are very popular in Japan is the visual novel. These kinds of games use still **manga**[13] images, have background music, and usually

◀ *No One But You*, a Japanese visual novel

Key Words

1. engaging 吸引人的 (a.) 2. dimension 層面 (n.) 3. interactive 互動的 (a.) 4. reveal 揭露 (v.)
5. plot 情節 (n.) 6. narrative 敘述 (n.) 7. feature 特徵 (n.) 8. revolutionary 革命的 (a.)
9. option 選項 (n.) 10. eventually 最終地 (adv.) 11. input 輸入 (v.) 12. variation 變化 (n.)
13. manga 日本漫畫 (n.) 14. occasionally 偶爾 (adv.) 15. strand 支線 (n.)

involve very little game play. **Occasionally**[14], readers are expected to make a choice between plot **strands**[15], but otherwise the experience is all about the story. Most PC games now sold in Japan are visual novels.

6   Whatever ends up becoming the future of books, be it on paper or on screen, it seems readers will never tire of finding new ways to get drawn into a juicy plot.

Choose Your Own Adventure
(cc by Nathan Penlington)

Questions

_____ 1. Which of the following is the main topic of this article? ◆Main Idea◆
   a People love traditionally written books.
   b Readers love getting involved in stories.
   c Interactive fiction is just a fantasy.
   d Books are not available to everyone.

_____ 2. What does this article primarily discuss? ◆Subject Matter◆
   a A new kind of sport.   b A form of entertainment.
   c A natural phenomenon.   d A tourist destination.

_____ 3. Which of the following statements is NOT true? ◆Supporting Details◆
   a Readers have been directly involving themselves in plots for years.
   b Japanese gamers love visual novels.
   c The text adventure was one of the first kinds of video games.
   d A *Choose Your Own Adventure* book only has one ending.

_____ 4. Which of the following is inferred by the article? ◆Inference◆
   a No one will read books made of paper in the future.
   b It's only through fusing with video games that books have survived into the twenty-first century.
   c In the future, readers will be able to get more involved in books than ever before.
   d People who use interactive books hate books made of paper.

_____ 5. What does the word **bookworm** in the first paragraph most likely mean?
◆Words in Context◆
   a A kind of insect that eats paper.
   b Someone who loves reading.
   c Someone who works in a library.
   d A device that scans text into a computer.

_____ 6. What phrase does the author use to suggest an amazing possibility?
◆Clarifying Devices◆
   a What if.   b Even though.   c Whatever.   d In addition.

Week 7 Day 5

Environment

◀ Reprintable paper only keeps its text for five to 10 days.

41
The End of Ink?

❶ Suppose you had only a single math notebook for your entire school career. Or could take yesterday's paper to a shop each morning and have it **reprinted**¹ with today's news. Thanks to light-printable paper, such things might be possible very soon!

❷ After years of effort, researchers in the United States and China have developed a remarkable chemical **compound**². When applied to **ordinary**³ paper, this compound makes the paper **printable**⁴ by **ultraviolet**⁵ (UV) light rather than ink. It looks and feels like any paper, but only keeps its text for five to 10 days. If you don't need the text for that long, heating the paper will erase it in 10 minutes. Either way, it can be printed on over 80 times with no loss of quality!

▲ The invention is to use UV light rather than ink to print.

❸ The benefits of such an **invention**⁶ are obvious. Newspapers, magazines, posters, notebooks, and supermarket product life **labels**⁷ are just a few of the many **temporary**⁸ information sources we use. Wouldn't it be great if we could keep on using them over and over again?

❹ Then there are the environmental advantages. Paper production is a major source of pollution, and even recycling paper pollutes due to its ink **removal**⁹ process. In some countries, one third of all trees cut down are used for paper and **cardboard**¹⁰. And where does all that paper end up? Mostly in **landfills**¹¹, where it accounts for 40 percent of dumped trash. The more we learn about reprintable paper, the more reason there is to love it!

❺ For now, however, **widespread**¹² use of this new technology is still just a dream. Although reprintable paper only costs about as much as ordinary paper, **laser**¹³ printers which can print it quickly don't exist yet. And since a blue **pigment** is one **component**¹⁴ of the light-printable compound, most UV printing is still either blue on

Key Words

❶ reprint 重印 (v.) ❷ compound 化合物 (n.) ❸ ordinary 一般的；普通的 (a.)
❹ printable 可印的 (a.) ❺ ultraviolet 紫外線的 (a.) ❻ invention 發明 (n.) ❼ label 商標；標籤 (n.)
❽ temporary 暫時的 (a.) ❾ removal 移除 (n.) ❿ cardboard 硬紙板 (n.) ⓫ landfill 垃圾掩埋場 (n.)
⓬ widespread 廣泛的 (a.) ⓭ laser 雷射 (n.) ⓮ component 成分 (n.) ⓯ reproduce 複製；繁殖 (v.)

white or white on blue. This means that only text and drawings can currently be **reproduced**[15] using this method.

6   Nevertheless, UV printing is an exciting new development which we should all keep an eye on. Who knows? One day there might be an edition of this book which you can have reprinted after you've finished reading it!

Questions

____ 1. What is the main idea of the fourth paragraph of this passage? •Main Idea•
   a Light-printable paper is much better than ordinary paper.
   b People are cutting down too many trees to make paper.
   c Recycling paper is more harmful than paper production.
   d The production, recycling, and disposal of paper all pollute.

____ 2. What does this passage mainly describe? •Subject Matter•
   a The different ways in which people use paper.
   b A group of researchers in the United States and China.
   c A new type of laser printer which will soon be available.
   d A new technology which could change many things.

____ 3. What is something UV printing cannot do yet? •Supporting Details•
   a Reproduce a page of text from a book.
   b Reproduce a full-color photograph.
   c Erase itself after a few days.
   d Print a white drawing on a blue background.

____ 4. What can we assume about UV printing from the article? •Inference•
   a It was discovered by accident during an unrelated experiment.
   b The idea was only very recently developed, and is already successful.
   c Everyone will have access to this technology within a year.
   d It was first thought of years ago, and is only now becoming possible.

____ 5. What is a **pigment**? •Words in Context•
   a A substance that gives things their coloring.
   b An animal from which we get pork and ham.
   c A type of printing technology.
   d A text or drawing reproduced by UV printing.

____ 6. What is one likely result of the introduction of UV printing? •Cause and Effect•
   a People will stop reading newspapers.
   b Everyone will buy a new laser printer.
   c Fewer trees will have to be cut down.
   d This book will erase itself in 10 days.

Week 7 Day 6

Arts & Literature

▶ Salvador Dalí (1904–1989)

42

A Method in the Madness

1. Clocks melt like cheese on a hot summer's day, elephants with matchstick-thin legs carry **pyramid**[1]-shaped **monuments**[2] on their backs, floating **rhinoceros**[3] horns form a figure staring out to sea—images like these, pulled from the irrational corners of the mind, were the mysterious subjects of Salvador Dalí.

2. With his unique dress sense, curled **mustache**[4], and eyes wide open as if constantly **startled**[5], Salvador Dalí lived his artistic ideas as well as painted them. He presented a lecture while wearing a deep-sea diving suit (including the helmet), resulting in his audience hearing only **muffled**[6] sounds from within. He invited an art critic to **strip**[7] naked while he himself took photos. The camera, however, had no film inside. He designed **bizarre**[8] art objects like the famous *Lobster Telephone*. Why, he questioned, was he never given a boiled telephone when he asked for a lobster in a restaurant?

3. The reason behind Dalí's strange behavior was that he considered himself the physical representation of the **surrealist**[9] movement. "I myself am surrealism," he declared as he was being **expelled**[10] from the surrealist group.

4. Dalí's version of surrealism involved finding links between things which the **rational**[11] mind usually would not connect. To do this he used a technique he called the **paranoiac**[12]-critical method. By **inducing**[13] a state of extreme **distrust**[14] and fear of the world around him, objects would take on new forms and become unstuck from their place in the rational world. The method can be compared to how to see different shapes in clouds, or faces in rocks, and allowed Dalí to create what he referred to as "hand-painted dream photographs," a reflection of his inner mind.

5. Born in 1904 in northeastern Spain, Dalí's artistic talents were encouraged by his mother, and he

▶ *Rinoceronte vestido con puntillas*
(cc by Manuel González Olaechea y Franco)

Key Words

1. **pyramid** 金字塔 (n.) 2. **monument** 紀念碑 (n.) 3. **rhinoceros** 犀牛 (n.) 4. **mustache** 八字鬍 (n.)
5. **startle** 使驚嚇 (v.) 6. **muffle** 消音 (v.) 7. **strip** 脫光衣服 (v.) 8. **bizarre** 奇異的 (a.)
9. **surrealist** 超現實主義的 (a.) 10. **expel** 驅逐 (v.) 11. **rational** 理智的 (a.) 12. **paranoiac** 偏執狂的 (a.)
13. **induce** 引誘 (v.) 14. **distrust** 懷疑 (n.) 15. **geometry** 幾何學 (n.) 16. **illusion** 錯覺 (n.)
17. **ridiculous** 荒謬的 (a.) 18. **sane** 神智清楚的 (a.)

studied art in Madrid. He was an extremely talented technical drawer, a skill that would be used to great effect in his paintings, which often used complex **geometry**[15] and visual **illusions**[16].

Dalí's works explore both the **ridiculous**[17] and terrifying aspects of the illogical. Some people called him **insane**, but Dalí simply replied, "There is only one difference between a madman and me. The madman thinks he is **sane**[18]. I know I am mad."

▼ Nobility of Time

Questions

____ 1. Which of the following is the main topic of the article? •Main Idea•
   a The early life of Salvador Dalí.
   b Dalí's art and his approach to surrealism.
   c Dalí's time in the surrealist group.
   d The bizarre behavior of Salvador Dalí.

____ 2. What is the purpose of this passage? •Subject Matter•
   a To describe modern Spanish art to the reader.
   b To expose the strange behavior of artists.
   c To provide a summary of surrealist theory.
   d To introduce Dalí, his work, and his ideas about art.

____ 3. Which of the following statements is NOT true? •Supporting Details•
   a Dalí's works often used complex shapes and visual tricks.
   b Dalí was primarily active as an artist in the nineteenth century.
   c Dalí's subject matter was the illogical and irrational.
   d Dalí was a talented technical drawer, trained in Madrid.

____ 4. What does this article imply about Dalí's works? •Inference•
   a They are simplistic and painted with little skill.
   b They are sometimes difficult to understand.
   c They mostly consist of art objects.
   d They do not attract the attention of serious art lovers.

____ 5. What does the word **insane** in the final paragraph mean? •Words in Context•
   a Intelligent.   b Foolish.   c Crazy.   d Arrogant.

____ 6. Which of the following is a commonly held opinion about Dalí? •Fact or Opinion•
   a Dalí was completely mad.   b Dalí was expelled from the surrealist group.
   c Dalí studied art in Madrid.   d Dalí was born in 1904 in Spain.

Salvador Dalí

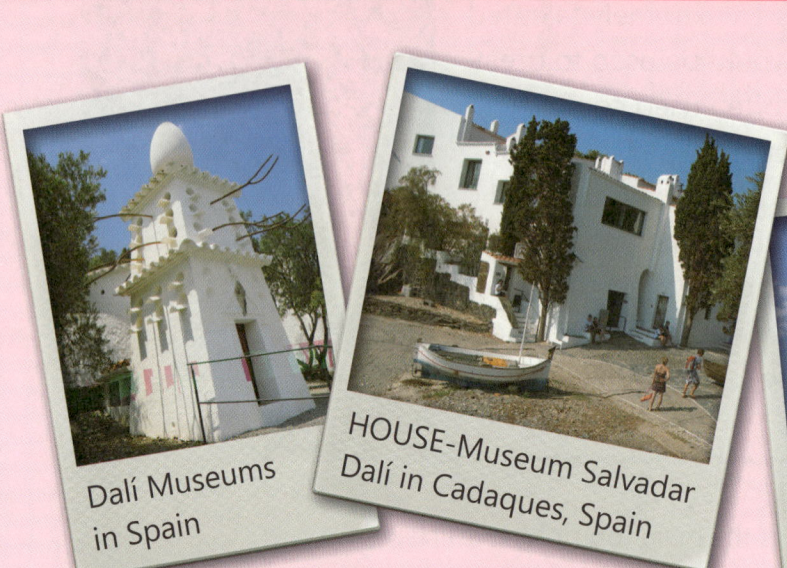

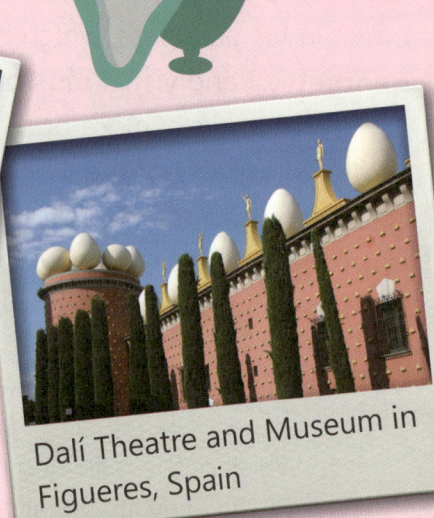

Dalí Museums in Spain

HOUSE-Museum Salvadar Dalí in Cadaques, Spain

Dalí Theatre and Museum in Figueres, Spain

▲ Soft Construction with Boiled Beans (Premonition of Civil War)

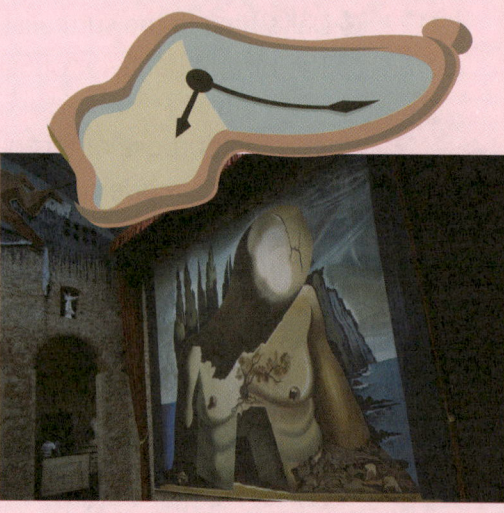

▲ Design for Set Curtain for Labyrinth I

▲ The Persistence of Memory

▲ The Temptation of Saint Anthony

▲ Portrait of Picasso

Week 8

Day 1 Geography	43	Walking on the Moon	108
Day 2 Culture	44	Say It With Your Fingers—Carefully!	110
Day 3 Business	45	Profit for a Cause	112
Day 4 Nature	46	A Beautiful Menace Under the Ice	114
Day 5 Technology	47	The Eyes Have It!	116
Day 6 Sports	48	Learn to Fight Like an Israeli	118

Week 8 Day 1

Geography

43 Walking on the Moon

▼ fairy chimneys

1   Cappadocia has a **landscape**[1] unlike anything you've seen before. Located in central Turkey, this region is famous for its natural rock **formations**[2]. Some visitors say that visiting Cappadocia is like visiting the moon.

2   How did Cappadocia become so **exceptional**[3]? Both nature and **humanity**[4] **had a hand in** it. Take the "fairy **chimneys**[5]" that the region is famous for. These are **pillars**[6] of rock that have been **eroded**[7] by thousands of years of wind and rain. They can stand as high as 40 meters tall. Some of them have a cone of harder rock at the top. It can look a bit like a hat sometimes. This cone takes longer to erode than the softer rock **underneath**[8].

3   Now, here's where humanity comes into the picture. The region of Cappadocia was located on the ancient Silk Road. For thousands of years, traders and soldiers from Europe and Asia passed through the area. Some decided to put down roots, and since Cappadocia's landscape is desert-like, without any trees, they faced a **housing**[9] problem. To solve it, settlers picked up **shovels**[10] and started digging. They dug into the larger fairy chimneys and built a complex system of caves to live in. Their work left the region's rock formations dotted with holes. The end result is a landscape that's truly jaw-dropping.

4   Fast-forward to the present, and some of these caves have been **converted**[11] into hotel **suites**[12]. Any visitor can try that "cave experience," and live like the settlers did thousands of years ago. But there's one important difference: now you can have a **mattress**[13], a pillow, and a blanket!

5   One of the best ways to discover these natural wonders is to take a hot air balloon ride. Balloon ride operators are common throughout Cappadocia.

▼ Balloon ride operators are common throughout Cappadocia.

Key Words

1. landscape 景觀；景色 (n.)
2. formation 結構 (n.)
3. exceptional 特別的；特殊的 (a.)
4. humanity 人文；人性 (n.)
5. chimney 煙囪 (n.)
6. pillar 柱子 (n.)
7. erode 侵蝕；腐蝕 (v.)
8. underneath 下面的；底下的 (a.)
9. housing 房屋；住宅 (n.)
10. shovel 鏟子；鐵鍬 (n.)
11. convert 轉變為 (v.)
12. suite 套房 (n.)
13. mattress 床墊 (n.)
14. soak 沉浸；浸泡 (v.)
15. fancy 時髦的 (a.)
16. champagne 香檳 (n.)

▼ housing cave in Cappadocia

Tourists can take a 1-2 hour ride and **soak**[14] in the sights from high in the sky. These tours can be very **fancy**[15]. Some even offer buffets and **champagne**[16] toasts. If you want something more private, there are tours focusing on special occasions like honeymoons or marriage proposals. Wouldn't it be romantic to have such a great surprise up in the air!

Questions

1. Which sentence is closest in meaning to the main point? ◆Main Idea◆
   a. Cappadocia was once on the ancient Silk Road.
   b. Several natural wonders can be found in Cappadocia.
   c. Cappadocia is a desert-like landscape without any trees.
   d. Fairy chimneys are pillars of rock with cones on top.

2. What's another possible title for this article? ◆Subject Matter◆
   a. Traveling Turkey in a Balloon.
   b. Erosion—Nature's Sculptor.
   c. An Unforgettable Landscape.
   d. My Life in a Cave.

3. Why did settlers in Cappadocia build their homes in caves? ◆Supporting Details◆
   a. There were no building materials available.
   b. It was the only way to beat the desert heat.
   c. For protection against passing soldiers.
   d. There was fresh water in the caves.

4. Which of the following is probably true about Cappadocia? ◆Inference◆
   a. Hot air balloon rides are popular with tourists there.
   b. It will disappear within the next 10 years.
   c. It's a very dangerous place to live.
   d. There is no electricity there.

5. What does the phrase **have a hand in** mean in the second paragraph? ◆Words in Context◆
   a. To delay something.
   b. To leave something.
   c. To contribute to something.
   d. To shrink something.

6. Which of the following statements is a fact? ◆Fact or Opinion◆
   a. Cappadocia has a landscape that's truly jaw-dropping.
   b. Cappadocia is unlike anything you've seen before.
   c. Cappadocia was located on the ancient Silk Road.
   d. Fairy chimneys can look a bit like a hat sometimes.

Week 8 Day 1 Walking on the Moon

Week 8 Day 2

Culture

◀ In the West, this gesture means "okay."

44
Say It With Your Fingers—Carefully!

1   Being in a place where you can't speak the local language can be **frustrating**[1]. It's only natural in such situations to attempt to communicate through body language. Hand gestures are indeed **universal**[2], but their meanings **vary**[3] as much as speech from place to place.

2   Take the gesture made by pressing the tips of your thumb and forefinger together while extending your other fingers. In the West, this is instantly recognized as meaning "okay." In Brazil, it is instantly recognized as an insult. In some East Asian countries, it means money. Just imagine the **potential misunderstandings**[4]!

3   Trying to call someone over to you can be just as confusing, depending on where you are. Westerners do it with a hooked forefinger and a raised **palm**[5]. Asians, on the other . . . uh, hand, find this rude, as they consider it suitable only for calling dogs. To **summon**[6] another person, they turn the palm down and wave all four fingers pressed together. This is exactly how Western people tell someone to go away!

4   One hand gesture that *does* translate is a raised middle finger with the back of the hand facing **outward**[7]. Considered extremely **offensive**[8], this is the American version of a gesture to which the British add a raised forefinger, forming a V. By turning his *palm* outward, however, the late British **Prime Minister**[9] Winston Churchill made this a victory sign during World War II. Twenty-five years later, American **hippies**[10] used the same gesture to **symbolize**[11] their wish for peace during the Vietnam War. Nowadays, Vietnamese and other East Asians flash "peace fingers" automatically anytime they have their pictures taken. Confused yet?

▶ Winston Churchill making the "V" sign, which meant victory during World War II

Key Words

1. frustrating 挫折的 (a.)   2. universal 普遍的 (a.)   3. vary 變化；不同於 (v.)
4. misunderstanding 誤解；誤會 (n.)   5. palm 手掌 (n.)   6. summon 召喚 (v.)
7. outward 向外地 (adv.)   8. offensive 冒犯的；無理的 (a.)   9. prime minister 首相 (n.)
10. hippie 嬉皮 (n.)   11. symbolize 象徵 (v.)   12. cross-culture 跨文化的 (a.)
13. instinctive 本能的；直覺的 (a.)   14. verbally 口頭地 (adv.)   15. hazardous 危險的 (a.)

◀ East Asians make the V gesture when they have their pictures taken.

[5] Even the simplest hand gestures can cause **cross-cultural**[12] problems. In the West, a thumb up has a positive meaning and a thumb down a negative one. In the Middle East, a thumb up has a negative meaning and a thumb down has no meaning at all. Might this be part of the reason for the seemingly endless trouble between these two societies?

[6] Body language may be an **instinctive**[13] option when we can't communicate **verbally**[14], but it can also be very **hazardous**[15]. My advice? The next time you travel abroad, take a phrase book!

Questions

____ 1. What is the main idea of this article? ⸺⸺⸺⸺⸺⸺⸺⸺⸺ ◆Main Idea◆
   a Middle Eastern people consider a thumb up offensive.
   b Most familiar hand gestures come from the West.
   c Hand gestures have different meanings in different places.
   d It is common for people to communicate through body language.

____ 2. What is this article primarily about? ⸺⸺⸺⸺⸺⸺⸺⸺⸺ ◆Subject Matter◆
   a Different ways of communicating.
   b Different cultures around the world.
   c How Winston Churchill won World War II.
   d The frustrating aspects of traveling.

____ 3. Which of the following might cause embarrassment to an Asian person traveling in the West? ⸺⸺⸺⸺⸺⸺⸺⸺⸺ ◆Supporting Details◆
   a Showing a thumb down to indicate that something is bad.
   b Making a "peace" sign when his or her picture is taken.
   c Using a phrasebook to try to speak to someone.
   d Calling someone over the way people in Asia usually do.

____ 4. What does the writer of this article probably believe? ⸺⸺⸺⸺⸺⸺ ◆Inference◆
   a Watching people get into trouble with hand gestures is fun.
   b People should know what hand gestures mean before using them.
   c Hand gestures should never be used under any circumstances.
   d British people don't understand the meanings of hand gestures.

____ 5. What does **potential** mean? ⸺⸺⸺⸺⸺⸺⸺⸺⸺⸺⸺ ◆Words in Context◆
   a Insulting.   b Possible.   c Confusing.   d Recognizable.

____ 6. How can the writer's tone in this article best be described? ⸺⸺⸺ ◆Author's Tone◆
   a Enthusiastic.   b Worried.   c Annoyed.   d Humorous.

45 Profit for a Cause

▶ social enterprise diagram

① Can **capitalism**[1] be a force for good in matters of the environment and social justice? This is the question at the heart of the social **enterprise**[2] movement. If you were to ask any social **entrepreneur** who's working hard to start their own business, they would surely say "yes."

② In some ways, a social enterprise is exactly like a regular enterprise. It provides a product or service, employs workers, and aims to make a profit. But there is one major difference: a social enterprise is **striving**[3] to make the world a better place. You might be thinking: "Doesn't every enterprise want to make the world a better place? **Corporations**[4] like Apple **donate**[5] millions of dollars to **charity**[6]." That's true, and it touches upon the central debate in the social enterprise movement.

③ There's a lot of **disagreement**[7] over what exactly **constitutes**[8] a social enterprise. To some people, it's an enterprise that invests all of its profit into social **welfare**[9]. Think of a **thrift**[10] store that takes its profits and funds a local food bank. This is the "purest" **interpretation**[11], but it still raises a few difficult questions. For example, should the thrift store expand and open new locations? Doing so might save more people from hunger. Yet the more money it **devotes**[12] to expansion, the more it looks like a regular corporation.

④ Others define social enterprise as a corporation whose goal is to provide social or environmental benefits. An example of this would be a factory that converts dangerous waste into a useful product. The factory operates like any other corporation, but it just so happens to be benefiting the local population. Another interpretation of social enterprise is one that hires **vulnerable**[13] people who struggle in the **mainstream**[14] economy. An example of this is the Children Are Us Foundation in Taiwan. This foundation runs bakeries **staffed**[15] by mentally challenged young adults.

▶ a seller of The Big Issue, one of the UK's leading social businesses, founded in 1991

Key Words

1. capitalism 資本主義 (n.)　2. enterprise 企業 (n.)　3. strive 奮鬥；努力 (v.)
4. corporation 公司；企業 (n.)　5. donate 捐獻 (v.)　6. charity 慈善 (n.)　7. disagreement 意見不一 (n.)
8. constitute 構成；組成 (v.)　9. welfare 福利 (n.)　10. thrift 節儉 (n.)　11. interpretation 解釋；闡明 (n.)
12. devote 奉獻 (v.)　13. vulnerable 脆弱的；易受傷的 (a.)　14. mainstream 主流的 (a.)
15. staff (為機構) 配備職員 (v.)　16. generosity 慷慨 (n.)

▶ The Co-operative Group values their social responsibilities more than profits.
(cc by The Co-operative)

[5] With all this disagreement, it's almost like anything can be a social enterprise. But what we're really doing here is just putting a new name on an old phenomenon. Social enterprises have been around for thousands of years. In the past, it was simply called neighbors helping out neighbors. You might even say that "social enterprise" is as old as human **generosity**[16].

Questions

____ 1. Which sentence is closest in meaning to the main point? ◆Main Idea◆
   a Social enterprise can mean many different things.
   b Social enterprises have been around for thousands of years.
   c Corporations like Apple donate millions of dollars to charity.
   d A social enterprise employs workers and makes a profit.

____ 2. What does this passage describe? ◆Subject Matter◆
   a An invention.   b A social benefit.
   c A type of company.   d A foundation.

____ 3. According to the article, which is NOT a possible interpretation of social enterprise? ◆Supporting Details◆
   a An enterprise that operates around the world.
   b An enterprise that hires vulnerable workers.
   c An enterprise that spends its profits helping people.
   d An enterprise whose goal is to improve welfare.

____ 4. Which of the following is something that the writer would likely believe? ◆Inference◆
   a Social enterprises are too expensive.
   b Social enterprises are good for society.
   c Social enterprises can't survive in the mainstream economy.
   d Social enterprises should never hire vulnerable workers.

____ 5. What does **entrepreneur** in the first paragraph mean? ◆Words in Context◆
   a Someone who has retired.
   b Someone who has lost all of their money.
   c Someone with a high level of education.
   d Someone who starts their own business.

____ 6. How does the writer capture the reader's attention in the final paragraph? ◆Clarifying Devices◆
   a By telling a joke.   b By offering an opinion.
   c By providing statistics.   d By sharing a personal story.

Week 8 Day 4

Nature

46   A Beautiful Menace[1] Under the Ice

[1] While exploring the Canadian north, photographer Paul Zizka came across a wonderful sight. It wasn't the snow-capped mountains, the pine trees, or the **tranquil**[2] lakes. Rather it was some bubbles that caught Paul's eye. These bubbles were visible just under the icy surface of a lake. There were hundreds of them, all frozen in place. They looked like strange sea creatures, maybe even **alien**[3] life.

[2] What the photographer had discovered is actually a gas called **methane**[4]. Methane is a **greenhouse**[5] gas that's far more powerful than carbon dioxide. By some **estimates**[6], it's 25 times more powerful. It's also highly **flammable** and can explode when released. Methane bubbles are formed by **bacteria**[7] at the bottom of lakes. These bacteria **consume**[8] plant matter and releases methane as part of their **digestion**[9] process. You might say it's a bacterium's way of **farting**[10]. In warmer weather, these methane bubbles float to the surface and are released into the **atmosphere**[11]. But when the water is frozen, the bubbles get trapped in the ice.

[3] But methane bubbles are far more than just a pretty picture. In actual fact, they're a serious threat to all of us. Methane is a gas that **contributes**[12] to global warming. Some parts of the planet are frozen all year round. It's called "**permafrost**[13]." As the planet heats up, this permafrost melts, releasing methane bubbles from lakes and rivers. The release of this methane causes more global warming, which melts more frozen lakes and rivers. The process is called a "**feedback**[14] cycle," because the effect contributes to the cause. According to one scientist, frozen methane is a climate time bomb waiting to go off.

Methane CH$_4$

▶ Methane emitted from animals contributes to global warming.

Key Words

① menace 威脅 (n.)　② tranquil 寧靜的；平靜的 (a.)　③ alien 外星的 (a.)　④ methane 甲烷 (n.)
⑤ greenhouse 溫室 (n.)　⑥ estimate 預估；預測 (n.)　⑦ bacteria 細菌（複數）(n.)
⑧ consume 吸收；消化 (v.)　⑨ digestion 消化 (n.)　⑩ fart 放屁 (v.)　⑪ atmosphere 大氣 (n.)
⑫ contribute 造成 (v.)　⑬ permafrost 永凍土層 (n.)　⑭ feedback 反饋；回饋 (n.)　⑮ preserve 保存 (v.)

◀ bubbles of methane gas
frozen into clear ice

[4]   The methane feedback cycle is yet another reason why the fight against global warming is so important. We all must do our part to solve the problem. This could mean planting a tree or even just walking to school or work every day. Doing so will help **preserve**[15] the natural beauty of these frozen bubbles. It will also help save the entire planet. Let's keep these dangerous bacteria farts where they belong: safely under the ice!

Questions

____ 1. Which sentence is closest in meaning to the main point? ◆Main Idea◆
   a We should do what we can to make a positive difference.
   b Methane bubbles may be beautiful, but they're also dangerous.
   c Methane bubbles are the main cause of global warming.
   d As the planet heats up, the permafrost melts.

____ 2. What is this article about? ◆Subject Matter◆
   a A type of gas.   b The permafrost.
   c A photographer.   d The Canadian north.

____ 3. According to the article, which of the following is NOT true about methane?
   ◆Supporting Details◆
   a It can get trapped in ice.
   b It is 25 times more powerful than carbon.
   c It does not contribute to global warming.
   d It is created by bacteria at the bottom of lakes.

____ 4. Which of the following does the writer probably believe? ◆Inference◆
   a The permafrost should be allowed to melt.
   b Global warming is not a threat.
   c The environment should be protected.
   d Carbon is more powerful than methane.

____ 5. What does **flammable** mean in the second paragraph? ◆Words in Context◆
   a Easily lit on fire.   b Heavy.
   c Bright.   d Carrying a strong smell.

____ 6. How does the writer capture the reader's attention in the first paragraph?
   ◆Clarifying Devices◆
   a By telling a story.   b By providing statistics.
   c By making an argument.   d By telling a joke.

Week 8 Day 5
Technology

47
(047)

The Eyes Have It!

[1] If you've ever tried to read or watch something on a smartphone in bright sunlight, you know it's not easy. People usually need **shade**[1] to see screens clearly, especially small screens. And if the sun is right **overhead**[2], your eyes can get a **nasty**[3] **blast**[4] of **glare**[5]. Then you won't be seeing *anything* for a minute or two!

[2] That's all changing right now, however, thanks to moths. Yes, moths. Taking inspiration from these **nocturnal** insects, scientists in Taiwan and the United States have found a solution to midday glare.

[3] The technology that **enables**[6] people to watch TV on the street in daylight is actually based on what allows moths to see at night. **Microscopic**[7] structures on moths' eyes let light in but don't reflect it back out. For the insects, this has a double benefit, enabling them to see in darkness while making them less visible to **predators**[8]. But when similar tiny structures are pressed into a thin, flexible **film**[9], they trap sunlight and **thereby**[10] prevent glare. This means that surfaces coated with such film can be clearly seen even under bright skies.

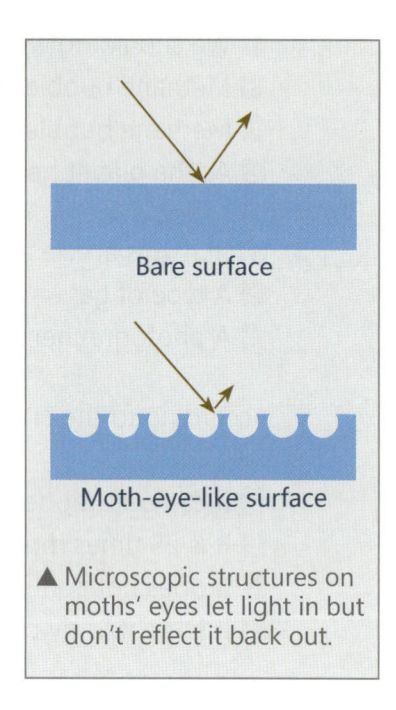

Bare surface

Moth-eye-like surface

▲ Microscopic structures on moths' eyes let light in but don't reflect it back out.

[4] "Moth eye" film was originally developed for use on solar energy panels, which are more efficient when they're non-**reflective**[11]. Now, however, it's ready to take on a variety of new uses. In addition to smartphone screens, **windowpanes**[12], road signs, watches, **speedometers**[13], and **fuel**[14] **gauges**[15] could all be improved by this inexpensive material. Researchers claim that "moth eye" film offers *10 times* better readability in clear weather and five times better

Key Words

① shade 陰影 (n.)　② overhead 頭頂上的 (a.)　③ nasty 棘手的；難處理的 (a.)
④ blast（突然）炸開；一陣 (n.)　⑤ glare 刺眼的強光 (n.)　⑥ enable 使能夠 (v.)
⑦ microscopic 極小的 (a.)　⑧ predator 獵食者 (n.)　⑨ film 薄膜 (n.)　⑩ thereby 因此；從而 (adv.)
⑪ reflective 反射的 (a.)　⑫ windowpane 玻璃窗 (n.)　⑬ speedometer 速度計 (n.)　⑭ fuel 燃料 (n.)
⑮ gauge 表；測量儀器 (n.)　⑯ gadget 小裝置 (n.)

even in direct sunlight. Since it's self-cleaning, dirt, dust, and fingerprints won't be problems anymore either.

[5] Perhaps the best thing about "moth eye" film is that you won't have to buy a new scooter or phone to get it. It can be stuck onto the surfaces of old **gadgets**[16] like any screen protector. In the future, however, it may become part of the manufacturing process and already be on products when you buy them.

[6] So the next time you see a moth, be sure to thank it for giving us humans a very helpful idea!

▲ "Moth eye" film can be attached to the surface of smartphone as a screen protector.

Questions

____ 1. What is the main idea of this passage? ◆Main Idea◆
   a Moths can see in the dark, but human beings can't.
   b Using your smartphone on a sunny day can be dangerous.
   c There is now a product that reduces glare on surfaces.
   d Dirt, dust, and fingerprints aren't problems anymore.

____ 2. What is this passage primarily about? ◆Subject Matter◆
   a A type of film.
   b A type of smartphone.
   c A type of insect.
   d A type of scientist.

____ 3. Which of the following statements is NOT true about "moth eye" film? ◆Supporting Details◆
   a It can be applied to devices that people already own.
   b It was originally developed for use on windowpanes.
   c It is thin, flexible, and inexpensive.
   d It traps sunlight and doesn't reflect it back out.

____ 4. What can we assume about "moth eye" film from the article? ◆Inference◆
   a It doesn't work in bright sunlight.
   b It is already available.
   c It only works on solar energy panels.
   d It has to be cleaned often.

____ 5. What does **nocturnal** mean? ◆Words in Context◆
   a Having eyes that don't reflect light.
   b Only active in the summertime.
   c Mostly active during the night.
   d More efficient when it's non-reflective.

____ 6. How can the writer's tone in this passage best be described? ◆Author's Tone◆
   a Humorous.   b Critical.   c Uninterested.   d Enthusiastic.

48 Learn to Fight Like an Israeli

▼ Imi Lichtenfeld (left) (1910–1998)

1   The story of Krav Maga is right out of a Hollywood movie. It begins with a man who grew up in **desperate**¹ times. His name was Emrich "Imi" Lichtenfeld. Imi was a **martial**² artist, **boxer**³, and **acrobat**⁴. He was also Jewish, which was very dangerous in 1930s Czechoslovakia. Facing **violent**⁵ threats over his religion, Imi decided to do something about it. He got together with other Jewish boxers and started working on a way to **defend**⁶ their people. The goal was to strip the "art" away from martial art. They wanted to create a fighting style that was **practical**⁷, effective, and easily taught to others. Their style came to be known as Krav Maga.

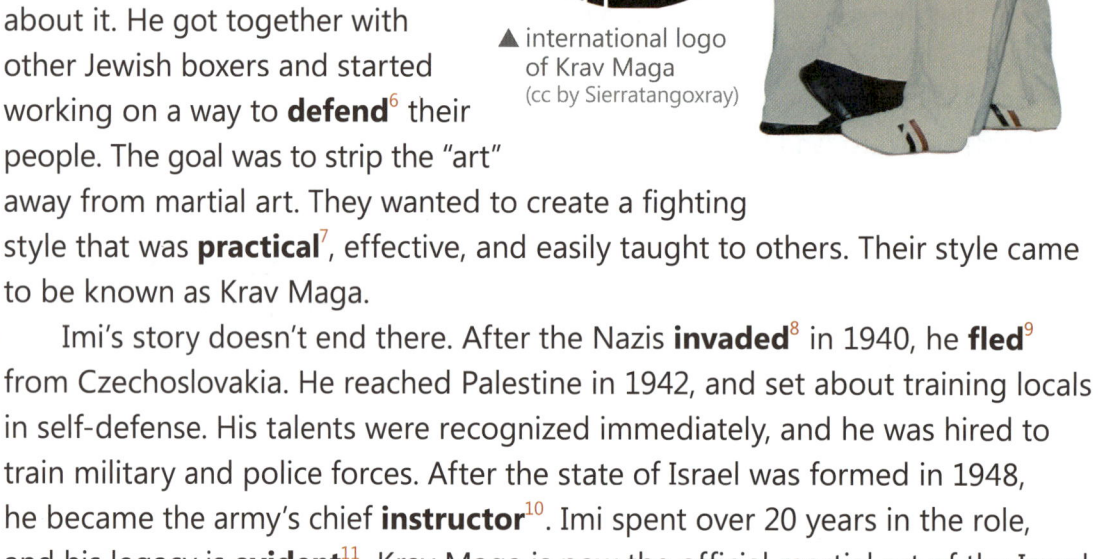

▲ international logo of Krav Maga (cc by Sierratangoxray)

2   Imi's story doesn't end there. After the Nazis **invaded**⁸ in 1940, he **fled**⁹ from Czechoslovakia. He reached Palestine in 1942, and set about training locals in self-defense. His talents were recognized immediately, and he was hired to train military and police forces. After the state of Israel was formed in 1948, he became the army's chief **instructor**¹⁰. Imi spent over 20 years in the role, and his legacy is **evident**¹¹. Krav Maga is now the official martial art of the Israel Defense Forces.

3   Krav Maga is practical above all. Imi drew heavily from other martial arts when developing it, but he only took techniques that were efficient and easy to understand. Therefore, everything in Krav Maga is useful in an actual fight. It teaches how to defend against weapons like knives and guns. It shows how to

Key Words

1. **desperate** 情勢危急的 (a.)　2. **martial** 軍隊的；軍事的 (a.)　3. **boxer** 拳擊手 (n.)
4. **acrobat** 雜技演員 (n.)　5. **violent** 暴力的 (a.)　6. **defend** 防禦 (v.)　7. **practical** 實用的 (a.)
8. **invade** 入侵 (v.)　9. **flee** 逃跑；撤退 (v.)　10. **instructor** 教練 (n.)　11. **evident** 明顯的 (a.)
12. **household** 家庭的 (a.)　13. **put a premium on** 鼓勵；強調　14. **out of commission** 失去行為能力

turn any **household**[12] object into a weapon. It also **puts a premium on**[13] swift strikes that can take an attacker **out of commission**[14]. A Krav Maga fighter will always target **vulnerable** spots like the eyes, neck, face, or knee.

❹ Krav Maga is also a fighting style that anyone can learn. Imi wanted to develop something that wasn't complicated and easy to learn. Men, women, and children of all ages and body types can train in Krav Maga, but that doesn't mean the training will be easy!

◀ Krav Maga is useful in real fights.

Week 8 Day 6 — Learn to Fight Like an Israeli

Questions

____ 1. Which sentence is closest in meaning to the main point? ◆Main Idea◆
   a Krav Maga training is not easy.
   b Krav Maga is a practical and accessible martial art.
   c A Krav Maga fighter targets vulnerable spots.
   d Emrich "Imi" Lichtenfeld invented Krav Maga.

____ 2. What does this passage describe? ◆Subject Matter◆
   a A person.
   b A fighting style.
   c A weapon.
   d The Israel Defense Forces.

____ 3. Which of the following is NOT true about Imi's life? ◆Supporting Details◆
   a He grew up in Czechoslovakia.
   b He was a boxer and a martial artist.
   c He fought against the Nazis in 1940.
   d He taught Krav Maga to the Israel army.

____ 4. Which of the following is probably NOT a principle of Krav Maga? ◆Inference◆
   a Strike your opponent when they least expect it.
   b Bow to your opponent before the fight starts.
   c Keep fighting until your opponent cannot threaten you anymore.
   d Always check your surroundings for weapons and escape routes.

____ 5. What's another word for **vulnerable** in the third paragraph? ◆Words in Context◆
   a Fragile.
   b Complicated.
   c Rare.
   d Ugly.

____ 6. What is the writer's tone in this passage? ◆Author's Tone◆
   a Tragic.
   b Comic.
   c Serious.
   d Angry.

Other Styles of Martial Arts

▼ tai chi

◀ karate

▼ wrestling

▼ Muay Thai

▼ boxing

▼ kalaripayattu

▼ judo

▼ tae kwon do

▶ sambo

120

Week 9

Day 1 Health & Body	49 **An Oil to Go Nuts For**	122
Day 2 Geography	50 **Towering Beauties**	124
Day 3 Culture	51 **A Mystical, Magical Soup**	126
Day 4 History	52 **Gold Fever**	128
Day 5 Environment	53 **Building a Greener Future**	130
Day 6 Health & Body	54 **Hidden Dangers**	132

Health & Body

Week 9 Day 1

▼ Coconut oil can help reduce inflammation, swelling, and pain.

▶ inflammation

49 🎧 049

An Oil to Go Nuts[1] For

[1] Whether in a newspaper or a magazine, you've probably heard of coconut oil. It's a new health **craze**[2] that's catching on around the world.

[2] Doctors have found that coconut oil is high in healthy **fatty acids**[3] that are easily digested. Energy from these acids is less likely to be converted into fat. It's also energy that is easily burned when exercising. But the benefits of coconut oil don't stop there—not even close! Studies have revealed the various ways in which coconut oil improves overall health. For one, coconut oil is high in natural **saturated fats**[4]. These fats increase healthy **cholesterol**[5], which prevents heart disease and high blood pressure. Coconut oil is also rich in **antioxidants**[6] that help reduce **inflammation**[7]. People who suffer from **arthritis**[8] and other inflammatory diseases sometimes report reduced **swelling**[9] and pain. Coconut oil is also believed to help prevent some types of cancer.

[3] As if that's not enough, coconut oil can also benefit your everyday life. Studies have shown that coconut oil can improve memory function in older people. It can also increase **metabolism**[10], which leads to better energy and **endurance**[11]. It even **restores**[12] skin and leaves it looking younger. No wonder they call coconut oil a superfood: it's creating super-people!

[4] Of course, not everyone agrees on the subject of coconut oil. There are a few doctors and scientists who **haven't seen the light** yet. For example, the American Heart Association claims that coconut oil is a "troubling" source of saturated fat. Others say that the benefits of coconut oil have been **exaggerated**[13], and that more research is needed. Then there are **journalists**[14] who believe that the coconut oil trend is hurting farmers worldwide.

Key Words

1. go nuts 陷入瘋狂 2. craze 瘋狂；熱潮 (n.) 3. fatty acid 脂肪酸 (n.)
4. saturated fat 飽和脂肪 (n.) 5. cholesterol 膽固醇 (n.) 6. antioxidant 抗氧化劑 (n.)
7. inflammation 發炎 (n.) 8. arthritis 關節炎 (n.) 9. swelling 腫脹處；腫塊 (n.)
10. metabolism 新陳代謝 (n.) 11. endurance 耐力 (n.) 12. restore 恢復；復原 (v.)
13. exaggerate 誇大 (v.) 14. journalist 記者 (n.) 15. incredible 不可思議的 (a.)

▼ swelling

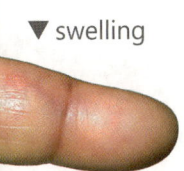

[5] In reality, the truth is somewhere in the middle. Coconut oil has been proven to have some **incredible**[15] health benefits. But like anything else in life, it's possible to have too much of a good thing.

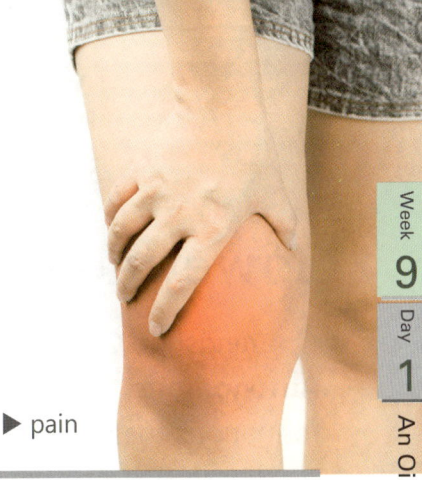

▶ pain

Questions

____ 1. Which sentence is closest to the main point? ◆Main Idea◆
   a Coconut oil restores skin and leaves it looking younger.
   b People think the benefits of coconut oil have been exaggerated.
   c It's possible to have too much of a good thing.
   d Coconut oil is a superfood with some doubters.

____ 2. What would be another title for this article? ◆Subject Matter◆
   a The Oil That Does It All.
   b Everyday Health Tips.
   c A World of Healthy Nuts.
   d How to Improve Your Energy.

____ 3. According to the article, which of the following is NOT a health benefit of coconut oil? ◆Supporting Details◆
   a Better skin.
   b Improved memory.
   c Deeper sleeps.
   d Cancer prevention.

____ 4. What can we infer from the second paragraph? ◆Inference◆
   a Coconut oil is popular with runners.
   b Coconut oil needs to be studied further.
   c Coconut oil is dangerous.
   d Coconut oil is very expensive.

____ 5. What does it mean that doctors and scientists **haven't seen the light,** as stated in the fourth paragraph? ◆Words in Context◆
   a They haven't been properly trained.
   b They haven't realized something.
   c They haven't been outside.
   d They haven't worked before.

____ 6. Which of the following is an opinion? ◆Fact or Opinion◆
   a Coconut oil is rich in antioxidants.
   b Coconut oil is high in natural saturated fats.
   c The truth is somewhere in the middle.
   d Not everyone agrees on the subject of coconut oil.

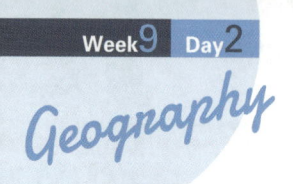

50 Towering Beauties

1 Yangshuo County in China's Guangxi **Autonomous**[1] Region has some truly unique rock formations that make for some of the most interesting geography in the world.

2 Located in Southeast China, Yangshuo is home to extremely **picturesque**[2] natural **scenery**[3]. Its landscape is teeming with unique rock formations that are called **karsts**[4]. These rocks **protrude**[5] out of the earth in a big way. They look like stone pillars that have grown to be **massive**[6] just like a tree might. Strangely enough, the two ingredients for this **peculiar**[7] geography are extremely simple: water and time.

3 It took a long time for Yangshuo to inherit its unique geography. Millions of years ago, the Guilin area used to be a **gulf**[8]. This meant that Guilin's hills were **submerged**[9] underwater. This water slowly eroded them and fashioned them into pillar shapes. After the water **receded**[10], wind and rain continued to eat away at them and contribute to Yangshuo's unique look. **Ultimately**[11], the rock formations that we see today in Yangshuo County were tens of millions of years in the making!

4 There are a few particularly **notable**[12] karst formations within Yangshuo County. The first of them is called Nine Horse Mural Hill. This landmark is a giant stone cliff that faces the Li River. It got its name from the fact that some people can see nine horses in various poses in the rock patterns. Sunshine reflecting off the cliff face has been known to **dazzle**[13] **spectators**[14] with a rainbow of many colors. These colors also change depending on the weather and the time of day.

5 Elephant Trunk Hill is another famous karst formation in Yangshuo County. It is a limestone **arch**[15] at the **junction**[16] of the Li and Taohuajiang rivers.

Key Words

1. autonomous 自治的 (a.)
2. picturesque 如畫般的 (a.)
3. scenery 風景 (n.)
4. karst 喀斯特地形 (n.)
5. protrude 突出 (v.)
6. massive 巨大的 (a.)
7. peculiar 奇特的 (a.)
8. gulf 海灣 (n.)
9. submerge 淹沒 (v.)
10. recede 向後退 (v.)
11. ultimately 最終地 (adv.)
12. notable 著名的 (a.)
13. dazzle 使目眩眼花 (v.)
14. spectator 觀眾 (n.)
15. arch 拱門 (n.)
16. junction 連接處 (n.)
17. exquisite 精緻的 (a.)

◀ Moon Hill

6 The arch looks like an elephant that has come to drink from the river. Under the arch, there is a crescent-shaped pool that looks like a moon when light strikes it from a certain angle. While Yangshuo has some of the world's most **exquisite**[17] karst formations, there are several other worldwide spots that share similar geography. Ha Long Bay in Vietnam and Gunung Mulu in Malaysia are two other popular examples of karst formations that have been dazzling human eyes for thousands of years.

Questions

_____ 1. What would you say is the main idea of the article? ◆Main Idea◆
   a It's important to plan before going on vacation.
   b Yangshuo has very special geography.
   c China has lots of interesting places to visit.
   d Karsts are strange rock formations that can only be found in China.

_____ 2. What is this article about? ◆Subject Matter◆
   a A place near Asia.
   b A place in China.
   c An interesting landmark.
   d Water erosion.

_____ 3. Which of the following statements is NOT true? ◆Supporting Details◆
   a Karsts are formed by water erosion over a long period of time.
   b Yangshuo is home to many karst formations.
   c Vietnam has karst formations.
   d Karsts can form in a couple of years.

_____ 4. What can we infer about Yangshuo from the article? ◆Inference◆
   a It has a very large population.
   b It is close to a large body of water.
   c It is an extremely expensive place to visit.
   d It has had these karst formations for over a billion years.

_____ 5. What does the word **eroded** in the third paragraph mean? ◆Words in Context◆
   a Gradually destroyed something.
   b Re-created something perfectly.
   c Infected.
   d Discolored.

_____ 6. How does the author present the information in the article? ◆Text Form◆
   a As a series of facts and explanations.
   b As two sides of an argument.
   c As a series of examples supporting a point.
   d As a timeline of events.

Week 9 Day 3

Culture

▶ astrology

51 A Mystical, Magical Soup

[051]

① Take a **pinch**[1] of Eastern philosophy, ancient **rituals**[2], pseudoscience, **superstition**[3], and Native American spiritualism. Mix them all together with a sprinkling of **astrology**[4], belief in **psychic**[5] powers, and some self-help psychology, and the New Age movement is what you should call the resulting soup.

② New Age is a mishmash of a variety of different spiritual, mystical, and magical traditions that has become an **umbrella term**[6] for almost any kind of beliefs outside the established world religions. New Age usually embraces beliefs that promote spirituality or the idea that the whole universe is connected in some kind of meaningful way. It is, however, fairly nonspecific and has absorbed countless different belief systems regardless of their origins or **contexts**[7].

③ **Conversely**[8] to science and mainstream religions, New Age primarily promotes the existence of magic over science or the **divine**[9]. This can be seen especially in the healing beliefs associated with New Age, such as crystal healing. This is where crystals are thought to hold magical powers and, when put on the body, create a protective, healing magical field. The all-**inclusive**[10] nature of New Age has even led it to **incorporate**[11] common **conspiracy**[12] theories such as the belief in UFOs and mysteries like the supposed mystical powers of Stonehenge.

Stonehenge

④ Psychologist Michael D. Langone suggests that people turn to New Age because they have spiritual **impulses**[13], but do not want to get involved with the **complexities**[14] and **commitments**[15] of the major religions. Also, due to the

▶ crystal healing

Key Words

① pinch 一撮；一把 (n.)　② ritual 儀式 (n.)　③ superstition 迷信 (n.)　④ astrology 占星術 (n.)
⑤ psychic 通靈的 (a.)　⑥ umbrella term 概括性術語 (n.)　⑦ context 來龍去脈 (n.)
⑧ conversely 相反地 (adv.)　⑨ divine 神的 (a.)　⑩ inclusive 包括在內的 (a.)　⑪ incorporate 包含 (v.)
⑫ conspiracy 陰謀 (n.)　⑬ impulse 衝動 (n.)　⑭ complexity 複雜 (n.)　⑮ commitment 奉獻 (n.)
⑯ exploitation 利用 (n.)　⑰ distort 曲解 (v.)　⑱ adept 擅長的 (a.)

all-inclusive nature of New Age, there is something for everyone, and once someone accepts one belief as true, it becomes easier and easier to accept the other more ridiculous ones as true also.

5 Some Native American groups have become increasingly offended by the apparent **exploitation**[16] of their traditional beliefs. They see the New Age movement as using practices specific to Native American culture simply for profit or **distorting**[17] them to suit personal needs. As a result, people who claim to practice or be **adept**[18] at Native American spiritual healing but who are not themselves Native American have been labeled "plastic medicine men."

▼ Native Americans were offended by the exploitation of their traditional beliefs.

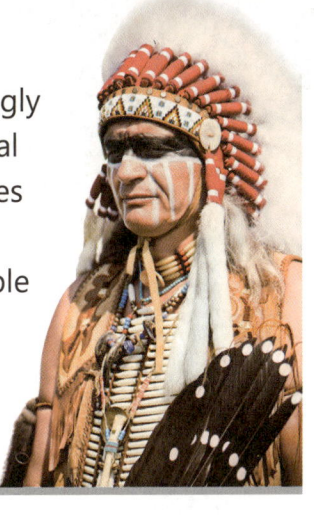

Questions

_____ 1. Which of the following is the main topic of the article? ◆Main Idea◆
 a What New Age really is.
 b People who believe in New Age.
 c The influence of Native American religions on the New Age movement.
 d The pros and cons of being a New Age believer.

_____ 2. What is this article about? ◆Subject Matter◆
 a A hobby.
 b A belief system.
 c A kind of medicine.
 d Magical landmarks.

_____ 3. Which of the following statements is NOT true? ◆Supporting Details◆
 a New Age attracts people with spiritual impulses.
 b Native American groups have been offended by New Age practices.
 c New Age thought often promotes magic over real science.
 d New Age discourages the idea that everything in the universe is connected.

_____ 4. What can we infer from this article? ◆Inference◆
 a Michael D. Langone is a New Age believer.
 b The term "plastic medicine men" is a critical one.
 c If you follow the New Age movement, you'll likely see a UFO.
 d New Age believers are in possession of secret knowledge that no one else has.

_____ 5. The title uses the word mystical. What does **mystical** mean? ◆Words in Context◆
 a Mysterious.   b Lucky.   c Scientific.   d Punctual.

_____ 6. Which of these best describes the author's tone in this article? ◆Author's Tone◆
 a Tragic.   b Wondering.   c Depressed.   d Skeptical.

52 Gold Fever

🎧 052

❶ In a tent **nestled**[1] deep within the Canadian **wilderness**[2], a **prospector**[3] named John **heaves**[4] a **sigh**[5]. It's 1865, and he's caught up in his third gold rush. This time, it's Big Bend Country in Canada, but it could be anywhere. After all, it's always the same story. Some lucky soul discovers a gold **nugget**[6], and before you know it, people are flooding in from all around the world. They all come with the same dream, but only a few of them get to walk away rich.

❷ He closes his eyes and listens to the rain pounding on his tent. He remembers his first chance, the Georgia gold rush of 1829. He was just a boy back then, swept up in his father's gold fever. The **trek** to Georgia was hard, and by the time they got there, thousands of other miners had already arrived. The early comers had already **uncovered**[7] most of the convenient gold by **panning**[8] for it in Georgia's rivers. Panning was a cheap and simple technique by which you used a pan to search for gold in the riverbed. The Georgia that John and his father discovered was one with no easy gold left. Only rich people could **retrieve**[9] what remained, because they had enough money to buy the **equipment**[10] necessary to dig underground.

▼ panning for gold

▲ advertisement about sailing to California, circa 1850

❸ Although his father died poor having never discovered his pot of gold, John **inherited**[11] his gold fever. In 1849, John was one of 90,000 people who traveled west during the California gold rush. This was the biggest gold rush of all time. It wasn't easy to get to California overland because there were no railways, so John took a ship that sailed from the east coast of America all the way

Key Words

❶ nestle 處於；位在 (v.)　❷ wilderness 荒野 (n.)　❸ prospector 探勘者 (n.)　❹ heave 發出（嘆息）(v.)
❺ sigh 嘆息 (n.)　❻ nugget 金礦 (n.)　❼ uncover 發掘；挖出 (v.)　❽ pan 淘金 (v.)
❾ retrieve 收回 (v.)　❿ equipment 裝備 (n.)　⓫ inherit 繼承 (v.)　⓬ continent 大陸 (n.)
⓭ stake a claim 宣稱（所有權）　⓮ dysentery 痢疾 (n.)

▶ gold nuggets

around the southern tip of the **continent**[12] of South America. Once he arrived, he set out for the mountains immediately. Since all of the land was owned by the government, prospectors were allowed to keep whatever gold they found. They just had to **stake a claim**[13] to prove they got there first. Unfortunately, the only thing that John ever found was a terrible case of **dysentery**[14] in San Francisco, the city that the gold rush built.

Week 9 Day 4 Gold Fever

Questions

____ 1. Which of the following is the main topic of this article? ◆Main Idea◆
   a Important gold rushes in nineteenth century North America.
   b The life of a prospector during the California gold rush.
   c Mining techniques of North American gold rushes.
   d Facts and fiction about the North American gold rush.

____ 2. What is this article mainly about? ◆Subject Matter◆
   a California.
   b Gold.
   c A prospector named John.
   d Big Bend Country.

____ 3. Which of the following is NOT true? ◆Supporting Details◆
   a The government owned most of the land in the California gold rush.
   b The California gold rush was the biggest of all time.
   c People flooded to places where gold had been discovered to get rich quickly.
   d Over 90,000 people flooded to Georgia during the gold rush of 1829.

____ 4. What does this article imply? ◆Inference◆
   a Gold fever is a real disease that sometimes causes paralysis.
   b San Francisco was a small town before the California gold rush.
   c Only poor people made fortunes during the California gold rush.
   d Big Bend Country was the last gold rush in North American history.

____ 5. The second paragraph mentions that the trek to Georgia was hard. What is a **trek**? ◆Words in Context◆
   a An easy journey.
   b A difficult journey.
   c A journey to a new continent.
   d A trip to a newly discovered place.

____ 6. Why did John have to travel all the way around the southern tip of South America by boat to get to California? ◆Cause and Effect◆
   a He had made very little money in Georgia.
   b There were no railways at that time.
   c All the land in California was owned by the government.
   d He inherited his father's gold fever.

129

Week 9 Day 5

Environment

▶ Cherokee Lofts is a Leadership in Energy and Environmental Design (LEED) Platinum Certified building.

53 Building a Greener Future

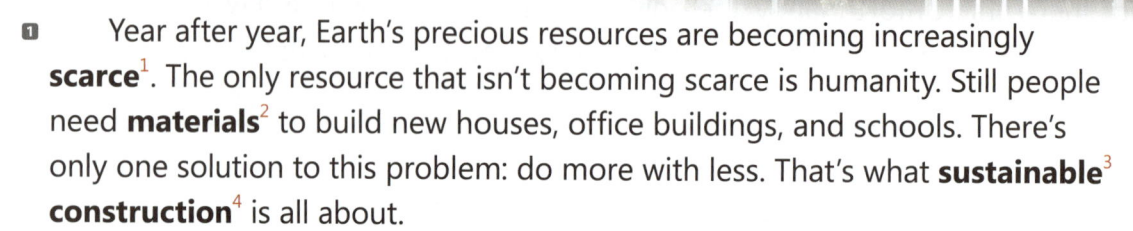

[053]

1 Year after year, Earth's precious resources are becoming increasingly **scarce**[1]. The only resource that isn't becoming scarce is humanity. Still people need **materials**[2] to build new houses, office buildings, and schools. There's only one solution to this problem: do more with less. That's what **sustainable**[3] **construction**[4] is all about.

2 **Advocates**[5] of sustainable construction believe the entire building process can be done without harming the environment, and by doing so, the earth is kept sustainable for future generations. To make these green buildings possible, however, the process must be **implemented**[6] from **conception**.

3 Picture a city government that wants to build a green office building. The first thing these city planners would do is select a site with a small environmental impact. Ideally, they would choose a site that had already been developed. Thus keeping the forests and **grasslands**[7] protected.

4 Next, city planners would turn their attention toward the construction process. Only green materials could be used to build their office towers. These include wood, steel, and other components that have been recycled from **demolished**[8] buildings. If possible, they have been **manufactured**[9], **recovered**[10], or **resourced**[11] locally. The closer that these green materials are to the construction site, the less energy is wasted getting them to where they're needed.

5 **Maintenance**[12] costs are the next important factors that need to be considered. City planners would design heating and cooling systems that use as little energy as possible. They would install solar roof **panels**[13] that will absorb the heat from the sun to power the building. Toilets and sinks designed to **minimize**[14] water waste would be installed throughout the building. These **efficiencies**[15] don't just help to protect the environment; they can save money over the long run as well.

Key Words

1. scarce 缺乏的 (a.) 2. material 材料 (n.) 3. sustainable 永續的 (a.)
4. construction 工程；建設 (n.) 5. advocate 擁護者 (n.) 6. implement 執行 (v.)
7. grassland 綠地 (n.) 8. demolish 拆除；拆毀 (v.) 9. manufacture 製造 (v.) 10. recover 修復 (v.)
11. resource 提供資源；援助 (v.) 12. maintenance 維修 (n.) 13. panel 壁板 (n.)
14. minimize 使減到最少 (v.) 15. efficiency 效率 (n.) 16. pollutant 污染源 (n.)

▶ The National Assembly for Wales uses traditional Welsh materials such as slate and Welsh oak.

[6] Finally, city planners would be aware of the fact that their new building may be demolished one day. Therefore, construction materials that can be reused after demolition would be selected. They would also make sure that the building doesn't contain any harmful **pollutants**[16] that could be released into the air during the demolition process.

[7] After all this was finished, the city planners would relax and maybe even throw a party. They have designed a building that was green at every step—the golden rule of sustainable construction.

Questions

____ 1. What would you say is the main topic of the article? ◆Main Idea◆
  a An analysis of different construction methods.
  b A case study of sustainable construction.
  c The benefits and drawbacks of sustainable construction.
  d A brief history of sustainable construction.

____ 2. What is this article about? ◆Subject Matter◆
  a A way to build buildings.   b Types of buildings.
  c Environmentalism.   d Recycling.

____ 3. Which of the following statements is NOT true? ◆Supporting Details◆
  a Sustainable construction focuses on every step of the building process.
  b The farther the building materials are from the construction site, the better.
  c Sustainable construction determines which toilets are used in a building.
  d Natural habitats are an important consideration to sustainable construction.

____ 4. Why have people started paying attention to sustainable construction recently?
  ◆Inference◆
  a Green office buildings are much more modern than any other kind.
  b Earth's resources are diminishing every passing year.
  c Governments can save a lot of money by using green building techniques.
  d It takes a lot of work to knock down old buildings.

____ 5. What does the word **conception** in the second paragraph mean?
  ◆Words in Context◆
  a A structure.   b A destruction.   c An idea.   d A deception.

____ 6. How does this passage start? ◆Clarifying Devices◆
  a By using contrasts of time.   b By presenting one specific case.
  c By stating a scientific fact.   d By referring to documents.

131

Week 9 Day 6
Health & Body

◀ English muffin

54
Hidden Dangers

1   Becky is a 35-year-old woman who is trying to lose weight and lead a healthy life. Every morning, she eats an English muffin for breakfast. English muffins, like various other breads, pastas, and dessert products, are often produced using **refined**[1] grains. These grains are heavily processed and have fewer **nutrients**[2] than whole grains. They have been linked to several health problems, including heart attacks, **diabetes**[3], and high cholesterol.

2   Becky packs a sandwich for lunch every day. Since she's trying to lose weight, she doesn't put butter or **mayonnaise**[4] on it. However, her sandwich always contains meat that is heavily processed and **loaded with sodium**[5]. Even though all of us need sodium to live, too much sodium in our body can lead to high blood pressure, **fluid retention**[6], and dizziness.

3   Going for a jog after work is Becky's favorite way to **unwind**[7] after a long, hard day. **As sure as the sun sets in the west**, Becky will reach for an energy drink after every run. She is completely unaware that the benefits of her run are being eroded by the high-fructose corn **syrup**[8] that she's drinking. High-fructose corn syrup is used as a sweetener in a wide range of foods, from soft drinks to breakfast cereals. Studies have linked its **consumption**[8] to **obesity**[10], **cavities**[11], and poor **nutrition**[12].

4   Becky likes to cook dinner for her family. Even though the meals she cooks are often very nutritious, she tends to use a lot of margarine. Studies have shown that the high levels of trans fats in margarine can **boost**[13] bad cholesterol and lower good cholesterol. People with high levels of bad cholesterol are more likely to have heart disease, cancer, and even depression.

▲ fresh and unprocessed food

Key Words

① refine 精製 (v.)   ② nutrient 養分 (n.)   ③ diabetes 糖尿病 (n.)   ④ mayonnaise 美乃滋 (n.)
⑤ sodium 鈉 (n.)   ⑥ fluid retention 水腫 (n.)   ⑦ unwind 放鬆 (v.)   ⑧ syrup 糖漿 (n.)
⑨ consumption 攝取 (n.)   ⑩ obesity 過胖 (n.)   ⑪ cavity 蛀牙 (n.)   ⑫ nutrition 營養 (n.)
⑬ boost 增加 (v.)   ⑭ fascinating 極好的 (a.)   ⑮ highlight 強調 (v.)   ⑯ deficiency 不足 (n.)

5   Becky may have gone on like this forever if not for a phone call from her mom one Sunday evening. Her mom informed her that she had read a **fascinating**[14] article in an English textbook that **highlighted**[15] the nutritional **deficiencies**[16] of everyday foods. "This article says that there's an easy way to be healthy," Becky's mom explained. "All you need to do is eat fresh foods that are not highly processed!"

▲ Margarine contains high levels of trans fats.

Week 9 Day 6 Hidden Dangers

Questions

____ 1. Which of the following is the main topic of this article? ············ ◆Main Idea◆
   a The dangers of not knowing about your food.
   b Becky's routine for losing weight.
   c How to eat healthy and lose weight.
   d The importance of eating fresh foods.

____ 2. What is this article about? ············ ◆Subject Matter◆
   a Harmful foods.   b A woman named Becky.
   c Good and bad cholesterol.   d Losing weight.

____ 3. Which of the following statements is NOT true? ············ ◆Supporting Details◆
   a Energy drinks sometimes contain high-fructose corn syrup.
   b Trans fats have been linked to depression.
   c Whole grains are healthier than refined grains.
   d Becky read a fascinating article in an English textbook.

____ 4. Which of the following would it be a good idea to do according to the article?
   ············ ◆Inference◆
   a Research and learn about your favorite foods.
   b Stop eating margarine and butter completely.
   c Add more sodium to your meals.
   d Start jogging every day after work or school.

____ 5. In paragraph two, the writer says that Becky's sandwich is always loaded with sodium. What does the phrase **loaded with** mean? ············ ◆Words in Context◆
   a Full of.   b Lacking in.   c Made of.   d Dipped in.

____ 6. What kind of phrase is **as sure as the sun sets in the west**, as used in paragraph three? ············ ◆Clarifying Devices◆
   a A contrast.   b A simile.   c A quote.   d A definition.

133

BAD FOOD

▲ eggs Benedict with smoked salmon on English muffin

▲ ham

▲ hot dogs

▲ instant noodles

GOOD FOOD

▲ fruits

▲ vegetables

▲ whole grain pasta

Week 10

Day 1 Environment	55	Is It Getting Darker in Here?	136
Day 2 Technology	56	Building the Future	138
Day 3 Language	57	The Great Absorber	140
Day 4 Environment	58	A Floating Landfill	142
Day 5 Technology	59	Water for Everyone	144
Day 6 Health & Body	60	Old Ways, New World	146

Week 10 Day 1

Environment

55 Is It Getting Darker in Here?

1. In the mid-1980s, a Japanese researcher named Atsumu Ohmura made a **stunning**[1] discovery. According to his data, the amount of solar **radiation**[2] reaching the earth's surface had **declined**[3] by 10% over the past 30 years. He had discovered what the science community now calls "global **dimming**[4]."

2. Global dimming is the reduction of overall sunlight reaching the earth's surface, and less sunlight means less heat. Scientists believe that certain pollutants in the earth's atmosphere, like carbon and **sulphates**[5], cause global dimming. These pollutants create clouds that are bigger and more **absorbent**[6], which means they can **reflect**[7] more sunlight back into space. Simply put, harmful **pollution**[8] in our atmosphere may have also been cooling down the planet for hundreds of years.

3. Governments around the world have **restricted**[9] these pollutants over the past decade, **reversing**[10] the process of global dimming. **Climatologists**[11] observing this **transition**[12] have discovered that global dimming impacts global warming more than we previously thought.

4. Think of global dimming and global warming as two different processes that occur at the same time. Global warming heats up the planet and global dimming cools it down. As global dimming slowly disappears, the true **extent**[13] of global warming is gradually revealed.

5. So, does this mean we should actually increase the amount of these pollutants in our atmosphere in order to combat global warming? Some scientists believe that this is exactly what we should do. It's not even a new idea. In 1974, Russian climatologist Mikhail Budyko suggested that we burn **sulfur**[14] in the atmosphere in order to create a **haze**[15] that will protect us from global warming. However, several other scientists believe that an increase in these pollutants would cause too many health problems, like **asthma** and other **respiratory**[16] illnesses.

Key Words

1. stunning 令人震驚的 (a.) 2. radiation 輻射 (n.) 3. decline 下降 (v.) 4. dim 變暗淡 (v.)
5. sulphate 硫酸鹽 (n.) 6. absorbent 能吸收的 (a.) 7. reflect 反射 (v.) 8. pollution 汙染 (n.)
9. restrict 限制 (v.) 10. reverse 反轉 (v.) 11. climatologist 氣候學家 (n.) 12. transition 過渡 (n.)
13. extent 程度 (n.) 14. sulfur 硫 (n.) 15. haze 霧霾 (n.) 16. respiratory 呼吸道的 (a.)
17. prediction 預言 (n.)

▶ Haze is a likely contributor to global dimming.

6   The discovery of global dimming shows us how little we know about how our climate works. After all, solar radiation had been falling steadily for decades before anyone even noticed. Given the fact that most global warming **predictions**[17] don't even take global dimming into account, is the world about to get a lot hotter, a lot faster than we think?

Questions

____ 1. Which of the following can summarize this article? ················ ◆Main Idea◆
   a There is still a lot we don't know about our climate.
   b There is nothing we don't know about our climate.
   c Pollution can be very harmful to human health.
   d Global warming will be solved by global dimming.

____ 2. What is this article about? ················ ◆Subject Matter◆
   a Global warming.   b Global dimming.
   c Pollutants.   d Solar radiation.

____ 3. Which of the following statements is true? ················ ◆Supporting Details◆
   a Mikhail Budyko discovered global dimming in 1985.
   b Asthma can be caused by pollutants in the atmosphere.
   c Global dimming can't stop the effects of global warming.
   d Atsumu Ohmura discovered an increase in solar radiation.

____ 4. Which of the following can we infer from this article? ················ ◆Inference◆
   a There weren't a lot of people studying global dimming.
   b There aren't a lot of people studying global warming.
   c Global dimming is more important than global warming.
   d Russia is leading the world in global warming research.

____ 5. What does the word **asthma** in the fifth paragraph mean? ········ ◆Words in Context◆
   a A disease that affects the eyes.   b A disease that affects the liver.
   c A disease that affects the lungs.   d A disease that affects the skin.

____ 6. Why does the writer phrase the first sentence of the fifth paragraph as a question? ················ ◆Clarifying Devices◆
   a To emphasize that it sounds like a strange plan.
   b To emphasize that is sounds like a bad plan.
   c To emphasize that it sounds like a good plan.
   d To help the reader make a logical conclusion.

Week 10 Day 1 Is It Getting Darker in Here?

137

Week 10 Day 2

Technology

▶ 3-D printing is now yesterday's news.

56 Building the Future

[1] Three-dimensional printing, which was, not too long ago, a part of science fiction, is now used practically everywhere—from the **aerospace**[1] industry, to medicine and education. This amazing technology, which allows anyone to print an entire object, is now yesterday's news. The next big thing in printing, however, is **on the horizon**. How is it different from 3-D printing? Well, it not only uses the three **dimensions**[2] of space but also the fourth dimension—time.

[2] Four-dimensional printing involves printing materials that are able to change over time in **reaction**[3] to different outside **stimuli**[4]—for example, temperature, water, or air pressure. Why is this useful? Construction is, in fact, an incredibly **inefficient**[5] industry. It takes a long time to **assemble**[6] a piece of furniture, build a house, or lay down a water pipe. If the environment changes, damage occurs, or you're not happy with how your work looks, you have to start all over again. Rather than **adapting**[7] or changing, building materials tend to stay the same shape—but not 4-D printed materials. These materials are **essentially**[8] programmable. Think self-assembling furniture, self-fixing water pipes, even self-**reconfiguring**[9] buildings that can take measures against natural **disasters**[10]. Four-dimensional printing even allows us to take construction into outer space, where the **hostile**[11] environment makes traditional construction incredibly **problematic**[12]. Think of 4-D printed materials as robots, just without wires or electricity. Who knows, in the future we may even be able to print material capable of conscious thought!

▲ 4-D printing involves printing materials that are able to change over time in reaction to different outside stimuli.

[3] So where did the idea for this kind of adaptable material come from? As with most things, Mother Nature got there first. DNA, RNA, and **proteins**[13], which make life possible and are found in all of our bodies, are essentially long strings of self-reconfiguring material. They can fold themselves, fix themselves,

Key Words

① aerospace 航太空業的 (a.)　② dimension 維度；空間 (n.)　③ reaction 反應 (n.)
④ stimulus 刺激 (n.)　⑤ inefficient 低效率的 (a.)　⑥ assemble 組裝；裝配 (v.)　⑦ adapt 適應 (v.)
⑧ essentially 本質上；根本上 (adv.)　⑨ reconfigure 重組；重設 (v.)　⑩ disaster 災難 (n.)
⑪ hostile 有敵意的 (a.)　⑫ problematic 有問題的 (a.)　⑬ protein 蛋白質 (n.)　⑭ replicate 複製；再生 (v.
⑮ attribute 特性；特質 (n.)　⑯ micro 微觀的 (a.)　⑰ molecule 分子 (n.)　⑱ macro 宏觀的 (a.)

▶ DNA is essentially long string of self-reconfiguring material.

DNA

replicate[14] themselves, and do so with little energy and no mistakes.

④ The trick is to translate those **attributes**[15] from the **micro**[16] world of **molecules**[17] into the **macro**[18] world of construction. Of course, that's easier said than done. But rest assured that some of the best material scientists in the world are working on it. Soon enough, cities won't need us to build them they'll build themselves.

Week 10 Day 2 Building the Future

Questions

____ 1. What is the writer's main message in this article? ◆Main Idea◆
   a Three-dimensional printing is fairly commonplace nowadays.
   b Four-dimensional printing will produce materials that can build themselves.
   c Material scientists are working hard on new building technologies.
   d Mother Nature often inspires new inventions.

____ 2. What is this article about? ◆Subject Matter◆
   a A novel innovation.   b Mother Nature.
   c The history of printing.   d Cities of the future.

____ 3. Which of the following is NOT true? ◆Supporting Details◆
   a Three-dimensional printing is used in medicine.
   b The current construction industry is very inefficient.
   c Four-dimension printed materials can reconfigure themselves.
   d Four-dimension printed materials need electricity to work.

____ 4. From the article, which of these can we infer about 4-D printed materials? ◆Inference◆
   a They will be cheaper than ordinary building materials.
   b They will not be used as material for furniture.
   c They will be used extensively in space.
   d They will not be used to build buildings.

____ 5. What does the phrase **on the horizon** mean in the first paragraph? ◆Words in Context◆
   a About to happen.   b Never going to happen.
   c Unlikely to happen.   d Happened a long time ago.

____ 6. How does the writer end the article? ◆Clarifying Devices◆
   a With a prediction.   b With a statistic.
   c With a famous quotation.   d With a warning.

Week 10 Day 3

Language

57 The Great Absorber

▶ Roman Baths

①   The story of English is one of a language constantly **evolving**[1] and absorbing outside influences. It begins thousands of years ago when the Celtic-speaking Britons **inhabited**[2] Britain. Their lives were turned upside down in AD 43, when the island was **conquered**[3] by the Roman Empire. These Roman soldiers didn't just bring weapons, but their Latin language as well. This was the first army to **alter**[4] the course of Britain's linguistic development. It wouldn't be the last.

②   As the Roman Empire **crumbled**[5] in the fifth century, it **withdrew**[6] its armies from Britain. However, it wasn't long before they were replaced by invading tribes from Germany such as the Angles, Saxons, and Jutes. These Anglo-Saxons brought their own German **dialect**[7] with them. Over the years, it **blended**[8] with the Celtic and Roman influences on the island. As a result, Old English was born. By AD 600, Old English had become distinct from dialects that were spoken in Germany.

③   In AD 787, Vikings arrived from Denmark and Norway. They set up **permanent**[9] settlements in the north of Britain and even ruled over the entire island briefly in the early eleventh century. The Viking period created more cultural mixing, and it exposed Old English to various Scandinavian words. For example, this is where the **pronouns**[10] *they*, *them*, and *their* came from.

④   One of the last **contributions**[11] to Old English was the Norman **conquest**[12] of Britain in 1066. The Norman conquerors brought the French language with them. As a result, English absorbed several French words, like *liberty*, *continue*, and *journey* to name a few.

⑤   The Middle English era lasted from AD 1100 to 1500. It was a period when the **elites** spoke French but the **peasants**[13] spoke English. As a result, Middle English grammar

▲ Norman ships

Key Words

① evolve 演變 (v.)   ② inhabit 居住；棲息 (v.)   ③ conquer 征服 (v.)   ④ alter 改變；修改 (v.)
⑤ crumble 崩潰；粉碎 (v.)   ⑥ withdraw 撤退 (v.)   ⑦ dialect 方言 (n.)   ⑧ blend 使混和 (v.)
⑨ permanent 永久的 (a.)   ⑩ pronoun 代名詞 (n.)   ⑪ contribution 貢獻 (n.)   ⑫ conquest 征服 (n.)
⑬ peasant 農民 (n.)   ⑭ simplify 簡化 (v.)   ⑮ vowel 母音 (n.)   ⑯ prose 散文 (n.)

▶ Geoffrey Chaucer
(1342–1400)

was **simplified**[14], and it lost many of the complex rules that once existed in Old English. **Vowel**[15] sounds also became simplified during The Great Vowel Shift, which occurred from 1350 to 1500.

The last dramatic change in the evolution of English took place in 1474. That was when the first printing press was brought into England. Thereafter, standard spelling and grammar could be delivered to the masses via the **prose**[16] of Chaucer, Milton, and Shakespeare. Modern English was born.

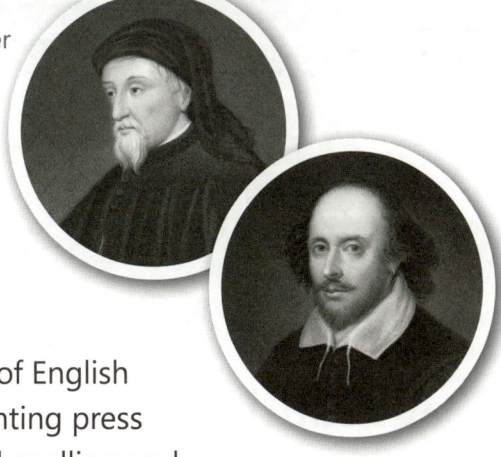

▲ William Shakespeare
(1564–1616)

Questions

____ 1. Which of the following is the main topic of this article? ◆Main Idea◆
   a The story of where Middle English came from.
   b The story of where Old English came from.
   c The story of how a language can absorb from other languages.
   d The story of how English got its simple grammar.

____ 2. What does this article focus on? ◆Subject Matter◆
   a The history of English.
   b How the Roman Empire crumbled.
   c The arrival of Vikings in England.
   d The simplification of English grammar.

____ 3. Which of the following is NOT true? ◆Supporting Details◆
   a The Roman Empire invaded Britain in AD 43.
   b English was influenced by Scandinavian languages.
   c Middle English grammar is simpler than Old English grammar.
   d Rome ruled Britain for over 800 years.

____ 4. What can we infer from this article? ◆Inference◆
   a The Norman people came from France.
   b Britons spoke some Latin before the Romans arrived.
   c Old English is easy for modern speakers to read.
   d Chaucer is a relatively unknown author.

____ 5. What does the word **elites** mean? ◆Words in Context◆
   a Diligent and hardworking people.
   b The white-collar working class.
   c Rich and powerful people.
   d Middle-class factory workers.

____ 6. Which of these best describes the form of the article? ◆Text Form◆
   a A biography.
   b An opinion piece.
   c A piece of short fiction.
   d A timeline of events.

Week 10 Day 4

Environment

58 A Floating[1] Landfill[2]

1 Did you know that the world's biggest landfill isn't even on dry land? It's actually the Great Pacific Garbage **Patch**[3], a **sprawl**[4] of floating garbage located in the waters between Japan and California.

2 The Great Pacific Garbage Patch is made up of trash that has been dumped by ships, **expelled**[5] by **sewers**[6], or just thrown into the ocean. Garbage from all over the world gets caught up in ocean **currents**[7] and **herded**[8] to the same spot. Some experts say that the Great Pacific Garbage Patch is the size of Texas. Others claim that it could be twice the size of the United States. What everyone can agree on is that the plastic in the garbage patch is not going away anytime soon.

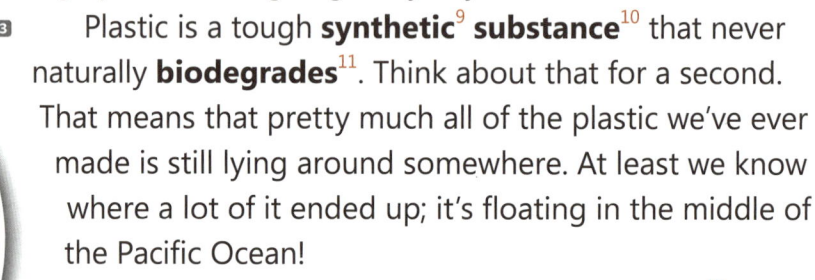

▲ The Great Pacific Garbage Patch is located within the North Pacific Gyre, one of the five major oceanic gyres.

3 Plastic is a tough **synthetic**[9] **substance**[10] that never naturally **biodegrades**[11]. Think about that for a second. That means that pretty much all of the plastic we've ever made is still lying around somewhere. At least we know where a lot of it ended up; it's floating in the middle of the Pacific Ocean!

4 Plastic doesn't just threaten ocean **ecology**[12] but human health as well. While plastic does not biodegrade, sunlight can still break it down into smaller and smaller pieces. The smaller these pieces get, the easier it is for fish and other sea life to mistake them for food. This means that the next fish you eat may have eaten some LEGO **fragments** in the Great Pacific Garbage Patch.

▲ It's easy for sea creatures to mistake plastic for food.

Key Words

❶ float 漂浮 (v.)　❷ landfill 垃圾場 (n.)　❸ patch 片狀物 (n.)　❹ sprawl 蔓延 (n.)　❺ expel 排出 (v.)
❻ sewer 下水道；排水管 (n.)　❼ current 洋流 (n.)　❽ herd 趕到一處 (v.)　❾ synthetic 合成的 (a.)
❿ substance 物質 (n.)　⓫ biodegrade 生物分解 (v.)　⓬ ecology 生態系 (n.)　⓭ disperse 分散 (v.)
⓮ reusable 可重複使用的 (a.)　⓯ moderate 中等的；適度的 (a.)

[5]   Cleaning up the garbage patch won't be easy, though some organizations are trying. First of all, it's hard to see, so the media doesn't pay attention to it. It's not a giant island of garbage. Rather, it's an underwater sprawl of tiny fragments of plastic and other trash. These tiny, **dispersed**[13] fragments of trash also make it hard for us to clean up. Therefore, if we really want to clean up our oceans, we need to stop using so much plastic and to recycle whenever we can. Maybe all it takes is some effort and a few **reusable**[14] bags, and 10 years from now, the Great Pacific Garbage Patch will have become the **Moderate**[15] Pacific Garbage Patch.

Questions

____ 1. Which of the following is the main topic of this article? ◆Main Idea◆
   a A serious problem in one of our planet's oceans.
   b How plastic harms ocean ecology.
   c The movement of the Great Pacific Garbage Patch.
   d How plastic threatens human health.

____ 2. What is this article about? ◆Subject Matter◆
   a Recycling.   b Plastic.   c Garbage trucks.   d Ocean pollution.

____ 3. Which of the following statements is true? ◆Supporting Details◆
   a It takes 20 years for plastic to biodegrade.
   b There is a lot of plastic in the Great Pacific Garbage Patch.
   c Experts agree on the size of the Great Pacific Garbage Patch.
   d Fish will avoid eating the plastic floating in the world's oceans.

____ 4. Which statement is most likely true about the Great Pacific Garbage Patch? ◆Inference◆
   a It has existed for a long time.
   b It will shrink in the next 10 years.
   c It will float south over the next 10 years.
   d It will float north over the next 10 years.

____ 5. What does the word **fragments** in the fourth paragraph mean? ◆Words in Context◆
   a Large pieces.   b The most important pieces.
   c Complete pieces.   d Very small pieces.

____ 6. How is this article best described? ◆Clarifying Devices◆
   a A warning to readers.   b A biased opinion.
   c A brief anecdote.   d A biography.

Water for Everyone

1 Humans need clean drinking water to survive. When our water supply is **contaminated**[1] or we drink from unsafe sources, we risk illness. **Components**[2] in unclean water such as bacteria and **parasites**[3] can have a variety of harmful effects. Waterborne diseases threaten the lives of millions of people every year. Even those who survive such illness can be left with serious medical conditions and financial burden.

2 Some communities use water filtration and treatment systems to **purify**[4] water before **distributing**[5] it to the public. Some people boil water before consuming it to kill any **pathogens**[6] that it might contain. Others rely on purchasing bottled water that has already been treated. However, still others, especially in developing countries, have no reliable access to safe drinking water.

▲ LifeStraw (cc by Edyta Materka)

3 A Swiss company, Vestergaard Frandsen, decided to develop a water **filter**[7] that could help these people. In 2005, they came out with a product called LifeStraw. It is a straw-like tube with special **fibers**[8] to physically filter water. LifeStraw filters more than 99% of bacteria and parasites from the water that passes through it. LifeStraw is powered by **suction**[9] and requires no electricity or pumping. Because LifeStraw uses chemicals and has no moving parts, it is both safe and **durable**[10].

4 One straw can provide one person with one year's worth of clean drinking water. Cleaning the filter after each use is easy and can even increase its use. All you have to do is blow air through the **mouthpiece**[11]. Any water that is still inside will **flush**[12] back out the bottom. After a LifeStraw has filtered 1,000 **liters**[13] of water, the filter stops letting water through. This prevents people from unknowingly consuming contaminated water.

5 LifeStraws have also been used for emergency response and **humanitarian**[14] aid. Every year, natural disasters unexpectedly **disrupt** communities worldwide.

Key Words

1. contaminate 汙染 (v.) 2. component 成分；要素 (n.) 3. parasite 寄生蟲 (n.) 4. purify 淨化 (v.)
5. distribute 分配 (v.) 6. pathogen 病原體 (n.) 7. filter 濾器 (n.) 8. fiber 纖維 (n.)
9. suction 吸；抽吸 (n.) 10. durable 耐用的 (a.) 11. mouthpiece 吹口 (n.) 12. flush 沖水 (v.)
13. liter 公升 (n.) 14. humanitarian 人道主義的 (a.) 15. hurricane 颶風 (n.) 16. tornado 龍捲風 (n.)
17. structural 結構上的 (a.)

▶ Natural disasters can contaminate water supplies.

Hurricanes[15] and floods contaminate water supplies, while earthquakes and **tornados**[16] cause significant **structural**[17] damage. Communities affected by such disasters can be left without safe water access for months or more. This leads to problems with not only personal health, but also disease outbreaks. Regardless of circumstance, a LifeStraw can provide anyone anywhere with the ability to drink clean water.

Questions

_____ 1. Which of the following is the main idea of this article? ◆Main Idea◆
   a Life can still be difficult after recovering from a waterborne disease.
   b Many people in developing countries do not have access to clean water.
   c Water filtration products can help prevent disease.
   d Natural disasters can ruin communities.

_____ 2. What is this article about? ◆Subject Matter◆
   a Switzerland.
   b A water filtration technology.
   c Natural disasters.
   d Humanitarian aid.

_____ 3. Which of the following statements is NOT true? ◆Supporting Details◆
   a Bacteria and parasites in water can make people sick.
   b Some people boil water to make it safe to drink.
   c A person could use a LifeStraw for a year before needing to replace it.
   d LifeStraw requires electricity to work.

_____ 4. What information can we infer from the fourth paragraph? ◆Inference◆
   a Each LifeStraw filters up to 1,000 liters of water.
   b Blowing through a straw is fun to do.
   c Cleaning your LifeStraw after each use is not beneficial.
   d You can use the same LifeStraw every day for many years.

_____ 5. The fifth paragraph mentions that natural disaster unexpectedly disrupt communities worldwide. What does **disrupt** mean? ◆Words in Context◆
   a Improve.
   b Cause a disturbance in.
   c Bring economic growth to.
   d Shame.

_____ 6. In the first paragraph, how does the writer set up the topic of the article? ◆Clarifying Devices◆
   a By giving an anecdote.
   b By telling a joke.
   c By providing background information.
   d By listing examples of similar products.

Week 10 Day 5 Water for Everyone

Week 10 Day 6

Health & Body

▶ Chinese herbal medicine

60
🎧 060

Old Ways, New World

❶ Traditional medicine has been used in China for around 3,000 years and is deeply rooted in the **spiritual**[1] and **philosophical**[2] aspects of Chinese culture. One of the oldest works on the subject is the *Yellow Emperor's Inner Canon*, which dates from the first century BC. It lays down the basic principles on which traditional Chinese medicine is based, including yin and yang, qi, and the five elements. It also provides a detailed discussion on early methods of **acupuncture**[3]—the practice of **inserting**[4] thin needles of varying lengths into different parts of a patient's body.

❷ Chinese medicine is based on the principle that the body's **internal**[5] systems are governed by the balance of five universal elements: metal, wood, water, fire, and earth. The balance of these within the body affects the overall **equilibrium**[6] of yin and yang, and any imbalance can cause the body's flow of qi, or vital energy, to become blocked, resulting in disease and the **deterioration**[7] of one's health. Qi can be **stimulated**[8] by the use of acupuncture, which encourages the flow by inserting thin needles into certain points on the body. Other methods such as taking **herbal**[9] **concoctions**[10] and cupping, where hot glass cups are applied to the skin and **suck**[11] blood into certain areas, also improve the flow of qi.

❸ In the West, Chinese medicine has gone from being a treatment solely for Chinese immigrants uncomfortable with Western techniques to being an ever more popular form of **alternative**[12] medicine. More than 70% of people in developed countries have tried alternative medicine, and the industry is showing steady growth due to the belief that traditional **remedies**[13] have fewer **side effects** than chemical drugs.

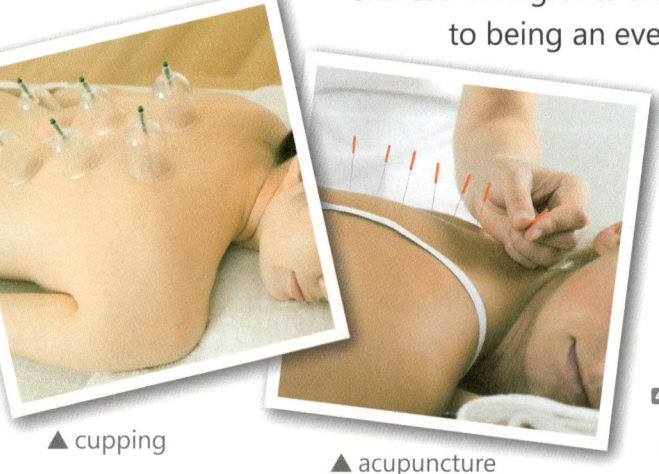

❹ Even though most Western doctors **dismiss**[14] the effects of acupuncture

▲ cupping

▲ acupuncture

Key Words

❶ spiritual 精神的 (a.)　❷ philosophical 哲學的 (a.)　❸ acupuncture 針灸 (n.)　❹ insert 插入 (v.)
❺ internal 內部的 (a.)　❻ equilibrium 平衡 (n.)　❼ deterioration 惡化 (n.)　❽ stimulate 刺激 (v.)
❾ herbal 草本的 (a.)　❿ concoction 調製品 (n.)　⓫ suck 吸 (v.)　⓬ alternative 替代的 (a.)
⓭ remedy 治療 (n.)　⓮ dismiss 對……不予理會 (v.)　⓯ publicize 宣傳；公布 (v.)
⓰ integrate 整合 (v.)　⓱ stroke 中風 (n.)

▶ the five universal elements: metal, wood, water, fire, and earth

and cupping as mostly psychological, many Hollywood celebrities who actively **publicize**¹⁵ these treatments have made them more and more fashionable.

[5] A major step toward **integrating**¹⁶ Western and Chinese medicine came in 2006. NeuroAiD, a drug made using Chinese herbs, showed proven results in assisting the recovery of **stroke**¹⁷ victims.

[6] The World Health Organization has also encouraged the use of effective and tested traditional medicines, meaning that in the future certain Chinese remedies may become largely accepted by Western doctors.

Week 10 Day 6 Old Ways, New World

Questions

____ 1. Which of the following best summarizes the article? ◆Main Idea◆
   a Chinese medicine and Chinese philosophy are strongly connected.
   b Stimulating qi can balance the body's yin and yang.
   c Chinese medicine is becoming more and more popular in the West.
   d Many Hollywood celebrities actively promote acupuncture.

____ 2. What is this article about? ◆Subject Matter◆
   a The advantages of herbal medicine.   b An ancient custom.
   c New cures for strokes.   d An alternative kind of medicine.

____ 3. Which of the following statements is NOT true? ◆Supporting Details◆
   a Chinese medicine originated a few centuries ago.
   b NeuroAiD is a traditional Chinese medicine that has been established as effective.
   c Methods of acupuncture are discussed in the *Yellow Emperor's Inner Canon*.
   d Over half of the people in developed countries have tried alternative medicine.

____ 4. What can we infer from this article? ◆Inference◆
   a Traditional Chinese medicine is completely useless and ineffective.
   b Western doctors are quickly choosing Chinese medicine over Western medicine.
   c Traditional medicine will soon stop being used in China.
   d Western doctors have found it difficult to accept traditional Chinese medicine in the past.

____ 5. What does the phrase **side effects** mean in the third paragraph? ◆Words in Context◆
   a Effective elements.   b Artificial colorings.
   c Undesirable outcome.   d Natural ingredients.

____ 6. Which of these best describes the author's tone in this piece? ◆Author's Tone◆
   a Pessimistic and disappointed.   b Informative and impartial.
   c Humorous and mocking.   d Angry and outraged.

147

Chinese Medicine and Chinese Food Therapy

▼ ginger tea

Ginger

In traditional Chinese medicine, ginger is warm in nature.
Ginger tea is often used to treat colds and the flu.

Chinese ginseng is said to improve memory and thinking.

▲ ginseng wine
(cc by Junho Jung)

Ginseng

Angelica Root

The Chinese angelica is supposed to strengthen the blood.
It is used to treat women's illnesses, such as period pains.

◄ soup made with Silkie chicken, angelica roots, and goji
(cc by wokkingmum)

Goji

148

Week 11

Day 1　Geography	**61**　Witness the Strange and Wonderful	150
Day 2　Mystery	**62**　Paranormal Activity	152
Day 3　Health & Body	**63**　Listen to Your Heart	154
Day 4　Geography	**64**　The Siege of Beijing	156
Day 5　Health & Body	**65**　The Food Poisoner	158
Day 6　Sports	**66**　The Sport of CEOs	160

Week 11　Day 1

Geography

◀ dragon blood tree

61

Witness[1] the Strange and Wonderful

❶　　Socotra lies about 380 km south of the Arabian **Peninsula**[2] in the Indian Ocean. It is a small island, only 132 km long, and has been isolated from the **mainland**[3] for about seven million years. It is this **isolation**[4] that has allowed Socotra to become one of the world's most unique places. The island has diverse and **distinctive**[5] plant life that gives it the appearance of an alien world straight out of the imagination of a science fiction writer.

❷　　Over 300 of the 825 plant species on Socotra can only be found on the island. Nowhere else in the world can boast such bizarre, otherworldly natural flora. Take the dragon blood tree (so called because of its blood-red sap) for example. Its branches **sprout**[6] upwards in an umbrella-like **dome**[7] while the leaves create a **dense**[8] covering that **resembles**[9] a well-mowed lawn. Hundreds of these trees dot the island like **fleets**[10] of grounded UFOs.

❸　　Another even more alien-looking plant is the desert rose, whose leathery body **bulges**[11] out from the rocks like an almost-bursting elephant's leg. The beautiful pink flowers that grow near the top seem almost clownish, while the thick body is perfectly evolved for storing water in the island's hot, dry climate.

▲ desert rose

❹　　Birdlife is also incredibly diverse and some rare species **thrive**[12] in the fish-filled ocean surrounding the island. There are over 1,000 **endangered**[13] Egyptian vultures living on Socotra—the most concentrated population of this dying species in the world.

❺　　The people of Socotra are mostly fishermen, farmers, and fruit growers, and while taking photos of the island's remarkable natural beauty is encouraged,

Key Words

❶ witness 目睹 (v.)　❷ peninsula 半島 (n.)　❸ mainland 大陸 (n.)　❹ isolation 隔離 (n.)
❺ distinctive 有特色的 (a.)　❻ sprout 發芽 (v.)　❼ dome 圓頂 (n.)　❽ dense 密集 (n.)
❾ resemble 像；類似 (v.)　❿ fleet 艦隊 (n.)　⓫ bulge 凸起 (v.)　⓬ thrive 生長茂盛 (v.)
⓭ endangered 瀕臨絕種的 (a.)　⓮ offensive 冒犯的 (a.)　⓯ tricky 難處理的 (a.)　⓰ overbook 過量預訂

it is considered extremely **offensive**[14] to take any photos of the island's women.

[6] Visiting the island can be **tricky**[15] as even though there are daily flights, they are often **overbooked**[16], meaning that it's not unusual to be delayed a day or more. Transport on the island has improved a lot over the past few years, but it's still inconvenient to get around, and the only places to stay outside the biggest town, Hadibu, are campsites dotted around the island. Sometimes, though, witnessing the strange and wonderful is worth a little inconvenience.

▼ Egyptian vulture

Questions

____ 1. Which of the following is the main topic of the article? ◆Main Idea◆
   a The people of Socotra.
   b The alien environment of Socotra.
   c The best time to visit Socotra.
   d Transportation problems on Socotra.

____ 2. What does this article focus on? ◆Subject Matter◆
   a A unique island.
   b A rare bird.
   c The religion of Islam.
   d The dragon blood tree.

____ 3. Which of the following statements is NOT true? ◆Supporting Details◆
   a Socotra is located in the Indian Ocean.
   b The desert rose has adapted to the island's harsh climate.
   c No people live on the island of Socotra.
   d Socotra is home to the rare Egyptian vultures.

____ 4. Which of the following does the fifth paragraph imply? ◆Inference◆
   a Life on Socotra is easy and relaxing.
   b The people of Socotra do not like people taking pictures of the island.
   c Most people on Socotra work in offices.
   d The women of Socotra are usually not willing to have their photos taken.

____ 5. What does **flora** mean in the second paragraph? ◆Words in Context◆
   a Plant life.
   b Tourists.
   c Animals.
   d Technology.

____ 6. According to the author, which of the following is the root cause of Socotra's uniqueness? ◆Cause and Effect◆
   a It's plant life.
   b It's long isolation.
   c It's small size.
   d It's people.

Week 11 Day 2

Mystery

62 Paranormal[1] Activity

▼ representation of the Mothman (cc by Tim Bertelink)

[1] The word "paranormal" is made up of two parts: *para* and *normal*. In Greek, *para* means "beside," or "beyond." Paranormal describes ghosts, alien **abductions**[2], magic, and mind reading—almost anything that modern science cannot explain. So basically, the paranormal **spooks**[3] us out but also makes us feel a bit curious at the same time.

[2] One example of the paranormal occurred on June 30, 1908, in the snowy woodlands of Russia. There was an **explosion**[4] that was 1,000 times more powerful than the **nuclear**[5] bomb that **detonated** over Hiroshima in 1945. This Tunguska event created a huge ring of fiery **devastation**[6], and scientists still can't explain how it happened. Some believe it was a **comet**[7] that never made impact, but what if it's actually **evidence**[8] of advanced alien technology?

[3] Then there's the unsolved **mystery**[9] of the Mothman sightings. Starting in 1966, a series of reports describing a giant winged creature appeared in West Virginia in the United States. These sightings mysteriously stopped right after the **collapse**[10] of the Silver Bridge in 1967, a disaster that killed 46 people. There are those who believe that the Mothman was sent to warn local townspeople of the coming disaster. Others believe that the Mothman might have been what destroyed the bridge in the first place. These **lingering**[11] questions are why the legend of the Mothman is still considered to be an unsolved paranormal mystery by many people throughout the United States.

[4] And what about those unexplained balls of light that can materialize in the middle of **nowhere**[12], far away from any electric lights. Are these spooklights proof that ghosts exist? One famous example of this phenomenon is the spooklight near Hornet, Missouri, in the United States. This **creepy**[13] white light looks like it's dancing up and down. It has shown

Key Words

① paranormal 超自然的 (a.)　② abduction 綁架 (n.)　③ spook 使驚嚇 (v.)　④ explosion 爆炸 (n.)
⑤ nuclear 核子的 (a.)　⑥ devastation 毀滅 (v.)　⑦ comet 彗星 (n.)　⑧ evidence 證據 (n.)
⑨ mystery 神祕的事物 (n.)　⑩ collapse 倒塌 (n.)　⑪ lingering 持續的 (a.)
⑫ nowhere 無處 (adv.)　⑬ creepy 毛骨悚然的 (a.)　⑭ homeland 家園 (n.)

◀ the Tunguska event

▼ Some believe that the Tunguska event is an impact event.

up constantly in the woods outside of town since the late nineteenth century. Some locals say that it's the ghost of two Native American lovers who died after being expelled from their **homeland**[14]. Others believe that it's the lantern of a miner who got lost hundreds of years ago. Whatever it is, the Hornet Spooklight is keeping people guessing.

Week 11 Day 2 Paranormal Activity

Questions

____ 1. What would you say is the main idea of the article? •Main Idea•
   a Paranormal activity only occurs in North America.
   b There are some things that science can't explain.
   c Science can explain the Hornet spooklight.
   d Adults don't believe in paranormal mysteries.

____ 2. What is this article mainly about? •Subject Matter•
   a Monstrous creatures.
   b The Tunguska event.
   c Unexplained phenomena.
   d Strange lights.

____ 3. Which of the following statements is NOT true? •Supporting Details•
   a In 1908, there was an explosion that was bigger than Hiroshima.
   b Some believe a town in Missouri is haunted by a miner.
   c The Mothman has been captured and photographed.
   d Some people call mysterious lights "spooklights."

____ 4. What can we infer about the Mothman from this article? •Inference•
   a It is seen as a hero by some people.
   b It only comes out during the night.
   c It looks more like a hummingbird than a moth.
   d It is an alien from another planet.

____ 5. What does the word **detonated** in the second paragraph mean? •Words in Context•
   a Cracked in two.
   b Exploded.
   c Malfunctioned.
   d Buried.

____ 6. How does the writer develop this article? •Clarifying Devices•
   a By using first-person experiences.
   b By using multiple examples.
   c By using famous quotations.
   d By using a narrative essay.

Week 11 Day 3
Health & Body

▶ Smartphones and smart watches can help monitor medical conditions.

63
Listen to Your Heart

[1] Smartphones have completely **transformed**[1] the way we look at telephones. From its **humble**[2] beginnings as a communication tool, the phone has evolved into a movie theater, music studio, library, and now a **portable**[3] hospital.

[2] A number of apps have been invented that can check a patient's heart rate. In the past, patients were required to wear **sensitive**[4] **pads**[5] on their **torso**, close to the heart, but this is no longer necessary. If the app user feels chest pain, they can take their own **pulse**[6] by placing their finger on the smartphone's camera, or laying the phone against their chest. Wearing a smart watch, instead of using a phone, is even more effective as the apps can monitor heart rate all the time, not only when pain is felt.

[3] If there are any **abnormal**[7] signs, the phone can automatically send an SMS to the patient's doctor. Experts have said that this could help save valuable time in **diagnosing**[8] a condition, as doctors would not have to **wade**[9] through piles of information in order to observe the problem.

[4] Obviously these apps have been designed **specifically**[10] for patients with heart conditions, and the ability to **monitor**[11] their hearts as they go about their daily lives is a major advantage in **combating**[12] heart disease. But these revolutionary apps have found some other **applications**[13], too.

[5] People without serious health issues, but who like to keep track of how their lifestyle affects their well-being, use these apps for more general health monitoring. Other uses include performance **assessment**[14] for athletes, diet monitoring for overweight people, and even a driving safety system.

[6] Imagine a device that "could be used in combination with cameras and other **mechanisms**[15] in the car," says David Atenza, who works on smartphone medical technology. "The driver could be monitored for hunger, tiredness, and any other things that affect driving ability."

▶ stethoscope

Key Words

1. transform 使徹底改變 (v.)   2. humble 普通的 (a.)   3. portable 便於攜帶的 (a.)
4. sensitive 敏感的；靈敏的 (a.)   5. pad 墊；襯墊 (n.)   6. pulse 脈搏 (n.)   7. abnormal 不正常的 (a.)
8. diagnose 診斷 (v.)   9. wade 費力地做 (v.)   10. specifically 特別地 (adv.)   11. monitor 監控 (v.)
12. combat 戰鬥 (v.)   13. application 應用 (n.)   14. assessment 評估 (n.)   15. mechanism 機制 (n.)

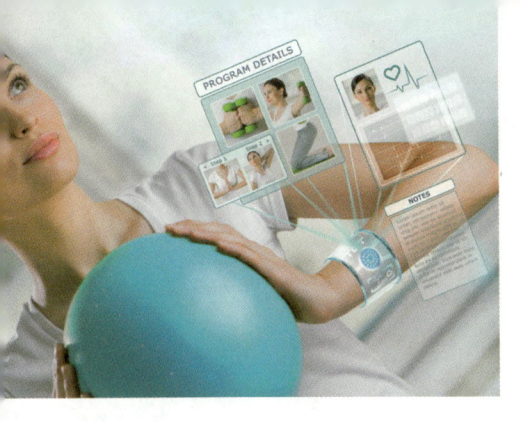

◀ Medical apps can be used for general health monitoring as well.

7 At the moment, there is a huge **wave of interest** in producing these kinds of medical apps. Products like the iStethoscope, which allows you to listen to your heart through the phone's microphone, are already popular. The hope is that in the future this type of technology will allow doctors to save lives faster and more efficiently than ever before.

Questions

_____ 1. What is the main idea of this article? •Main Idea•
   a Smartphones are very versatile tools.
   b Smartphones can be used to stop car accidents.
   c Smartphones are revolutionizing medicine.
   d The evolution of the smartphone.

_____ 2. Which of the following could be an alternative title for this passage?
   •Subject Matter•
   a Doctors Get Lazy.
   b Keeping an Eye on Patients.
   c Everyone's a Doctor.
   d A Smart Diagnosis.

_____ 3. Which of the following statements is NOT true? •Supporting Details•
   a Smartphones can check a patient's heart condition.
   b The apps have many other uses besides medical ones.
   c The apps will save doctors a lot of time.
   d Medical app users have to wear sensitive pads on their body.

_____ 4. How will this device most likely affect patients? •Inference•
   a They will not worry anymore about their condition.
   b They will spend less time visiting the hospital for tests.
   c They will begin to doubt doctors' ability to diagnose.
   d They will need to spend more money to pay medical bills.

_____ 5. What is the meaning of **torso** in paragraph two? •Words in Context•
   a The inside of the mouth.
   b Between the waist and the feet.
   c Between the neck and the waist.
   d The hands, feet, and head.

_____ 6. What does the phrase a **wave of interest** in the last paragraph imply?
   •Clarifying Devices•
   a A disappearance of interest.
   b An interest in marine science.
   c A sudden rise in interest.
   d A sudden drop in interest.

Week 11 Day 4

Geography

▶ map of Beijing and the Gobi Desert (cc by Christophe cagé)

64

The Siege[1] of Beijing

❶ Beijing is a city under siege, and the threat isn't coming from any country or group of **rebels**[2]. It's not people at all. Rather, it's the Gobi Desert, and it's slowly winning the fight.

❷ Every year, the Gobi Desert expands more than 3,300 square kilometers. On the eastern side it is pushing closer to Beijing, and experts worry the city could be on the **verge**[3] of **desertification**[4]. While alarming, this phenomenon is not exactly new. It's actually been going on for quite a long time. Back in 2006, the Chinese government announced that 27 percent of China's **landmass**[5] was desert, up from 18 percent in 1994. In other words, it only took 12 years for nine percent of China's landmass to be swallowed up by growing deserts. However, since 2006 the rate of **expansion**[6] seems to be less **drastic**[7]—but it certainly hasn't stopped.

❸ When it comes to the expansion of the Gobi Desert, the list of contributing factors is quite long. Two of the biggest ones are the presence of too many **grazing**[8] animals and widespread **deforestation**[9]. The growth of China's cities has also contributed to the problem by increasing demands on underground water supplies. This has left the soil more **vulnerable**[10] to desertification.

❹ The Chinese government is **determined**[11] to win its battle against the sandy **menace**, and to do so, it has decided to fight nature with nature. The Green Wall of China is a government program that aims to build a massive **barrier**[12] of trees to protect China's cities from desertification. The program was started in 1978. Its goal is to plant a 4,480-kilometer wall of trees by 2050, that **spans**[13] all the way from Xinjiang to Heilongjiang. By then, they expect forests to cover 42 percent of China's landmass. This **ambitious**[14] project will also help in the fight against global warming.

Key Words

❶ siege 圍困 (n.)　❷ rebel 反叛者 (n.)　❸ verge 邊緣 (n.)　❹ desertification 沙漠化 (n.)
❺ landmass 整片陸地 (n.)　❻ expansion 擴張；擴大 (n.)　❼ drastic 激烈的；猛烈的 (a.)
❽ graze（牛羊等）吃草 (v.)　❾ deforestation 森林砍伐 (n.)　❿ vulnerable 脆弱的；易受傷的 (a.)
⓫ determine 決定；決心 (v.)　⓬ barrier 障礙 (n.)　⓭ span 橫跨 (v.)　⓮ ambitious 野心勃勃的 (a.)
⓯ skeptical 懷疑的 (a.)　⓰ breed 品種 (n.)

[5] But will the Green Wall be enough to save Beijing? Some experts remain **skeptical**[15]. They argue that trees are easy to plant but hard to take care of over the long term, especially when the trees being planted are non-native **breeds**[16] that aren't suited to the environment. If they're right, then violent sandstorms will be the least of Beijing's problems. Residents could one day wake up to find their houses have been buried in sand.

a serious sandstorm hits Beijing in 2010

Questions

_____ 1. Which of the following is the main topic of this article? ◆Main Idea◆
   a Beijing's fight against illegal hunting.
   b Beijing's weapon in the war against global warming.
   c Beijing's fight against an expanding desert.
   d Beijing's fight against sandstorms.

_____ 2. What is this article about? ◆Subject Matter◆
   a Desertification in China.
   b Planting trees.
   c Global warming.
   d Beijing's reconstruction.

_____ 3. Which of the following statements is true? ◆Supporting Details◆
   a Beijing never experiences sandstorms.
   b The Gobi desert is shrinking very quickly.
   c Some experts doubt that the Green Wall will work.
   d China's government has no plan to stop the growth of the Gobi Desert.

_____ 4. Which statement is most likely true? ◆Inference◆
   a Desertification has been a problem since at least 1978.
   b The Green Wall has completely failed to contain the Gobi Desert.
   c Chinese officials don't think desertification is a problem.
   d China is the only country in the world with a desertification problem.

_____ 5. In the fourth paragraph, the author writes that the Chinese government is determined to win its battle against "the sandy menace." What is a **menace**?
   ◆Words in Context◆
   a A danger.   b A plan.   c A solution.   d A mystery.

_____ 6. How does the author develop the main idea of this passage? ◆Clarifying Devices◆
   a By explaining a natural process.
   b By using examples to prove a point.
   c By telling a story.
   d By giving a description.

Health & Body

Week 11 Day 5

▶ salmonella

65

The Food Poisoner

1 Salmonella is a **noxious**[1] little bacteria that has been infecting humans and other **mammals**[2] for thousands of years. How does it make us sick? Often via eating contaminated foods such as eggs, meat, **poultry**[3], and even fruits and vegetables. Symptoms of salmonella poisoning include **diarrhea**[4], **dehydration**[5], fever, and **vomiting**[6]. Occasionally, salmonella can cause serious **complications**[7] if it travels from the **intestines**[8] into the bloodstream without being treated with **antibiotics**[9]. In some cases, it can even be deadly.

▲ Salmonella can contaminate foods such as eggs and meat.

2 Salmonella is not rare. Quite the contrary, it is the most common foodborne illness in the United States. America's Centers for Disease Control (CDC) estimates that 19,336 people were **hospitalized**[10] and 378 died as a result of salmonella poisoning in 2011.

3 Deadly salmonella **outbreaks** are big news in America. Every year, there are a few **high-profile**[11] outbreaks that result in food products being recalled. In 2011 alone there were salmonella outbreaks involving pine nuts, boiled chicken livers, papayas, alfalfa sprouts, and turkey burgers.

4 Unfortunately, scientists are predicting that future outbreaks of salmonella will be more deadly. This is due to the bacteria's growing **resistance**[12] to antibiotics. **Clinical**[13] studies have shown that the more a bacteria is exposed to a certain kind of antibiotic, the less effective that antibiotic is. Scientists in Asia, America, and Europe have already discovered a few **strains**[14] of salmonella that are highly resistant to most kinds of antibiotics.

5 Some scientists believe that this resistance is being caused by excessive use of antibiotics in large-scale chicken farms, or factory farms. In fact, the World Health Organization has been **issuing**[15] warnings over the use of antibiotics in factory farming for several years.

6 The fight against salmonella and several other food safety issues can be **boiled down**[16] to a simple **equation**[17]: the more food that's produced, the less safe it is. For example, a food company wants to produce more chickens

Key Words

[1] noxious 有毒的 (a.) [2] mammal 哺乳動物 (n.) [3] poultry 家禽肉 (n.) [4] diarrhea 腹瀉 (n.)
[5] dehydration 脫水 (n.) [6] vomit 嘔吐 (v.) [7] complication 併發症 (n.) [8] intestine 腸 (n.)
[9] antibiotics 抗生素 (n.) [10] hospitalize 使住院治療 (v.) [11] high-profile 備受矚目的 (a.)
[12] resistance 抵抗 (n.) [13] clinical 臨床的 (a.) [14] strain 品種 (n.) [15] issue 發布 (v.)
[16] boil down 簡化 [17] equation 相等；均衡 (n.) [18] inject 注射 (v.)

to make more of a profit. However, so many chickens packed together breed disease. To keep the chickens healthy, the company **injects**[18] them with antibiotics, and voilà, an antibiotic resistant outbreak of salmonella.

7   To beat salmonella, we may need to start putting food safety before food industry profits.

▼ Resistance is caused by the excessive use of antibiotics on large-scale chicken farms.

Week 11 Day 5 The Food Poisoner

Questions

____ 1. Which of the following is the main topic of this article? ◆Main Idea◆
   a The health risk posed by salmonella poisoning.
   b The growing threat of salmonella poisoning.
   c The benefits and drawbacks of factory farming.
   d The evolution of salmonella bacteria.

____ 2. What is this article about? ◆Subject Matter◆
   a The food industry.   b Factory farming.
   c A type of bacterium.   d Antibiotics.

____ 3. Which of the following is NOT true? ◆Supporting Details◆
   a Salmonella has been infecting mammals for thousands of years.
   b Factory farming may cause resistance to antibiotics.
   c Salmonella poisoning can occasionally cause death.
   d Salmonella bacteria has only been discovered in America.

____ 4. Which of the following is probably true? ◆Inference◆
   a Other kinds of foodborne bacteria are developing drug resistances.
   b Salmonella poisoning can be spread person-to-person like the flu.
   c Salmonella did not exist before factory farms were invented.
   d Salmonella poisoning results in fewer and fewer hospitalizations every year.

____ 5. In the third paragraph, a deadly salmonella outbreak is mentioned. What is an **outbreak**? ◆Words in Context◆
   a A sudden rise in the occurrence of something.
   b An occurrence of something that is expected beforehand.
   c A surprising decrease in an activity.
   d One reported case of a deadly disease.

____ 6. Which of these statements from the article is an opinion? ◆Fact or Opinion◆
   a In 2011, 378 people died in the United States as a result of salmonella.
   b Future outbreaks of salmonella will be more deadly.
   c Salmonella has been affecting humans for thousands of years.
   d Salmonella is the most common foodborne illness in the United States.

159

Week 11 Day 6

Sports

◀ a putter for the final tap into the hole

66 ∩066
The Sport of CEOs

1   Golf is a businessman's game. Big money deals are struck on the golf course, and a trip to the golf club is just another name for a business meeting. The connection between golf and business is such that, according to a recent survey, CEOs who play better golf actually make more money than those whose scores are too high.

2   Too high? Golf is one of the few sports where a low score is **preferable**[1] to a high one. Players try to hit the ball into a hole on the course in as few **strokes**[2] as possible. To make things more interesting, the course **is** often **littered with**[3] **obstacles**[4] such as areas of long grass (known as the **rough**[5]) and sand pits (or **bunkers**[6]).

3   Golfers hit the ball using a variety of clubs, each suitable for a particular area of the course. A driver, for example, is heavy and large-headed and is used for long-distance shots, while a putter is used for the final **tap**[7] into the hole.

4   The scoring system in golf is littered with odd sounding names. The target number of shots for each hole is called "par." For an easy hole, this number might be three, for very difficult holes, par is as high as six. If the player is skilled, he may sink the ball in fewer strokes than the average par. A score of one below par is called a "birdie," and two below an "eagle," while one over par is a bogey.

5   Modern golf **originated**[8] in fifteenth century Scotland (though a similar game existed in the Tang Dynasty of China), where it was played by the rich and poor alike. In the 1800s however, wealthy members of the middle class became fond of escaping the city and playing golf together in the countryside. These golf clubs, which had expensive membership fees and formal dress **codes**[9], eventually became the **norm**[10], and golf passed into the **realm**[11] of the elite.

Key Words

1. preferable 偏愛的 (a.)   2. stroke 揮桿 (n.)   3. be littered with 到處都是   4. obstacle 障礙物 (n.)
5. rough 深草區 (n.)   6. bunker 沙坑 (n.)   7. tap 輕敲 (n.)   8. originate 發源 (v.)   9. code 規則 (n.)
10. norm 基準 (n.)   11. realm 領域 (n.)   12. reputation 名聲 (n.)   13. exclusive 排他的 (a.)

◀ A trip to the golf club is just another name for a business meeting.

6   Golf's **reputation**[12] for being **exclusive**[13] to the mostly male business class has become so rooted in public opinion that a popular joke about the word "golf" is that it's an **acronym** for "Gentlemen Only, Ladies Forbidden."

Week 11 Day 6 The Sport of CEOs

Questions

____ 1. What would you say is the main idea of the article? ・・・・・・・・・・・・・・・・・・・・・・・・・・・・・・・・・・・・・◆Main Idea◆
   a The rules of golf are fairly simple.
   b Business and golf have a strong relationship.
   c Women seldom play golf.
   d Golf was first played in ancient China.

____ 2. Which of the following could be another title for this article? ・・・・・・・◆Subject Matter◆
   a Golf for Beginners.   b Why Women Can't Play Golf.
   c How to Be a Better CEO.   d The Business of Golf.

____ 3. According to the article, which of the following statements is NOT true?
   ・・・◆Supporting Details◆
   a The word "golf" comes from "Gentlemen Only, Ladies Forbidden."
   b CEOs who play golf well are often richer than those who don't.
   c The best score in a game of golf is the lowest score.
   d Golfers use different kinds of clubs for different obstacles.

____ 4. Which of the following can be inferred from the passage? ・・・・・・・・・・・・・・・・・◆Inference◆
   a To be a good golfer you must be a successful businessman.
   b Poor people are not as talented at golf as the rich.
   c To be a successful businessman, it's beneficial to play golf.
   d Golfers have a fondness for birds, especially eagles.

____ 5. What does the word **acronym** in the last paragraph mean? ・・・・・・・◆Words in Context◆
   a An incorrect spelling of a word.
   b A word formed by a phrase's initials.
   c A slang phrase used by common people.
   d An official title used in competitions.

____ 6. The author writes that in the 1800s, wealthy people began gathering in clubs in the countryside to play golf together. What was the effect of this trend?
   ・・◆Cause and Effect◆
   a Golf was played in Scotland.
   b Golf was played by rich and poor alike.
   c Golf's scoring system developed some strange names.
   d Golf became a sport for the elites only.

Golf Field

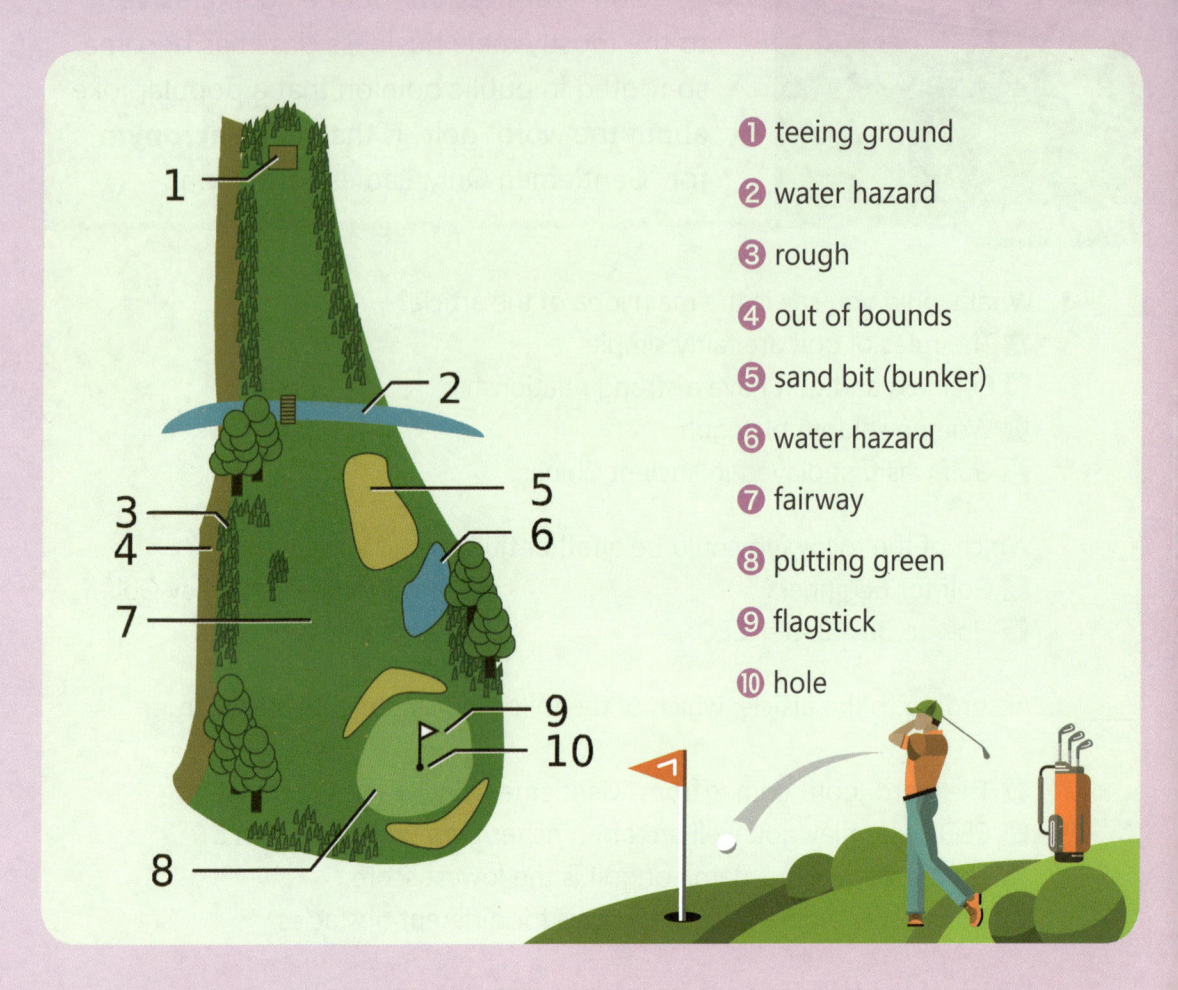

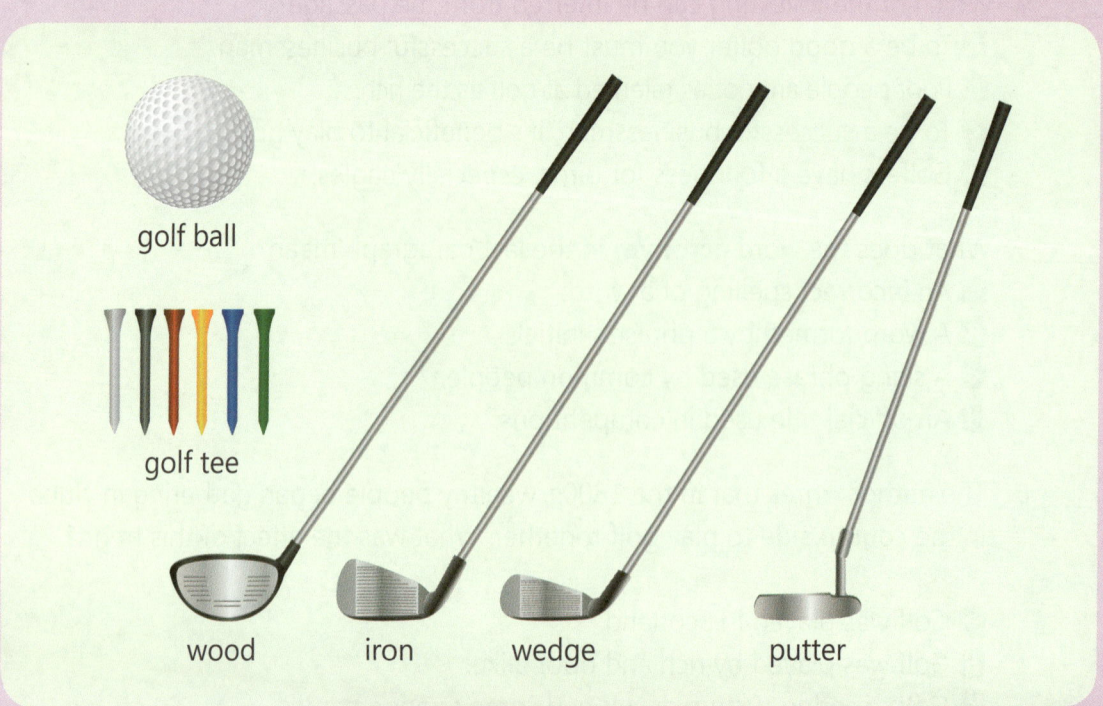

1. teeing ground
2. water hazard
3. rough
4. out of bounds
5. sand bit (bunker)
6. water hazard
7. fairway
8. putting green
9. flagstick
10. hole

golf ball

golf tee

wood

iron

wedge

putter

Week 12

Day 1 Language	67 In Danger of Falling Silent	164
Day 2 Health & Body	68 Doctor, Doctor!	166
Day 3 Mystery	69 Gone and Back Again	168
Day 4 People	70 An African Hero	170
Day 5 Entertainment	71 Come Watch Me Play	172
Day 6 People	72 Dancing Queen	174

Week 12 Day 1

Language

◀ the Hebrew language

67
In Danger of Falling Silent

1. There are over 6,000 languages spoken in the world today. More than 1,000 of them are locked away in the heads of **elderly**[1] people who cannot pass them on to the next generation. If current rates of language **extinction**[2] continue, anywhere from 50 to 90 percent of these languages will be gone forever by 2050. We are living in an age of mass language extinction.

2. To some, this isn't considered to be a problem. Quite the **contrary**[3], it's an **indication**[4] of global progress. They argue that the fewer languages, the greater the number of people who can actually communicate with each other. Communication breeds understanding, so the world will be a more peaceful place as a result.

3. Others aren't so sure. Professor Wade Davis believes that a language takes a piece of humanity's **heritage**[5] with it when it dies. To him, languages represent the complex web of human imagination. If one language gets **plucked**[6] from that web, a way of thinking disappears along with it. In other words, the fewer languages there are in the world, the less **imaginative**[7] and creative we are as a species.

4. It's going to take a lot of effort to **rein in** language extinction. The United Nation's list of dying languages is rather long. Taiwan's Thao language and China's Manchu made it onto the list. Saving these languages isn't just a matter of time and money. Governments need to **foster**[8] the belief that these dying languages are worth saving.

5. The good news is that there have been success stories in the past. Hebrew was saved from the **brink**[9] of extinction by the hard work of an **academic**[10] named Eliezer Ben-Yehuda in the nineteenth century. He took an ancient language

▲ Thao people of Sun Moon Lake, Taiwan

Key Words

① elderly 年長的 (a.)　② extinction 滅絕 (n.)　③ contrary 相反 (n.)　④ indication 徵兆 (n.)
⑤ heritage 遺產 (n.)　⑥ pluck 拔 (v.)　⑦ imaginative 想像的 (a.)　⑧ foster 培養 (v.)
⑨ brink 邊緣 (n.)　⑩ academic 學者 (n.)　⑪ humankind 人類 (n.)　⑫ inheritance 遺產 (n.)
⑬ squander 揮霍 (v.)

▶ the Manchu language

and transformed it into something that could be used in everyday life. Eventually, his efforts paid off as Hebrew is now spoken by over nine million people.

6   We should think of all the world's languages as **humankind's**[11] cultural **inheritance**[12]. They tell us stories about where we came from, the gods we believe in, what it is to be human, and the environment around us. We're **squandering**[13] our inheritance, and when it's gone, it's gone forever.

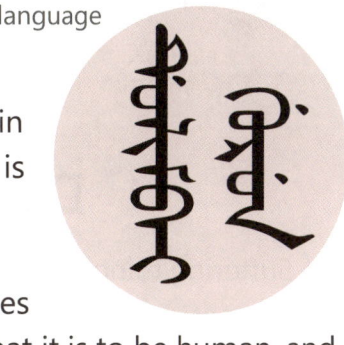

Week 12 Day 1 In Danger of Falling Silent

Questions

____ 1. Which of the following is the main topic of this article? ◆Main Idea◆
   a The struggle to boost global communication.
   b The struggle to save our cultural inheritance.
   c The struggle to save money on language textbooks.
   d The revival of the Hebrew language.

____ 2. What is this article about? ◆Subject Matter◆
   a The United Nations.   b Dying languages.
   c Hebrew.   d Culture.

____ 3. Which of the following statements is NOT true? ◆Supporting Details◆
   a There are over 6,000 languages spoken in the world today.
   b Some people believe that language extinction is a good thing.
   c Hebrew was saved from the brink of extinction.
   d Taiwan does not have any dying languages.

____ 4. Which of the following is likely true? ◆Inference◆
   a Many governments don't view language extinction as a problem.
   b Professor Wade Davis only speaks one language.
   c Language extinction cannot be stopped.
   d Dead languages can always be revived.

____ 5. The fourth paragraph of this article mentions that it will be hard to rein in language extinction. What does the phrase **rein in** mean? ◆Words in Context◆
   a To lose control over something.
   b To gain control over something.
   c To learn about something.
   d To speed something up.

____ 6. What tone does the author take in this article? ◆Author's Tone◆
   a Playful.   b Surprised.   c Concerned.   d Uncaring.

165

Week 12 Day 2

Health & Body

▶ emergency button

68
Doctor, Doctor!

❶ Suffering minor aches and pains is a normal part of being human. Our bodies constantly exhibit mild signs of **discomfort**[1], and usually we ignore these as being what they are—nothing serious. But what if every tiny ache, every **twinge**[2] of pain, and every harmless **ailment**[3] was, in your eyes, the sign of a **terminal**[4] illness? That's the kind of mental **torment**[5] sufferers of health **anxiety**[6], or **hypochondria**[7], have to deal with on a permanent basis.

❷ Hypochondriacs are constantly afraid that they may have a terrible disease and become obsessed with checking their bodies for symptoms. Even the most **innocuous** symptoms can, to a health anxiety sufferer, lead to a cycle of obsessive behavior, driving them **insane**[8] with worry. To a sufferer, a cough is sure to be lung cancer, a headache is a brain **tumor**[9], and stomach pains most certainly are proof of an **ulcer**[10].

❸ According to some **statistics**[11], six percent of patients who visit doctors have health anxiety and not only do they cause themselves **undue**[12] **distress**[13], they also take up unnecessary amounts of doctors' time and medical resources.

❹ The problem has gotten worse since medical information has become readily available on the Internet. Hypochondriacs are now able to find **obscure**[14] diseases that seem to fit their symptoms, and they **convince**[15] themselves that they are one of the rare sufferers.

❺ It's important to note that hypochondriacs do not make up their symptoms. But while the symptoms may be real, their exaggerated self-diagnosis is often the problem.

❻ The condition has been linked to obsessive-compulsive disorder, a form of anxiety that makes people obsess about the tiniest things and exhibit bizarre behavior as a result, like turning light switches on and off 10 times before they leave the room.

▼ Hypochondriacs are constantly afraid that they may have a terrible disease.

Key Words

❶ discomfort 不適 (n.)　❷ twinge 劇痛 (n.)　❸ ailment 小病 (n.)　❹ terminal 末期的 (a.)
❺ torment 痛苦的根源 (n.)　❻ anxiety 焦慮 (n.)　❼ hypochondria 慮病症 (n.)　❽ insane 瘋狂的 (a.)
❾ tumor 腫瘤 (n.)　❿ ulcer 潰瘍 (n.)　⓫ statistics 統計資料 (n.)　⓬ undue 過分的 (a.)
⓭ distress 苦惱 (n.)　⓮ obscure 不清楚的 (a.)　⓯ convince 說服 (v.)　⓰ refer 轉診；轉介 (v.)
⓱ therapist 治療師 (n.)

▶ Doctors usually refer health anxiety cases to behavioral therapists, who can help patients with their condition.

The same kind of obsessive behavior is thought to be at the root of health anxiety.

7   One of the main problems doctors have in treating hypochondriacs is that they often don't trust doctors' advice and, even when constantly assured that they are not sick, will still be doubtful. Doctors usually **refer**[16] health anxiety cases to behavioral **therapists**[17] who can better help patients come to terms with their condition.

Questions

_____ 1. How would you summarize the article? ◆Main Idea◆
  a There is a cure for health anxiety.
  b New research is needed for hypochondria.
  c Hypochondria causes real suffering.
  d There are few people with health anxiety in modern society.

_____ 2. What is this article about? ◆Subject Matter◆
  a A mental disorder.   b A rare illness.
  c Doctor-patient relationships.   d Hospital facilities.

_____ 3. Which of the following statements is NOT true? ◆Supporting Details◆
  a Doctors often refer patients with health anxiety to therapists.
  b Hypochondriacs make up their symptoms.
  c Even the most harmless symptoms can cause distress to a hypochondriac.
  d Heath anxiety is linked to obsessive-compulsive disorder.

_____ 4. According to the article, which of these would probably be true of a hypochondriac? ◆Inference◆
  a If a doctor said he was fine, he would not believe it.
  b He would not research his symptoms on the Internet.
  c If he had a serious symptom, he would not worry.
  d He would feel better after seeing a doctor.

_____ 5. What does the word **innocuous** in the second paragraph most likely mean? ◆Words in Context◆
  a Painful.   b Harmless.   c Obvious.   d Foolish.

_____ 6. How does the writer illustrate the mindset of hypochondriacs in the second paragraph? ◆Clarifying Devices◆
  a By using a simile.   b By using a narrative essay.
  c By using a quotation.   d By using exaggeration.

Week 12 Day 3

Mystery

69 Gone and Back Again

1 What if death is not really the end? That's what billions of people around the world believe. Some are looking forward to an **eternity**¹ in Heaven. Others are worried about ending up in Hell. And still others believe that they'll end up right back where they started—on Earth. The idea of being **reborn**² after dying is called **reincarnation**³. It has been a part of the Buddhist and Hindu **religions**⁴ for thousands of years.

2 Reincarnation may be a matter of belief, but that doesn't mean there isn't any evidence. There have been hundreds of cases of **suspected**⁵ reincarnation over the years. Some of these **incidents**⁶ remain unexplained to this very day. Are these stories the **smoking gun** that proves reincarnation exists? Decide for yourself.

3 Take the story of a young American boy named Ryan. At just four years of age, Ryan started begging his parents to take him home. His parents were **confused**⁷; he was **already** home. They asked: "Where is your home?" He replied it was a big house in Hollywood. Ryan's mom started taking books on Hollywood from the library. One day she showed Ryan a picture from a movie set. Ryan pointed at one of the actors and said: "That guy's me! The old me!"

4 Then there's the strange **tale**⁸ of James Leininger. Like many little boys, James loved planes, but he knew much more about them than he should, even down to the technical details. One day, James started having **nightmares**⁹. The dream was always the same. He would get shot down by a plane with a red

◀ Reincarnation is a part of the Buddhist and Hindu religions.

Key Words

❶ eternity 永恆；永世 (n.) ❷ reborn 重生 (v.) ❸ reincarnation 轉世 (n.) ❹ religion 宗教 (n.)
❺ suspected 疑似的；可疑的 (a.) ❻ incident 事件 (n.) ❼ confused 困惑的 (a.)
❽ tale 故事 (n.) ❾ nightmare 惡夢 (n.) ❿ launch 發射 (v.) ⓫ incredible 不可思議的 (a.)
⓬ trauma 創傷 (n.)

sun on it. In the nightmare, his plane was called *Corsair* and he **launched**[10] from a boat called *Natoma*. The **incredible**[11] thing is that both actually existed. They match the fate of James Huston, a pilot who died in World War II. Could it be that James was experiencing **trauma**[12] from a past life?

[5]   There are hundreds of stories like these from all around the world. The facts on reincarnation are out there for anyone who wants to search for them.

The Vought F4U Corsair is an American fighter aircraft that actually existed and widely used in World War II.

Questions

___ 1. Which sentence is closest in meaning to the main point? ◆Main Idea◆
  a Reincarnation is a part of major world religions.
  b James Leininger was really a World War II pilot named James Huston.
  c Many people believe in reincarnation around the world.
  d Most reincarnation cases remain unexplained.

___ 2. What is another possible title for this article? ◆Subject Matter◆
  a Discovering Our Past Lives.   b Sharing Our Stories of Survival.
  c The Traumas of World War II.   d Take Me Home to Hollywood.

___ 3. According to the article, which of the following is NOT true? ◆Supporting Details◆
  a Reincarnation is a part of the Buddhist religion.
  b There is no evidence of suspected reincarnation.
  c Ryan believed he was a Hollywood actor in a previous life.
  d James Leininger dreamed about a plane called *Corsair*.

___ 4. Which of the following can we infer from this article? ◆Inference◆
  a The writer doesn't believe in reincarnation.
  b Reincarnation is something that can't be scientifically explained.
  c James Leininger's parents taught him everything he knows about planes.
  d Reincarnation is dangerous and needs to be studied.

___ 5. What does **smoking gun** mean in the second paragraph? ◆Words in Context◆
  a Strong evidence.   b Dangerous weapon.
  c Useful tool.   d Old belief.

___ 6. Why does the word **already** appear in bold in the third paragraph? ◆Clarifying Devices◆
  a To emphasize the word.   b To quote someone.
  c To show it's a title.   d To show it's from another language.

Week 12 Day 4

People

▶ Wangari Maathai (1940–2011)

70
An African Hero

1. If Kenya's Wangari Maathai kept a **trophy**[1] case for her international awards, it would be as big as a house. Yet all these awards resulted from a very simple **concept**[2]: the importance of planting trees.

2. Her story starts in 1940, when she was born in a small village in Kenya. Her early **upbringing**[3] occurred in an area rich with natural beauty and **wildlife**[4]. This taught her to love nature from a very early age. In 1960, she was one of 300 Kenyans selected for a special **scholarship**[5] to study in America. Ten years of **rigorous**[6] study later, she became the first East African woman to receive a doctorate degree.

3. Wangari Maathai was active in the National **Council**[7] of Women of Kenya (NCWK) in the 1970s. Her early work with the NCWK convinced her that the environment was the key to improving the lives of poor women.

4. Next, she put her theory into practice. She began planting trees in 1976 and established the Green Belt Movement in 1977. By 1986, her movement had spread to the rest of the continent. To date, it has planted over 40 million trees in Africa. As if that wasn't enough, their goal for the next decade is to plant over one billion trees worldwide.

5. Though Ms. Maathai's **activism**[8] began with the environment, it eventually expanded into political matters. This got her into trouble with Kenya's ruling elite. Between 1982 and 2001, she was beaten up, arrested, forced into hiding, and even had to **barricade herself in**[9] her house at one point. However, in 2002 democracy **prevailed**[10], and Ms. Maathai was elected to Kenya's **parliament**[11]. The very next year, she was **appointed**[12] Assistant **Minister**[13] for the Environment and Natural Resources.

6. In 2004, Wangari Maathai was awarded the Nobel Peace Prize in **recognition**[14] of her efforts to promote environmental protection, women's rights, and

▲ Green Belt Movement tree nursery in Tumutumu Hills, Kenya (photo by Ariel Poster)

Key Words

1. trophy 獎盃 (n.) 2. concept 概念 (n.) 3. upbringing 教養 (n.) 4. wildlife 野生動物 (n.)
5. scholarship 獎學金 (n.) 6. rigorous 嚴格的 (a.) 7. council 議會 (n.) 8. activism 行動主義 (n.)
9. barricade oneself in 把自己關在裡面 10. prevail 佔優勢 (v.) 11. parliament 議會 (n.)
12. appoint 任命 (v.) 13. minister 部長 (n.) 14. recognition 認可 (n.) 15. ovarian 卵巢的 (a.)

▶ Wangari Maathai memorial trees and garden at the University of Pittsburgh

political freedom. It marked the first time the prize was awarded to an African woman.

7   Africa lost one of its most brilliant **activists** in September 2011 when Wangari Maathai died of **ovarian**[15] cancer. She may be gone, but her message of political freedom and caring for our environment live on in the Green Belt Movement.

Questions

____ 1. Which of the following is the main topic of this article? •Main Idea•
  a The life and times of an African activist.
  b The importance of planting trees.
  c Major changes in Kenya's politics.
  d The history of the Green Belt Movement.

____ 2. What is this article about? •Subject Matter•
  a Trees.
  b The Green Belt Movement.
  c Wangari Maathai.
  d Kenya.

____ 3. Which of the following statements is NOT true? •Supporting Details•
  a Wangari Maathai was born in Kenya in 1940.
  b Wangari Maathai studied in America.
  c Wangari Maathai was elected president of Kenya.
  d Wangari Maathai won the Nobel Peace Prize in 2004.

____ 4. What can we infer from this article? •Inference•
  a Kenya has the highest unemployment rate in Africa.
  b Kenya is the most developed country in Africa.
  c Kenya had an oppressive political system.
  d Wangari Maathai had a university degree in physics.

____ 5. The last paragraph mentions that Africa lost one of its most brilliant activists. What does an **activist** do? •Words in Context•
  a Work hard to accomplish a political or environmental goal.
  b Organize sports activities in the community where he or she lives.
  c Go to jail for something that he or she believed in.
  d Receive awards from the government for community service.

____ 6. What was the root cause of Wangari Maathai's love of nature? •Cause and Effect•
  a Attending university in America.
  b Winning a Nobel Peace Prize.
  c Joining the National Council of Women of Kenya.
  d Growing up in an area rich with natural beauty and wildlife.

Week 12 Day 5

Entertainment

▶ video game live streamer

71 🎧 071

Come Watch Me Play

❶ Wouldn't it be great to just play video games for a living? For many young people, that's the dream. A few years ago, many would have laughed at such a ridiculous **fantasy**¹, but the world has changed. Nowadays, playing video games for a living is not only possible, but also has the potential to make you a very comfortable living, too. It's all thanks to video game live **streaming**².

❷ Video game live streaming is simply the act of **broadcasting**³ **footage**⁴ of yourself playing a video game live over the Internet. And though you might struggle to believe it, viewers actually come in their millions to watch these streamers at play.

❸ What is it, then, that draws so many viewers to watch people playing video games? As with any form of reality **entertainment**⁵, it comes down to our very human love of people-watching. Viewers are drawn by the streamers' personalities, in-game **commentary**⁶, and humor, as well as their gaming skills.

❹ The streamers themselves make their money through sharing in advertising **revenue**⁷ from the streaming sites, **sponsorships**⁸ from gaming organizations, and even **donations**⁹ from their fans. According to the US-based website Twitch, one of the world's top live-streaming websites, the most successful live-streamers make more than **six figures** a year.

❺ Of course, only very few of the top streamers make that much money, and before you decide to start your own streaming channel, there are risks to consider.

❻ **Amateur**¹⁰ streamers often spend long hours online with few breaks, as any time they spend away from their channel marks an opportunity for them to lose viewers. As a result, the lifestyle of the average **aspiring**¹¹ streamer is not the healthiest.

❼ Streamers are also at risk of online **stalking**¹². Some viewers become so **obsessed**¹³ with their favorite streamer that they attempt to find and befriend

▲ Streamers' personalities, in-game commentary, and gaming skills can draw millions to watch them pla

Key Words

❶ fantasy 幻想 (n.)　❷ streaming 線上收聽（看）(n.)　❸ broadcast 播送；播放 (v.)
❹ footage 影片；片段 (n.)　❺ entertainment 娛樂 (n.)　❻ commentary 評論 (n.)
❼ revenue 收益 (n.)　❽ sponsorship 贊助 (n.)　❾ donation 捐款 (n.)　❿ amateur 業餘的 (a.)
⓫ aspiring 野心勃勃的 (a.)　⓬ stalk 跟蹤 (v.)　⓭ obsess 使著迷 (v.)　⓮ flatter 奉承；討好 (v.)
⓯ prospect 預期；期望 (n.)　⓰ pastime 消遣；娛樂 (n.)

▶ Twitch website homepage

them, which, though **flattering**[14], is not always a welcome **prospect**[15].

Despite the risks, streaming remains a popular **pastime**[16] for many gamers. Even if they have few followers, the joy of being able to share their passion with the world is enough and that is something all of us, gamers or not, can surely relate to.

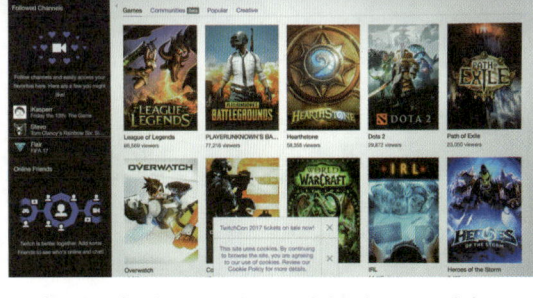

Questions

____ 1. Which of the following comes closest to expressing the article's main idea?
  ◆Main Idea◆
   a Lots of people go online to watch strangers play video games live.
   b Video game streamers often lead unhealthy lifestyles.
   c Video game streaming is a new money-making opportunity for gamers.
   d New streamers need to spend a lot of time online getting followers.

____ 2. What is the article about? ◆Subject Matter◆
   a Online gaming.
   b Video game live streaming.
   c New ways to make money.
   d A popular video game streamer.

____ 3. Which of these is NOT mentioned as a way in which video game streamers make money? ◆Supporting Details◆
   a Fan donations.
   b Advertising revenue.
   c Sponsorships.
   d Selling second hand games.

____ 4. Which of these people would probably be the most popular video game live streamer? ◆Inference◆
   a A moderately skilled gamer who doesn't talk much.
   b A talkative, highly skilled gamer with a good sense of humor.
   c A miserable gamer who always loses and never makes jokes.
   d A highly skilled gamer who only streams once a month.

____ 5. In paragraph four, the author says that the most successful streamers make "more than six figures a year." What does the phrase **six figures** refer to here?
  ◆Words in Context◆
   a An amount of money.
   b A number of games.
   c An amount of time.
   d A number of followers.

____ 6. How does the writer introduce the topic in the first paragraph? ◆Clarifying Devices◆
   a By giving the reader a warning.
   b By posing a difficult moral question.
   c By giving the reader a piece of advice.
   d By contrasting the past and the present.

Week 12 Day 5 Come Watch Me Play

72

Dancing Queen

▶ Martha Graham, 1922

1. In 1970, at the age of 76, Martha Graham performed her final dance. For the **legendary**[1] American dancer and **choreographer**[2], it was a transition that she would find very difficult to go through. Having spent over half a century as a dancer, when the time finally came to hang up her dancing shoes, Graham sank into **depression**[3] and **alcoholism**[4], feeling that her raison d'être had been taken away from her by age.

2. By the time it came for Graham to retire from dancing, she had danced at the White House for eight different presidents and choreographed countless highly influential performances. Her dance company, the Martha Graham Dance Company, which is now one of the oldest dance companies in America, had toured Asia, the Middle East, and Europe, earning her global **acclaim**[5].

3. But watching young dancers take roles that had once been meant for her was almost overwhelmingly sad for the aging Graham. "I believe in never looking back, never **indulging**[6] in **nostalgia**[7], or **reminiscing**[8]," she said. "Yet how can you avoid it when you look on stage and see a dancer made up to look as you did 30 years ago, dancing a ballet you created with someone you were then deeply in love with?"

4. Graham's approach to modern dance was innovative in that she challenged the fluidity and grace of ballet, **confronting**[9] tradition with sharp, sexual movements. Her actions expressed violent passions, inner **turmoil**[10], and psychological torment, all **vividly**[11] expressed through her ability to display extreme **tension**[12] and release with her body. Freedom of movement was central to her philosophy. "It's not my job to look beautiful," she said. "It's my job to look interesting." For subject matter she took stories from **mythology**[13], folk tales,

Key Words

① legendary 傳說的 (a.)　② choreographer 編舞家 (n.)　③ depression 沮喪 (n.)
④ alcoholism 酗酒 (n.)　⑤ acclaim 喝采 (n.)　⑥ indulge 沉迷於 (v.)　⑦ nostalgia 懷舊 (n.)
⑧ reminisce 追憶 (v.)　⑨ confront 對抗 (v.)　⑩ turmoil 混亂 (n.)　⑪ vividly 栩栩如生地 (adv.)
⑫ tension 張力；緊張 (n.)　⑬ mythology 神話 (n.)　⑭ abuse 濫用 (n.)　⑮ enroll 註冊 (v.)

▼ Martha Graham, 1948

and history, and often wove strong social commentary into her choreography.

5　　Alcohol **abuse**[14] after her retirement sent her to the hospital, but she recovered and even began writing again, continuing to contribute to choreography until her death in 1991. Her influence on modern dance has been compared to Picasso's influence on art, something she could never have expected when, as an aspiring young performer, she **enrolled**[15] in a dance school at the late age of 22, which many considered far too old for a dancer.

Questions

1. Which of the following is the main topic of the article? ◆Main Idea◆
   a. The early life of Martha Graham.
   b. Martha Graham's problems with alcohol.
   c. The later life and legacy of Martha Graham.
   d. The famous quotes of Martha Graham.

2. What is this article about? ◆Subject Matter◆
   a. Old age.
   b. A performing artist.
   c. The history of dance.
   d. Depression.

3. Which of the following statements is NOT true? ◆Supporting Details◆
   a. Martha Graham began dancing at a relatively late age.
   b. Martha Graham died in 1991.
   c. Martha Graham's approach to dancing was very traditional.
   d. Martha Graham danced for several US presidents.

4. What does the last paragraph imply? ◆Inference◆
   a. Martha Graham is considered a bigger influence in the art world than Picasso.
   b. Martha Graham continued dancing after her stay in a hospital.
   c. Martha Graham began to dislike dancing in her later life.
   d. Martha Graham's success went far beyond her and others' expectations.

5. What does **raison d'être** in the first paragraph mean? ◆Words in Context◆
   a. Reason for performing.
   b. Reason for living.
   c. Reason for drinking.
   d. Reason for dying.

6. How does the writer treat his subject matter? ◆Clarifying Devices◆
   a. With humor.
   b. With admiration.
   c. With disapproval.
   d. With carelessness.

Martha Graham Dance Company

◀ Martha Graham School headquarters in 1994, at 316 East 63rd Street, New York. Though the school has since moved from this location, this is the last studio that Martha Graham herself taught in.

▲ *Visionary Recital* (photograph by Carl Van Vechten)

Week 13

Day 1 Technology	73 People Power	178
Day 2 Language	74 Communication Breakdown	180
Day 3 Mystery	75 The Skull and Bones Society	182
Day 4 Nature	76 The Cold-Blooded Collapse	184
Day 5 Arts & Literature	77 Writing the Unexpected	186
Day 6 Geography	78 Something in the Wind	188
Day 7 Culture	79 Tears for Hire	190

Week 13 Day 1

Technology

▶ Heat radiated by the human body can be an energy source.

73 🎧 073
People Power

1 In a world where oil and gas are increasingly scarce, companies are **scrambling**[1] to find innovative new ways to conserve energy and save money. A Swedish company called Jernhusen has taken things one step further. They have discovered how to **harness**[2] an energy source that is **abundant**[3] yet often **overlooked**[4]—the heat **radiated**[5] by the human body.

2 Jernhusen is a real **estate**[6] company that owns Stockholm's Central Station, the largest railway station in Sweden. Over 250,000 **commuters**[7] come through here every single day. Some of them stay for a while to have a coffee, a quick bite, or maybe even catch a nap while they wait for an afternoon train. All of them put together radiate enough heat to keep the station warm and **toasty**[8] despite the **harsh**[9] Swedish winter outside.

3 Jernhusen engineers discovered that this heat could be used for another purpose. They built an innovative new heating system that uses the **accumulated**[10] body heat in Stockholm Central Station to heat up large tanks of water. Once it's hot enough, the water is then **pumped**[11] 100 yards across the street, where it's used to heat another office building that is owned by Jernhusen. The system cost a mere US$30,000 to **install**[12], and it is estimated that it will reduce energy costs by 30 percent every year.

4 Sweden isn't the only country going ahead with this innovative new technology. A similar **scheme**[13] has also been implemented in Paris, where body heat from the Metro is harnessed and pumped into public housing buildings. The Mall of America in Minnesota is another example of a heating system that takes advantage of body heat. In fact, its combination of **skylights**[14] and body heat has been a little too effective. There are times when the mall needs to turn on the air-conditioning during wintertime in order to maintain a comfortable temperature for shoppers.

▼ hall of Stockholm Central Station

Key Words

1. scramble 爭搶 (v.)　2. harness 利用 (v.)　3. abundant 充足的 (a.)　4. overlook 忽略 (v.)
5. radiate 散發 (v.)　6. estate 地產；財產 (n.)　7. commuter 通勤者 (n.)　8. toasty 暖烘烘的 (a.)
9. harsh 嚴酷的 (a.)　10. accumulate 累積 (v.)　11. pump 抽送 (v.)　12. install 安裝 (v.)
13. scheme 計畫 (n.)　14. skylight 天窗 (n.)　15. feasible 可行的 (a.)

▼ The combination of skylights and body heat has been too effective in the Mall of America, Minnesota.

5 While body heating systems are an innovative new approach, they do have some **drawbacks**. The heat cannot travel very far before it starts to cool off. What's more, body heat systems are not economically **feasible**[15] in warmer climates and locations with cheaper conventional energy sources like oil and gas.

Week 13 Day 1 People Power

Questions

_____ 1. Which of the following can summarize this article? ········· ◆Main Idea◆
   a Humans produce a lot of body heat.
   b Buildings can be heated from unlikely sources.
   c Innovative new technologies come from Sweden.
   d Jernhusen is the company of the future.

_____ 2. What does this article focus on? ········· ◆Subject Matter◆
   a Sweden.   b Jernhusen.   c Body heat systems.   d Green technologies

_____ 3. Which of the following is true? ········· ◆Supporting Details◆
   a The Mall of America in Minnesota has conventional heating.
   b Stockholm Central Station uses skylights for heating.
   c Body heat can be used to save money on energy costs.
   d Over 250,000 people sleep in Stockholm Central Station every night.

_____ 4. What can we infer from this article? ········· ◆Inference◆
   a The Mall of America's body heat system worked better than expected.
   b Body heat from New York could be pumped to Buffalo.
   c Body heat can be stored in containers for future use.
   d There are too many drawbacks for body heating to be effective.

_____ 5. The last paragraph of this article mentions that body heating systems have drawbacks. What is a **drawback**? ········· ◆Words in Context◆
   a An advantage   b A disadvantage.
   c An obscure feature.   d A hidden danger.

_____ 6. Which of the following is a statement of opinion? ········· ◆Fact or Opinion◆
   a Jernhusen is a real estate company that owns Stockholm's Central Station.
   b The body heat system in Stockholm's Central Station will likely reduce energy costs by 30 percent every year.
   c Over 250,000 commuters pass through Stockholm's Central Station every single day.
   d The body heat system in Stockholm Central Station cost a US$30,000 to install.

179

Week 13 Day 2

Language

74 Communication Breakdown

🎧 074

[1] So, you want to learn a new language. Good for you! But there's something you should know: not all languages are created equal. Some of them will have you happily communicating with native speakers in a few weeks, and others will make you **toil**[1] for an entire year before you can even start complaining about the weather. Read on if that's the kind of challenge you're looking for. These are the hardest languages in the world.

[2] First off, there's Arabic. This language is so difficult that it will give even the cleverest students nightmares. Letters can be written in four different ways depending on their position in a word and the present verb **tense**[2] has 13 different forms. There are also as many **dialects**[3] spread around the world as there are days in a month.

[3] If that sounds too easy for you, you might want to try Cantonese. You can **embark on**[4] the **monotonous**[5] process of **memorizing**[6] 25,000 written characters. And don't forget to master the nine tones as well. At least **grammar**[7] won't be a problem. With no verb **transformations**[8], **genders**[9], or tenses, Chinese grammar is some of the simplest in the world.

[4] Japanese is another Asian language that will take a lot of toil to master. It's almost like the opposite of Cantonese. **Pronunciation**[10] is easy, and there are few tones, but the verb tenses will make you want to pull your hair out. What's more, you have to learn a whole new verb tense if you want people to stop thinking that you're rude.

[5] If you'd rather learn a tongue-**twisting**[11] European language, then Hungarian is a good choice. Hungarian nouns have 18 different cases. Memorizing them won't be your only problem. To speak Hungarian properly, you need to become familiar with all of the different sounds that your

▶ Arabic alphabet

Key Words

① **toil** 苦幹 (v.)　② **tense** 時態 (n.)　③ **dialect** 方言 (n.)　④ **embark on** 開始；著手做
⑤ **monotonous** 單調的 (a.)　⑥ **memorize** 背熟 (v.)　⑦ **grammar** 文法 (n.)
⑧ **transformation** 變化；轉變 (n.)　⑨ **gender** 性別 (n.)　⑩ **pronunciation** 發音 (n.)
⑪ **twist** 扭轉 (v.)　⑫ **appeal** 吸引 (v.)　⑬ **fluency** 流暢 (n.)

▶ Japanese alphabet

throat can produce. Hungarian pronunciation can be extremely difficult for non-native speakers.

6   If none of these **appeal**[12] to you, there are plenty of other languages in the running for world's hardest. Finnish, Polish, Estonian, Navajo, Basque, and Icelandic are only a few of them. Just remember: no matter what language you decide to study, **perseverance** is the key to **fluency**[13].

Questions

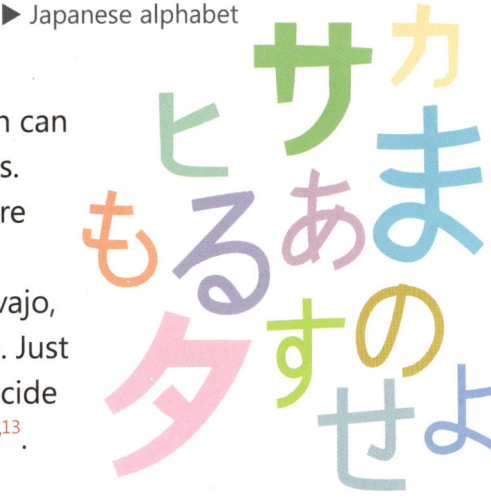

____ 1. Which of the following is the main topic of this article? ◆Main Idea◆
   a A list of the hardest languages in the world.
   b A guide to mastering difficult languages.
   c A list of the hardest languages in Asia.
   d A list of the most useful languages in the world.

____ 2. What does this article focus on? ◆Subject Matter◆
   a Nightmares.
   b Characters.
   c Difficult ways of expression.
   d Grammar.

____ 3. Which of the following statements is NOT true? ◆Supporting Details◆
   a Hungarian is a difficult language to learn.
   b Arabic letters can be written in four different ways.
   c Chinese grammar is considered to be difficult.
   d Finnish, Polish, and Navajo are considered to be difficult languages.

____ 4. What does this article imply? ◆Inference◆
   a Lots of foreigners can speak Chinese without being able to read it.
   b Europe is home to some of the hardest languages in the world.
   c The older the language, the harder it is for people to master.
   d Once you've mastered one difficult language, the next one is much harder.

____ 5. The last sentence of this article mentions that perseverance is the key to fluency. What does **perseverance** mean? ◆Words in Context◆
   a Being unable to sleep.
   b Being persistent and not giving up.
   c Not working very hard.
   d The act of speaking a lot.

____ 6. Which of the following best describes the form of the article? ◆Text Form◆
   a A biography.   b A list of examples.   c A timeline.   d A narrative.

Week 13 Day 3

Mystery

75 The Skull and Bones Society

◀ the Skull and Bones Hall, known as the Tomb

▲ logo of Skull and Bones

▲ 15 Bonesmen showing human bones and a grandfather clock at 8 p.m.

❶ Outside a room guarded by an iron door, 15 new members nervously await their initiation. They can hear strange noises, cries, and screams coming from within the **sanctum**. One enters. He sees robed figures, men in **skeleton**[1] **costumes**[2], and a man dressed as the devil; they push him to a table and **chant**[3] "Read!" He reads the secret **oath**[4]. The robed figures grab him and push him toward a picture of Eulogia—the society's own goddess of **eloquence**[5]. "Eulogia! Eulogia!" the figures chant.

❷ He is rushed outside, where the figures scream, **wail**[6], and **urge**[7] him toward a white tent. "The hangman equals death," they shout. "The devil equals death! Death equals death!" In the tent he picks up a **thigh**[8] bone. Out in the open again, he sees a terrifying scene before him. A **butcher**[9] towers over a figure covered in fake blood. The **initiate**[10] approaches a skull on the ground near the butcher, kneels, and kisses it. The butcher **enacts**[11] cutting the figure's throat, a motion that symbolizes the initiate's death to the **barbarian**[12] world and rebirth into The Order.

❸ The Skull and Bones is Yale's oldest secret society, with nearly 200 years of hidden tradition and a habit of producing some of America's most important future leaders.

❹ This disturbing description of the society's initiation ritual has been pieced together by journalists from countless interviews and secret recordings. No one except true members of the society really know what goes on behind the doors of the Skull and Bones club. The members are sworn to secrecy, keeping the society's inner workings quiet under strict **vows**[13] of silence.

❺ While it may be just an **eccentric**[14] debate society that meets every Thursday and Sunday evening, the Skull and Bones club's **obsession**[15] with death and connection with turning out America's power elite separate it from other college societies.

Key Words

① skeleton 骨骸 (n.)　② costume 服裝 (n.)　③ chant 吟誦 (v.)　④ oath 誓約 (n.)
⑤ eloquence 雄辯 (n.)　⑥ wail 嚎啕 (v.)　⑦ urge 催促 (v.)　⑧ thigh 大腿 (n.)　⑨ butcher 屠夫 (n.)
⑩ initiate 入會者 (n.)　⑪ enact 上演 (v.)　⑫ barbarian 野蠻人 (n.)　⑬ vow 誓言 (n.)
⑭ eccentric 古怪的 (a.)　⑮ obsession 迷戀 (n.)　⑯ opponent 對手 (n.)

◀ George W. Bush, former Bonesman

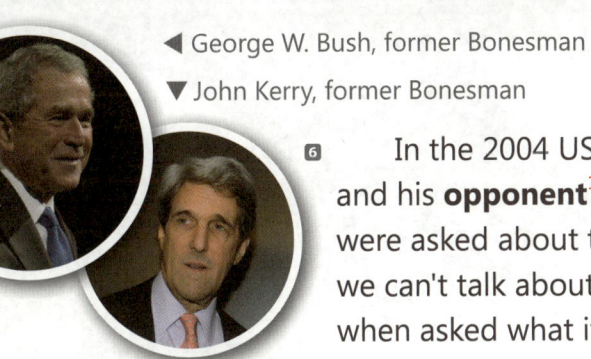

▼ John Kerry, former Bonesman

6 In the 2004 US presidential election, George W. Bush and his **opponent**[16] John Kerry (both former Bonesmen) were asked about their time in the society. "It's so secret we can't talk about it," said President Bush. While Kerry, when asked what it meant that both had been initiated into the society, replied, "Not much, because it's a secret."

Week 13 Day 3 The Skull and Bones Society

Questions

____ 1. Which of the following is the main idea of the article? ············· ◆Main Idea◆
  a The Skull and Bones society is based in Yale.
  b New members are put through a bizarre initiation process.
  c The Skull and Bones society is secretive, strange and powerful.
  d Yale University has many secret societies.

____ 2. What is this article about? ············· ◆Subject Matter◆
  a The society's rituals and secretive nature.
  b The society's famous former members.
  c How and when the society began.
  d The costumes worn at the initiation ceremony.

____ 3. Which of the following statements is NOT true? ············· ◆Supporting Details◆
  a The Skull and Bones society is the oldest secret society in America.
  b The Skull and Bones society initiates fifteen new members at a time.
  c Former president George W. Bush was once a member of the society.
  d Initiates must kiss a skull before they can become members.

____ 4. Who is most likely to be invited to become a member of the Skull and Bones society? ············· ◆Inference◆
  a A radical, prize-winning student poet.
  b A student who organizes antigovernment protests.
  c A student from a poor background studying medicine.
  d A student with great political potential.

____ 5. What does the word **sanctum** in the first paragraph mean? ······· ◆Words in Context◆
  a A courtyard.　　b A private room.　　c A box or container.　　d A castle.

____ 6. Why does the writer use the present tense to narrate the events in the first and second paragraphs? ············· ◆Clarifying Devices◆
  a It makes the order of the events clearer.
  b It gives the reader an objective view of events.
  c It makes the action feel more immediate.
  d It allows the writer to be more descriptive.

Week 13 Day 4
Nature

▶ frog
▼ toad

76 🎧 076
The Cold-Blooded Collapse

❶ Frogs, **toads**[1], and **salamanders**[2] were the earliest **vertebrate**[3] life-forms to walk on land. This **accomplishment**[4] happened about 350 million years ago. Since then, **amphibians**[5] have gone **extinct**[6] at a rate of one species every 250 years. That is until humanity arrived and altered Earth's natural balance.

❷ Recently, the extinction rate of amphibians has increased dramatically. Since 1980, over 200 species of amphibians have disappeared from the planet forever, and it's about to get a lot worse. Another 1,856 species are currently facing the threat of extinction. These shocking numbers are causing a worldwide **scramble**[7] as scientists desperately seek to understand what is behind this amphibian collapse.

❸ It seems that mass amphibian extinction is being caused by several factors. First and foremost is the destruction of natural **habitats**. As humans continue to tear down forests and build houses in their place, we **disrupt**[8] **ecology**[9] all over the planet. Global warming is also adding to the damage. Frogs, toads, and salamanders have evolved in a highly **specialized**[10] way in order to live in specific habitats. **Subtle**[11] changes in global temperatures can disrupt their ability to survive.

❹ It's not just humans who are the problem. A deadly disease called **chytridiomycosis**[12] has **ravaged**[13] amphibian populations in the Americas and Australia. Amphibians that are infected with this fungus die within weeks. Scientists don't even know where it came from, let alone how to stop it.

▲ a frog infected with chytridiomycosis (cc by Forrest Brem)

❺ Scientists often classify amphibians as bio-**indicators**[14]. This means that they're more sensitive to changes in their environment than other organisms are.

Key Words

❶ toad 蟾蜍 (n.)　❷ salamander 蠑螈 (n.)　❸ vertebrate 脊椎動物的 (a.)　❹ accomplishment 成就 (n.)
❺ amphibian 兩棲動物 (n.)　❻ extinct 絕種的 (a.)　❼ scramble 混亂 (n.)　❽ disrupt 擾亂 (v.)
❾ ecology 生態系 (n.)　❿ specialized 專門的；專業的 (a.)　⓫ subtle 微妙的 (a.)
⓬ chytridiomycosis 壺病菌 (n.)　⓭ ravage 毀滅 (v.)　⓮ indicator 指標 (n.)　⓯ astonish 使吃驚 (v.)

◀ salamander

Frogs, toads, and salamanders are like an early-warning system that can show us what will happen to other species that suffer similar environmental destruction. Therefore, since amphibians are going extinct at an **astonishing**[15] rate, it's quite possible that birds and mammals won't be far behind.

6   We may also be losing a wealth of medical science from amphibian collapse. Around 10 percent of all of the Nobel Prizes in Physiology or Medicine have involved research on amphibians. That means that every species that disappears is one that might have cured a terrible disease.

Questions

____ 1. Which of the following is the main topic of this article? ◆Main Idea◆
  a A profile of amphibian species.
  b Causes of mass amphibian extinction.
  c The effects of mass amphibian extinction.
  d An analysis of mass amphibian extinction.

____ 2. What is this article about? ◆Subject Matter◆
  a Biology.
  b Chytridiomycosis.
  c Amphibian extinction.
  d Medical advances.

____ 3. Which of the following statements is NOT true? ◆Supporting Details◆
  a Currently, 1,856 amphibian species are threatened.
  b Amphibians are known as bio-indicators.
  c Amphibians have helped produce medical discoveries.
  d Global warming doesn't affect amphibians.

____ 4. What can we infer from this article? ◆Inference◆
  a Amphibians are more threatened than birds or mammals.
  b Chytridiomycosis can spread to people.
  c Amphibian collapse is a natural process.
  d Humans cannot be affected by environmental destruction.

____ 5. The third paragraph of this article mentions habitats. What is a **habitat**?
  ◆Words in Context◆
  a A frog.   b A home.   c A disease.   d A lake.

____ 6. Which of these is NOT a cause of amphibian collapse, according to the article?
  ◆Cause and Effect◆
  a Global warming.
  b Bio-indicator.
  c Habitat destruction.
  d Chytridiomycosis.

Week 13 Day 5

Arts & Literature

▶ Rampo Edogawa (1894–1965)

77
Writing the Unexpected

1   With his deep understanding of **horror**[1] and the **grotesque** and his talent for unexpected **plot**[2] twists, Edogawa Rampo took the Japanese mystery **genre**[3] to terrifying new territories. Born Hirai Taro, he published his first story in 1923 under the name Edogawa Rampo—a play on the name Edgar Allan Poe. Rampo gained success by combining the **suspense**[4]-filled style of Western mystery stories with his own **bizarre**[5] imagination.

2   In his story "The Human Chair," for example, Rampo describes an ugly chair maker who **craves**[6] human contact and designs a **luxurious**[7] sofa for a hotel. He alters the inside of the sofa so that he himself can climb inside. The sofa is then taken to the hotel with its maker hiding just beneath the surface. In the hotel, guests sit on him unaware that the chair is in fact hiding a man. The sofa is eventually sold to another **household**[8], where a young woman lives. The story itself takes the form of a letter being read by a young female writer, and as she reads on, it becomes more and more apparent that the chair she is sitting on is hiding the twisted chair maker beneath its surface. Though the story doesn't end here (there is one more delicious twist before the reader turns the final page), it shows just how smoothly Rampo is able to **manipulate**[9] his readers' most basic emotions of fear and **dread**[10].

▲ The Black Lizard and Beast in the Shadows
▲ Youth Detective Squad 
▲ Japanese Tales of Mystery and Imagination 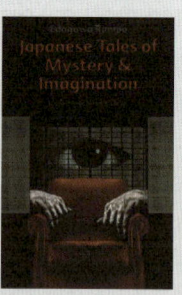

3   Another story, "The Red **Chamber**[11]," focuses on a group of men who come together to tell horror stories. One new member

Key Words

1. horror 恐怖 (n.) 2. plot 情節 (n.) 3. genre 種類 (n.) 4. suspense 懸疑 (n.)
5. bizarre 奇異的 (a.) 6. crave 渴望 (v.) 7. luxurious 豪華的 (a.) 8. household 家庭 (n.)
9. manipulate 操作 (v.) 10. dread 懼怕 (n.) 11. chamber 房間 (n.) 12. murderer 殺人犯 (n.)
13. ingenious 巧妙的 (a.) 14. sleeve 袖 (n.)

begins by revealing that he is a **murderer**[12] and has killed 99 people but has done so in a way so **ingenious**[13] that the police will never catch him. He tricks people into deadly situations by lying or suggesting actions that will certainly cause their deaths. He sees himself as the perfect murderer, and in the end tricks a servant into killing him, thus bringing his total murders to 100. Once again, though, there is in fact one more twist in the story before the final sentence. It's important to remember that even when you think the story's over, Rampo always has a final surprise up his **sleeve**[14].

▶ statue of Edogawa Rampo, Mie Prefecture

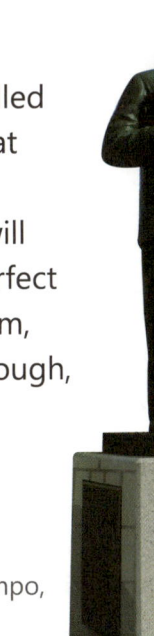

Questions

____ 1. Which of the following is the main topic of the article? ······ ◆Main Idea◆
  a The life of Edogawa Rampo.
  b The character of Edogawa Rampo.
  c The critics' opinion of Edogawa Rampo.
  d The terrifying tales of Edogawa Rampo.

____ 2. What does this article mostly focus on? ······ ◆Subject Matter◆
  a The works of one author.
  b Writers of Japanese horror stories.
  c Fear as a harmful emotion.
  d Places with mysterious stories attached.

____ 3. Which of the following statements is NOT true? ······ ◆Supporting Details◆
  a Rampo used a style similar to that of Western mystery stories.
  b The story "The Human Chair" takes the form of a diary entry.
  c The story "The Red Chamber" ends with a plot twist.
  d "The Human Chair" is about a strange chair maker.

____ 4. What can we infer from this article? ······ ◆Inference◆
  a "The Red Chamber" ends with the death of the main character.
  b The writer of the article does not like Poe's stories.
  c Rampo kept his manuscripts in his sleeves.
  d Rampo was an admirer of the American writer Edgar Allan Poe.

____ 5. What does the word **grotesque** in the first paragraph mean? ······ ◆Words in Context◆
  a Monstrous.   b Ordinary.   c Medical.   d Wild.

____ 6. What do paragraphs two and three primarily consist of? ······ ◆Clarifying Devices◆
  a Instructions.   b Statistics.   c Narratives.   d Quotations.

Week 13 Day 6

Geography

▶ Asian brown cloud

78 Something in the Wind

[1]   A vast brown cloud of smog, dust, and other pollutants hangs over the Indian subcontinent **like** a **filthy**[1] **smear**[2] of mud in the sky. It is the **accumulation**[3] of decades of fossil-fuel abuse and vehicle **emissions**. In recent years, it has begun to affect the weather to such an **extent**[4] that it endangers the lives of millions and can potentially cause billions of dollars' worth of damage.

[2]   A study has concluded that the so-called "Asian brown cloud" has directly increased the **intensity**[5] of the area's tropical **cyclones**[6], particularly those forming over the Arabian Sea on India's west coast.

[3]   In India, harmful chemical emissions are now six times higher than they were in the 1950s. This increased **concentration**[7] of harmful **particles**[8] in the air acts like a **sponge**[9] that absorbs the sun's rays, affecting the area in which the sun can reach and heat the surface of the sea. This has caused an atmospheric **disturbance**[10] that has reduced the **vertical**[11] **wind shear**[12] in the area. Vertical wind shear is the difference in speed or direction between winds at different **altitudes**[13]. High vertical wind shear is an important factor in weakening the formation of cyclones. As the wind shear decreases, cyclones in the area can strengthen to a degree that can cause major problems when they hit land.

[4]   Cyclones are caused by hot air rising from the ocean surface. Cold air rushes in to replace it and heats up, and this cycle eventually causes a violent **circulation**[14] of wind and storms. Cyclones need to form vertically, so if the winds higher up in the atmosphere are traveling faster or in different directions to those in the lower atmosphere, this vertical formation will be disrupted, and the cyclone will **disintegrate**[15].

[5]   In the past, strong winds traveling in opposite directions (high vertical wind shear) would **substantially**[16] reduce the frequency of cyclone formation in the Arabian Sea. However, with the brown cloud weakening the wind shear, cyclones

▼ chemical emissions

Key Words

1. filthy 骯髒的 (a.)   2. smear 汙跡 (n.)   3. accumulation 堆積 (n.)   4. extent 程度 (n.)
5. intensity 強度 (n.)   6. cyclone 氣旋 (n.)   7. concentration 集中 (n.)   8. particle 粒子 (n.)
9. sponge 海綿 (n.)   10. disturbance 擾亂 (n.)   11. vertical 垂直的 (a.)   12. wind shear 風切 (n.)
13. altitude 高度 (n.)   14. circulation 循環 (n.)   15. disintegrate 分解 (v.)
16. substantially 大致上；基本上 (adv.)   17. tackle 著手處理 (v.)

◀ Cyclone Phet in 2010

in this area have grown in intensity. Cyclone Gonu, in 2007, was the strongest ever cyclone in the area, causing $4.4 billion worth of damages and killing 78 people. It was followed in 2010 by Cyclone Phet, which caused 47 deaths. To get these storms under control, India must **tackle**[17] the causes of the brown cloud—which, in such a rapidly developing country, may be easier said than done.

Questions

____ 1. Which of the following is the main idea of the article? ◆Main Idea◆
   a The Asian brown cloud is partly a result of vehicle emissions.
   b Many people have been killed by cyclones in recent years.
   c Pollution in India has increased dramatically since the 50s.
   d Pollution in India is affecting the weather in serious ways.

____ 2. What is this article about? ◆Subject Matter◆
   a How, why, and when cyclones form.
   b The relationship between cyclones and the Asian brown cloud.
   c Scientists who conducted a study into cyclones.
   d The cost of damage caused by cyclones around the Arabian Sea.

____ 3. Which of the following statements is NOT true? ◆Supporting Details◆
   a High vertical wind shear disrupts cyclone formation.
   b The Asian brown cloud has weakened the area's vertical wind shear.
   c In the past, the vertical wind shear over the Arabian Sea was low.
   d The Asian brown cloud absorbs the sun's rays.

____ 4. In the passage, what is implied about pollution? ◆Inference◆
   a It can cause extreme weather.   b It stops cyclones forming.
   c It doesn't influence the weather.   d It is primarily an Asian phenomenon.

____ 5. What does the word **emissions** mean in the first paragraph? ◆Words in Context◆
   a Strong violent winds often found over oceans.
   b Substances discharged into the atmosphere.
   c People who campaign on environmental issues.
   d Instruments used for studying extreme weather.

____ 6. In the first paragraph, what does the writer indicate with the word **like**?
   ◆Clarifying Devices◆
   a An example.   b A personal preference.
   c A contradiction.   d A comparison.

Week 13 Day 7

Culture

▼ Professional mourners kneel and wail in agony over the deceased. (photo by Liu Jun-Lin)

▼ Professional mourners attend funerals to grieve on behalf of the family of the deceased. (photo by Liu Jun-Lin)

79
(079)

Tears for Hire

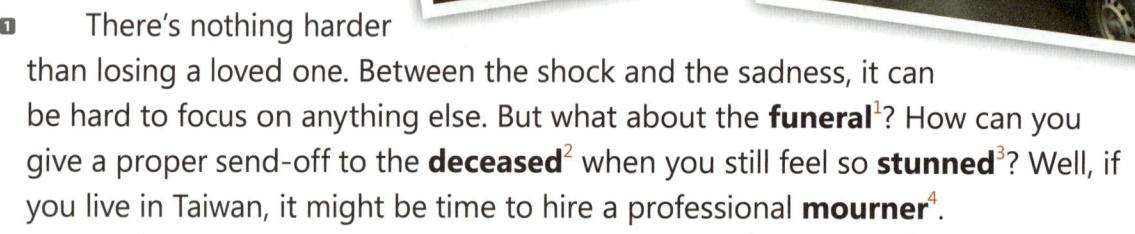

1   There's nothing harder than losing a loved one. Between the shock and the sadness, it can be hard to focus on anything else. But what about the **funeral**[1]? How can you give a proper send-off to the **deceased**[2] when you still feel so **stunned**[3]? Well, if you live in Taiwan, it might be time to hire a professional **mourner**[4].

2   Professional mourners attend funerals to **grieve**[5] on **behalf**[6] of the family of the deceased. Dressed in white robes, they will kneel and **wail**[7] in **agony**[8] over someone they never met. Their performance serves two purposes. First, it shows that the deceased was a wonderful person who will be greatly missed. Second, it **spares**[9] the family from having to "perform" while they're still dealing with their loss.

3   **Mourning**[10] can be big money in Taiwan. A family can pay over NT$200,000 for a funeral **parade**[11] that includes professional mourners. You might be thinking: "That's a lot of money! Professional mourners really have it made!" But the job is actually much harder than it looks. You must be able to change your **emotional**[12] state instantly, **shifting**[13] from happy to sad. You also need to know how to read a crowd. Professional mourners need to strike a perfect balance in their grieving. They must show sadness and agony, but not have it appear too **exaggerated**[14] or humorous. Going too far risks **insulting**[15] the family and their lost loved one in the afterlife.

4   The idea of professional mourners may seem strange to some cultures. It's not unusual for Taiwan's mourners to show up in **zany**[16] news articles. However, this is not a joke or some money-making trick. The practice is thousands of years old, and rooted in ancient Chinese culture. Parents used to marry off

Key Words

❶ funeral 葬禮 (n.)   ❷ deceased 亡者 (n.)   ❸ stunned 目瞪口呆的 (a.)   ❹ mourner 哀悼者；送葬者 (n
❺ grieve 悲痛 (v.)   ❻ behalf 代表 (n.)   ❼ wail 慟哭 (v.)   ❽ agony 極度痛苦 (n.)   ❾ spare 使避免 (v.)
❿ mourn 哀悼 (v.)   ⓫ parade 遊行 (n.)   ⓬ emotional 情緒化的 (a.)   ⓭ shift 轉換 (v.)
⓮ exaggerate 誇大 (v.)   ⓯ insult 侮辱 (v.)   ⓰ zany 稀奇古怪的 (a.)

▼ a terra cotta mourner, 1550–1295 BC (cc by Rama)

their daughters to distant lands. When a parent died, it wasn't easy for the daughters to come home and mourn them. Therefore, someone was hired nearby to mourn in her place. The practice wasn't just limited to China. There are examples of professional mourners in ancient Greece, India, and some African countries as well.

Questions

____ 1. Which sentence is closest in meaning to the main point? ◆Main Idea◆
   a It is very hard for people to lose their loved ones.
   b Professional mourning is an ancient custom that's still popular.
   c A funeral parade can cost a family a fortune.
   d Professional mourners make a lot of money in Taiwan.

____ 2. What does this passage describe? ◆Subject Matter◆
   a A funeral parade.   b An emotion.   c A job.   d The deceased.

____ 3. According to the article, which of the following is a benefit provided by professional mourners? ◆Supporting Details◆
   a They make a lot of money for the family.
   b They help the family get over their loss.
   c They help reduce the cost of the funeral.
   d They show that the deceased was a great person.

____ 4. What can we infer from the third paragraph? ◆Inference◆
   a Being a professional mourner takes some serious skills.
   b All professional mourners are children.
   c A professional mourner can never sit down.
   d Many professional mourners are scared of crowds.

____ 5. What does it mean to **have it made**, as in the third paragraph? ◆Words in Context◆
   a You are guaranteed to be successful.
   b You are seeing something for the first time.
   c You are preserving old traditions.
   d You are doing a job that you love.

____ 6. How does the writer begin the passage? ◆Clarifying Devices◆
   a By listing the steps in a process.
   b By encouraging us to imagine how something feels.
   c By describing the history of professional mourning.
   d By telling a personal story about their life.

Funerary Practices in Different Cultures

- burial/interment
- cremation
- burial at sea/river
- sky burial
- burial in a coral reef
- flower burial

(cc by Vladimir Menkov)

192

Week 14

Day 1 Health & Body	80 **A Challenging Diagnosis**	194
Day 2 Nature	81 **Synthetic Signal Blockers**	196
Day 3 Mystery	82 **Can the Future Really be Known?**	198
Day 4 Social Behavior	83 **Breaking the Habit**	200
Day 5 Environment	84 **The Stolen Hour**	202
Day 6 People	85 **The Heroes Who Heal**	204
Day 7 Sports	86 **En Garde!**	206

Health & Body

A Challenging Diagnosis[1]

1. I told the patient that I needed to fill out some paperwork, but in reality I'm not sure how I should **proceed**[2] on this one. It might just be a classic case of the mental disorder called **schizophrenia**[3], but something doesn't seem right.

2. While no one is totally sure what causes schizophrenia, we do know some things that increase the chances of getting the disease. There are definitely a few **red flags**[4] in this patient's background. First of all, his sister has been diagnosed with schizophrenia, meaning he has a 6.5% chance of developing it himself. What's more, the patient has a history of drug abuse involving **marijuana**[5] and **cocaine**[6]. That can be another **contributing**[7] factor. He's also twenty years old, which is about the time when schizophrenia usually starts to manifest itself.

3. It's certainly true that his symptoms don't **resemble**[8] the **paranoid**[9] type of schizophrenia. He isn't hearing any voices in his head, thinking he's better than everyone else, or becoming **suspicious**[10] that people are out to get him. However, he is definitely displaying symptoms of other kinds of schizophrenia. He has **isolated**[11] himself from his friends, doesn't display much emotion, and can't sleep at night. Most troubling, he's having problems **formulating**[12] sentences. His speech is becoming distorted because his mind cannot think in an **orderly**[13] and logical fashion. This might be a sign that he's developing a case of disorganized schizophrenia.

▼ Patients with schizophrenia suffer from hallucinations.

4. He could be one of the 3.2 million Americans who suffer from schizophrenia, or he could just be a depressed young man who has fried his brain with illegal drugs.

5. I always want to be absolutely sure before I diagnose schizophrenia because the

Key Words

1. diagnosis 診斷 (n.) ❷ proceed 繼續進行 (v.) ❸ schizophrenia 思覺失調症 (n.)
4. red flag 示警紅旗 (n.) ❺ marijuana 大麻 (n.) ❻ cocaine 古柯鹼 (n.) ❼ contribute 造成 (v.)
8. resemble 類似 (v.) ❾ paranoid 偏執的 (a.) ❿ suspicious 多疑的 (a.) ⓫ isolate 使孤立 (v.)
12. formulate 系統地闡述 (v.) ⓭ orderly 有條理的 (a.) ⓮ antipsychotic 抗精神病的 (a.)
15. prescribe 開藥方 (v.) ⓰ tremor 顫抖 (n.) ⓱ medicate 用藥治療 (v.)

antipsychotic[14] drugs used to treat it can be very damaging. The last person I **prescribed**[15] antipsychotic drugs to suffered from side effects such as dizziness, **tremors**[16], and weight gain. He even started to move in slow motion sometimes. On the other hand, bad things can happen if schizophrenia goes untreated. Not only do most patients eventually try to **medicate**[17] themselves with illegal drugs, but over one-third of them will attempt suicide at some point during their illness.

[6] I think I'll wait and see how his symptoms develop. I'll tell him to come back in a month.

▶ self-portrait of a person with schizophrenia

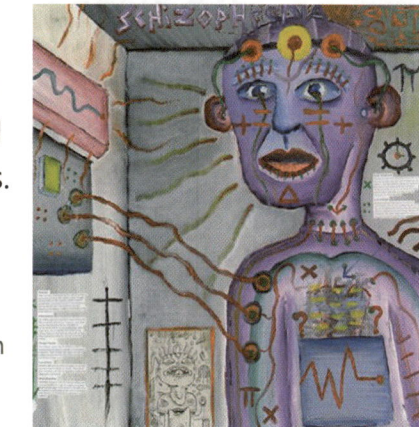

Questions

1. What would you say is the main idea of the article? ◆Main Idea◆
   a. A doctor considers how to diagnose his patient.
   b. A doctor worries about his patient's drug abuse.
   c. A doctor struggles with his own mental disorder.
   d. A doctor diagnoses his patient with a mental disorder.

2. What does article focus on? ◆Subject Matter◆
   a. Marijuana.   b. Patients.   c. Schizophrenia.   d. Drug abuse.

3. Which of the following statements is NOT true? ◆Supporting Details◆
   a. Over two million Americans suffer from schizophrenia.
   b. Hearing voices is a symptom of paranoid schizophrenia.
   c. Distorted speech is a symptom of disorganized schizophrenia.
   d. Drug abuse does not increase chances of schizophrenia.

4. What can we infer about schizophrenia from this article? ◆Inference◆
   a. It is contagious.   b. It is hard to treat.
   c. It has no possible treatment.   d. It goes away on its own eventually.

5. What does the word **distorted** in the third paragraph most likely mean?
   ◆Words in Context◆
   a. Changed from its normal state.   b. Extremely loud.
   c. Extremely soft.   d. Full of long pauses.

6. What form does this article take? ◆Text Form◆
   a. An encyclopedia entry.   b. A personal narrative.
   c. A formal letter.   d. An interview.

Week 14 | Day 2

Nature

81 Synthetic[1] Signal Blockers

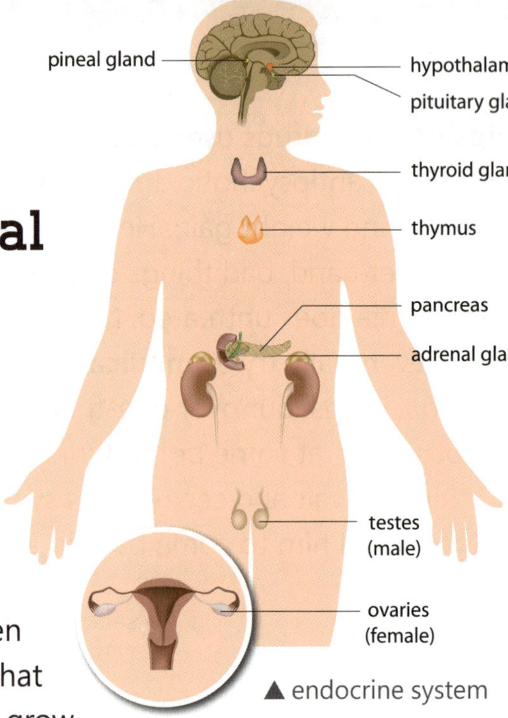

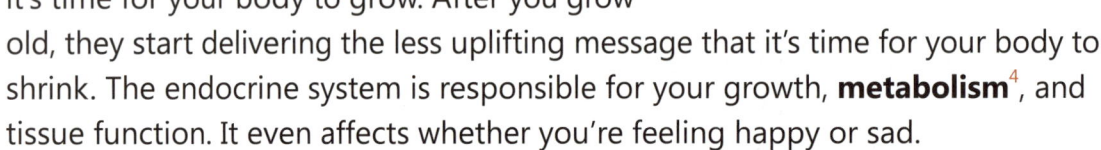

[081]

pineal gland
hypothalamus
pituitary gland
thyroid gland
thymus
pancreas
adrenal glands
testes (male)
ovaries (female)

▲ endocrine system

1 The human **endocrine**[2] system is a complex series of glands and pathways that help **hormones**[3] travel from one point in our body to another. Think of these hormones like workers in a tiny biological postal service. Their function is to deliver **messages**. For example, when you're young, they deliver the message that it's time for your body to grow. After you grow old, they start delivering the less uplifting message that it's time for your body to shrink. The endocrine system is responsible for your growth, **metabolism**[4], and tissue function. It even affects whether you're feeling happy or sad.

2 What happens when something starts **interfering**[5] with the endocrine system? That's what scientists around the world are currently trying to figure out. They are studying the chemicals that block our body's biological postal service. These endocrine **disruptors**[6] are synthetic chemicals that humans have created. They have **seeped**[7] into natural environments all around the world. Endocrine disruptors are known to harm living organisms, and they have been linked to cancer and other **reproductive**[8] **disabilities**[9] in humans.

3 Dichlorodiphenyltrichloroethane, or DDT, is a classic example of a synthetic chemical that is an endocrine disruptor. It was **banned**[10] in the United States in 1972 after it was discovered that DDT caused birds to lay eggs with soft shells. DDT also harms human reproductive health. It is still being used in some parts of Africa.

4 The World Health Organization (WHO) has released several reports **outlining**[11] the threat that endocrine disruptors pose to wildlife. These reports show that **mammals**[12], **reptiles**[13], birds, and fish species are suffering from altered gender ratios, reproductive deficiencies, and growth disorders. However, the results aren't totally **conclusive**[14]. Currently, there are so many pollutants in

Key Words

1. synthetic 合成的 (a.)   2. endocrine 內分泌的 (a.)   3. hormone 荷爾蒙 (n.)
4. metabolism 新陳代謝 (n.)   5. interfere 妨礙 (v.)   6. disruptor 干擾素 (n.)   7. seep 滲出 (v.)
8. reproductive 生殖的 (a.)   9. disability 殘疾 (n.)   10. ban 禁止 (v.)   11. outline 概述 (v.)
12. mammal 哺乳類 (n.)   13. reptile 爬蟲類 (n.)   14. conclusive 決定性的 (a.)   15. laboratory 實驗室 (n.)

196

◀ DDT causes birds to lay eggs with soft shells. (cc by Ryan Somma)

natural environments that it's difficult for these studies to determine what is and isn't being caused by endocrine disruptors.

[5] Only studies that have been conducted in **laboratories**[15] have proven that endocrine disruptors can harm humans. So far, there have been no conclusive studies linking human disease to endocrine disruptors that already exist in our environment. However, several studies have proven that endocrine disruptors are negatively impacting mammal species in their natural habitats. Since humans are mammals, doesn't that mean that we're in trouble, too?

Questions

____ 1. Which of the following is the main topic of this article? ◆Main Idea◆
   a Endocrine disruptors as a threat to humans.
   b Endocrine disruptors' threat to wildlife.
   c An analysis of various endocrine disruptors.
   d An explanation of the endocrine system.

____ 2. What is this article about? ◆Subject Matter◆
   a Certain pollutants.　　　　　b The endocrine system.
   c The life cycle of birds.　　　d Reproductive health.

____ 3. Which of the following is NOT true? ◆Supporting Details◆
   a Endocrine disruptors have been proven to harm mammals.
   b Hormones are a part of the human endocrine system.
   c Endocrine disruptors are man-made synthetic chemicals.
   d WHO has concluded that endocrine disruptors are not a problem.

____ 4. Which of the following is likely true? ◆Inference◆
   a The benefits of DDT outweigh the drawbacks.
   b There have been other chemicals like DDT.
   c All endocrine disruptors occur naturally.
   d WHO studies aren't thorough enough.

____ 5. What does the word **messages** in the first paragraph refer to? ◆Words in Context◆
   a Noxious poison.　　　　　b Biological information.
   c Important nutrients.　　　d Oxygen molecules.

____ 6. Which of the following best describes the author's tone by the end of the article? ◆Author's Tone◆
   a Playful.　　b Concerned.　　c Celebratory.　　d Uncaring.

Week 14 Day 3

Mystery

▼ preface to *The Prophecies*   ▶ portrait of Nostradamus

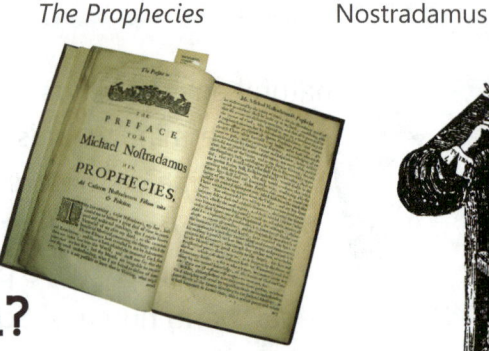

82
[082]

Can the Future Really be Known?

1   Some say Nostradamus (1503–1566) predicted the French Revolution, the rise of Adolf Hitler, the 9/11 attacks in the United States, and Donald Trump's **presidency**[1]. Others dismiss his **predictions**[2] as nonsense.

2   His most famous work, *The Prophecies* (published between 1555 and 1558), contains a future history of the world up to the year 3797. His most famous predictions (though there are over 1,000 in *The Prophecies*) are probably the following two: "Beasts mad with hunger will swim across rivers / Most of the battle will be against Hister," and "At forty-five degrees, the sky will burn / Fire will approach the great new city."

3   Believers are quick to point out the similarity between "Hister" and "Hitler," convinced that Nostradamus named the infamous **dictator**[3]. However, "Hister" was the ancient name for the Danube River in central Europe, and has nothing to do with Hitler. The second **prophecy**[4] is supposed to be a description of 9/11, and the "new city" New York, which lies at **latitude**[5] 45°. In fact, New York is at latitude 40° 43', and the "new city" probably refers to Naples, whose Greek name, Neapolis, actually means "new city."

4   The main **criticism**[6] of Nostradamus's prophecies is that they are often **repetitions**[7] of past events projected into the future in the **assumption**[8] that history will repeat itself. It's also convenient that he left his prophecies undated and in no particular order. It has been suggested that the famous 9/11 prophecy is a repetition of the 1139 **invasion**[9] of Naples in the same year that the nearby volcano Mount Vesuvius **erupted**[10].

5   His general statements, their **overinterpretation**[11], and lines taken out of context have all fed the myth of Nostradamus's mystical ability to see into the future.

6   In 2000, after George Bush was elected president of the United States, a **verse**[12] apparently written by Nostradamus was **circulated**[13] around the

Key Words

[1] **presidency** 總統職務 (n.)   [2] **prediction** 預言 (n.)   [3] **dictator** 獨裁者 (n.)
[4] **prophecy** 預言；先知 (n.)   [5] **latitude** 緯度 (n.)   [6] **criticism** 批評 (n.)   [7] **repetition** 重複 (n.)
[8] **assumption** 假設 (n.)   [9] **invasion** 入侵 (n.)   [10] **erupt** 噴出 (v.)   [11] **overinterpretation** 過度詮釋 (n.)
[12] **verse** 詩 (n.)   [13] **circulate** 流通 (v.)   [14] **millennium** 千禧年 (n.)   [15] **foreseer** 預言家 (n.)

▶ Nostradamus predicted Donald Trump 400 years ago.

Internet, predicting Bush's election. "Come the **millennium**[14], month 12 / In the home of the greatest power / The village idiot will come forth / To be acclaimed the leader." Incredible accuracy! It was later revealed, however, that this was written not by the great **foreseer**[15], but rather by an Internet **prankster** looking for a laugh.

Questions

___ 1. What is the main idea of this article? ◆Main Idea◆
   a Nostradamus wrote a book called *The Prophecies*, containing 1,000 predictions.
   b Many of Nostradamus's predictions are repetitions of past events projected into the future.
   c Despite believers' insistence, the evidence for doubting Nostradamus's powers is very strong.
   d Nostradamus predicted some of the modern world's most important events.

___ 2. What is the main focus of this article? ◆Subject Matter◆
   a The evidence against Nostradamus's powers.
   b The style and structure of *The Prophecies*.
   c The 9/11 attacks in the United States.
   d The election of George Bush in 2000.

___ 3. Which of the following statements is NOT true? ◆Supporting Details◆
   a Nostradamus's statements are often taken out of context.
   b New York City lies at latitude 45°.
   c Nostradamus did not predict the election of George Bush.
   d The word "Hister" refers to a river, not to a dictator.

___ 4. Which of the following statements is probably true? ◆Inference◆
   a Nostradamus was very unpopular during his lifetime.
   b Nostradamus was an uneducated man.
   c Nostradamus admitted that his prophecies were nonsense.
   d Nostradamus had a good knowledge of history.

___ 5. In the last paragraph, the writer mentions an Internet prankster. Who is a **prankster**? ◆Words in Context◆
   a A joker.   b A historian.   c A fan.   d A believer.

___ 6. How does the writer end the article? ◆Clarifying Devices◆
   a With an unanswered question.   b With a suggestion.
   c With a warning.   d With a revelation.

Week 14 Day 4

Social Behavior

83 Breaking the Habit

▶ Frequent, excessive hand washing occurs in some people with OCD.

1 I'm Dave. I'm Dave. I'm Dave. Whoops, sorry about that. Looks like it happened again! My **obsessive**[1]-**compulsive**[2] **disorder**[3] (OCD) sometimes makes me write things three times for good luck.

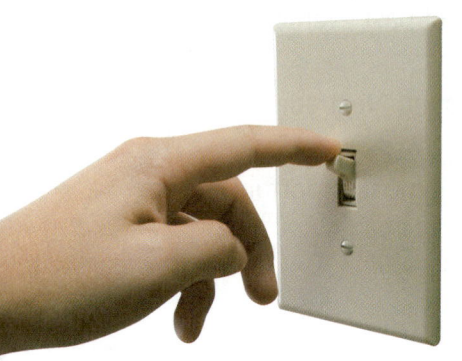

2 I was first diagnosed with OCD five years ago. My problems began when I found myself developing all of these **weird**[4] habits that I couldn't control. For example, I would be scared to go to bed if I didn't turn the lights on and off five times. That's also when I started saying and writing everything three times in a row. And let me **assure**[5] you, this makes it hard to have normal conversations with people.

▲ The habit of turning lights on and off helps put the minds of OCD sufferers at ease.

3 The doctor told me that OCD is very common. In fact, it's diagnosed almost as frequently as **asthma**[6]. He said that it was nothing to be **ashamed**[7] of. All of us have habits in life, like checking to make sure the door is locked before going to sleep. People with obsessive-compulsive disorder have habits that are . . . Well, let's just say their habits are a bit more **exotic** than normal people's.

4 He also told me that symptoms vary from person to person. Some OCD sufferers **occasionally**[8] have a thought that won't go away. It may make them uncomfortable or **anxious**[9] for a while, but it will eventually disappear. Other people experience much more serious OCD symptoms. They might have uncomfortable thoughts that make them anxious all of the time. They tend to develop habits in order to help put their mind at ease. One minute they're feeling nervous, and the next they're washing their hands for two hours before they'll even touch their lunch.

Key Words

❶ obsessive 過於執著的 (a.) ❷ compulsive 強迫性的 (a.) ❸ disorder 失調 (n.) ❹ weird 怪異的 (a.)
❺ assure 確保 (v.) ❻ asthma 氣喘 (n.) ❼ ashamed 羞愧的 (a.) ❽ occasionally 偶爾 (adv.)
❾ anxious 焦慮的 (a.) ❿ undergo 經歷；接受 (v.) ⓫ ritual 儀式 (n.) ⓬ exposure 暴露 (n.)
⓭ therapy 療法 (n.) ⓮ trigger 引起 (v.) ⓯ urge 衝動 (n.)

[5]   I know what you're thinking: Why aren't I writing everything in this article three times in a row? Well, the doctor didn't just tell me what OCD was; he also told me how I could treat it. I **underwent**[10] two kinds of treatment—**ritual**[11] prevention and **exposure**[12] **therapy**[13]. These treatments exposed me to circumstances that **triggered**[14] my habits. Think of it as getting practice resisting the **urge**[15] to indulge in my exotic habits. So far, the treatment has worked very well, but there's still some work to do. Still some work to—Hah! Gotcha!

▶ Excessive nail biting is another symptom of OCD.

Questions

____ 1. Which of the following can summarize this article? ·········· ◆Main Idea◆
- a Universal habits.
- b One person's experience with OCD.
- c The life and times of Dave.
- d How to conquer your own anxiety.

____ 2. Which of the following could be another title for this article? ········ ◆Subject Matter◆
- a My OCD View of the World.
- b Dave's Struggles to Make Friends.
- c Notice Your Everyday Habits.
- d Treatment Options for OCD.

____ 3. Which of the following statements is true? ·········· ◆Supporting Details◆
- a Dave discovered that his OCD cannot be cured.
- b OCD is diagnosed far less often than asthma.
- c OCD symptoms are usually the same for everyone.
- d Ritual prevention and exposure therapy were effective for Dave.

____ 4. What can we infer from this article? ·········· ◆Inference◆
- a OCD makes people go crazy all the time.
- b OCD treatment can take a long time.
- c OCD treatment is very expensive.
- d OCD treatment is very inexpensive.

____ 5. In the third paragraph, what does the word **exotic** mean? ········ ◆Words in Context◆
- a Harmful.
- b Unusual.
- c Long-lasting.
- d Exaggerated.

____ 6. Which of the following actions mentioned in the article is caused by OCD?
·········· ◆Cause and Effect◆
- a Having a normal conversation with people.
- b Making weird thoughts go away.
- c Getting diagnosed by a doctor.
- d Turning the light on and off five times.

Week 14 Day 4 Breaking the Habit

Week 14 Day 5

Environment

84 The Stolen Hour

[1] "Give us back our stolen hour!" Britons demanded as they **protested**[1] against the introduction of Daylight Saving Time (DST) in the 1900s. The idea of altering the clocks to move an hour of daylight from the morning to the evening during summer has been **controversial**[2] throughout its history. People have argued that the practice saves energy, reduces crime, and prevents traffic accidents. Others are not so convinced, and studies **conducted**[3] over the past decade have shown mixed results.

[2] The idea was first **implemented**[4] in Germany during World War I in an attempt to **conserve**[5] coal during wartime. Britain soon followed with its own Summer Time but so did **confusion**[6] and **chaos**[7], with some **institutions**[8] following the changes and some simply ignoring them. One writer **resented**[9] the laws in a more **poetic**[10] manner, expressing his **distaste**[11] at being forced to favor the sun over the moon.

[3] Despite the early controversy, more than 70 countries currently use DST. The United States moves its clocks forward an hour at 2 a.m. on the second Sunday in March and back an hour on the first Sunday in November. Some states, however, still do not apply DST, and in the past even some areas within individual states refused to **observe**[12] DST while the rest of the state did.

[4] It was originally thought that DST would reduce energy consumption as people would use less electric lighting in the evening due to the increased hours of daylight. However, recent studies have suggested that this benefit has been **offset** by the increased use of home air conditioners, which people use for longer on long summer evenings.

[5] Brighter evenings have reduced the number of traffic accidents in countries which observe DST, but studies have also noticed a **spike**[13] in the number of accidents during the week after the clocks change, possibly due to the sudden **interruption**[14] of people's sleeping patterns.

▶ The United States moves its clocks forward an hour at 2 a.m. on the second Sunday in March and back an hour on the first Sunday in November.

Key Words

[1] protest 抗議 (v.)　[2] controversial 有爭議的 (a.)　[3] conduct 進行 (v.)　[4] implement 實行 (v.)
[5] conserve 節省 (v.)　[6] confusion 困惑 (n.)　[7] chaos 混亂 (n.)　[8] institution 機構 (n.)
[9] resent 憤慨 (v.)　[10] poetic 有詩意的 (a.)　[11] distaste 嫌惡 (n.)　[12] observe 遵行 (v.)
[13] spike 突增；尖刺 (n.)　[14] interruption 中斷 (n.)　[15] civilian 平民 (n.)

▶ Brighter evenings have reduced the number of traffic accidents in countries that observe DST.

6   One certain good thing to come out of DST, however, happened in 1999, when a group of West Bank terrorists (on DST) delivered bombs to a cell in Israel (not on DST) but ignored the time difference when setting the timers for their bombs. The bombs went off one hour earlier than planned, killing three terrorists instead of the intended **civilians**[15].

Questions

____ 1. Which of the following is the main topic of the article? ◆Main Idea◆
   a The question of Daylight Saving Time.
   b The benefits of Daylight Saving Time.
   c Daylight Saving Time and its effect on terrorism.
   d Daylight Saving Time in the United States.

____ 2. What is this article about? ◆Subject Matter◆
   a A national pastime.
   b Germany during WWI.
   c A theory about the nature of time.
   d Making summer evenings longer.

____ 3. Which of the following statements is NOT true? ◆Supporting Details◆
   a Germany implemented DST to save on coal.
   b Britain implemented DST before Germany.
   c A terrorist plot failed because of DST.
   d DST interrupts people's sleeping patterns.

____ 4. What can we possibly conclude from this article? ◆Inference◆
   a DST has stopped being a controversial subject.
   b DST caused an increase in the use of home air conditioners.
   c Americans have mixed opinions about DST.
   d All countries that use DST change their clocks at the same time as the United States does.

____ 5. What does the word **offset** in the fourth paragraph most likely mean?
   ◆Words in Context◆
   a Increased.   **b** Countered.   **c** Recorded.   **d** Used.

____ 6. What was the original cause of DST? ◆Cause and Effect◆
   a A desire for fewer traffic accidents.
   b A desire for more sunlight.
   c A desire to reduce crime.
   d A desire to conserve energy resources.

Week 14 Day 5 The Stolen Hour

Week 14 Day 6

People

85 The Heroes Who Heal

◀ countries in which Doctors Without Borders has operated (cc by M.alnuaimy)

1 In 1971 a group of French doctors and journalists created an international organization that would provide emergency medical care to victims of war, natural disasters, or disease regardless of their race, religion, or political beliefs. They named the organization Médecins Sans Frontières, or Doctors Without Borders, as it has become known in the United States.

2 Made up of all kinds of **specialists**[1] from every aspect of the health industry, the organization provides vital medical support in some of the world's most **deprived**[2] and war-torn countries.

3 These doctors, nurses, **administrators**[3], and planning experts are active in over 70 countries and operate under a firm **code**[4] of **ethics**[5], which requires them to treat everyone equally without showing discrimination. The organization also remains strictly politically and religiously **neutral**[6] and does not take sides in war. It does this so that it can remain free of any **constraints**[7] that could affect its ability to give aid where it's most needed.

4 It also maintains its independence by making private donations its main source of income. There are over 5.7 million private **donors**[8] that come from countries all around the world. Only 10 percent of its funds come from governments.

5 Often first on the scene in any crisis, Doctors Without Borders is constantly in the thick of disasters, be they man-made or natural, sometimes witnessing scenes of real **brutality**[9] and violence. In order to provide the best medical care, they are continually in touch with local people on the ground. As such, they have a unique and **thorough**[10] **perspective**[11] on the world's most desperate situations.

6 Using this firsthand knowledge, the organization frequently speaks out against human rights abuses, medical **neglect**[12], and instances of violence that do not get sufficient attention from the media.

Key Words

1 specialist 專家 (n.)　2 deprived 貧困的 (a.)　3 administrator 行政人員 (n.)　4 code 規範 (n.)
5 ethic 倫理標準 (n.)　6 neutral 中立的 (a.)　7 constraint 限制 (n.)　8 donor 捐贈者 (n.)
9 brutality 殘忍 (n.)　10 thorough 徹底的 (a.)　11 perspective 看法 (n.)　12 neglect 忽視 (n.)
13 intervention 侵略 (n.)　14 massacre 大屠殺 (n.)　15 condemn 譴責 (v.)
16 humanitarian 人道主義的 (a.)

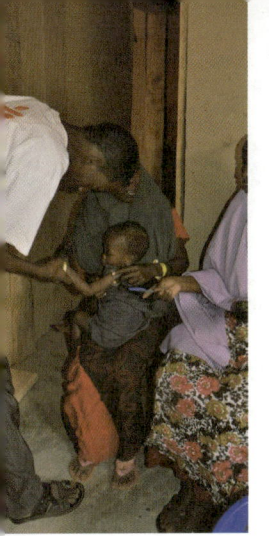

◀ an MSF health worker examines a child (cc by DFID)

[7] A peaceful organization, they have only ever called for military **intervention**[13] once, during the 1994 **massacres**[14] in Rwanda. However, they have also strongly **condemned**[15] the actions of the governments of several African and Asian countries, often working directly with the United Nations.

[8] In 1999, the organization was awarded the Nobel Peace Prize for its exceptional **humanitarian**[16] work around the world. And, true to form, it used the money to fund the fight against neglected diseases.

Questions

____ 1. What would you say is the main idea of the article? ◆Main Idea◆
   a Doctors Without Borders won a Nobel Prize for its work.
   b Many people donate money to Doctors Without Borders.
   c Doctors Without Borders has huge political influence.
   d Doctors Without Borders helps countless people around the world.

____ 2. What is this article about? ◆Subject Matter◆
   a War crimes.
   b French hospitals.
   c The importance of the media.
   d An international aid organization.

____ 3. Which of the following statements is NOT true about Doctors Without Borders? ◆Supporting Details◆
   a It is politically and religiously neutral.
   b It has never suggested military intervention.
   c It is active in over 70 countries.
   d It operates under a strict ethical code.

____ 4. Which of the following is probably true? ◆Inference◆
   a Working for Doctors Without Borders is dangerous.
   b Doctors Without Borders spends its money unwisely.
   c The UN considers Doctors Without Borders unreliable.
   d Doctors Without Borders has little effect on people's lives.

____ 5. What does the word **discrimination** in paragraph three mean? ◆Words in Context◆
   a Medical training.
   b Biased treatment.
   c Considerate behavior.
   d Intelligence.

____ 6. Which of the following best describes the passage? ◆Text Form◆
   a An informative article.
   b A retelling of a myth.
   c An opinion piece.
   d An article giving advice.

Week 14 Day 7

Sports

▶ medieval fencing

86

En Garde!

1. "Sir, I **demand satisfaction**[1]!" This cry, heard among the upper classes of early modern England, would be shouted by a man who felt his honor had been insulted. Unless an apology was swiftly offered by the offending party, a **duel** would follow to settle the score, sometimes resulting in death.

2. Fencing, a sport in which two people **engage**[2] in close combat using one of three different kinds of swords, is the modern **manifestation**[3] of these duels, which were fought in countries all over Europe.

3. Fencers stand on a **piste**[4], which is a long strip usually 2 meters wide and 14 meters long, with two lines on either side of the midpoint where the fencers take their starting positions. Fencers stand on these lines and **salute**[5] each other, then, the **referee**[6] calls "*En garde!*" This is the signal for the fencers to put on their protective masks and raise their swords. After the match begins, whoever manages to score a hit (called a "touch") on their opponent's body gains a point, and five points wins a match.

4. In **medieval**[7] Europe, skill with a sword became unnecessary as the use of armor demanded strength, **hacking**[8], and heavy weapons to cut through an opponent's tough metal suit. However, the development of guns made armor useless, and swordplay became popular once again during the fifteenth century. The development of the rapier—a long, light sword—in the sixteenth century caused swordsmen to emphasize skill, speed, and technique over power. Later swords developed from the rapier were even lighter and pointed rather than sharp-edged, which encouraged **thrusting**[9] attacks rather than **slashing**[10].

5. Modern fencing weapons consist of three swords: the **foil**[11], the **épée**[12], and the **saber**[13]. The foil is light, flexible and pointed, the épée is slightly heavier, and the saber is an edged weapon, making

Key Words

1. demand satisfaction 要求決鬥   2. engage 從事 (v.)   3. manifestation 表現形式 (n.)
4. piste 擊劍劍道 (n.)   5. salute 行禮；致意 (v.)   6. referee 裁判 (n.)   7. medieval 中世紀的 (a.)
8. hack 劈；砍 (v.)   9. thrust 刺 (v.)   10. slash 猛砍 (v.)   11. foil 鈍劍 (n.)   12. épée 銳劍 (n.)
13. saber 軍刀 (n.)   14. stab 刺 (v.)

▶ Modern fencing counts on electronic scoring system to detect hits.

it perfect for cutting as well as **stabbing**[14]. In the past, fencing matches were scored by judges who would watch the match and shout if they saw a hit. However, this was unreliable and was replaced by the current electronic scoring system in which a flashing light is triggered when the system detects a hit, truly bringing the art of dueling into the modern era.

Questions

____ 1. Which of the following is the main idea of the article? ◆Main Idea◆
   a Fencing developed from early forms of close combat but is now a thoroughly modern sport.
   b Fencing regained popularity after guns made armor useless.
   c Fencers face each other with their swords raised.
   d Fencing is a sport which uses three kinds of swords.

____ 2. What is this article primarily about? ◆Subject Matter◆
   a Ancient ways of settling an argument.   b Different types of swords.
   c Electronic scoring.   d Competitive sword fighting.

____ 3. Which of the following statements is NOT true? ◆Supporting Details◆
   a Fencers must salute each other before starting a match.
   b Matches are usually played to five points.
   c Medieval armor could be pierced with a light sword.
   d Scoring a fencing match using judges was not always accurate.

____ 4. What does the last paragraph imply? ◆Inference◆
   a The modern scoring system is more accurate than the traditional one.
   b The traditional scoring system was more accurate than the modern one.
   c The traditional and modern scoring systems are equally accurate.
   d The modern scoring system is disliked by many fencers.

____ 5. What does the word **duel** in the first paragraph mean? ◆Words in Context◆
   a A serious talk between two people.   b A fight between two people.
   c A joke shared between two people.   d A formal dinner for two people.

____ 6. Which of the following best describes the article? ◆Text Form◆
   a A personal narrative about fencing for the first time.
   b A step-by-step guide to learning how to fence.
   c A biography of a famous fencer.
   d A brief introduction to the sport of fencing.

Three Swords of Modern Fencing

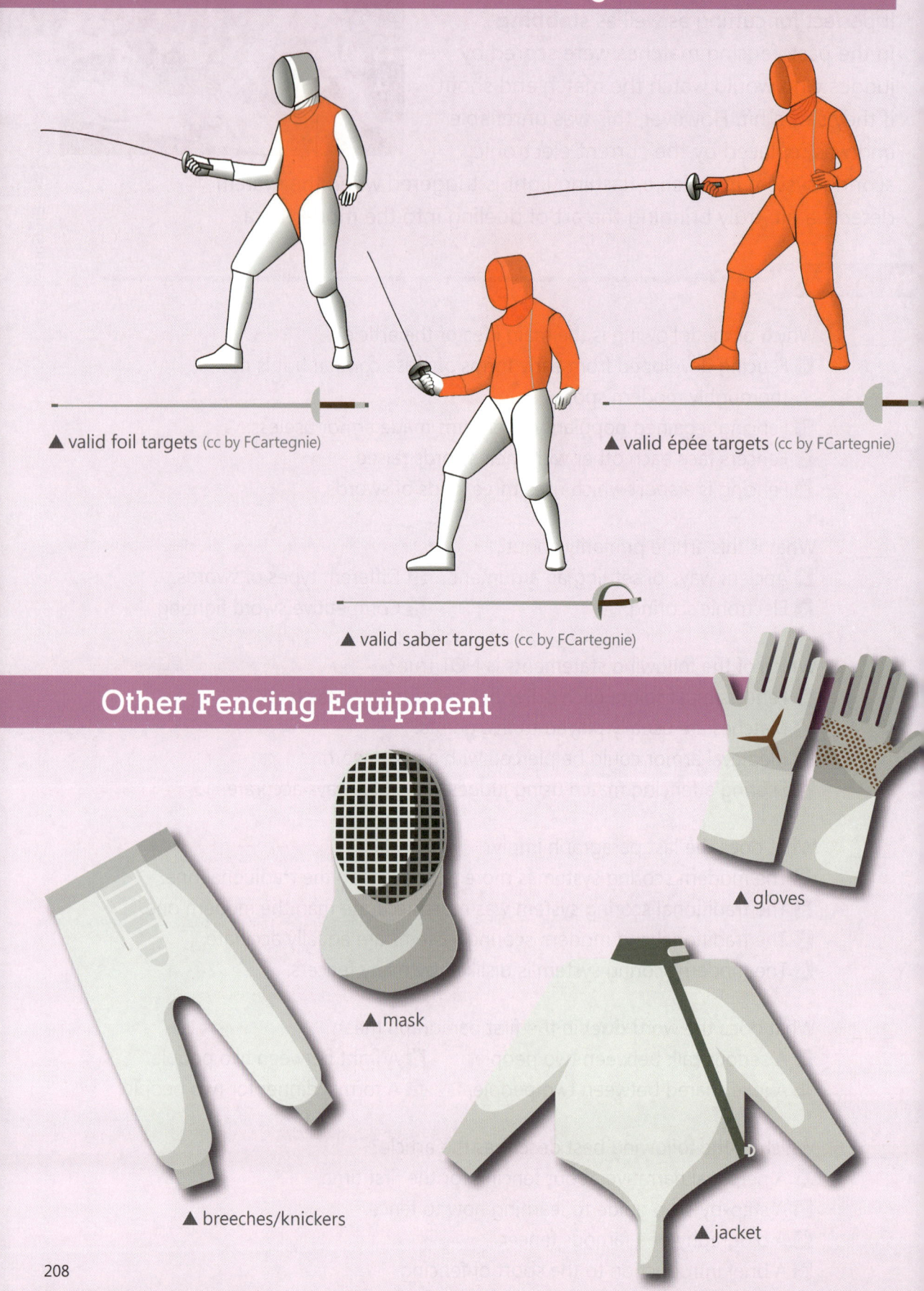

▲ valid foil targets (cc by FCartegnie)

▲ valid épée targets (cc by FCartegnie)

▲ valid saber targets (cc by FCartegnie)

Other Fencing Equipment

▲ gloves

▲ mask

▲ breeches/knickers

▲ jacket

Week 15

Day 1 Mystery	87	**Speaking Spooks**	210
Day 2 Social Behavior	88	**The Magic Social Number**	212
Day 3 People	89	**Education Where It's Needed Most**	214
Day 4 Sports	90	**Korean Combat!**	216
Day 5 Animals	91	**A Tale of Two Chimps**	218
Day 6 Social Behavior	92	**Trapped in a Small Space**	220
Day 7 Science	93	**Journey to the Center of the Earth**	222

Week 15　Day 1

Mystery

87
Speaking Spooks[1]

[1] In 1848, two sisters, Kate and Margaret Fox, said they could communicate with the dead. They claimed to hear loud **tapping**[2] sounds coming from their house in Hydesville, New York. People who visited them confirmed the tapping and that the girls could indeed communicate with the noisy spirit.

[2] Before long, thousands of **mediums**[3] had emerged who claimed **miraculous**[4] powers of being able to speak to the dead. In darkened rooms, with a small group of people, they would attempt to reach **departed**[5] loved ones.

▲ the Fox sisters: Margaret, Kate, and Leah (from left to right)

[3] Mediums would use many different methods to indicate that a spirit was present. Bells and balls were placed on the table, and as the medium spoke, the ball would move around, or the bell would ring without being touched. Some mediums would use spirit slates—two blank chalkboards tied together that, after calling a spirit, would be opened to **reveal**[6] a message written on the inside. However, many of these methods were **exposed**[7] as common magic tricks.

[4] Many modern **séances**[8] now take place in front of large audiences, with the medium providing personal messages from the spirit world. The medium often displays an **uncanny** knowledge of the **deceased**[9] as well as the audience member—sure proof that he is **genuinely**[10] talking to the spirits!

[5] However, **skeptics**[11] insist that mediums are simply using a **linguistic**[12] trick called "cold reading," which gives the impression of telling someone information, when actually the information is mostly being provided by the audience member himself.

[6] For example, a medium might claim to be hearing from a spirit whose name begins with P and who is repeatedly saying the number five. An audience

Key Words

❶ spook 鬼魂 (n.)　❷ tap 輕拍 (v.)　❸ medium 靈媒 (n.)　❹ miraculous 神奇的 (a.)
❺ departed 去世的 (a.)　❻ reveal 顯露 (v.)　❼ expose 使暴露 (v.)　❽ séance 降靈會 (n.)
❾ deceased 亡者 (n.)　❿ genuinely 真誠地 (adv.)　⓫ skeptic 懷疑者 (n.)　⓬ linguistic 語言的 (a.)
⓭ phenomenon 現象 (n.)　⓮ confess 坦承 (v.)　⓯ crack 使霹啪作響 (v.)

member picks up on this information and says, "That must be my father, Peter, who had five brothers." In fact, the letter P and number five could have applied to many audience members; meanwhile, the medium has actually not given any details at all, only appeared to do so.

[7] It may not come as a surprise, then, that in 1888 Margaret Fox, who had started the entire **phenomenon**[13], **confessed**[14] that the mysterious tapping was nothing more than she and her sister **cracking**[15] the joints of their toes.

▼ Ouija Board, used by mediums for communicating with the dead

Questions

____ 1. Which of the following is the main question that the article tries to answer? ◆Main Idea◆
   a How did the Fox sisters perform séances?
   b Are séances real or fake?
   c Are modern séances more effective?
   d What is the secret of the spirit slate?

____ 2. What is this article about? ◆Subject Matter◆
   a A dying language.
   b Different attitudes toward death.
   c Superstition in America.
   d A bizarre form of communication.

____ 3. Which of the following statements is NOT true? ◆Supporting Details◆
   a Many people believed the Fox sisters could contact the dead.
   b Séances do not take place in modern society.
   c Mediums used to use bells to prove spirits were present.
   d Many of the old mediums' methods were exposed as tricks.

____ 4. Which of the following does this article imply? ◆Inference◆
   a Modern mediums are not actually talking to the dead.
   b The nineteenth century mediums were certainly genuine.
   c To talk to the dead you need to use a chalkboard.
   d Margaret Fox's confession was false.

____ 5. What does the word **uncanny** in the fourth paragraph mean? ◆Words in Context◆
   a Simple.   b Ridiculous.   c Mysterious.   d Ordinary.

____ 6. Which of these best describes the author's tone towards the end of this article? ◆Author's Tone◆
   a Cheerful.   b Skeptical.   c Full of awe.   d Curious.

Week 15 Day 1 Speaking Spooks

Week 15 Day 2

Social Behavior

▶ People tend to form natural groups of about 150 people.

88

The Magic Social Number

1. From the earliest point in our **evolution**[1], we have been social animals. Living in hunter-gatherer groups, we created small societies based on complex **interpersonal** relationships and developed a broader **collective**[2] of ideas **dictating**[3] the rules of our social world.

2. Creating and maintaining these **bonds**[4] requires a skill that sociologists have termed "social action." These are actions which **take into account**[5] the reactions of others and can be altered according to these reactions. This cause-and-effect-based behavior results in firm social structures within which individuals can better organize their lives, and set and achieve goals.

3. During the past 200 years, however, people have gone from living in relatively small **rural**[6] societies to living in cities filled with millions of people. It is estimated that by 2050, 70 percent of the world's population will live in cities. So how do human beings, who for most of our evolutionary history have lived in small societies, **cope**[7] with the emergence of these city-centered super societies?

4. Robin Dunbar, a professor of evolutionary **anthropology**[8] at the University of Oxford, has suggested that there is actually a limit to the number of people we can maintain meaningful social **interactions**[9] with. Dunbar says that human beings tend to form natural groups of about 150 people. This number is roughly the size of traditional hunter-gatherer tribes, the average size of a medieval village, and the number of friends the average person stays in contact with on Facebook.

5. Dunbar has divided this number into layers of **intimate**[10] friends, good friends, friends, and **acquaintances**[11]. The level of **intimacy**[12] required between these 150 people is described by Dunbar as "people you wouldn't feel embarrassed about joining if you happened to find them at the bar in the **transit**[13] **lounge**[14] of Hong Kong airport at 3 a.m."

6. In recent years, people's social groups have tended to become stretched over countries or even continents due to job **migration**[15], attending universities far from home, and the Internet revolution.

Key Words

1. evolution 演化 (n.) 2. collective 集體 (n.) 3. dictate 規定 (v.) 4. bond 聯繫 (n.)
5. take into account 考慮到 6. rural 農村的 (a.) 7. cope 應對 (v.) 8. anthropology 人類學 (n.)
9. interaction 互動 (n.) 10. intimate 親密的 (a.) 11. acquaintance 泛泛之交 (n.) 12. intimacy 親密 (n.)
13. transit 轉機;過境 (n.) 14. lounge 休息室 (n.) 15. migration 遷移 (n.)

◀ expansion of people's social groups

7 This has led to theorists questioning the concept of community and its future, fearing that as the world grows farther apart, a lack of social interactions may leave us feeling quite alone in a very crowded world.

Questions

____ 1. What is the main idea of the article? ◆Main Idea◆
  a People keep in contact with around 150 friends on Facebook.
  b Human beings' social groups have limits and are gradually growing farther apart.
  c People used to live in small rural communities but now more and more live in cities.
  d Human beings are social animals.

____ 2. What does this article focus on? ◆Subject Matter◆
  a The social groups of human beings.
  b Ancient hunter-gatherer tribes.
  c Robin Dunbar.
  d The increase in the world's population.

____ 3. Which of the following statements is NOT true? ◆Supporting Details◆
  a Dunbar estimates that humans form social groups of 150 people.
  b Job migration is partly responsible for the spreading out of social groups.
  c The average size of a medieval village mirrors the size of our social groups.
  d Social action destroys firm social structures and causes us to lead disorganized lives.

____ 4. What can we infer from this article? ◆Inference◆
  a Our minds have not evolved to deal with large city-based societies.
  b People without a concrete social group are happier than people with one.
  c People will decide to stop living in cities by 2050.
  d Dunbar's theory is not widely accepted.

____ 5. What does the word **interpersonal** in the first paragraph most likely mean? ◆Words in Context◆
  a Existing only for individual gain.
  b Understood but not spoken of.
  c Based on the need for entertainment.
  d Involving people.

____ 6. Which of these is an effect of humans having lived in small communities for thousands of years? ◆Cause and Effect◆
  a People have intimate friends, good friends, and acquaintances.
  b Many people live in cities filled with millions of people.
  c We tend to form natural groups of about 150 people.
  d People's social groups have become stretched over many countries.

Week 15 Day 2 The Magic Social Number

213

Week 15 Day 3

People

89 Education Where It's Needed Most

◀ Adam Braun

1. After a near-death experience inspired him to see the world, Adam Braun began **backpacking**¹ in some of the world's poorest countries. He traveled from the deprived **townships**² of South Africa to the starving streets of Cambodia. But it was in India where the idea for Pencils of Promise **struck**³ him. A small **beggar**⁴ boy held out his hand for some money. Instead of immediately giving money, Braun asked the boy what he wanted most in the world. "A pencil," the boy replied.

2. From that moment on, Braun would buy large **stacks**⁵ of pencils and pens wherever he went and would give them to the children who lived on the street. He quickly realized that pencils, the tools for an education, were far more valuable to these children than anything else.

3. In 2008, just before his 25th birthday, Braun put $25 into a savings account in the hope of starting a fund to build just one school in a poor area of the world. The reaction to his **pledge**⁶, however, was quite **extraordinary**⁷.

4. Within six months he had raised over $50,000 and had 75 **volunteers**⁸ ready to start building a preschool in Laos.

5. "It was funded by 2,000 individual contributions of less than $100 each. That is the **grassroots**-style movement we hope to create and build upon as we grow," Braun said, encouraging the **involvement**⁹ of people at a local level.

6. The first school, built in 2009, was a great success. It took only three months to build and cost $18,000. This cost included teachers' salaries, school materials, and three years' **maintenance**¹⁰ costs. One of Pencils of Promise's policies is that the community in which the school is built must fund 10% of the project. They can do this by providing workers and building materials, and this **ensures**¹¹ that the whole community is involved in and cares about the project.

Key Words

1. backpacking 背包旅行 (n.) 2. township（非洲）黑人城鎮 (n.) 3. strike 使……產生想法 (v.)
4. beggar 乞丐 (n.) 5. stack 一疊；一堆 (n.) 6. pledge 誓約 (n.) 7. extraordinary 不同凡響的 (a.)
8. volunteer 義工；志願者 (n.) 9. involvement 參與 (n.) 10. maintenance 維護；保養 (n.)
11. ensure 保證 (v.) 12. construction 建造 (n.) 13. scarce 缺乏的 (a.) 14. plentiful 豐富的 (a.)

▶ children in India

[7] But the organization is much more than just a **construction**[12] company. It now trains teachers and provides long-term support for schools in Laos, Ghana, Guatemala, and Nicaragua, regularly checking in and testing students to ensure that standards remain high. It has also started a program called WASH, ensuring clean bathrooms are available and teaching children about water and health.

[8] So far, Pencils of Promise has built over 400 schools, taking education to places where money is **scarce**[13] but the desire for education is **plentiful**[14].

Questions

____ 1. What would you say is the main idea of the article? ◆Main Idea◆
   a Pencils of Promise builds schools in Asia.
   b Pencils of Promise builds schools in the world's poorest areas.
   c Pencils of Promise was founded by a man named Adam Braun.
   d Pencils of Promise built its first school in Laos.

____ 2. What is this article about? ◆Subject Matter◆
   a A construction company.   b Global poverty.
   c Education around the world.   d A charitable organization.

____ 3. Which of the following statements is NOT true? ◆Supporting Details◆
   a The first school built was funded by one wealthy donor.
   b Pencils of Promise regularly returns to its community school.
   c Adam Braun was inspired to travel the world after almost dying.
   d Members of the village provide help building their new school.

____ 4. Which statement is most likely true about Pencils of Promise? ◆Inference◆
   a They prefer to employ US teachers over locals.
   b They have received a lot of negative feedback.
   c They make contact with experts in the schools' communities.
   d They prefer to build schools in countries that have English as a first language.

____ 5. What is the meaning of **grassroots** in the fifth paragraph? ◆Words in Context◆
   a Using only natural products.   b Using people at a local level.
   c Using small businesses.   d Using money from unknown sources.

____ 6. How is the development of the article presented? ◆Clarifying Devices◆
   a In reverse historical order.   b In random order.
   c In order of importance.   d In chronological order.

Korean Combat!

1 With over 30 million **practitioners**[1] spread across five continents, tae kwon do has become one of the most popular **martial**[2] arts on the planet. But did you know that tae kwon do is not just one, but nine different schools (kwans) of Korean martial arts, each with its own long history?

2 The story of tae kwon do begins around the sixth century AD. Back then, the Korean **peninsula**[3] was divided into three kingdoms: Silla, Koguryŏ and Paekche. Silla, the smallest kingdom, was worried about being conquered by its larger neighbors. This constant fear caused it to establish a group of elite **warriors**[4] called the Hwarang, or "flower boys." These Hwarang didn't just **pioneer**[5] **unarmed**[6] combat techniques that focused on the foot, much like modern-day tae kwon do does. They also established a code of ethics that emphasized honor and **obedience**[7]. Eventually, the flower boys helped Silla to defeat its neighbors and **unify**[8] Korea under the Koryŏ dynasty in AD 918.

3 Korean martial arts continued to **flourish**[9] under the Koryŏ dynasty. This is when early styles like subak and tae kyon made their first appearances. Their popularity spread like **wildfire**[10] after the king established regular martial arts competitions and ordered that all soldiers be trained in the art of unarmed combat.

4 The rise of Japanese influence in Korea after 1910 marked a turning point in tae kwon do's historical development. This was a time when Korean martial arts were banned and Japanese styles such as karate were encouraged as **alternatives**[11]. As a result, Korean martial arts absorbed some Japanese styles and **tactics**[12].

5 After Korea was **liberated**[13] in 1945, Korean martial arts were once again allowed to flourish, but there was a **diverse** set of nine different schools at this point, each

Key Words

❶ practitioner 實踐者 (n.)　❷ martial 軍事的 (a.)　❸ peninsula 半島 (n.)　❹ warrior 戰士 (n.)
❺ pioneer 當先驅 (v.)　❻ unarmed 徒手的 (a.)　❼ obedience 服從 (n.)　❽ unify 統一 (v.)
❾ flourish 興旺 (v.)　❿ wildfire 野火 (n.)　⓫ alternative 選擇 (n.)　⓬ tactic 戰術 (n.)
⓭ liberate 解放 (v.)　⓮ standardize 標準化 (v.)　⓯ simplify 簡化 (v.)　⓰ accessible 可接近的 (a.)

▼ Different belt colors mean different ranks.

with its own fighting styles, tactics, and philosophies. **Ultimately**, these nine schools were combined into one when the Korea Tae Kwon Do Association was established in 1961. This started the process of **standardizing**[14] and **simplifying**[15] teaching methods, making the martial art more **accessible**[16] to international audiences.

6 So next time you head out to your tae kwon do *dojang* for some practice, don't forget that you're studying the sum of over 1,000 years of fighting wisdom.

Questions

____ 1. Which of the following is the main topic of this article? ◆Main Idea◆
   a The history of Korea.
   b The history of Korean martial arts.
   c The history of tae kyon.
   d The history of the Three Kingdoms.

____ 2. What is this article about? ◆Subject Matter◆
   a Uniforms.
   b Martial arts.
   c Ancient customs.
   d Korea.

____ 3. Which of the following statements is true? ◆Supporting Details◆
   a Korea is the birthplace of martial arts.
   b People practice tae kwon do at a dojo.
   c The Kingdom of Koguryŏ established the Hwarang.
   d Tae kwon do was created from nine different schools.

____ 4. Which of the following is most likely true? ◆Inference◆
   a China has the most tae kwon do practitioners.
   b Korea has the most tae kwon do practitioners.
   c Taiwan has the most tae kwon do practitioners.
   d Japan has the most tae kwon do practitioners.

____ 5. The fifth paragraph of this article mentions that there was a diverse set of nine different schools. What does **diverse** mean? ◆Words in Context◆
   a Many different kinds.
   b All the same kind.
   c Very powerful.
   d Very old.

____ 6. Why does the writer use the word **ultimately** in the fifth paragraph?
   ◆Clarifying Devices◆
   a To emphasize the importance of an event.
   b To indicate the timing of an event.
   c To emphasize the unimportance of an event.
   d To draw attention to an event.

Week 15 Day 4 Korean Combat!

Week 15 Day 5

Animals

91
(091)

A Tale of Two Chimps

[1] Researchers at the University of Atlanta have discovered a side of **chimpanzees**[1] that no one has seen before. Apparently, these distant relatives of human beings may not be as selfish and cruel as we thought.

[2] Since chimpanzees are our closest living relatives, we tend to label them as the source of all of humanity's failings. So, it's true that we can be greedy, but chimpanzees are greedier. We can also be **vengeful**[2], but our talent for revenge is nothing compared to what chimpanzees display in the wild. And that's just to name a few **flaws**[3]. Basically, when we think of the goodness of humankind, we think of the things that we've **accomplished**[4] in spite of what we share with chimpanzees.

[3] This negative view of chimpanzees is often **reinforced**[5] by various studies. Chimp society is often regarded as **fission**[6]-**fusion**[7]. This means that the only **substantial**[8] social bonds in chimp society are those that exist between mothers and their **offspring**. Every other member of chimpanzee society would stab the next chimp in the back if there was a banana in it for them. Chimps have also been observed waging war for territory and killing each other for no **apparent**[9] reason.

[4] However, a **groundbreaking**[10] study of chimpanzee behavior performed by the University of Atlanta is challenging these **conventional**[11] views. Researchers performed an experiment for which two chimps were placed in two rooms separated by a wire mesh. A bucket full of different colored **tokens**[12] was placed in front of each chimp. When a chimp handed a green token to the researchers, it would be rewarded with a treat. If it chose a blue token on the other hand, both chimps would get a treat. Under these circumstances, the chimps consistently chose blue tokens. They would rather help out

▼ a group of chimpanzees

Key Words

[1] chimpanzee 黑猩猩 (n.)　[2] vengeful 圖謀報復的 (a.)　[3] flaw 錯誤 (n.)
[4] accomplish 完成 (v.)　[5] reinforce 加強 (v.)　[6] fission 分裂 (n.)　[7] fusion 聯合 (n.)
[8] substantial 實在的 (a.)　[9] apparent 顯而易見的 (a.)　[10] groundbreaking 開創性的 (a.)
[11] conventional 習慣的 (a.)　[12] token 代幣 (n.)　[13] welfare 福利 (n.)　[14] ethical 倫理的 (a.)

▶ The only substantial social bonds in chimp society is between mothers and their offspring.

their fellow chimp than dine alone. According to the researchers who organized this study, this proves that chimpanzees can put group **welfare**[13] ahead of their own individual needs. In other words, it shows that chimpanzee behavior can be **ethical**[14]. They may not choose the action that benefits the group every single time, but then again—neither do humans.

Questions

_____ 1. What would you say is the main topic of the article? ◆Main Idea◆
  a The evil nature of chimpanzees.
  b The good nature of chimpanzees.
  c Finding the true nature of chimpanzees.
  d The similarities between humans and chimpanzees.

_____ 2. What is this article about? ◆Subject Matter◆
  a Chimpanzee diet.
  b Chimpanzee behavior.
  c Chimpanzee history.
  d Chimpanzee biology.

_____ 3. Which of the following is NOT true? ◆Supporting Details◆
  a Chimpanzees have been known to wage war.
  b Chimpanzee society is described as fission-fusion.
  c Chimpanzees will never help a fellow chimpanzee.
  d Chimpanzees can be greedy sometimes.

_____ 4. What can we infer about chimpanzees from this article? ◆Inference◆
  a They cause disagreements in academic circles.
  b They are considered to be the most peaceful great ape.
  c They are the least-studied great ape.
  d They hunt by night and sleep by day.

_____ 5. What does the word **offspring** in the third paragraph mean? ◆Words in Context◆
  a Children and descendants.
  b Sisters and brothers.
  c Uncles and aunts.
  d Friends.

_____ 6. Which of the following is a statement of fact? ◆Fact or Opinion◆
  a Chimpanzees are our closest living relatives.
  b Chimpanzees are selfish and cruel.
  c Chimpanzees are greedier than humans.
  d Chimpanzees are more vengeful than humans.

Week 15 Day 6

Social Behavior

92 Trapped in a Small Space

▶ Claustrophobia is the fear of being enclosed or trapped in a small space. (cc by Laura Lewis)

1 Were you ever trapped in a small space as a child? Did you ever find yourself accidentally locked in a dark room or fall into a deep pool with no way out? For many people, these kinds of terrifying childhood experiences do not **fade away**[1] with time. Instead they can leave behind a sometimes **crippling**[2] condition called **claustrophobia**[3].

2 Claustrophobia is the **irrational**[4] fear of **confined** spaces. Sufferers can become extremely **panicked**[5] at even the thought of entering such a small space. Entering an elevator, taking the subway, or sitting on an airplane are all situations that can fill sufferers with a deep sense of **terror**[6]. It is estimated that six percent of the world's population suffers from claustrophobia, though only a small number seek any kind of treatment.

3 Claustrophobia occurs because the mind **associates**[7] small spaces with that terrible childhood memory of being trapped, triggering a **hysterical**[8] reaction whenever a confined space is **encountered**[9]. This usually results in a panic attack which can cause the sufferer to sweat, feel light-headed or sick, begin to shake, and sometimes even **faint**[10].

4 For extreme sufferers, this condition can cause serious problems in their social lives, and often results in the sufferer **deliberately**[11] avoiding certain situations because he or she fears experiencing a panic attack. Sufferers can also become depressed, feeling their lives are **dominated**[12] by fear. They can become afraid of being in a crowded room at a party, and in some very extreme cases even fear a closed door.

5 One branch of research has suggested that claustrophobia is, in fact, a fear that's hidden in all of us. Fearing dangerous confined spaces was actually

Key Words

❶ fade away 逐漸消失　❷ crippling 嚴重的 (a.)　❸ claustrophobia 幽閉恐懼症 (n.)
❹ irrational 不理智的 (a.)　❺ panic 驚恐 (v.)　❻ terror 驚駭 (n.)　❼ associate 聯想 (v.)
❽ hysterical 歇斯底里的 (a.)　❾ encounter 遇到 (v.)　❿ faint 昏厥 (v.)　⓫ deliberately 蓄意地 (adv.)
⓬ dominate 支配 (v.)　⓭ prone 易於……的 (a.)　⓮ phobia 恐懼症 (n.)　⓯ session（授課活動等的）時間

◀ Entering an elevator can be terrifying for sufferers of claustrophobia.

an important evolutionary advantage in early humans, and so we are now naturally **prone**[13] to this kind of **phobia**[14].

[6] The most effective treatment for claustrophobia has been exposure therapy. This kind of therapy gradually exposes the sufferer to the thing that they fear. The first **session**[15] may introduce the subject to an elevator, convincing them that there is nothing to fear at being inside. Then the therapist gradually exposes the patient to smaller and smaller spaces until the subject is completely comfortable in even the most confined spaces.

Questions

____ 1. Which of the following is the main idea of the article? ◆Main Idea◆
   a Claustrophobia affects six percent of the world's population.
   b Claustrophobia is a fear of small spaces, which causes major problems for many people.
   c Therapists can treat claustrophobia with exposure therapy.
   d Some memories are difficult to forget and can cause problems in later life.

____ 2. What is this article about? ◆Subject Matter◆
   a How memory works.
   b Human evolution.
   c The pros and cons of fear.
   d A psychological condition.

____ 3. Which of the following statements is NOT true? ◆Supporting Details◆
   a Claustrophobia is usually caused by childhood trauma.
   b Claustrophobia is a treatable condition.
   c Claustrophobia does not affect the social lives of sufferers.
   d It is thought that humans are naturally inclined to suffer from claustrophobia.

____ 4. What can we infer from the last paragraph about curing someone of claustrophobia? ◆Inference◆
   a It is impossible.
   b It is a slow process.
   c It is a dangerous process.
   d It is expensive.

____ 5. What does the word **confined** in the second paragraph mean? ◆Words in Context◆
   a Restricted.
   b Vast.
   c Decorated.
   d Foreign.

____ 6. What does the article mostly resemble? ◆Text Form◆
   a An instruction booklet.
   b A timeline of events.
   c An information pamphlet.
   d A short story.

93 Journey to the Center of the Earth

[1] Have you ever thought about how deep people can go toward the center of planet Earth? Just about every child has dreamed about digging a hole and coming out the other side of the planet. What's down there, and what would it look like? Well, Earth isn't just made up of stone and rock. It actually has three **distinct layers**[1], and each one of them has its own physical **properties**[2].

[2] First, there's the outer layer. This is called Earth's **crust**[3]. It's made of **solid**[4] rock, and is divided into massive **tectonic**[5] plates. Sometimes, energy from deep within the planet causes these plates to **shift**[6], and an earthquake is the result. On average, the earth's crust is about 80 km thick. It can be as thin as 5 km at the bottom of the ocean.

[3] The layer under Earth's crust is the **mantle**[7]. It is **composed**[8] of an upper and lower section. In total, it's about 2,900 km thick. The harder upper part of the mantle and the earth's crust are **collectively**[9] known as the **lithosphere**[10], after the Greek word for "rocky." The inner mantle is liquid that **swirls**[11] and flows like honey. It is made up of **silicon**[12], oxygen, iron, and **magnesium**[13].

[4] Sometimes, shifts in tectonic plates can create a passageway for superheated **lava**[14] from the inner mantle to escape to the planet's surface. This is where volcanoes come from. Think of a volcanic **eruption**[15] as Earth bleeding.

[5] Then there's the **core**[16] in the very center of the planet. This part is still somewhat of a mystery to scientists, but it is widely accepted that its **density**[17] is very high. Experts also believe that the center of Earth is made of iron and **nickel**[18]. It is said to be around the same temperature as the surface of the sun.

◀ plate boundary

Key Words

1. layer 地層 (n.) 2. property 特性 (n.) 3. crust 外殼；地殼 (n.) 4. solid 固體的 (a.)
5. tectonic 地殼構造的 (a.) 6. shift 移動 (v.) 7. mantle 地函 (n.) 8. compose 組成 (v.)
9. collectively 集合地 (adv.) 10. lithosphere 岩石圈 (n.) 11. swirl 旋轉 (v.) 12. silicon 矽 (n.)
13. magnesium 鎂 (n.) 14. lava 熔岩 (n.) 15. eruption 爆發 (n.) 16. core 地核 (n.)
17. density 密度 (n.) 18. nickel 鎳 (n.)

6. So next time when you hear of someone wanting to dig to the other side of the world, make sure you tell him he might want to bring a first aid kit and wear a T-shirt. It can get pretty hot down there.

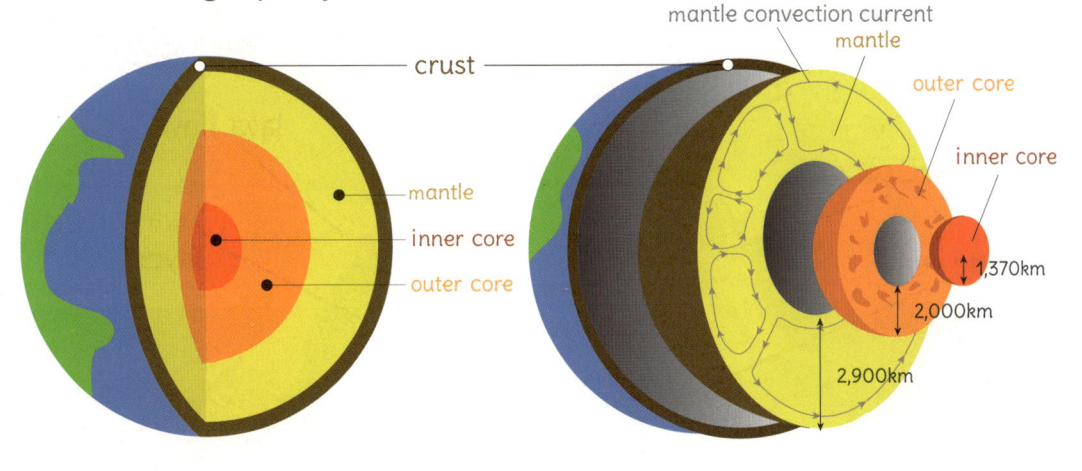

Questions

___ 1. What would you say is the main focus of the article? ◆Main Idea◆
   a A description of what our planet is made of.
   b An analysis of the history of our planet.
   c An analysis of planets in our solar system.
   d A description of the earth's core.

___ 2. What is this article about? ◆Subject Matter◆
   a Meteorology.   b Geology.   c History.   d Rocks.

___ 3. Which of the following statements is NOT true? ◆Supporting Details◆
   a Earth is composed of three main layers.
   b The center of our planet is called the core.
   c Earth's core is extremely hot.
   d It's impossible for tectonic plates to shift.

___ 4. What can we infer about Earth's core from this article? ◆Inference◆
   a It is hotter than the Sun.
   b It is twice the size of the Moon.
   c It has never been seen.
   d It has three layers.

___ 5. What does the word **distinct** in the first paragraph most likely mean?
   ◆Words in Context◆
   a Different.   b Similar.   c Unknown.   d Dangerous.

___ 6. On what kind of tone does the author end the article? ◆Author's Tone◆
   a A humorous one.   b A serious one.
   c A tragic one.   d A worried one.

Structure of a Volcano

- crater
- main vent
- parasitic cone
- side vent
- gas and volcanic ash
- lava flow
- lava and pyroclastic layers
- laccolith
- dike
- magma chamber
- sill
- sedimentary rock
- mantle

▶ The Kilauea volcano erupts on the island of Hawaii.

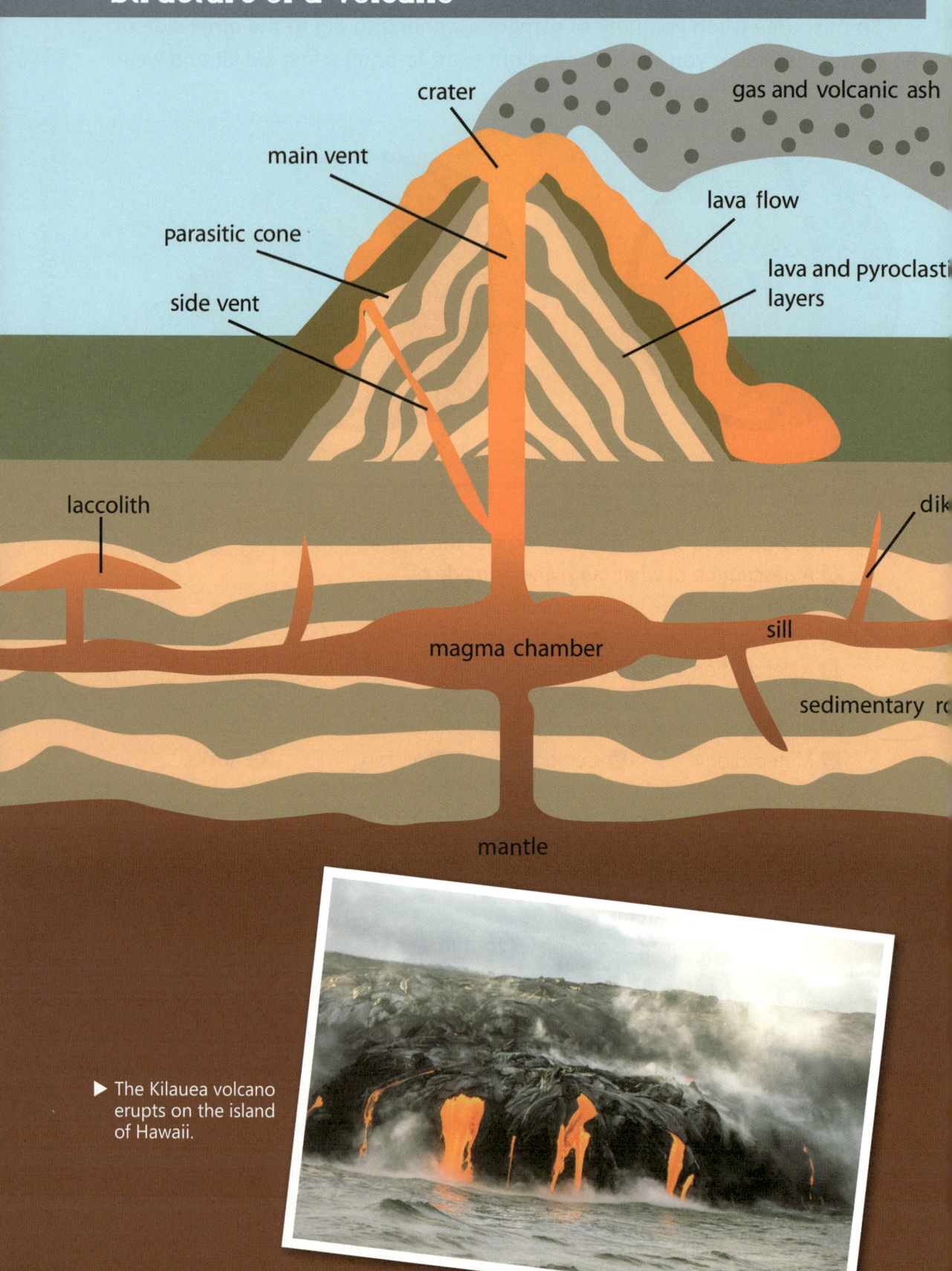

Week 16

Day 1 Language	94 Humanity's First Words	226
Day 2 Nature	95 Troubled Waters	228
Day 3 Social Behavior	96 Part of the Herd	230
Day 4 Science	97 The Hobbit	232
Day 5 Social Behavior	98 On Human Kindness	234
Day 6 Sports	99 Loose Your Arrows!	236
Day 7 Science	100 Cracking the Case	238

Humanity's[1] First Words

1. The origin of language is a puzzle that has **baffled**[2] theorists for hundreds of years. How did early humans go from producing animal-like **howls**[3] and grunts to expressing **abstract**[4] ideas and passing on complex skills? So far there has been no universally agreed upon conclusion, and the puzzle has been called "the hardest problem in science."

2. There are two main approaches to **tackling**[5] the problem. The first **assumes**[6] that language gradually evolved from preexisting systems used by our **primate**[7] **ancestors**[8], such as mating calls or warning signals. The second is that language suddenly came out of nowhere, caused by a **random**[9] **mutation**[10] that reorganized the brain and emerged almost perfectly formed in a very short period of time.

3. Some scientists suggest that a basic form of language existed with early humans such as *Homo ergaster* (1.8 million years ago). This basic language was somewhere between a primate form of communication and modern language. It was probably mainly made up of commands and suggestions and also depended heavily on gestures.

4. Studies of chimpanzees have suggested that the emergence of language is linked to our ability to trust each other within a community. Chimps use a variety of sounds and calls to signal different meanings, but they also try to use these signals to **deceive**[11] their fellows. Therefore, any sound whose meaning could be easily faked is often ignored and treated as a deception. It is only in a community in which the members trust each other enough to allow **signals**[12] that express things other than **involuntary** natural or emotional reactions that language can flourish.

5. However, a phenomenon in Nicaragua has lent **credibility**[13] to the theory that language may have appeared relatively suddenly. In 1980, an **institute**[14] for the deaf was created in Nicaragua. The school focused on lip-reading, but the children, when allowed to play together, began creating their own basic sign language. The next generation of children built on this basic language, and it became more and more complex. This suggested

▲ *Homo ergaster*

Key Words

1. humanity 人類 (n.) 2. baffle 使迷惑 (v.) 3. howl 嚎叫 (n.) 4. abstract 抽象的 (a.)
5. tackle 著手處理 (v.) 6. assume 假定 (v.) 7. primate 靈長類 (n.) 8. ancestor 祖先 (n.)
9. random 隨機的 (a.) 10. mutation 突變 (n.) 11. deceive 欺騙 (v.) 12. signal 訊號 (n.)
13. credibility 可信度 (n.) 14. institute 學院 (n.) 15. innate 天生的 (a.) 16. sophisticated 複雜的 (a.)

◀ Humans have a kind of innate grammar for building complex languages.

that humans have a kind of **innate**[15] grammar, and that it was possibly a mutation in the brain of early humans that gave rise to this remarkable ability to form **sophisticated**[16] languages from scratch.

Questions

____ 1. What is the main idea of the article? ··· ◆Main Idea◆
   a. Chimpanzees often try to deceive each other and as a result cannot develop language.
   b. A study of Nicaraguan sign language has pointed to the origins of language in early humans.
   c. How language began is a complex problem with many conflicting theories.
   d. *Homo ergaster* possessed a basic language more sophisticated than primate communication.

____ 2. What is this article mainly about? ·································· ◆Subject Matter◆
   a. A scientific problem.
   b. Wild animals.
   c. Sign language.
   d. The human brain.

____ 3. Which of the following statements is NOT true? ················· ◆Supporting Details◆
   a. The language of the early human species was not very descriptive.
   b. Deaf children in Nicaragua developed a language identical to that of *Homo ergaster*.
   c. The development of language may have depended on humans' ability to trust one another.
   d. The two main approaches to the origin of language problem both have evidence to support them.

____ 4. What does this article suggest? ·· ◆Inference◆
   a. Modern humans have a genetic ability to create languages.
   b. Wild apes can be taught to use human language.
   c. The origin of language is a question that is almost solved.
   d. The phenomenon observed in Nicaragua was a deliberate experiment.

____ 5. What does **involuntary** in the fourth paragraph mean? ········· ◆Words in Context◆
   a. Loud and confident.
   b. Out of one's control.
   c. Complicated.
   d. Impolite toward others.

____ 6. Which of these is an effect of humanity's ability to create languages?
   ··· ◆Cause and Effect◆
   a. Humans in communities tend to trust each other.
   b. A mutation formed in the human brain.
   c. Early human communication probably depended heavily on gestures.
   d. Humans can express abstract ideas and pass on complex skills.

Week 16 Day 1 Humanity's First Words

Week 16 | Day 2

Nature

95 Troubled Waters

▼ eutrophication (cc by F. Lamiot)

1   There is an environmental crisis that is **brewing**[1] deep within the rivers, lakes, and oceans of our planet. It's called **eutrophication**[2], and it's what happens when **excessive**[3] amounts of **nitrates**[4] or **phosphates**[5] are added to a body of water.

2   Eutrophication can **ravage** entire food chains in underwater ecosystems because it alters the delicate balance of life at its most basic level. Simple plant life like **algae**[6] **thrives**[7] in water that has undergone eutrophication. In fact, algae and **phytoplankton**[8] grow so rapidly that nothing else can survive. As the algae grows and expands, it sucks all of the oxygen out of the water, **suffocating**[9] more complicated forms of plant life. Consequently, fish and other **aquatic**[10] life forms lose their primary source of food and starve to death.

3   As if that wasn't scary enough, scientists have also discovered that eutrophication is increasing **acidity**[11] in the world's oceans. A recent study by the University of Georgia found that eutrophication increases the amount of carbon dioxide that oceans are able to absorb from the atmosphere. It concluded that the continued eutrophication of coastal waters could lead to the collapse of several species of crabs, snails, **clams**[12], and coral.

4   Eutrophication can occur in **freshwater**[13] systems just as easily as it can in the open ocean. Surveys have shown that 54% of the lakes in Asia are eutrophic, as well as 53% in Europe and 48% in North America. Some of the world's largest and most **well-known**[14] lakes are also considered to be eutrophic, such as Lake Erie in the United States and Tai Lake in China. Eutrophic water can be dangerous to drink. Thus, the more eutrophication there is in freshwater lakes, the less drinking water there will be for a global population that is already starting to get thirsty.

Key Words

❶ brew 醞釀 (v.)   ❷ eutrophication 優養化 (n.)   ❸ excessive 過度的 (a.)   ❹ nitrate 硝酸鹽 (n.)
❺ phosphate 磷酸鹽 (n.)   ❻ algae 藻類（複數）(n.)   ❼ thrive 茂盛生長 (v.)
❽ phytoplankton 浮游植物 (n.)   ❾ suffocate 使窒息 (v.)   ❿ aquatic 水生的 (a.)   ⓫ acidity 酸度 (n.)
⓬ clam 蛤蜊 (n.)   ⓭ freshwater 淡水 (n.)   ⓮ well-known 眾所周知的 (a.)   ⓯ fertilizer 肥料 (n.)

▶ Most fertilizers contain either phosphates or nitrates, the two chemicals that cause eutrophication.

[5]   Though eutrophication can occur naturally, this crisis is the direct result of human activity. Farming in particular is thought to be a main reason why eutrophication is increasing. Most **fertilizers**[15] contain either phosphates or nitrates, the two chemicals that cause eutrophication. According to some estimates, over 600,000,000 tonnes of phosphates were added to the earth's surface between 1950 and 1995. With numbers like these, it's not hard to see why eutrophication is becoming so widespread.

Week 16 Day 2 Troubled Waters

Questions

____ 1. Which of the following can summarize this article? ◆Main Idea◆
   a Human activity is threatening underwater ecosystems.
   b Fish and plants are dying in lakes around the world.
   c The amount of algae is rising in coastal waters.
   d Too much algae can be bad for human health.

____ 2. What is this article about? ◆Subject Matter◆
   a Algae.
   b Phosphates and nitrates.
   c Eutrophication.
   d Aquatic ecosystems.

____ 3. Which of the following is true? ◆Supporting Details◆
   a Too much algae growth should not be considered a problem.
   b Eutrophication is in decline worldwide.
   c Eutrophication threatens several species with extinction.
   d Eutrophication is not caused by human activity.

____ 4. Which of the following is likely true? ◆Inference◆
   a It will be hard to bring eutrophication under control.
   b Eutrophication can only occur in the open ocean.
   c Eutrophication will eventually disappear on its own.
   d Human activities have nothing to do with eutrophication.

____ 5. In the second paragraph, the writer mentions that eutrophication can ravage entire food chains. What does the word **ravage** mean? ◆Words in Context◆
   a Totally destroy.
   b Make stronger.
   c Break in half.
   d Become angry at.

____ 6. How does the writer develop this article? ◆Clarifying Devices◆
   a By using facts and statistics.
   b By using personal observations.
   c By using comparisons of time.
   d By using narrative storytelling.

Week 16 Day 3

Social Behavior

▶ a herd of zebras

96 Part of the Herd

1   It is said that there's safety in numbers. Fish collect in huge **shoals**[1], and zebras come together in large groups, blending into an uncountable mass to confuse **predators**. This kind of herd behavior, while apparently beneficial to the whole group, actually has a more selfish **motive**[2]. Though a flock of birds may look majestic and **graceful**[3], seemingly moving as if with one mind, each individual animal is in fact looking out for itself and itself alone. Each animal is trying to get as close to the center of the herd as possible, effectively using its fellows as living **shields**[4]. It is of course the unfortunate individual on the outer edges that inevitably gets eaten. Herd behavior is also seen in humans, with similarly selfish motives and potentially **destructive**[5] results.

2   Crashes on the stock market are a result of human herd behavior. Panicked investors try to sell their stock before others, resulting in a financial disaster caused by individual fear. People have been **trampled**[6] to death in supermarkets during **frantic**[7] shopping seasons in a **bid**[8] to get that last-in-stock product.

3   Being a part of a huge crowd can cause people to behave in ways that they wouldn't otherwise behave. An individual becomes less aware of the true effects of his or her actions, depending on raw emotion rather than reason and looking to the majority for signals on how to proceed. This kind of behavior has been labeled **mob**[9] **mentality**[10] and has led to acts of violence and destruction that people would not usually be willing to perform.

4   An experiment by a British **illusionist**[11] recently explored the dark side of herd behavior. He set up a fake TV show for which the audience members were asked to vote for what should happen to an unsuspecting member of the public. They were given

◀ Panicked investors try to sell their stock before others when stock market crashes.

Key Words

1. shoal （魚）群 (n.)   2. motive 動機 (n.)   3. graceful 優美的 (a.)   4. shield 盾牌 (n.)
5. destructive 毀滅性的 (a.)   6. trample 踐踏 (v.)   7. frantic 發狂似的 (a.)   8. bid 出價 (n.)
9. mob 烏合之眾 (n.)   10. mentality 心理 (n.)   11. illusionist 幻術家 (n.)   12. unpleasant 令人不悅的 (a.)
13. property 財產 (n.)   14. kidnap 綁架 (v.)   15. anonymous 匿名的 (a.)

◀ People can behave cruelly when they are anonymous.

choices between something nice and something **unpleasant**[12], and as the show progressed the audience increasingly voted for the unpleasant option, resulting in the victim having his **property**[13] destroyed, being told he had been fired, and in the end being **kidnapped**[14]. This was done to show how uncharacteristically people can behave when they are an **anonymous**[15] part of a crowd.

Questions

1. Which of the following is the main topic of this article? ◆Main Idea◆
   a The benefits of herd behavior.
   b The true nature of herd behavior.
   c Herd behavior in wild animals.
   d Experiments on herd behavior.

2. What is this article mainly about? ◆Subject Matter◆
   a A bodily reaction.
   b A basic behavior.
   c Similarities between animals and humans.
   d The stock market.

3. Which of the following statements is NOT true? ◆Supporting Details◆
   a An animal on the edge of the herd is more likely to be eaten.
   b People behave differently when they are part of a crowd.
   c Herd behavior is only seen in animals.
   d People have been killed because of herd behavior.

4. Which of the following is probably true? ◆Inference◆
   a Studying herd behavior only has applications in the animal kingdom.
   b Herd behavior is easy to control and damage is usually minimal.
   c There would be more acts of violence if there were no herd behavior.
   d Subjects of the TV show experiment were unaware that they were being tested.

5. What does the word **predator** in the first paragraph mean? ◆Words in Context◆
   a A creature that hunts others for food.
   b A type of large cargo ship.
   c A fast-running flightless bird.
   d A person that eats only vegetables.

6. Which of these is a statement of opinion? ◆Fact or Opinion◆
   a Herd behavior in animals confuses predators.
   b A flock of birds is engaging in herd behavior.
   c Each bird in a flock is trying to get close to the center.
   d A flock of birds looks majestic and graceful.

Week 16 Day 4

Science

97 The Hobbit

▼ the Liang Bua, a limestone cave where remains of *Homo floresiensis* were found (cc by Rosino)

1   It lived over 12,000 years ago and was only the size of a three-year-old human child, and yet it hunted **dwarf**[1] elephants weighing 1,000 kg and lived **alongside**[2] giant dog-sized rats and killer lizards. *Homo floresiensis*, nicknamed the "Hobbit" because of its small size, lived on the island of Flores, Indonesia, and may have been the last species of early humans to interact with modern humans, *Homo sapiens*.

2   The species is probably **descended**[3] from *Homo erectus*, an ancestor it shared with modern humans, which arrived on Flores around one million years ago. Hundreds of thousands of years later, *Homo erectus* had **evolved**[4] into the tiny Hobbit probably because of a phenomenon known as **insular**[5] **dwarfism**[6]. On small islands, survival favors those who need a lower energy **intake**[7] from the limited food available. Animals therefore tend to develop smaller body sizes.

3   The species was discovered in 2003 by **archaeologists**[8] **excavating**[9] a cave. They found a female skeleton, one meter tall, buried in the sediment covering the cave floor. Originally, they mistook it for that of a child. Later, eight additional skeletons were found in the cave along with stone tools and dwarf elephant bones.

4   *Homo floresiensis* differed from modern humans not only in height. Their arms were longer, and they had large feet and teeth, though not much of a chin. Their brains, however, were far smaller than ours and smaller even than the average chimpanzee's. In spite of this, they used sophisticated tools, fire, and probably even had language, **evidenced**[10] by their complex group hunting strategies.

5   Most evidence points to *Homo floresiensis* becoming extinct about 12,000 years ago after a volcanic eruption destroyed many of the island's **inhabitants**[11]. Modern human **remains**[12] have been found dating from around 11,000 years ago, but not before, so it is unclear whether the two species ever **mingled**[13].

Key Words

1. dwarf 矮小的 (a.)   2. alongside 與……一起 (prep.)   3. descend 來自於 (v.)   4. evolve 演化 (v.)
5. insular 島嶼的 (a.)   6. dwarfism 侏儒 (n.)   7. intake 吸收 (n.)   8. archaeologist 考古學家 (n.)
9. excavate 挖掘 (v.)   10. evidence 證明 (v.)   11. inhabitant 居民；棲居的動物 (n.)
12. remains 遺留物（複數）(n.)   13. mingle 使混合 (v.)   14. primitive 原始的 (a.)   15. infer 推論 (v.)

▶ Kelimutu volcano in central Flores island, Indonesia

6 However, Flores's modern-day inhabitants have legends that tell of small, hairy humanlike creatures who lived in caves and spoke a strange **primitive**[14] language. These creatures were thought to be alive as recent as the nineteenth century, leading archaeologists to **infer**[15] that perhaps they were the surviving decedents of *Homo floresiensis*, and may still be living in the poorly explored forests of Indonesia.

▲ skull of *Homo floresiensis*
(cc by Ryan Somma)

Week 16 Day 4 The Hobbit

Questions

____ 1. Which of the following is the main topic of the article? ◆Main Idea◆
   a The beauty of Flores Island.
   b The history of early humans.
   c The ancient inhabitants of Flores.
   d Archaeology in Indonesia.

____ 2. What does this article focus on? ◆Subject Matter◆
   a A scientific phenomenon.
   b A tourist destination.
   c Caves and forests in Indonesia.
   d Human evolution.

____ 3. Which of the following statements is NOT true? ◆Supporting Details◆
   a *Homo floresiensis* was shorter than modern humans.
   b *Homo floresiensis* was a solitary hunter.
   c *Homo floresiensis* evolved from *Homo erectus*.
   d *Homo floresiensis* inhabited Flores before modern humans.

____ 4. What does this article suggest? ◆Inference◆
   a Not all Hobbits were killed by the ancient volcanic eruption.
   b The people who discovered the Hobbits were unhappy with their discovery.
   c Modern humans are responsible for the extinction of the Hobbits.
   d *Homo floresiensis* lived in an easy and pleasant environment.

____ 5. What does the word **sediment** in the third paragraph most likely mean? ◆Words in Context◆
   a The roof or top part of a structure.
   b Equipment used for digging holes.
   c Matter that collects at the bottom of something.
   d A man-made container.

____ 6. Where would you be most likely to find this article? ◆Text Form◆
   a In a travel magazine.
   b In the letters section of a newspaper.
   c On the author's page of a book.
   d On an information board at a museum.

233

98 On Human Kindness

❶ Phrases we hear every day like "survival of the fittest" and "it's a dog-eat-dog world" don't really portray the full **spectrum**[1] of human behavior. After all, isn't it true that humans can be downright **decent** on occasion?

❷ Concern for the well-being of fellow humans is called **altruism**[2]. Real altruism is **motivated**[3] by the desire to help someone who's in need. It's not motivated by personal reward or feelings of **loyalty**[4] or duty. Think of altruism as that warm, **fuzzy**[5] feeling that builds inside you when you help relieve human suffering. If you've never felt anything like that before, you might just be too **insensitive**[6].

❸ Altruism is not **restricted**[7] to any one culture or religion. Quite the contrary, it is somewhat of a universal ethical **doctrine**[8] that has existed throughout the history of **mankind**[9].

❹ Buddhism **preaches**[10] love and **compassion**[11] for all things equally. Consequently, a Buddhist will extend a helping hand to any stranger just the same as he would to a member of his own family. This is an example of altruism.

❺ The *Sahih Al-Bukhari*, an Islamic text, states, "None of you truly believes until he loves his brother what he loves for himself." In other words, if one truly believes in God, he will be altruistic toward his fellow man.

❻ Judaism portrays altruism as the desired goal of creation. It is one of several religious traditions that believe human kindness is a **manifestation**[12] of God in our world. Therefore, we are kind because there is a piece of God in every one of us.

❼ Christianity contains a well-known saying that goes something like this: treat your neighbor the same way that you treat yourself. It is another religious tradition that teaches to love others is godly.

▶ Giving alms to the poor is considered an altruistic action.

Key Words

❶ spectrum 範圍 (n.)　❷ altruism 利他主義 (n.)　❸ motivate 激發 (v.)　❹ loyalty 忠誠 (n.)
❺ fuzzy 模糊的 (a.)　❻ insensitive 不敏感的 (a.)　❼ restrict 限制 (v.)　❽ doctrine 教義 (n.)
❾ mankind 人類 (n.)　❿ preach 講道 (v.)　⓫ compassion 慈悲 (n.)　⓬ manifestation 展現 (n.)
⓭ trait 特徵 (n.)　⓮ distressed 痛苦的 (a.)

▼ Buddhism preaches love and compassion for all things equally.

8   Whether the source of our altruism is spiritual or the result of evolution, it doesn't matter. What is important is that altruism is a human **trait**[13] that has been with us through history and doesn't look like it will be going anywhere.

9   As such, maybe we should introduce some new phrases like "survival of the nicest" or "it's a dog-aid-**distressed**[14] dog world."

Week 16 Day 5 On Human Kindness

Questions

___ 1. What would you say is the main topic of the article? ◆Main Idea◆
  a An examination of altruism in world religions.
  b An examination of altruism in early humans.
  c An examination of world religions.
  d The historical origins of altruism.

___ 2. What is this article about? ◆Subject Matter◆
  a Being cruel to people.
  b Being nice to people.
  c Dog-eat-dog world.
  d Duty.

___ 3. Which of the following is NOT true? ◆Supporting Details◆
  a Altruism exists in most of the major world religions.
  b Altruism is not motivated by duty.
  c Christianity believes in treating people nicely.
  d Buddhism was the first religion to practice altruism.

___ 4. What can we infer about altruism from this article? ◆Inference◆
  a It exists in Hinduism as well.
  b It was invented in the thirteenth century.
  c It was invented by Judaism.
  d It is punished in most religions.

___ 5. The first paragraph mentions humans can be downright decent on occasion. What does **decent** mean? ◆Words in Context◆
  a Behaving like a mean person.
  b Behaving in a moral and responsible way.
  c Behaving in a fierce and threatening manner.
  d Behaving like a child.

___ 6. Which of the following best describes the author's tone in the article?
 ◆Author's Tone◆
  a Encouraging.   b Pessimistic.   c Uncaring.   d Academic.

235

Week 16 Day 6

Sports

99

Loose Your Arrows!

[1] **Archery**[1] is the practice of firing an arrow into a target, living or otherwise, using a bow. The origins of archery possibly date back as far as 50,000 BC, a theory supported by the discovery of **prehistoric**[2] stone **arrowheads**[3] in Africa. Since its **invention**[4], archery has been used primarily in hunting and war. The Mongol armies of Genghis Khan conquered Asia with their **devastating**[5] **mounted**[6] archers, and many gods and heroes of myth and legend are **depicted**[7] as archers. The Greek demigod Hercules, the Chinese hero Houyi (who shot down nine of the ten suns), and the English folk hero Robin Hood are just some of the many archers celebrated in popular legends.

[2] Despite the strong start, bows gradually lost their **prominence**[8] as the long-range weapon of choice after the rapid development of **portable**[9] **firearms**[10] in the fifteenth and sixteenth centuries. Soldiers could be trained to use guns much faster, and their ability to **pierce**[11] armor easily caused the bow to become quickly **obsolete**. As such, modern archery is treated as a competitive sport rather than a **combative**[12] skill, with participants firing at targets placed at set distances, then scored depending on their **accuracy**[13].

[3] Commonly, an archer stands with his or her side facing the target with both feet at shoulder-width apart, providing a stable base for the shooter. The arrow is then loaded into the bow in a process called "**nocking**[14] the arrow." The nock is the small groove at the end of the arrow that the string of the bow fits into. The bow is then raised, and the arrow is drawn back in one smooth motion. The left arm should be locked in a straight position, pointing toward the target, while the right arm, which draws the bow, should be bent with the elbow at shoulder

▲ mounted archery

Key Words

① archery 射箭 (n.)　② prehistoric 史前的 (a.)　③ arrowhead 箭頭 (n.)　④ invention 發明 (n.)
⑤ devastating 毀滅性的 (a.)　⑥ mount 騎上（馬）(v.)　⑦ depict 描述 (v.)　⑧ prominence 傑出 (n.)
⑨ portable 便於攜帶的 (a.)　⑩ firearm 槍枝 (n.)　⑪ pierce 刺穿 (v.)　⑫ combative 好戰的 (a.)
⑬ accuracy 精確 (n.)　⑭ nock 將（箭）搭上弦 (v.)　⑮ astonishing 令人驚訝的 (a.)

height and in line with the arrow. If the drawing arm is too far back, the arrow will not fly straight on release.

You may be surprised to find out that the world record for the furthest arrow ever shot using a handheld, pulled bow is an **astonishing**[15] 1,222.01 meters — that's over a kilometer! Not bad for just wood, string, and an arm, don't you think?

▶ Robin Hood

Questions

____ 1. Which of the following best summarizes the article? ◆Main Idea◆
   a Archery features heavily in many myths and legends.
   b Archery has a long history and requires great skill to perform well.
   c Archery world records are often very impressive.
   d Archery slowly went out of fashion after the development of guns.

____ 2. What is article about? ◆Subject Matter◆
   a A military strategy.
   b A legendary hero.
   c Constructing bows.
   d A competitive sport.

____ 3. Which of the following statements is NOT true? ◆Supporting Details◆
   a The origins of archery are found in Mongolia.
   b Archery went out of military use after firearms became common.
   c Modern archery is mostly competitive.
   d Chinese legend has a famous archer.

____ 4. Which of the following does archery mostly likely require? ◆Inference◆
   a Strong legs.
   b Extreme physical fitness.
   c Good aim.
   d Quick reactions.

____ 5. What does the word **obsolete** in the second paragraph mean? ◆Words in Context◆
   a Of interest to many people.
   b No longer in use.
   c Used by everyone.
   d Used only by the elite.

____ 6. What is cited in the article as being the cause of the decline of bows?
   ◆Cause and Effect◆
   a The discovery of prehistoric stone arrowheads in Africa.
   b The mounted archers of the Mongol army.
   c The Greek hero, Hercules.
   d The development of portable firearms.

Week 16　Day 7

Science

100 Cracking the Case

① It is China in the year 1247. Song Ci has just written *Washing Away of Wrongs*, a book that contains the first written accounts of **forensic**[1] science—the type of science that is used to answer legal questions. The book tells of an **investigator**[2] who travels to a remote village in order to solve a murder mystery. After examining the murder victim's wound, he tries out various weapons on animal **corpses**[3] to identify what kind of weapon the murderer used. He then gets the villagers to bring their **scythes**[4] to the center of town. Flies start to accumulate on one of the scythes because it still has **trace**[5] amounts of blood on it. The villager who owns the scythe breaks down and confesses to the murder.

② Hundreds of years pass. It's late nineteenth century France. Alexandre Lacassagne **conducts**[6] a study into the relationship between bullets and guns. His work lays the foundation for the modern practice of **ballistic**[7] fingerprinting, which is how investigators match bullets to the gun that fired them.

③ Next, Argentine policeman Juan Vucetich shocks the world in 1892 when he uses a **suspect's**[8] **fingerprints**[9] to **convict**[10] her for a murder. Mr. Vucetich's technique for classifying fingerprints would eventually spread to police departments all over the world.

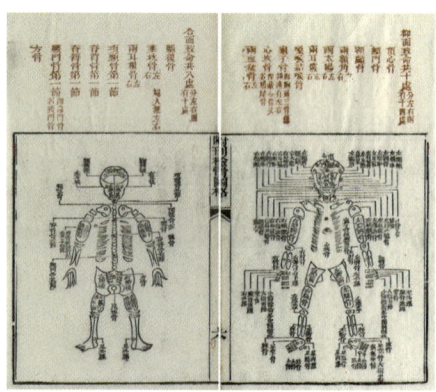

▲ *Washing Away of Wrongs* by Song Ci

④ Another **breakthrough** occurs in Germany about 15 years later. Margarethe Filbert's murderer is captured after investigators use soil samples taken from the murderer's shoes to **verify**[11] his movements on the day that the crime took place.

⑤ In 1987, a British man named Colin Pitchfork becomes the first criminal to be convicted using DNA fingerprinting evidence. Investigators believe that a 17-year-old

Key Words
❶ forensic 法醫的 (a.)　❷ investigator 調查者 (n.)　❸ corpse 屍體 (n.)　❹ scythe 鐮刀 (n.)
❺ trace 痕跡 (n.)　❻ conduct 進行 (v.)　❼ ballistic 彈道的 (a.)　❽ suspect 嫌疑犯 (n.)
❾ fingerprint 指紋 (n.)　❿ convict 證明……有罪 (v.)　⓫ verify 證明 (v.)　⓬ innocent 無罪的 (a.)
⓭ facilitate 促進 (v.)　⓮ database 資料庫 (n.)　⓯ tread 輪胎花紋 (n.)

▶ fingerprints taken circa 1859–1860

would have been wrongfully convicted for the double murders if not for the DNA evidence proving he was **innocent**[12].

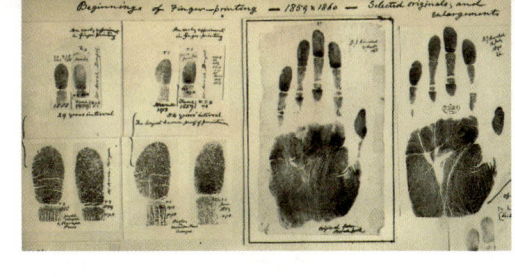

[6]   Nowadays, police forces the world over have taken these past breakthroughs and integrated them in order to **facilitate**[13] police work. For example, American government agencies have created vast **databases**[14] containing DNA, fingerprint, paint type, tire **tread**[15], and weapon and bullet manufacturing information.

[7]   It seems that the life of a criminal has gotten a lot harder since the days of just having to wash off your scythe thoroughly.

Questions

____ 1. Which of the following is the main topic of this article? ◆Main Idea◆
   a The importance of forensic science.
   b Important breakthroughs in forensic science.
   c A guide to forensic science.
   d Landmark cases in forensic science.

____ 2. What is this article about? ◆Subject Matter◆
   a Crime.   **b** Punishment.   **c** Forensic science.   **d** Scythe.

____ 3. Which of the following statements is NOT true? ◆Supporting Details◆
   a Ballistic fingerprinting was pioneered by a French policeman.
   b Fingerprinting was pioneered by an Argentine policeman.
   c The American government has various forensic science databases.
   d The first account of forensic science was written in France.

____ 4. Which of the following is most likely true? ◆Inference◆
   a Modern forensic science is practiced all over the world.
   b The Chinese gave up on forensic science in the nineteenth century.
   c DNA fingerprinting was invented in France.
   d Forensic science is a small part of modern police work.

____ 5. In the fourth paragraph, the writer mentions a breakthrough in Germany. What is a **breakthrough**? ◆Words in Context◆
   a A sudden setback.   **b** A sudden advance.
   c An unforeseen setback.   **d** A sudden rise in popularity.

____ 6. Which of the following best describes this article? ◆Clarifying Devices◆
   a A descriptive essay.   **b** A narrative timeline.
   c An argument.   **d** A biased point of view.

TRANSLATION

01 最甜美的毒藥 (P. 10)

說到巧克力成癮，狗跟人類沒有什麼分別。狗兒也愛巧克力的甜美可口。但是你知道嗎？巧克力對我們人類最好的朋友來說不啻於死刑。

巧克力含有咖啡因與可可鹼。這兩種成分使得睡前吃一條糖果棒，會讓你幾乎無法成眠。巧克力雖然會讓我們的心跳加速，卻不至於有害人體健康。除非吃上大量的巧克力，才可能因此生病。

但對狗而言則大大不同。狗的身體無法如人一般快速地代謝可可鹼，所以可可鹼會長時間停留在狗的體內。在人體內，巧克力帶來的興奮感大約維持20至40分鐘，但是在狗的體內卻會持續好幾天。

巧克力中毒的症狀非常嚴重。初期包括嘔吐、尿量過多、躁動。當狗的血液吸收更多可可鹼，會出現更嚴重的症狀，包括暈眩、肌肉抽搐以及癲癇發作。如果無法迅速送獸醫救治的話，狗有可能會陷入昏迷，最後死亡。

顯然，所有的巧克力對狗來說都有毒。然而某些種類的巧克力尤其危險。白巧克力的可可鹼含量很低，一條重20磅的狗，要吃55磅的白巧克力才會引起嚴重的症狀。而烘焙用巧克力則毒性較強，只要兩盎司的烘焙用巧克力，就會讓重20磅的狗出現嚴重的中毒症狀。一般而言，顏色愈深的巧克力，對狗的危害愈大。

你或許會認為，狗應該會自己遠離這麼危險的東西，但事實並非如此。狗跟我們一樣愛吃巧克力，牠們似乎不太在乎隨之而來的疼痛與痛苦。這也是為何你要小心不要讓你的狗有任何機會嘗到巧克力，即使只是一小口，狗也可能會因此愛上這個最甜美的毒藥。

02 建設美國的大亨 (P. 12)

想像在某個時代，人們在短短幾個星期內，從赤貧一躍成為鉅富，然後又一貧如洗。想像一個政客如股票可以被買賣的時代。這是美國在1870至1880年間的「鍍金時代」，亦是「強盜大亨」的時代。

強盜大亨是指一群在美國內戰後，突然暴富的商人。這些商人靠建設鐵路、油田、銀行、鋼鐵廠和港口而發財致富，最後也讓美國成為世界經濟強國。他們稱號中的「強盜」也表示了這群人中，某些為做生意巧取豪奪的手段，包括賄賂、偷竊、欺騙，以便擊垮競爭對手，進而壟斷市場。

傑‧古爾德是其中一個聲名狼藉的強盜大亨。他出生於1836年，受岳父任命，擔任一家經營不善的鐵路公司的經理前，他一直是個做小生意的商人。這機會是他事業的開始，他事業起飛的手法，是買賣鐵路公司，並犧牲大眾的利益。眾所周知，每當古爾德先生的公司需要通過某些法條時，他便會賄賂政府官員。1869年，他與其惡名昭彰的合夥人吉姆‧菲斯克企圖壟斷美國的黃金市場，進而引發了市場恐慌。他甚至涉嫌密謀綁架某位聲名狼藉的幕後金主，該金主收賄後逃逸至加拿大。根據2009年某個頗受歡迎的美國商業網站公布的名單，傑‧古爾德名列美國史上第八的惡劣總裁。

並非所有的強盜大亨都像傑‧古爾德這般惡名遠揚。事實上，當中有些人利用他們的財富造福社會。安德魯‧卡內基在鋼鐵業發跡致富，被視為美國史上的第二大富豪。然而，卡內基先生相信，「亡於富者，亡於恥焉」。這樣的理念促使他在死前將大部分的財富捐給社會公益。卡內基先生不僅在美國，也在加拿大、愛爾蘭、澳洲等國興建公立圖書館。他還捐了大筆財富給美國各地的學校與大學。

03 世界成年禮 (P. 14)

從孩童進入成年是一個漫長艱辛的過程。這次蛻變也深具社會意義，因此每個文化都有特殊的慶祝方式。成年禮會是你這輩子最快樂還是最悲慘的時刻，就要看你的文化背景了！

光是決定孩子「何時」變成大人，這問題本身就體現了文化之別。在馬來西亞，有些女孩在慶祝11歲生日時，會背誦伊斯蘭教聖書可蘭經的最後一個篇章，以證明此後即正式成為社會的一分子。在美國，「甜密十六歲」對許多女孩來說是很特別的生日，家人會為她們舉辦盛大的派對。美國人滿16歲之後就可以開車，因此有些幸運的女孩還會收到一輛車呢！

日本人慶祝女孩男孩邁入成年又更晚了些，是等到他們20歲的時候。在日本稱之為「成年禮」，這場盛事包括穿戴傳統服飾、在當地的政府機關舉行儀式、收受禮物，當然還會有一場大型派對。在日本，20歲是可以合法飲酒的年齡，所以酒後的宿醉也就在所難免了！

大多成年禮的傳統儀式僅持續一小段的時間，但有些卻可長達數年之久。北美的艾米許人因保留近兩百年的生活方式而聞名。艾米許人拒絕使用電、不開車、不崇尚時尚，有時甚至沒有熱自來水。然而，當滿16歲後，他們可在週末時自由選擇想做的事情。對他們來說，這意味著可以穿著時髦、使用便利的現代設施等等。有些艾米許青年選擇離開家園數年，有些甚至再也不回去。而想回歸艾米許社會的人得在26歲前做出決定。

不是所有的成年儀式都是令人開心的，至少對參與者來說並不是。在亞馬遜雨林裡，薩特瑪維部落的13歲男孩，得戴上裝滿蜇人螞蟻的手套長達10分鐘之久。另外有些部落的成年儀式則是在皮膚上刺青或是磨平牙齒，真痛！

無論是以何種方式或是在何處，每個人都會長大，成年儀式將永遠是人生的一部分，也包括你的！

04 搖籃到搖籃 (P. 16)

想像一下，你剛飛抵阿姆斯特丹史基浦機場，護照上蓋了海關印，從99％由可回收材質製成的行李輸送帶上領取行李。一走出機場，你搭上一輛不會造成汙染的電動計程車，然後乘車到2020號公園附近的旅館。這間旅館看起來跟一般的旅館沒什麼不同，但它可大有文章。用來打造這間旅館的建材並不屬於旅館。這些建材是租來的，只供旅館在營業期間使用。一旦旅館歇業，這些建材就得歸還給擁有者，然後再用來蓋其他的建築物。旅館內的任何維修也是比照辦理。

這些只是循環經濟的幾個例子，使用替代消費、以最小的破壞換取最大的效益。荷蘭是遵循這種新商業模式的世界領導者，但其他國家也開始跟進。

在循環經濟下，資源的使用壽命會儘量延長，廢物（如果有的話）的產生也會減到最低。聽起來像是大規模的資源回收，但循環經濟牽涉的更廣。傳統的資源回收會降低原材料的品質，但循環經濟是保持品質甚至增進其價值。為達到這樣的目的，通常會完全改變材料原本的樣貌。

以位在高雄的石安牧場為例，該牧場裡養殖了70萬隻雞。這些雞不只生產大量的雞蛋，產出的雞糞量也相當可觀。雞蛋會賣到商店與餐廳，而雞糞則直接運送到臺灣最大的沼氣發電廠，其位置就位於牧場中。在發電廠裡，雞糞與洗選蛋回收的廢水混合，產出的沼氣儲存在巨大的高壓儲氣槽中，產生的電力可供應附近一千戶的家庭使用。如果你是當地居民，你家的電視、冰箱以及智慧型手機可是名符其實地靠雞糞發電啊！

透過再次利用製造過程中產生的有毒廢棄物，同時減少對新資源的需求，循環經濟創造了雙贏的結果。除了著重在修復而不是替換，循環經濟挑戰了如何抓住人與企業的消費心態。科技已有卓越的進展，但大眾的態度是否也能跟著調整呢？

05 超級英雄拯救地球 (P. 18)

超人看起來不超過35歲（且從未改變過），但他不久就要80歲了。超人第一次現身是在1938年6月的《動作漫畫》創刊號裡。當年那本漫畫僅需10分美元，但是在2014年的時候，竟在eBay上以令人瞠目結舌的價格──3,207,852美元賣出。很顯然地，這位「鋼鐵英雄」，也是身價驚人的「黃金單身漢」！

成為世上最貴的一本漫畫已足以令人嘖嘖稱奇，但那其實只是《動作漫畫》的出版社DC漫畫眾多傳奇故事之一。在超人首次現身的一年內，蝙蝠俠出現在第二十七期的《偵探漫畫》裡。緊接著是號稱世上跑得最快的閃電俠，在1940年接力而出。然後是史上第一位女性超級英雄，神力女超人，於1941年現身。這些角色都獲得空前的歡迎，進而造就了所謂的「漫畫的黃金年代」。

但到了1940年代末期，超級英雄逐漸失去人氣。只有超人、蝙蝠俠以及神力女超人存活了下來，許多DC漫畫的其他角色則已消失無蹤。這家漫畫公司靠著旗下的喜劇、恐怖、科幻以及浪漫愛情類漫畫來抓住原有的粉絲。然而，1950年代對大部分的漫畫出版社來說都是艱辛的十年，DC漫畫也不例外。唯一的亮點是在1956年，新一代的閃電俠的誕生，有著新的故事背景、服裝和秘密身分。新一代閃電俠開啟了漫畫的「白銀時代」，只是當時大家還沒意識到。

諷刺的是，DC漫畫開創了新時代，但卻因此使他們失去美國漫畫產業的龍頭寶座。DC漫畫最強勁的對手漫威漫畫，從此稱霸了漫畫界30年。即使是超人或蝙蝠俠都無法勝過漫威旗下的蜘蛛人、X戰警、綠巨人浩克以及其他赫赫有名的角色。雖然DC漫畫在業界依然頗有份量，但在銷量上以極大的落差屈居第二。

此情形在1980年代晚期開始有了改變。蝙蝠俠系列電影的成功，重新燃起大眾對DC漫畫角色的興趣。超人與神力女超人也在登上了大螢幕後有了新的粉絲。DC漫畫跟漫威漫畫多年來為了銷量你來我往地較勁，就如同漫畫裡的超級英雄與超級惡棍，為了人類的安全不斷地爭戰。誰說人生不能如戲呢？

06 犯罪塗鴉的世界 (P. 20)

班克西是一位匿名的塗鴉藝術家，自1990年代初期開始活躍於英國的布里斯托，他的黑白模版技術拓印風格獨樹一幟，因為他必須迅速完成畫作，以避免被逮捕。據說模版技術拓印作畫的靈感，來自一次他為了躲避警察而藏身在垃圾車底下時，看到車身上打印的模板印刷序號。由於班克西偏好在公共場合的牆上作畫，有些人覺得他比較像罪犯，而非藝術家。

在布里斯托、紐約、倫敦和紐奧良的街道上都看得到班克西的創作。2005年，他甚至在以色列西岸的隔離牆上畫了一系列發人深省的畫作。很多人認為班克西是藝術天才，但這樣的信念也導出了一個困難的問題：「如果班克西算是藝術家，那所有牆上的塗鴉都可被視為藝術嗎？」班克西常常嘲弄何謂藝術的傳統觀點。他以出入各大博物館，把自己的作品掛在牆上而聞名。《蒙娜麗莎》的再創也曾成為他塗鴉的題材。

班克西的藝術創作也引出了另一個關鍵性的問題：藝術家真的重要嗎？沒人知道班克西到底是誰。他的身分充滿謎團，引起媒體公開揣測。2016年，倫敦瑪麗王后大學的科學家聲稱他們已經揭開班克西的真實身分。研究人員利用「地理剖繪」的方法，認為班克西就是布里斯托當地一位名叫羅賓‧格寧漢的藝術家。而格寧漢本人既沒承認也沒否定這個說法。其他人則臆測，班克西其實是一群塗鴉創作者，只是用同一個不公開的名字在運作。無論真相為何，班克西完全不想暴露身分。

不管班克西到底是誰，他的創作清楚傳達出反權威與反戰的訊息。或許班克西隱藏身分的作法才是他想傳達的最重要訊息。當藝術家不具名時，大眾就可以自己觀察畫作，而不因其身分而對作品的意義下任何不必要的結論。

07 微心靈控制 (P. 24)

在泰國熱帶雨林的深處，螞蟻群正面臨一項恐怖的危機。工蟻不回巢，而蟻后則把自己鎖在蟻室中，牠們全都害怕相同的東西──殭屍蟻！

螞蟻的恐慌是由一種特別詭異的真菌所造成的，其學名為蛇形蟲草屬真菌。這種真菌會控制螞蟻的心智，迫使牠做不願意做的事。

想像一下，有一隻純真的螞蟻，在晴天時外出散步，途中經過一具怪異的屍體，屍身上覆滿了蛇形蟲草屬真菌，卻也沒多加留意。在接下來的兩天裡，這隻螞蟻若無其事，繼續過著規律的生活。三天過去了，牠的身體開始經歷物理變化。真菌緩慢地破壞螞蟻的肌肉組織，並漸漸控制螞蟻的神經系統。幾天之後，螞蟻開始抽搐，失去控制身體的能力。

到了此時，真菌真正接管了螞蟻的身體，它強迫螞蟻爬上樹葉，咬住葉子。其中最怪異的事情可能就是，殭屍蟻總是會在豔陽高照的正午時分，咬下最後一口的樹葉之後死去。

接下來就是噁心的部分了。螞蟻死後，真菌撐破螞蟻的頭部，長出蘑菇狀的形體。在兩個星期間，真菌會將殭屍蟻的內臟轉化為糖分，供給自身生長。待時機成熟時，真菌便會釋放出新的孢子，毀滅附近的螞蟻。

蛇形蟲草屬真菌非常強大，它的威力可以摧毀一整個蟻群。不過，蟻群漸漸熟悉此種威脅，也會盡力保護自身安全。如果一隻健康的螞蟻看見另一隻螞蟻出現殭屍蟻的傾向，蟻群便會把受感染的螞蟻盡量拖離，遠離其他的螞蟻。與其讓整個蟻群暴露在殭屍孢子的危險中，不如放棄一隻被感染的螞蟻！

受到殭屍真菌威脅的不只是螞蟻。世界上存在著不同類型的蛇形蟲草屬真菌，各有其特定攻擊的昆蟲，例如蛾、螳螂，甚至是蜘蛛。

08 掙扎與天才 (P. 26)

「這世上沒有什麼比說實話來得困難，也沒有什麼比阿諛奉承來得容易。」杜斯妥也夫斯基在1866年出版的古典文學巨著《罪與罰》曾經這麼說過。當時他瀕臨破產，這位文學天才筆下的文句，反映他對人性深刻的了解。

1821年11月11日，杜斯妥也夫斯基這位俄國文學巨擘出生於莫斯科，父母是現今烏克蘭地區的移民。他在家中七個小孩中排行第二，出生後不久就罹患了顳葉癲癇，終其一生都為此病所苦。杜斯妥也夫斯基到學校學習他很討厭的數學，1841年至1844年間，他在俄國軍隊服役。退役後他開始寫小說。

自1849年起，杜斯妥也夫斯基被噩運纏身。就在這一年，他與一群知識分子一同在聖彼得堡遭到逮捕入獄，並且被判處死刑。當時俄國的統治者，沙皇尼古拉一世，非常恐懼革命。杜斯妥也夫斯基及其同夥的知識分子被帶到一處庭院，他們被綁在樑柱上，蒙住雙眼，宣布即將進行頭部槍決。但是子彈從未射出。這不過是場惡作劇，「假槍決」的目的是要給他們一個教訓。這段經歷使他的精神大受打擊，內心從此無法恢復寧靜。之後他被押送到西伯利亞，被迫在當地服勞役與兵役，直到1859年。

杜斯妥也夫斯基返回聖彼得堡後繼續寫作。然而景況並未好轉。1864年，在妻子與兄長逝世後，他開始積欠大筆債務，甚至還染上可怕的賭博惡習。據說他不得不匆忙寫完《罪與罰》的最後部分，因為他已經輸光了最後一個戈比（編註：俄羅斯法定貨幣盧布的輔助單位，1盧布＝100戈比）。

杜斯妥也夫斯基於1881年辭世。他在逝世的前幾年，寫下了幾部最著名的小說，像是《白癡》、《卡拉馬佐夫兄弟》，身後留下第二任妻子以及四名兒女。

09 被番茄染紅的街道 (P. 28)

八月的最後一個星期三，西班牙布尼奧爾的街道上滿是紅色的⋯⋯番茄汁。這是一年一度全球規模最大的食物大戰，二萬二千多名狼狽的參加者丟擲160噸壓爛的番茄。在前幾年，人數甚至高達五萬！而且大部分都是觀光客。現在，為了要控管人數，參加前必須事先購票。

早上十點，憂心忡忡的商家急忙把店面掩護好。備有消防水管的消防車已準備就緒，等著要把即將覆蓋眼前一切的濕滑番茄渣沖掉。大批群眾手舞足蹈，熱切歡呼著。

他們在等待「搶火腿」活動（一根油滋滋的長桿）開始。大多數的活動以鳴槍宣告開始，可是西班牙番茄節並不這麼做。他們會在鎮上豎起一根長桿，頂端綁著火腿，然後群眾開始往前衝，爭先恐後拼命地想要成為第一個爬上桿子頂端，搶下火腿的人。等火腿一被扔到地上，番茄大戰就可以拉開序幕了。

一輛輛卡車將過熟的番茄倒在廣場時，瘋狂的番茄大戰正式爆發。要不了多久，整個街道就被成千上萬、漫天飛舞的軟爛番茄給淹沒了。

一小時之後，筋疲力竭、從頭到腳都濕成紅通通的民眾開始慢慢散去。身經食物大戰的戰士步向河邊，掏洗頭髮裡的番茄籽以及臉上的果泥。

沒人確切知道番茄大戰是何時又為何開始舉辦的。一般會追溯到1940年代中期，對於第一次番茄大戰的起源倒是眾說紛紜，有許多不同的推測。有人說只是朋友間的嬉鬧，也有人說是針對議會議員的攻擊。甚至還有傳聞說是一臺卡車不小心把農產品傾倒了，大家忍不住就玩了起來。

這個節日實在太受歡迎了，別國甚至試著想要模仿。然而，有些國家的政府比喜歡作樂的西班牙人略顯嚴肅些。在邦加羅爾舉辦的印度版番茄節就遭到禁止，因為番茄農認為丟擲大量的農作物是浪費食物，堅決不能接受。

10 馬克出頭天 (P. 30)

2004年2月4日，有個哈佛學生在他的宿舍裡開創了一項網路風潮。網站名叫臉書，它改變了全世界人們溝通的方式。然而臉書並不是馬克・祖克柏對世界唯一的影響。

電腦一直是馬克・祖克柏生活中的固定課題。他從父親那裡學會寫基礎的電腦程式。年僅十二歲的他為家人寫了一個簡單的通訊軟體，ZuckNet。不久後，市面上如同AOL的即時通訊軟體便開始紅遍全國半邊天。

之後，馬克寫了另一個叫做Synapse的程式。Synapse利用人工智慧研究用戶收聽音樂的習慣。這個程式讓幾家像微軟這樣的大型軟體公司印象深刻，主動提供他工作機會。馬克拒絕了，因為他早已決定要繼續學業。跟ZuckNet一樣，繼馬可的Synapse之後，又有一個叫做Pandora的軟體開始廣受歡迎。

馬克對寫程式的熱忱在他就讀哈佛時開始茁壯。大學二年級的時候，他設計了一個電腦程式，可以幫助學生選課和找到學習小組。他也創造了讓使用者來評價大家相貌的Facemash，那就是臉書的前身。想當然爾，就在馬克創造了臉書後，很快就流傳開來。這次，是馬克自己設計的軟體在網路世界裡獨占鰲頭了。

至今，臉書仍是使用者最多的社群媒體，每月有超過二十億的用戶。但這對馬克來說不夠，他真心相信網路讓人們的生活更好。於是，他希望世界上每個人都能夠上網。2013年，馬克・祖克柏開了一家新公司，叫做 Internet.org，這家公司利用人工智慧、無人機，甚至是雷射來增加每個人上網的機會。

然而，馬克並非只專注於電腦，他和他的太太普莉希拉・陳也非常注重教育、健康、永續能源與人類平等等議題。他們共同成立了一個組織，叫做陳祖柏克計畫。透過這個組織，他們會在有生之年捐出99%的財富。每一個新計畫都將讓馬克・祖克柏繼續改變這個世界。

11 魔鏡啊魔鏡 (P. 32)

如果顧客在一家店裡，不必進更衣室就能試穿喜歡的衣服，那會是什麼樣子？或者更好一點，在自己的臥室就能進行試穿呢？科技的進步可以幫我們做到。全新的購物經驗即將進駐你周遭的購物商場，而且速度比你想像中還要快。

這項新科技叫做「虛擬試衣間」。想像一下，你站在一面全身鏡前，這面鏡子不但顯示出你的倒影，還列出可供購買的衣物。顧客只要簡單地用手往下移動，就可以一件一件地瀏覽衣服。顧客選定的衣物會以虛擬的方式穿在他們的倒影上，就可以看到自己在現實生活中穿著那些衣物的樣子了。如果顧客不喜歡這個顏色，也只要用手指點鏡子上的另一個地方，就可以另選新顏色了。

雖然這聽起像是科幻小說的情境，還處在遙不可及的未來，但這項科技其實已經出現了。全球已有百貨公司設有虛擬試衣間。世界級連鎖服飾店 Topshop，其莫斯科分店已經採用微軟的 Kinect 技術，推出了虛擬試衣間。位於紐約市的梅西百貨，亦於2010年試用了這項技術。他們安裝了「神奇魔鏡」，能讓顧客試穿店內所有的服飾。要是他們喜歡自己的打扮，便可將穿著虛擬新衣的影像發布到自己的臉書上。使用虛擬試衣間的顧客發現，他們省下了很多時間。虛擬試衣間能讓顧客縮小搜尋範圍，找出最喜歡的衣物，然後再將有意購買的衣物予以整理分類。

雖然世界各地已有商店開始實際應用這項科技，但它仍然未臻完美。舉例來說，衣服的影像看起來不自然，無法跟實物媲美，更不用說這項科技無法讓顧客體驗衣物穿在身上的實際感受。

12 是動物也是生態環境 (P. 34)

珊瑚看起來像植物，摸起來像石頭，且常在電視節目中介紹魚類和其他海洋生物時，被當作色彩繽紛的背景，但牠其實是動物。如果我們將珊瑚礁視為單一有機體，那麼牠是迄今地球上最大也最古老的生物。

珊瑚是水母和海葵的遠親，珊瑚雖屬無脊椎動物，但確實有那麼點骨架。石珊瑚（或稱硬珊瑚）的骨骼稱為珊瑚石，其成分為石灰岩（碳酸鈣）。而軟珊瑚則有著像樹木般的骨骼。只有石珊瑚會形成珊瑚礁，石珊瑚會在熱帶海域淺灘處把自己固定在石頭上。一株珊瑚可以分裂上千次，創造分身，珊瑚石相連在一起，形成一個珊瑚生物群。這個生物群其實是一隻動物，而且可以和其他珊瑚生物群相連成為珊瑚礁。有些珊瑚礁據信已有五萬多年的歷史了！

如果你曾在電視上觀看過海底生物，你大概會認為珊瑚有著繽紛的色彩。事實上，珊瑚是透明的，那些五彩繽紛的色調是靠著附著在牠們身上數十億的海藻（植物）形成。這其實是一種雙方互惠的關係。珊瑚可以藉著以牠們為宿主的海藻得到大部分的食物來源，但珊瑚自身也有毒性鉤狀的觸手。這些觸手通常活躍於夜間，在共生海藻進入休息狀態時，珊瑚的觸手就會捕捉浮游生物甚至是小魚。沒錯，珊瑚是吃肉的！

因為珊瑚必須居住在沿海地區，珊瑚覆蓋的範圍不到海底的百分之一，但牠們卻是四分之一海洋生物的食物供應來源。這樣問題就來了，因為珊瑚礁正快速地成為各種自然變化與人為威脅的受害者。汙染、風暴、全球氣候暖化、船隻以及廢土和泥沙往海洋的傾倒，這些對珊瑚都是致命的。即使水溫的微小變化，也會讓珊瑚失去保護牠們的共生海藻，最後恐怕導致為毀滅性的白化現象。

如果人類無法保護地球上最古老也最巨大的有機體，那我們還能做什麼呢？該是時候深思我們對環境所造成的影響了，特別是環境本身還是一隻動物啊。

13 最差男主角得獎的是…… (P. 38)

贏得奧斯卡金像獎是每個演員的夢想，對身處電影圈的人來說是最高的成就。金酸莓獎（又稱為 the Razzies）則與金像獎相反，是頒給電影製作裡表現最差勁者。

金酸莓獎的獎項類別有「最差電影」、「最差男主角」、「最差電影劇本」及「最差導演」等獎項。可想而知，大多數的演員都很怕獲得提名。

金酸莓獎首度於 1981 年在好萊塢作家約翰·威爾森的住所頒發。每年他都會在奧斯卡之夜舉辦晚餐派對。有一年他突發奇想，覺得辦一場假的頒獎典禮，慶祝該年度表現最糟糕的電影會很好玩。那一年，《青春歡唱》榮獲首屆金酸莓最差電影獎。威爾森拿掃帚柄和泡綿球來充當麥克風，他把賓客拉上舞台，發表滑稽的得獎感言。

由於威爾森的假頒獎典禮太好笑了，大家一致認為應該每年都要舉辦。1984 年，頒獎典禮從威爾森的住所移到了學校的禮堂，甚至還設法吸引了 CNN 的記者前往報導。

自此，金酸莓獎有了一批死忠的粉絲。趁媒體齊聚好萊塢之便，金酸莓獎於奧斯卡頒獎典禮的前一晚舉辦。如今，金酸莓獎不必與奧斯卡金像獎競爭，就已擁有屬於自己的光環。

2005 年，女演員荷莉·貝瑞親自出席金酸莓獎，受領「最差女主角」獎。她一手拿著她在 2002 年獲得的奧斯卡「最佳女主角」獎，另一手則握著金酸莓獎，對觀眾發表了另人捧腹大笑的得獎感言。有趣的是，在 2010 年，女演員珊卓·布拉克居然同時獲得奧斯卡金像獎與金酸莓獎。

不過，有些人認為金酸莓獎與約翰·威爾森對取笑表現最差的電影過於殘酷。威爾森對此表示，金酸莓獎就像是「地上的香蕉皮，而不是臉上的一記耳光」。雖然不是所有的好萊塢人士都贊同他的說法，但可以確定的是，在短時間內，金酸莓獎還是不會停止揶揄好萊塢的菁英。

14 天上的火河 (P. 40)

在委內瑞拉北邊，卡塔通博河流入馬拉開波湖的地方，終年有 300 個夜晚都有雷聲與閃電肆虐。這永恆的雷雨風暴，每晚有超過兩萬次的閃電照亮夜空，當地的部落稱之為「天上的火河」。

這個不凡自然現象最早的記錄始於 1597 年的一首詩，描述英國海盜法蘭西斯．德瑞克爵士的船，正謀畫攻擊此地，卻被不斷發出的閃電光芒照亮。結果，德瑞克爵士的突襲被發現並受到阻擋。

卡塔通博閃電的光芒是如此耀眼，即使在 500 公里外，加勒比海地區的阿魯巴島都看得見，為此它也有了另一個稱號，「馬拉開波燈塔」。

雖然這些閃電與一般雷雨中的閃電沒有太大不同，有些因素使得卡塔通博的雷雨特別壯觀。這個區域的大氣中蘊含豐富的天然氣，使得閃電能夠比平常更快速充電，因此能在較短的時間內放出較多次的閃電。除此之外，大氣中的塵埃微粒也時常讓閃電染上特殊的紅橘色調，這裡的一場雷雨甚至可以持續十小時之久。

盛行的理論是，由加勒比海向北吹進的暖風，與安地斯山下來向南的冷風混合，因而形成雷雨。

馬拉開波湖被周遭高度近五千公尺的山環繞，這樣的狀況將冷熱不一的空氣限制在這個相對較小的區域，造成強烈集中的氣候條件，是雷雨形成的最佳地點。

雷雨也是世界上形成天然臭氧的最佳資源之一。臭氧的形成是由於閃電將氧分子劈開，重新組成臭氧。新形成的臭氧通常停留在大氣層的底層，而它其實很少會上達臭氧層，進而協助修補臭氧破洞。

有個警告，要給那些熱切期盼親眼看見閃電奇景的人：遊客在委內瑞拉的這個地區得小心留意，這裡遍布毒販幫派與武裝匪徒，造訪這裡不但讓你嘆為觀止，也有潛在的危險。

15 大自然柔和的光輝 (P. 42)

不論是夜空中閃閃發亮的螢火蟲，或是照亮深海的鮟鱇魚，生物體所發出的光讓我們知道演化的過程是多麼的巧妙。

bioluminescence 這個字是由表示「有生命的」的希臘文，以及表示「光」的拉丁文所結合而成的。這個字用來形容某些生物透過螢火蟲螢光素、螢光素酶以及氧氣間的簡單化學反應所發出的光。

大多數的人認為發光的生物僅限於螢火蟲，但事實上有好幾種生物都能在黑暗中發光，包括魚類、鯨魚、烏賊魷魚、細菌，甚至是菇類。生物體發出的光也涵蓋光譜兩端的顏色，包括黑龍魚所發出的紅光，到弧菌的白光使海水看來宛如牛奶。

那麼，發光的目的何在？答案與生物的進演化有關。每一種生物，都是為了要在其環境中存活下來，而演化出發光的機制。

以螢火蟲為例，發光有許多目的。螢火蟲發光以吸引牠們想要的事物，例如獵物或配偶，此外，光同時也幫助牠們避開潛在的危險。捕食者知道這些讓生物發光的化學物質並不可口，因此牠們在獵捕螢火蟲前會再三考慮。

螢火蟲發光的目的相當直接明瞭，其他的物種可就複雜多了。例如在巴西發現的一種生物性發光蘑菇「夜光蘑菇」。由於夜光蘑菇不斷遭受昆蟲的威脅，因此會依靠自體發光來吸引那些吃昆蟲的動物。這樣的演化形式就像古老的格言所說的：「敵人的敵人就是朋友」。

櫛水母也演化出很棒的防衛手法。假使捕食者咬上一口發光的深海水母，牠們口中的大餐將會一路發光到胃裡。捕食者肚裡的亮光，在暗無天日的深海中相當危險。因此，之後捕食者在侵擾櫛水母前，都會三思而後行。

演化的過程十分驚人。如同自然界的商業大亨，發現市場缺口後，會以創新來填補。而且，既然演化能夠讓生物像燈泡一樣發光，還有什麼是演化做不到的呢？

16 可汗王國 (P. 44)

　　蒙古貧瘠的草原是世界上最偏僻的地區之一。然而在八百年前，這裡可是最大帝國版圖的中心。從1206年到1294年間，蒙古可汗（首領）征服的領土東起朝鮮（今韓國）、西迄匈牙利。蒙古帝國的版圖最大時可達2,400萬平方公里！

　　這一切都始於鐵木真，他是蒙古族的部落首領，在戰場上擊敗無數敵手。他一統蒙古，將各部落納入旗下，並為蒙古人制訂法治系統。沒聽說過他嗎？那成吉思汗這個名字呢？這是指「萬眾領袖」的意思，他在1206年的部落大會上獲得這個稱號，蒙古帝國自此誕生了。

　　在接下來的21年裡，成吉思汗的大軍朝四面八方而去。他們很快地就佔領了中國北方、俄國南部、中亞以及某些中東地區。當成吉思汗於1227年逝世後，這片領土隨即分裂成四大汗國，由他的後裔統治。

　　西元1229年，成吉思汗的第三個兒子窩闊台繼位成為新可汗。在他的領導下，蒙古帝國持續壯大，東歐、波斯和北朝鮮都成了蒙古帝國的領地。然而，在1241年窩闊台過世後，蒙古帝國便陷入長期的家族權力鬥爭中。

　　在成吉思汗孫子忽必烈的帶領下，蒙古帝國達到了巔峰。由於忽必烈將重心放在東亞，使得整個中國與朝鮮都納入版圖。他也征服了東南亞地區，但他卻沒能攻下日本與爪哇。到了1294年他去世的時候，蒙古帝國已然永久分裂，帝國的版圖不久即大幅縮小。到了西元1300年晚期，各個可汗所統治的領土幾乎比蒙古本身還小。

　　蒙古帝國是第一個也是唯一一個，橫跨如此大面積歐亞大陸的帝國。雖然蒙古帝國只維持了不到150年，但影響卻極為深遠。蒙古大軍的進逼促使（通常是強迫）當地大量人口離鄉背井。這造就了許多現代國家發跡的先河，如俄羅斯與伊朗。東方世界自可汗時代後已改變許多，若不是因蒙古帝國，東方世界也不會是現今的樣貌了。

17 失落在海底的城市 (P. 46)

　　當柏拉圖寫到一個存在於西元前360年，名為亞特蘭提斯的先進島國時，他可能不知道他的文字會成為這麼一個歷史謎團。甚至到了今天，在他最初寫作對話錄之後的兩千多年，我們仍然試圖發掘亞特蘭提斯究竟是事實還是虛構。

　　柏拉圖描繪了一個資源豐富與軍事力量強大的島國，並提到了亞特蘭提斯曾與據說也是柏拉圖出生地的雅典結盟。最後，亞特蘭提斯人背叛並大舉侵略其前盟友雅典，最終卻落敗。之後，亞特蘭提斯島遭受一連串自然災難侵襲，最後「被海水吞噬」。

　　有些人認為神祕的亞特蘭提斯根本就不存在。柏拉圖只是將亞特蘭提斯當成隱喻，來教導讀者道德的教訓。他們的論點得到兩項重要證據的支持：第一，眾所皆知，柏拉圖在其作品中經常使用隱喻；第二，柏拉圖聲稱，這些事件發生在西元前9000年。那時的雅典如果真有什麼，也不過只是一群繞著營火圍坐的人罷了。

　　也有人相信，柏拉圖的亞特蘭提斯實際上是另一個比喻，描述另一座完全不同的希臘島嶼的敗亡，島叫做席拉（現名聖托里尼）。在西元前1500年左右，發生了人類文明史上最大的火山爆發。它摧毀了席拉及其中大部分的邁諾安文明。這個理論的支持者並不把柏拉圖所寫到的西元前9000年當一回事，他們認為也許他只是那天太累了，不小心多加了一個零。

　　最後，還有一群人相信，柏拉圖對亞特蘭提斯的描述是確切的事實。對他們而言，這個高度進步的島國文明遺跡就在海底某處，只是等著被發現。而且，要發現它並不容易。大多數相信亞特蘭提斯存在的人，認為它就在地中海某處或其周圍地區；然而也有人聲稱它就在大西洋或瑞典外海的北海。所以要尋找的範圍可大了。

18 歡慶色彩 (P. 48)

帕德瑪睜開眼睛，掀開毛毯，飛奔下床。她期待許久的日子終於到了。這天是冬季的最後一個滿月，也是慶祝侯麗節，印度教五彩節的日子。

帕德瑪還來不及穿好衣服，桑傑就在窗外向她招手了。一瞬間她便跑下樓，衝出了門。她的母親甚至來不及斥責她別在侯麗節這天穿著漂亮的衣服出門。

帕德瑪跟桑傑手持水槍出發，還帶了紅、藍、黃三種叫做 gulal 的色粉。他們騎著腳踏車，跑遍大街小巷，尋找突襲的對象。遇到人時，他倆雙雙大喊「holi hai!」，並將水與一把把色粉潑灑在對方的身上。到最後，他們跑進敵方一群小孩當中，大戰就此全面爆發。戰爭結束後，敵我雙方的戰士看上去有如彩虹一般。

兩人回到帕德瑪的公寓吃午餐，桑傑今天能夠與帕德瑪的家人一塊用餐，因為在侯麗節期間，並不需要遵守種姓隔離的常規。兩個小孩一邊吃著糖果，帕德瑪的媽媽一邊告訴他們侯麗節的由來。

侯麗節是源自於一個名叫希蘭亞卡西普的暴君，及他妹妹侯麗卡的故事。有一天，暴君問他兒子普哈拉誰是最偉大的神。他兒子回答是至高無上的神毗濕奴，而非自己父親，暴君大怒，命令他妹妹侯麗卡殺死這個違逆自己的兒子。侯麗卡答應了，可是就在她把王子拖進火坑中時，諸神保護了王子不受火焚，而侯麗卡卻被燒成灰燼。

午餐後，帕德瑪與桑傑拿著水與色粉出去突襲更多人。那天晚上，生起了大營火，本地人都出來唱歌跳舞，一起享受這個盛宴。稍晚，帕德瑪回到床上，最後帶著微笑進入夢鄉。她已經開始期待著明年侯麗節的慶祝活動了。

19 陰間之窗 (P. 52)

鄰近土庫曼沙漠中的小村落達瓦札綠洲，一個寬328英呎的洞燒著紅色火光，周圍數英哩都清晰可見。看起來就像地獄開啟了入口，並且將地獄裡頭的一切都傾倒入人間一樣。

古希臘人的許多故事都敘述了英雄奮不顧身進入地獄，拯救愛人或質問死者。在義大利詩人但丁的描述中，也出現這樣的場景——他通過一個拱門，上面刻著「凡進入此門者，必放棄所有希望」。

進入地下世界的魅力，使很多地方都標榜著自己是「地獄之門」。或許是由於一些奇怪的自然現象（通常與火、煙或黑暗相關），或是因為地方上的傳說或迷信。

在這些「地獄之門」中，最具視覺震撼的就是位於土庫曼的達瓦札地獄之門，它已經持續燃燒長達40年之久。

這個地獄之門不是全然的自然現象。1971年，俄羅斯人在此處鑽探時，意外鑽穿蘊含天然氣的厚實礦床。鑽床底下的地面崩塌，整個工程設備因此掉進坑裡。

為了避免毒氣流瀉到大氣中，俄羅斯人決定在礦床上點火。他們認為這些天然氣會在幾天內燃燒殆盡，結果火光一路燃燒到了今天。

你不一定要有大坑的火，才能創造一個厲害的「地獄之門」神話。賓州的哈萊姆小鎮不只是名字不尋常，更有個令人混亂不解的故事，讓大家相信在小鎮附近的樹林裡真的可以找到地獄的入口。

傳說中，樹林裡有一個精神病收容所。為了防止病人逃跑，居民們圍著收容所建造了七扇門。有一天收容所發生大火，眾多的病人都因為這七道防止逃跑的大門而被活活燒死。

故事是這樣說的，假如有人找到這些大門，而且通過所有七道門，他們就會直接走進地獄。

20 小卻致命的生物 (P. 54)

這是個危險的世界，對小型動物而言更是如此。在野外，擁有致命的武器是很有價值的，可用以自衛或甚至狩獵。有些動物，例如從蛇到蝸牛，都擁有比獠牙或是利爪更為有效的武器——毒液，不論敵人有多強大，都可以致命。

世界上很多最具殺傷力的動物都居住在海裡。嚇人的箱型水母長約三公尺，牠的毒液可以在三分鐘內殺死敵人。有報告宣稱，自1954年以來，這種水母已經造成5,500多人死亡。雖然被螫時可以用醋治療，但是因為毒性發作太快，大多數的人還沒來得及靠岸就死在水裡。下次去游泳時，還是小心為妙。

東西好，包裝也總是小巧，毒液似乎也遵循這樣的道理。藍環章魚只有一個高爾夫球大，但是牠是世上最致命的動物之一。被牠咬一口，你可能根本不會察覺，因為傷口通常很小又不會疼痛，但這一小口的毒液卻足以殺死26個人。牠的毒液太強，使得大部分的人在幾分鐘內便死亡，更沒有解毒血清。不過，仍然有一線希望，如果受害者的心臟撐得夠久，毒液最終會排出體內，也不會留下後遺症。

絕大多數的生物在自我防衛時才會用上牠們的毒液，除非是受到挑釁，否則也不會主動攻擊，然而巴西遊走蜘蛛則因為天生好鬥的習性而特別危險。有幾點讓這種蜘蛛特別不受歡迎。第一，牠們喜歡四處移動，並且居住在人口稠密的地區，躲在房子、箱子以及汽車裡。第二，在所有的蜘蛛種類裡，這種蜘蛛的毒液最強。第三，牠們的體型很大，有時候大小如同人類的手掌。幸運的是，牠們咬人時多半不會釋放出毒液，因為牠們喜歡把毒液留著襲捕獵物。自從發現解毒血清後，也不曾傳出死亡案例，這更是讓人心安許多。

21 爬得越高，跌得越重 (P. 56)

擁有160年歷史的投資銀行「雷曼兄弟」，多年來安然度過許多次危機。雷曼兄弟挺過鐵路公司破產、美國經濟大蕭條，甚至是兩次世界大戰，顯得這家銀行屹立不搖。然而在2008年9月15日這天一切全都變了，雷曼兄弟的好運走到盡頭，成為了美國史上最大金額的破產案。

就在雷曼兄弟破產前的五年裡，投資銀行的業務蓬勃發展。2003到2004年間，該公司收購了一批次級房貸貸款機構。次級房貸是指為財務風險高的客戶所提供的高息貸款。大部分申請次級房貸的人，其收入並不足以清償貸款。但是，只要房地產的價格持續上揚，這應該不成問題。許多華爾街的公司都一頭栽進次級房貸的市場裡，雷曼兄弟也是其一，該公司從2005年到2007年的獲利也因此而屢創新高。

然而，在2008年年初起了天翻地覆的改變。房地產的價格開始下滑，一夕之間，全美國屋主背負的房貸遠超過其房地產本身的價值。2008年3月，另一家大型投資公司貝爾斯登也因為接觸了次級房貸而幾近破產。雷曼兄弟的股價開始逐漸下跌。

到了2008年9月，雷曼兄弟的股票已經墜入深淵，全球股市大幅下跌，這時的雷曼兄弟到處求援。為了阻止公司破產，雷曼兄弟找到可以買下公司的合作伙伴。他們向英國巴克萊銀行、美國銀行，甚至是韓國產業銀行請求協助，但還來不及達成協議，這間美國第四大投資銀行就破產。

即使美國政府積極紓困貝爾斯登、房利美和房地美等其他金融機構脫離財務困境，卻沒有對雷曼兄弟的倒閉伸出援手。之所以不出手相救，是因為雷曼兄弟缺乏有價值的資產。諷刺的是，許多屋主在這段期間內也因此破產。雷曼兄弟破產的消息一出，道瓊工業平均指數下跌了五百點，導致投資人全面恐慌，紛紛撤回在美國與世界各地的資金，就此揭開經濟大衰退的序幕。

22 月光下跳舞 (P. 58)

每個月，泰國的帕岸島哈林海灘都會舉辦一場月圓派對，那可說是東南亞最惡名昭彰的派對之一。在滿月的當晚，參加派對的人身穿閃亮的螢光衣、身上塗抹螢光顏料，群聚到沙灘上。火舞者表演危險又令人瞠目結舌的特技。DJ播放各類讓人暈頭轉向的音樂，小販的攤位上掛滿了明亮的燈光，超大瓶的甜雞尾酒就放在海灘桶裡販賣。

每個月有多達三萬人來此參加派對，大家都希望有一場難忘的體驗。雖然這場派對特別受到年輕背包客的歡迎，但不論年齡性別，任何人都可參加。參加月圓派對最大的樂趣是，你不知道在帕岸島巨大的滿月之下會與誰相遇，又或者你會結交什麼朋友，與誰擦出戀情的火花。大部分的人會一直跳舞跳到第二天天亮為止。

即便眾說紛紜，但沒有人知道這些派對到底是如何又是何時開始的。大部分的人認為是在1980年代晚期，從海灘上某個度假小屋所舉行的歡送會開始的。不管這些派對是何時或怎麼開始的，消息一下子就經由口耳相傳散布開來。很快地，這些派對不只變成定期舉行的活動，規模也愈來愈大，愈來愈狂野。

有些人可能會說，這些派對變得太受歡迎，當地居民開始抗議參加派對之人所製造的噪音與帶來的髒亂。因為大批尋歡作樂的人與毫無節制的飲酒，使得這些派對也開始變得愈來愈危險。破碎的玻璃對打赤腳的人來說是很大的問題，許多與火有關的景點與活動也造成不少輕微的燒傷。除此之外，小偷也會趁著觀光客整夜外出時闖空門，竊取貴重物品。

有鑑於此，目前尚不知道泰國政府還會允許派對繼續舉行多久。所以如果參加月圓派對是你畢生的願望之一，你可得趕快去參加了！

23 白色海洋 (P. 60)

一位地科學家形容烏尤尼鹽沼有如「平靜無浪的白色海洋」。想像一下站在 10,582 平方公里大，有如餐盤一樣平坦的白色荒蕪大地上，你可能就對於造訪位於南美洲玻利維亞烏尤尼鹽沼，意即世界上最大的鹽沼，有點概念了。

烏尤尼鹽沼是由巨大的史前湖泊逐漸乾涸而形成，被一層數公尺厚的堅硬鹽層覆蓋，鹽層表面下藏著 20 公尺深的鹽湖。這裡的景觀看起來像是南極洲而非南美洲，遊客很難說服自己腳下踩的是鹽，而不是雪。

鹽沼上零星點綴著一些小「島」，這些其實是一度被淹沒在湖面下的古代火山頂，但現在卻是千年仙人掌的絕佳生長地，這些仙人掌每年以一公分的速度生長。

這個區域的平坦度十分驚人，在面積廣達一個小國大小的土地上，高度差不超過 80 公分，使這裡成為人造衛星調整高度計的完美地點。人造衛星通常會利用海床來精準判斷在太空的高度，但鹽沼晴朗的氣候和單一的特質，讓鹽沼的高度判斷比海床準確五倍以上。

鹽沼也成為全南美最貧窮國家，玻利維亞的經濟命脈。據估計，世界上高達 70％ 的鋰存在於鹽沼堅硬表層下，高濃度的鹽水中。鋰是製造電池的必需物質，抽取的方式是在鹽沼表面鑿出小水塘，注入沼面下方的鹽水溶液，鋰和鹽就會在在陽光蒸發水分時被分離出來。

拜訪鹽沼的遊客們還可以看到粉紅色的南美洲紅鶴，每年 11 月在此地繁殖，以及有名的食鹽宮殿，一家完全由鹽所建造的飯店，那裡的重要規定是「請勿舔牆壁！」

24 熱情法式饗宴 (P. 62)

當你想到法國菜──濃郁的奶油、如奶油般滑順的醬汁、成堆的起司、多汁的紅肉──「心臟病」這個字會跳進腦中嗎？

這些字不該出現的，因為，儘管法國人吃的奶油是美國人四倍，吃的起司也幾乎是美國人的兩倍，法國人罹患心臟病的死亡率可不到美國的二分之一。

這樣的數據被稱為「法式矛盾」，科學家們歸因於各種的因素，從法國人較少吃甜食的習慣，到地中海型氣候可激勵人多運動等等。

這個與常識相違背的現象讓科學家深感困擾。法國人對紅酒的熱愛，最常被用來解釋這個有違直覺的現象。

研究顯示，適度飲用紅酒對健康及長壽有正面效果。科學家們一開始認為化學物質白藜蘆醇是主因，但紅酒中的白藜蘆醇含量似乎太低了，無法造成如法式矛盾這麼巨大的效果。

另外一種在葡萄酒中被找到的化學物質，原花青素，就具有足夠的量，可以有效保護人類血管的細胞。在人們最健康的法國地區，所產的葡萄酒，花青素含量也較高。無論支持這個現象的科學理論為何，葡萄酒能維持心臟健康的理論曝光後，使得美國的葡萄酒進口量激增。

其他試圖要解釋法式矛盾的理論認為，法國人簡單的飲食習慣，例如少量進食對健康有益。法國人不習慣兩餐之間吃點心，較少吃油炸食物以及兩餐間隔較久，都可以讓食物消化得更好。

此外，由於南法的晴朗天氣，法國人有許多機會從陽光中獲取較多的維生素 D。維生素 D 能夠預防動脈硬化，並且降低心肌梗塞的危機。

理論先丟一邊，看來如果你想要享受美食，又要擁有一顆健康心臟，投胎當法國人好像是比較簡單的方式。

25 不只一個你？ (P. 66)

你剛坐下打開課本，該是增進英文閱讀能力，學習一些新單字的時候了。但是可能有另一個版本的你決定今天不念書了。也可能還有另一個版本的你老早就放棄讀書，因為那個你在去年某個時候就決定要成為專業舞者。或許還有一個特別粗俗的你，寧可把書頁撕下來吃掉，也不想拿來學好英文。

這些聽起來可能有點瘋狂，但這個平行宇宙的理論，事實上已經在某些科學圈子中建立了良好的基礎。

想像有一疊牌，如果你把那疊牌洗上幾百幾千次，那你最後將得到各種可能的組合。一些量子物理學領域的專家相信，同樣的概念也適用於我們的宇宙。如果宇宙是無限的，那表示它將永續不停，粒子的各種可能組合必定存在於某處。

量子物理學也得到證據，發現物質可以同時以兩種狀態存在。2010 年，加州大學的研究員讓一小片金屬振動，卻同時保持靜止不動的狀態。如果他們的推論是正確的，那我們宇宙中所真實存在的事物，就是來自於觀察其中一個可能的狀態。我們觀察不到的其他可能的狀態，正由平行宇宙的某人所觀察。觀察眾多可能不同狀態之一的過程，讓我們的現實世界分裂成不同的平行宇宙。用最簡單的方式解釋，平行宇宙的理論假設我們的行動與決策，都可以以量子的層面測量。以外行人的話來說，大腦裡的粒子會因為你決定吃熱狗而做出特定反應。

許多相信平行宇宙這個理論存在的科學家承認，我們不太可能穿梭於平行宇宙之間。但一百年前，大部分的科學家也不相信太空旅行是可行的。或許最終有一天，你還是會遇上那個已經變成專業舞者的自己。

26 永久的大舌頭 (P. 68)

我們的身體聽到、理解與發出語言的方式相當複雜，如同其他繁複的過程，都會有不靈光的時候。這個現象就叫做語言障礙。在我們與他人溝通時，語言障礙有可能會造成嚴重的後果。

語言障礙有兩種形式：發展性與後天性。有些孩童在成長的過程中自然出現發展性語言障礙。這會影響到語言器官的發育，像是喉頭、聲帶或是大腦中負責溝通的區域。後天性語言障礙不分年齡，有可能發生在任何人的身上，通常是因為頭部創傷或腦部缺氧所造成。

某些語言障礙同時屬於發展性與後天性，好比口吃。口吃是語言不斷被打斷的失常狀態，像是單字的第一個音節不斷重複（ㄑ—ㄑ—去），或是拉長（做——）。有的時候連一個字都說不出口。

大多數的情況下，口吃這種發展性語言障礙，好發於三歲左右的男童身上。80％患有口吃的孩童會在成年之前不再口吃。但也有少數屬於後天性口吃的例子。在這些例子中，頭部創傷、中風或藥物使用都有可能導致成人突然口吃。

失語症是另一種後天性的語言障礙。跟後天性口吃非常類似，一個人在遭受頭部創傷或是中風後可能會出現失語症。失語症的症狀極為多樣。有些很單純，像是單字發音困難或是說不出完整的句子。有些則非常嚴重，包括無法閱讀或是書寫。還有一些特別怪異的症狀，像是用一些無意義的話來代替正確的詞彙。

好消息是治療語言障礙的方法一直在進步中，雖然多數的語言障礙無法根治，但通常可以減輕。語言治療師能幫助病患改善發音的準確度與清晰度，同樣重要的是，增進患者的自信心。

27 媲美汽車之父的伊隆・馬斯克 (P. 70)

若是伊隆・馬斯克的計畫得以實現，你和你的朋友很快就可以駕駛電動車了。如果是長途旅行，你會坐在封閉的行駛艙裡以極速旅行，比搭飛機還要更快更便宜。未來你甚至有可能在火星上擁有一間公寓！聽起來不可置信嗎？如果你曾經使用 PayPal 買東西，那麼你已經是馬斯克先生瞬息萬變世界裡的一員。

伊隆・馬斯克在1971年於南非出生，大學時在美國攻讀物理與經濟。他早期的興趣在綠色能源、太空旅行、網際網路與社會改革等領域。不可思議的是，他在這些領域中都產生極大的影響。

在創立一間成功的軟體公司並隨後賣出之後，馬斯克在2001年協助創辦了 PayPal。這間線上支付公司改變了人類交易的方式。

大部分的人都認為這樣已經算是很有成就了，但一年後，馬斯克成立了 SpaceX，一間火箭製造公司。他的目標是精進太空旅行的技術，而且他做到了。就在2012年，SpaceX 成為第一間在國際太空站實現太空船對接的私人公司！或許馬斯克想在2040年在火星建立人類殖民地的夢想並不瘋狂。

再回到地球上，馬斯克在2006年創辦太陽城。你想的沒錯，這是一間太陽能發電公司，目前位居全美第二大。可再生能源也是馬斯克在2008年接管特斯拉電動車的主要原因。特斯拉如今也讓其他汽車製造商使用他們的技術來發展各家的電動車。對伊隆・馬斯克來說，金錢似乎不代表一切，當然，他非常有錢！

馬斯克的點子源源不絕。對於「超迴路列車」運輸系統，馬斯克的設想是，搭載人的封閉行駛艙在管道中以時速1,200公里行進。比一般的商用飛機快了近50％！馬斯克也希望人工智慧能更廣泛地應用，並期待有一天能直接與人類的大腦連結。

若這想法是來自其他人，那聽起來就像是科幻小說。但若是來自馬斯克這位已有諸多豐功偉業的傑出人物，我們不能小看他想像出來的任何事物。

28 「面」對未來 (P. 72)

醒來發現自己換了一張臉,這根本就是惡夢或是科幻小說裡才會發生的事情。但是,對在意外中留下可怕的顏面傷疤和毀容的受害者來說,臉部移植是重拾正常生活的一線希望。

一般的臉部手術,是取病患的自體組織,再接到病患的臉上,這種手術稱之為皮膚移植(植皮)手術。然而,臉部移植手術是把別人的臉皮取下,然後直接接到病患的臉上。

最常見的誤解是,接受移植者看起來會跟捐贈者的臉一模一樣。其實不然,由於患者和捐贈者的骨架不同,所以會產生第三張「混血」的臉孔。

首次臉部移植成功的案例是發生在2005年,由一群法國醫師操刀完成。他們將一位腦死捐贈者的鼻子、嘴唇和下巴,移植給一位被狗猛烈攻擊臉部的38歲婦人。2010年,一位因槍擊意外而受傷的男性獲捐一張全新的臉,這是全臉移植的首例。

這種手術非常的複雜,因為得小心連接臉部皮膚下的神經、肌肉和血管。這需要非常高超的技巧,這樣病患以後做臉部表情時,看起來才會自然。這項手術非常艱難,有時甚至需要超過24小時才能完成。雖然手術不容易,但醫師還是推崇能讓臉部做出自然表情的臉部移植,勝過看起來像是戴了面具般的自體組織植皮手術。

對病患來說,其中一個最大的風險是對這張新臉的自體排斥。因此接受新臉的移植者必須終生服用特殊的藥物,以抑制免疫系統。2008年,一位被熊攻擊的中國籍患者換了新的臉頰、上唇和鼻子,卻因為他以中藥取代處方藥物而死亡。首次接受臉部移植的患者也在術後11年,即2016年過世。她的死因是藥物產生的併發症。

即使有這些風險,接受臉部移植手術的人仍然非常開心,因為他們能再次做一般人習以為常的事情,像是說話、吃東西和微笑。

29 太空深處的暗黑謎團 (P. 74)

問題:換一顆燈泡需要多少個天文學家?答案是:一個都不用。天文學家根本就不怕黑!撇開這個冷笑話不談,天文學家或許不怕黑,但是他們一定在暗物質這個議題上嚴重失眠。

暗物質的分布比我們宇宙中的普通物質更常見四倍,不過用望遠鏡不可能看的到,科學家只知道它存在,因為它會影響可見物質。

其實,「知道」這個詞也許是過於自信的說法。暗物質是一個想法、一種假說,實際上就是試著要把我們肉眼看得見的宇宙,與科學數據所顯示的宇宙,兩者之間的缺口填補起來的物質。不過,實驗尚未探測出暗物質粒子的存在,而這引起了一些科學家懷疑宇宙結構與宇宙形成的標準模型。

瑞士物理學家弗里茨・茲威基首次於1933年提出暗物質的存在。他觀察到有個星系團叫做「后髮座星系團」,其中包含了上千個星系,每個星系都有數十億顆星星,聚集在這漫無邊際的廣大宇宙群裡。在這其中,茲威基發現了令人費解、前後矛盾之處。

茲威基依據星團裡可見物質的數量,進行大規模的計算,並且計算星系團中群星移動的速度。他了解這一大群星系本身並沒有足夠的重力,能讓這些迅速移動的星系循著軌道運行。星系應該早就飛出星系團外了,而非留在軌道內。之後,茲威基依據星系運行的速度計算出星系團的質量,發現比依據可見物質所計算的,還要多出400倍以上的質量。他推算必定是某種看不見的物質,造成計算中的差異。

由於科學家十分難以探測出暗物質,因此暗物質形成與運作的新理論很少有結論。科學家必須根據暗物質對其他宇宙結構的間接影響來作出假設,這也代表了,暗物質的祕密可能還有很長的一段時間,都將處在黑暗中不為人所知。

30 死物藝術 (P. 76)

達米恩・赫斯特的鉅作不是那種你會想要掛在牆上的藝術品。一大群蒼蠅在乳牛頭上大快朵頤、從中間被切開的小牛，還有一顆鑲滿鑽石的頭骨，這些裝置藝術全都是他以現代視角詮釋藝術的例子。

赫斯特高中時的美術課差點被當掉，在上大學攻讀美術之前，他曾在工地工作過。求學時期，他也曾在太平間打工，也就是大體下葬前停放的地方。這份工作對他的作品有很大的影響，他的作品大多與死亡有關。他經常把死掉的動物拿來用，將動物的屍體保存在化學藥劑裡，然後再對大眾公開展示。身為欣然接受以死亡為主題的藝術家，赫斯特是英國最具影響力的當代藝術家之一，他的作品通常都是價值數百萬美元。

赫斯特第一個重要的作品叫做《千年》，是對生與死的評論。一個牛頭被蛆啃食著，蛆後來變成了蒼蠅，卻又被捕蚊燈殺死。有一些蒼蠅存活了下來並產卵，然後繼續著這個循環。藝術贊助家查爾斯・薩奇對這個概念的原創性相當驚豔，當下就買下這個作品。

薩奇自那時起便同意資助赫斯特的創作，赫斯特用這筆錢買了一條鯊魚，並將之泡在福馬林（又稱甲醛，是一種保存屍體不腐敗的化學藥劑）裡，然後命名為《生者對死者無動於衷》。2004 年，該作品以一千兩百萬美元賣出。即使兩人後來因為一連串的爭執而分道揚鑣，但薩奇仍堅稱赫斯特是個天才。

赫斯特在藝術上所呈現的獨特性引發了很多爭議，因為有許多作品都是由助理完成的。他著名的《點點畫》是由三百多個隨機點上的彩色點點組合而成，但其中只有五個點是出自於赫斯特本人之手。

赫斯特於 2012 年在泰特現代藝術館舉辦的回顧展，充分顯示出對他作品評價的兩極化：該展覽吸引了空前的人潮，但同時也引來大量的抨擊。不論是喜愛或是憎惡他，達米恩・赫斯特都是不會被輕易遺忘的紀錄保持人。

31 青春永駐 (P. 80)

你可曾想過永遠活著是什麼樣的感覺？對大部分人而言，這是不可能的夢想，但對一種水母來說，長生不死只是生命的一部分。這種水母被稱作「不朽的水母」，只有五毫米長，比你的指甲還小。

這種水母的特別之處在於牠可以藉由「反轉分化」的過程，改變細胞，逆轉生命週期。性成熟之後，牠可迫使自己的細胞慢慢變成自己的年輕版。將外傘和觸手縮回，並沉入海底變成不成熟的苗芽，或稱作水螅。這隻水螅可以再繁衍出與成熟水母完全相同的新水母。

這種反轉生命週期的好處之一，就是在食物缺乏或是情況危及時，牠們可以存活下去。藉由返回不成熟的水螅期，等待困境過去，直到狀況更穩定時再出現。

儘管可能會被其他海洋生物吃掉，渺小的水母得以藉此卓越的生存能力，排除萬難，開枝散葉到全世界。科學家懷疑，這種長生不死的物種，意外地被遠洋貨運船隻載往世界各地。船隻把水母吸進船體，接著將牠們帶到距離原本棲息地千萬哩之遠的地方。現在全世界很多海洋都有牠的蹤跡，因此有些人開始稱呼牠們為「入侵者」。

雖然一百多年前這個物種就已被發現，但直到最近，人們才開始注意到牠們令人讚嘆的能力。牠們能夠戲劇化地改變自我細胞的能力，已經引起亟欲找出癌症及心臟病解藥的科學家的極大興趣。如果能發現細胞如何轉換，或許可消弭現今的不治之症。

儘管科學家要花上好一陣子，才可能找出讓人類永遠不會因老化而死亡的方式，但是，毫無疑問地，這些長生不死的水母握有通往永生的解答。

32 永不止息的戰爭 (P. 82)

在遠古時代，猶太人居住的土地就是現今的以色列。這片土地於西元前一世紀被羅馬人征服，當時稱之為猶地亞。在接下來的兩千年間，這片小沙漠接連成為各帝國的屬地。隨著時間的變遷，猶太人大多遷移到世界各地。後來，阿拉伯人取而代之，他們將此地稱之為巴勒斯坦，並稱自己為巴勒斯坦人。

第二次世界大戰後，聯合國決定將大部分的巴勒斯坦歸還給猶太人，迫使無數的巴勒斯坦人離開家園。長期居住此地的巴勒斯坦人與新來的猶太人爆發了衝突。猶太人最終贏得了戰爭，以色列於1948年正式建國。

武裝衝突迅速地再次爆發，然而，這次是在以色列人與其周邊的阿拉伯國家之間。接下來的25年，這個地區發起一連串的戰爭。有些是猶太人挑起的，有些則是阿拉伯人。但是，以色列人贏得每場戰役，在以色列人嚴厲的統治下，巴勒斯坦百姓持續受苦。結果造成很多巴勒斯坦人投向恐怖主義，就為了要趕走猶太人。

到底該怎麼做呢？以色列堅持建國的權力，該地必須被認可為猶太國家，也堅持保有他們所征服的領地。而阿拉伯國家拒絕承認以色列，除非以色列歸還領地。他們也要求當時因以色列建國，而被驅逐的巴勒斯坦人的後裔，獲准回到原居地。

阿拉伯人與以色列人之間的衝突也影響到世界其他地方。以美國為首的西方國家，在政治、軍事以及經濟上完全支持以色列人。這讓許多阿拉伯人與其他穆斯林憎恨西方國家，甚至採取報復行動。在全球則有許多人非常同情巴勒斯坦人，他們不瞭解為何西方國家對以色列人的暴行視而不見，反稱以色列人為受害者。

根據現階段的政治局面，以阿雙方之間的衝突，態度愈來愈強硬，也愈來愈極端。不論接下來如何演變，這場永不止息的戰爭還將持續很長的一段時間。

33 下一個「亞特蘭提斯」？ (P. 84)

隨著時間一天天過去，人口逾八百萬的泰國首都一點一滴的沉入大海。曼谷正以每年1.5至5公分的速度下降當中。對興建在沼澤地上、海拔只有1.5公尺的曼谷來說，這樣的下降速率是相當可觀的。

曼谷會逐漸沉入泰國灣，是由好幾個因素造成。首先也是最重要的因素是都市化。每年，曼谷因為吸收來自周圍鄉村地區的移民而擴張。沉重的建物興建在灌溉渠道以及自然防洪工事的上方，導致海岸受到侵蝕。曼谷的居民愈多，意味著必須抽取愈多的地下水，供居民飲用；抽取愈多的地下水，曼谷下沉得愈快。這是難以阻擋的惡性循環。

更何況，下沉的過程是無法逆轉的。曼谷每下沉一英寸，就會永遠失去一英寸的土地。

曼谷正在下沉，而海平面卻正在上升。由於這種危險的組合，有些專家預測，不久之後，曼谷將會面臨一場大災難。有人認為，到了2030年，曼谷部分地區將會沉入水中。泰國國家災難示警中心的史密斯·哈馬薩羅加更進一步預測，在2100年，曼谷會成為下一個亞特蘭提斯。

如果泰國政府想要避免這場災難，必須迅速採取行動。其中一個計劃是在泰國灣興建海堤系統，以保護城市不受海平面上升的影響。然而，興建海堤需耗資數十億美元，而且一些傑出的科學界人士都認為，興建海堤可能毫無助益。他們提出，前幾次威脅曼谷的大洪水都是來自北方，而非來自南方。

另一個選擇是，泰國政府必須更強力控制曼谷的都市擴張，撤離湄南河畔的建物，轉而興建在地勢較高的地方。

挽救曼谷會是件費時、費錢又耗力的事。如果泰國政府拖延太久，他們可能就只剩下一種選擇：放棄這座「東方威尼斯」，在別處重建新的城市。

34 日本文學的超級巨星 (P. 86)

村上春樹擅於模糊真實與想像之間的界線，這項天賦讓他在太平洋兩岸家喻戶曉。是什麼原因讓這位日本作家，不僅在祖國紅透半邊天，同時也譽海外呢？

首先，村上春樹有著相當浪漫的背景。他出生於1949年，父母皆為日本文學教師，大學時期在東京攻讀戲劇。畢業後，在唱片行工作了一陣子，在1970年代中期決定與妻子一起開一間爵士酒吧。

1978年，村上春樹在看棒球比賽時，突然想要寫小說。那天晚上回到家以後，他拿了筆就開始寫。幾個月後，他將作品寄去參加文學競賽，結果出版社同意予以出版，這是村上春樹的第一部小說《聽風的歌》。雖然村上春樹之後一直都在寫作，他在日本仍沒什麼名氣，直到1987年《挪威的森林》出版。十年後，《發條鳥年代記》一出版，各國的讀者便愛上了他。2013年，《沒有色彩的多崎作和他的巡禮之年》在日本發行的頭三天就賣出了35萬本。

村上春樹的書在全球已被譯為50多種語言，許多人公開猜測他總有一天會贏得諾貝爾文學獎。看來，當年那場棒球比賽相當啟發人心！

全球的讀者也很喜歡村上春樹獨特的文學風格。他彷彿能看透我們身處的這個世界，進入下一個世界。這使他寫出來的小說成了讀者最純粹的逃避之所，讓讀者從現實的生活裡放個假。

村上春樹的散文融合了東西方的文化。他雖然受過日本的教養薰陶，在文化上卻頗受西方的影響。他從小到大讀的是西方文學作家，如馮內果與費茲傑羅等的作品，聽的是西方音樂，如賽隆尼斯・孟克、納京高、披頭四與巴布・迪倫等人的音樂。

東西文化交會的結果，讓這位作家在叛逆中長大，卻又生活在一個循規蹈矩的社會中。這樣的矛盾在他的小說中並未以政治觀點體現，而是化為現實與幻想之間的模糊界線。

35　稀土金屬 (P. 88)

稀土金屬（或稱稀土元素，簡稱 REEs）如鈧、釔等，其實並非真的特別稀有。這 17 種礦物大多像銅一樣非常普遍。最稀少的量也還比黃金高上兩百倍。大多數沒有化學學位的一般人，就算看到它們，可能也叫不出它們的名字，因為它們都是鮮為人知的化學元素。即便如此，這些稀土金屬對現代科技來說非常重要，從電池和檯燈，以及噴射機引擎到衛星通訊系統，全都需要稀土金屬。

雖然稀土金屬在地殼表層中很常見，卻很少會形成足夠大的礦藏以供開採，而通常是稀疏分布在地殼表層中，因此要獲得可以使用的量相當困難，這也就是為什麼它們會被認為是稀有的。

此外，對很多現在社會習以為常的東西（如智慧型手機、冰箱等）來說，稀土金屬是不可或缺的原料，因此造就了稀土金屬的價值。

可想而知，萃取、出口這些稀土金屬是非常有利可圖的生意。過去 20 多年來，主宰這產業的國家是中國，1990 年產出的稀土金屬占全球產量的 27%，如今來到了 90%。這讓中國壟斷了珍貴稀土金屬的全球供應量。

也因此中國在 2009 年引起爭議，因為倚賴中國供應稀土金屬的美國、歐盟和墨西哥向世界貿易組織抗議中國稀土金屬的出口量過低。

中國逐步地在減少稀土金屬的出口量，在 2011 年降到 35%，這項舉動使得稀土金屬的價格高漲。世界貿易組織在 2011 年裁定這項行為違反規定。中國提出抗議，解釋他們限制出口量是為了未來子孫保留天然資源。不過，2015 年，中國還是被迫解除稀土金屬出口量的限制。

雖然開採與加工取得稀土金屬是一項艱鉅且危險的工作，但全球對這些重要礦物的需求，在可見的未來仍將主宰全球貿易。

36　熱情的傳遞藝術 (P. 90)

大部分人一想到啦啦隊，想到的是精巧的動作、極度危險的特技和短短的裙子。但是啦啦隊真的就像在好萊塢電影《魅力四射》中所描述的這麼光鮮亮麗嗎？這個現在全世界共有 160 多萬人從事的獨特運動，究竟來自何處呢？

啦啦隊的故事起源於 19 世紀晚期的美國。在 1898 年，明尼蘇達大學一位名叫強尼・坎貝爾的學生，苦思該如何幫自己學校的足球隊在一場關鍵的比賽中打敗對手。他決定，最能夠幫助該隊的方式就是讓群眾更投入。在那場重要比賽的當天，他站在台上，帶領著群眾喊著「啦！啦！啦！明尼蘇達！」。他的熱情充滿感染力，而明尼蘇達足球隊也贏得了比賽。啦啦隊的概念由此而生。

1898 年之後，啦啦隊在美國各校如雨後春筍般冒出。不過早先這個運動完全由男性主導，直到 1923 年，明尼蘇達大學再次開創了新的潮流，引進了女子啦啦隊的概念。1940 年代，第二次世界大戰爆發，男人飄洋過海打仗，為了填補男人留下的空缺，女性有了許多進展，這就是為何啦啦隊演變成我們今日所知的以女子為主的運動。

女子成為啦啦隊員，啦啦隊的動作也隨之變化。舊式固定不動的單調加油方式很快地就被手臂動作、踢腿與翻筋斗所取代。隨著時代的變遷，這項運動不斷的演化。

1975 年，國際啦啦隊協會（UCA）首次舉辦訓練營，包括配有背景音樂的啦啦隊表演動作，又讓啦啦隊朝著目前的型態跨近了一步。這也奠定了競賽型啦啦隊的基礎。

1982 年，ESPN 轉播了第一屆啦啦隊國際錦標賽，讓這項運動走入鎂光燈下。自此以後，競賽型啦啦隊在美國大為流行，在世界各地也愈來愈受歡迎。估計世界各地大約有十萬名啦啦隊員，在澳洲、加拿大、日本、芬蘭、法國、德國和臺灣等地相互較勁。

37 全新的自己？(P. 94)

愈來愈多亞洲人發現，他們不用再留著天生的那張臉，或是因深夜喝了太多的珍珠奶茶而造就出來的大屁股。他們一直夢寐以求的身材，只要找個醫師就能辦到！

亞洲正迅速成為世界整形手術之都。30 年前，亞洲的整形率遠比西方來得低，因為當時人民的收入低、合格醫師較少，以及排斥外在虛榮心的文化因素。如今，如南韓和臺灣等國都是那些想要改變面貌與身材的人可去之處。在南韓，每 1000 人裡就有 20 人動過整形手術，大部分的人都是去江南（首爾的富人區）做的手術。愈來愈多來自越南、臺灣和日本的人都一窩蜂地跑到江南，這個地區有 500 多間診所能為客戶打造一個「全新的你」。

那麼，到底是什麼原因讓亞洲人這麼熱衷於整形呢？首先也是最主要的原因，是人們的手頭寬裕了。在亞洲，一張漂亮的臉成了成功的象徵，整形可以向世界展現你的成功。職場帶來的龐大壓力也成了去整形的因素，並不是只有男女藝人希望青春不老，一般人也有這樣的夢想。有些求職者為了避免在面對資歷相同，卻又長得比較漂亮的對手競爭時失去優勢，而選擇整形。

相較於西方人，亞洲人對整形的要求大不相同。西方顧客大多希望經由去除皺紋、眼袋脂肪等手術，讓自己看起來更年輕；亞洲客人則希望看起來像西方人。亞洲常見的整型手術有割雙眼皮、隆乳、小臉及縮唇手術。

整形其實也沒什麼值得驚奇的。畢竟，亞洲就是整形手術的發源地之一。在第四世紀的印度醫療古籍《蘇胥如塔·妙聞集》裡，就有一個章節敘述了當鼻子不幸被削掉之後，該如何重建的內容。

38 成為雕塑 (P. 96)

我們利用藝術傳達自己的想法、意見與經驗。藝術能幫助我們往外走，與他人建立聯繫。但為何藝術總被侷限於畫布上、書籍裡，或者是電影膠卷中呢？藝術為什麼不能包覆四面牆與天花板，或是擴張到一棟建築物那麼大呢？是的，這就是裝置藝術所做的事。

裝置藝術誕生於 1970 年代的觀念藝術運動。觀念藝術認為，比起美學或是藝術品的外觀，藝術品所傳達的想法更加重要。一件優質的觀念藝術會激發我們思考，雖然它的外表不一定讓我們驚艷。

採取雕塑的觀點來看裝置藝術，並將其概念反轉。當我們欣賞一件雕塑品時，通常是由外往內看。然而，在觀賞裝置藝術時，我們位在藝術品之內，被藝術品所環繞。在某種的程度上，我們成為雕塑的一部分。

華人藝術家艾未未於 2010 年展出的作品《葵花籽》，就是說明裝置藝術的一個好例子。艾未未將一億粒以陶瓷燒製而成的葵花籽，鋪在倫敦泰特現代美術館的地板上。每一粒獨一無二的葵花籽都是在中國一家小作坊手繪而成。在原本是發電廠的泰特現代美術館中，陶瓷葵花籽手繪的人情味，與冷硬的工業化空間，兩者的對比差異形成了展品的整體美感。這件作品也引起大眾對中國製造以及全球化現象的討論。

內萊·阿澤維多則是另一位知名的裝置藝術家。她到世界各地旅遊，創造出數百件小型冰雕人像。可以想見，一旦氣溫上升，她的作品一定會漸漸融化，但是，那正是藝術家要傳達的重要訊息。內萊鑄造這些「融化中的人」，就是為了讓大眾意識到全球暖化的威脅。

還有許多其他裝置藝術家試圖將我們拉進他們的雕塑作品中。派翠克·多爾迪使用各種樹枝和枝枒，建造出露天的大型房屋、茅舍、紀念碑，甚至是公路。在法國，吉爾勞姆·雷蒙以大量的中古車與卡車，創造出龐大機器人的景象。當世界就是你的畫布，沒有什麼事不可能。

39　抄襲致富 (P. 98)

在大企業的世界裡，有兩個可以遵循的主要策略：「應變策略」及「謹慎策略」。你會預期新興的企業使用應變策略。應變策略有彈性、實驗性質高、嘗試各種新方式以找出最佳的商業模式。但是在公司找出最能獲利的攻擊方式後，則改用謹慎策略。謹慎策略可以積極拓展，並以極快的速度推進贏家策略。

大多數的西方企業始於應變策略，再過渡至謹慎策略。然而中國在過去三十年來，歷經史無前例的擴展，被迫採取捷徑，也就是另一種發展策略。多數中國企業，並非由應變策略起家再轉型至謹慎策略，取而代之的是完全省略應變策略，並快速推向並非由自身所創建的謹慎策略。中國快速蓬勃的經濟也因此被戲稱為「抄襲經濟」。

由於這種「抄襲」策略，許多在中國的外國投資者已經察覺智慧財產權被侵害，並且提出異議，嚴禁大眾非經原作者允許，不得複製與發行產品。

美國駐中國大使駱家輝提出建言，認為中國如果不願意積極執行智慧財產權，許多有實力的中國年輕企業，只會遠走海外發展壯大，替發展中的中國經濟強權，製造出問題。不過中國發言人卻駁斥這樣的建言，堅稱這樣的限制只會箝制中國企業的發展。

以中國的汽車產業為例，中國的汽車數量從1977年的一百萬輛到目前約有近八千五百萬輛車，每年製造的汽車甚至比美國還多。主要的汽車大廠，像是BMW以及賓士，都曾指控某些中國企業剽竊他們的設計理念。不過在如此短暫的時間內，要因應如此大量的需求，這種抄襲策略似乎是必要的，儘管從西方國家的觀點，此舉並不可取。

40　書的探險 (P. 100)

書蟲最愛的，莫過於沉浸在迷人的小說世界裡。然而，在不久的將來，原本不起眼的紙本書將一頭栽進嶄新且刺激的互動式閱讀中。

如果你能收到書中主角寫給你的電子郵件，那會是什麼樣子？如果你實際親臨故事中提到的某個地點，從而開啟了一個全新的章節，那又會是什麼樣子？假設你在現實生活中執行某些任務，卻開啟了全新的故事秘密情節。想像一下，你把自己加進故事裡，真正地融入了故事的敘述中。這些都只是現在互動式書籍的讀者使用到的某些功能。讀者甚至可以下載互動故事的應用程式到手機上。

即便這聽起來是革命性的變化，但是這半個世紀以來，讀者其實一直都在參與故事情節的發展。《驚險岔路口》系列書於 1970 年代開始出版，讀者每讀幾頁後，就要進行選擇。例如會出現「如果你想審問園丁，請翻到第23頁。」這種句子，由讀者選擇故事接下來的走向為何。每個選擇最後都會引導讀者走向約40種不同結局中的一個。

電玩遊戲也使用了互動式小說。文字冒險遊戲是最早開發的其中一款電腦遊戲。玩家只要輸入「打開信箱」或是「走出屋子」等指令，就能推動情節。

現在在日本很熱門的視覺小說就是文字冒險遊戲的另一種變化。這類遊戲使用靜止的漫畫圖像，有背景音樂，遊戲的成分卻通常不多。讀者有時需要在支線劇情之間做出選擇，但除此之外全部的體驗都與故事內容有關。日本現在市面上販售的電腦遊戲大多屬於視覺小說。

不管書本未來會變成什麼樣子，紙本或螢幕，看來讀者永遠都會不厭其煩的找到讓自己沉浸在有趣情節中的新方式。

41　墨水的末日？ (P. 102)

假設在整個就學期間，你就只用一本數學筆記本，或是每天早上拿著昨天發行的報紙，到店裡去重印今天的新聞內容。由於光印刷再寫紙的問世，上述的假設可能很快就會成真！

經過多年的努力，美中兩國的研究員共同研發出一種很不尋常的化學物質。將之塗抹於一般紙張上時，就能摒棄油墨，改運用紫外線光進行印刷。這種紙的外觀與觸感與一般紙無異，可是印出來的文字只會維持五至十天。若是不需要保留這麼久的時間，只要將紙張加熱就能在10分鐘內消除字跡。不管怎樣，這種紙能重複印刷達80次以上且無損其品質！

此項發明的益處顯而易見。報紙、雜誌、海報、筆記、超市產品有效期的標籤等，不過是眾多僅需暫時資訊的幾個例子。如果這些紙張能重複印刷使用，那不是很棒嗎？

此外，還有環境上的優勢。紙張的生產是汙染的主要來源之一，而回收紙因其去除油墨的過程，同樣也會造成環境汙染。在某些國家，三分之一的林木遭到砍伐，以製作紙張及硬紙板。那些紙最後都到哪了？大多都在垃圾掩埋場，占了四成的垃圾傾倒量。我們愈認識這種可重複印刷的紙，就愈有理由愛上它！

然而，目前想要廣泛使用這項新科技還只是一個夢想。雖然可重複印刷的紙要價和普通紙差不多，但是能快速印刷的雷射光還不存在。由於藍色顏料是光印刷技術的一個要素，大部分的紫外線光印刷品依然不是白底藍字就是藍底白字。這表示目前只有文字和素描能以此方法重複印製。

不過，紫外線光印刷是一項令人興奮的新發展，我們都應該要密切關注。誰知道呢？或許有一天，這本書也會有個以紫外線光印刷的版本，而你在讀完本書後，就可以拿去重新印刷啦！

42　瘋狂有道 (P. 104)

炎炎夏日裡，時鐘像起司般融化；四肢如火柴棒纖細的大象，背上馱著金字塔型的紀念碑；漂浮的犀牛角，彷彿正張著眼睛瞪著外海──這些圖畫來自於腦海裡非理性的角落，都是薩爾瓦多‧達利創造的，富含神祕意味的題材。

獨樹一格的服裝品味，長而捲翹的八字鬍，眼睛睜得老大，好像不時受到驚嚇，達利不但在繪畫上，也在生活裡徹底實踐他的藝術理論。他曾穿著深海潛水衣（包括鋼盔）去講課，使得聽眾只能聽到他從鋼盔裡隱約傳來的聲音。他也曾邀請藝術評論家脫得一絲不掛讓他親自拍照，只不過，相機裡沒有裝上底片。他設計了奇異的藝術品，像是有名的《龍蝦電話》，他問道，為什麼餐廳從不在他點龍蝦時，給他一臺煮熟的電話？

達利怪異行為的背後原因，在於他將自己視為超現實主義運動的具體代表。當他被超現實主義團體除名時，他宣稱：「我本人就是超現實主義」。

達利的超現實主義包括尋找事物之間的連結，而理性往往無法聯想得到。為了達成目的，他採取了一種他稱之為「偏執批判」的方法。藉著誘發周遭世界極度的不信任與恐懼，物體產生新的型式，跳脫其在理性世界裡的位置。這個方法就像是如何在雲朵中找出不同形狀，或是在岩石裡看見臉，或是讓達利可以創造他所謂的「手繪夢想照片」，這是他真實內在的反映。

1904年，達利出生於西班牙北部，他的藝術天份得到媽媽的鼓勵，並於馬德里學習美術。他的繪畫技巧相當優異，往後也在作品裡發揮到極致，他的畫中常出現複雜的幾何概念和視覺幻象。

達利的作品探索了非邏輯中荒唐、嚇人的一面。有些人稱他瘋子，但達利直率地答道：「我和瘋子的唯一不同之處，就是瘋子認為自己正常，而我知道自己瘋了。」

43　漫步在月球 (P. 108)

卡帕多奇亞有你前所未見的景觀。卡帕多奇亞位於土耳其的中部地區，以其自然形成的岩石結構而聞名。有些遊客說，拜訪卡帕多奇亞就像拜訪月球一樣。

卡帕多奇亞究竟為何如此特別呢？究其原因，大自然和人文影響都脫不了關係。以該地區著名的「精靈煙囪」為例，這些石柱歷經數千年風吹雨打的侵蝕，高度達40公尺，有的頂端覆蓋著較硬的錐狀岩石，有時看起來有點像帽子。這種圓錐狀的岩石比下方較軟的岩石更耐侵蝕。

現在要說的是人文影響了。卡帕多奇亞地區就位在古絲綢之路上。幾千年來，這裡是歐亞商人與士兵的必經之處，有些人決定在此落地生根。但由於卡帕多奇亞沙漠般的地景，沒有任何樹木，這些人面臨了居住的難題。為了解決這個問題，開拓者拿起鐵鍬開始挖，他們挖的對象是較大的精靈煙囪，建造出一個有著複雜網絡的洞穴來定居。他們的做法使得此處的岩層佈滿星羅棋布的洞穴，最終形成了令人嘆為觀止的景觀。

快轉回到現在，這些洞穴裡有些已經被改造成了旅館套房。每個遊客都可以嘗試來個「洞穴體驗」，像數千年前的開拓者一樣住在洞穴裡。但還是有個重要的差別：現在你可有了床墊、枕頭和毛毯！

探索這些自然奇觀，其中一個最好的方法是搭乘熱氣球。熱氣球營運商在卡帕多奇亞十分常見，觀光客搭一至兩小時的熱氣球就能從高空俯瞰，沉浸在眼前的美景中。這些熱氣球之旅可以很豪華，有的甚至提供自助餐以及香檳祝酒。如果你想要比較私密一點的，那麼有專為像蜜月或求婚這類特殊場合而設計的行程。在高空中出現這麼突如其來的驚喜，不是很浪漫嗎！

44　比手畫腳要小心！ (P. 110)

　　身處異地卻又不會說當地的語言，通常會讓人很挫折。在這種情況下，自然會想要以肢體語言來溝通。打手勢確實是很普遍的辦法，但是其含義跟語言一樣會因地而異。

　　舉個例子來說，將大拇指指尖和食指指尖按在一起，同時伸出另外三指，在西方這會立即被理解為okay，表示「好」或「沒問題」的意思。但在巴西，大家的第一個反應則是受辱。而在某些東亞國家，這表示金錢。想像一下這可能會衍生出多少誤會！

　　光是召喚某人過來你這裡的手勢，也會因地域差異而讓人一頭霧水。西方人會舉起手掌，手心朝著自己，食指向內彎曲，做出勾食指的動作。亞洲人則認為這個手勢很沒有禮貌，因為那只適合用來召喚小狗。他們召喚他人的手勢是手心朝下，除了大拇指外的四指合在一起來回擺動。可是這卻正是西方人叫人走開的手勢！

　　有個手勢卻在各國都能充分表達它的意思，那就是手背朝外，舉起中指的手勢。美國人認為這個手勢無禮至極，對英國人來說，在這個手勢上加入一根豎起的食指，形成V字，也具有同樣無禮的涵義。然而在第二次世界大戰期間，已故的英國首相溫斯頓．邱吉爾就曾做出這個手勢，只不過他的手心是朝外的，後來成了表示勝利的手勢。25年後，美國的嬉皮在越戰期間，用同樣的手勢作為渴望和平的象徵。如今，越南人和其他東亞人只要拍照，就會不由自主地做出這個和平手勢。已經一頭霧水了嗎？

　　即使最簡單的手勢也會引起跨文化的問題。在西方，豎起大拇指有正面的意思，而大拇指向下則是負面的意思。在中東地區，豎起大拇指有負面的意思，而大拇指向下則毫無意義。這有可能就是導致兩個社群間紛爭不斷的部分原因嗎？

　　當語言無法溝通時，我們本能會選擇以肢體語言來進行溝通，不過這要冒很大的風險。我的建議？下次出國時，帶本常用語手冊吧！

45　為了理想營利 (P. 112)

　　資本主義能不能在環境與社會公義的議題上形成一股善的力量？這是社會企業運動的核心問題。隨便去問任何一個正在努力創業的社會企業家，他們肯定會說：「能」。

　　社會企業在某些地方跟一般企業沒什麼兩樣。其提供產品或服務、聘雇員工、旨在盈利。但是，有個最大的不同點：社會企業努力要讓這個世界變得更美好。你或許會想：不是每個企業都想讓世界變得更美好嗎？像蘋果這樣的大公司，捐了幾百萬美元給慈善機構。確實如此，而這涉及到社會企業運動的核心問題。

　　對於到底要如何定義社會企業，至今仍意見分歧。對有些人來說，社會企業是將所有營利投入社會福利的企業。不妨想想將收益用於資助當地食物銀行的舊貨店。這是對社會企業「最純粹」的詮釋，不過還是衍生出一些難題。例如，舊貨店該不該擴大開設分店？若開分店就能使更多人免於飢餓。然而，投入拓展的資金愈多，看起來就愈像是一般的企業。

　　有些人則將社會企業界定為一家企業，其目標是裨益社會或環境。將有害的廢棄物轉化為有用商品的工廠即是一例。工廠的營運跟其他公司一樣，卻又能惠及當地居民。社會企業的另一種解釋，則是聘雇在主流經濟中掙扎求生的弱勢族群。臺灣的喜憨兒基金會就是一例。該基金會經營烘焙坊，聘雇的員工都是有心智障礙的年輕人。

　　社會企業的定義如此分歧，好像隨便一家公司都可以成為社會企業一樣。不過，我們現在所做的就是拿新瓶裝舊酒。社會企業已經存在了好幾千年。只不過以往，我們簡稱為鄰里守望相助。甚至可以說，「社會企業」就跟人的樂善好施一樣歷史悠久。

46 冰下的美麗威脅 (P. 114)

攝影師保羅・奇茨卡在探索加拿大北部時，偶然發現了一個奇妙的景象。吸引保羅目光的不是白雪皚皚的山巒、不是松樹、也不是寧靜的湖泊，而是一些氣泡。這數百個氣泡就存在結冰的湖面下，一個個清晰可見，凍結在冰下，宛如怪異的海洋生物，也許更像外星生物。

攝影師所發現的氣泡其實是一種名為甲烷的氣體。甲烷是一種溫室效應氣體，其威力比二氧化碳還大。據估計，甲烷造成的溫室效應比二氧化碳大上25倍。甲烷屬於高度易燃的氣體，釋放時會引起爆炸。甲烷氣泡是湖底細菌釋放出來的氣體。這些細菌會分解植物，並在其消化的過程釋放出甲烷，你可以說這是細菌放屁的方式。天氣暖和時，這些甲烷氣泡就會浮出水面，釋放到大氣中。但是，當湖水結冰時，這些氣泡便被困在冰層裡。

甲烷氣泡可不僅是張美麗的照片。事實上，這些氣泡對於我們全人類來說，是個嚴重的威脅。甲烷是導致全球暖化的氣體。地球某些地區終年處在冰凍狀態，我們稱之為「永凍層」。隨著地球氣候溫度的上升，永凍層融化，從湖泊或河川裡釋放出甲烷氣泡。而甲烷氣泡的釋放導致更嚴重的溫室效應，使更多湖泊或河川融化。這個過程被稱之為「回饋循環」，乃因結果導致了成因，互為因果。根據某位科學家所言，冰凍的甲烷是氣候的定時炸彈，隨時都會引爆。

對抗全球暖化之所以如此重要，甲烷的回饋循環固然是原因之一。我們必須盡己所能解決這個問題。身體力行的做法可以是種一棵樹，或者是每天走路上班上學。如此一來，將有助於保存這些冰凍氣泡的自然美景，也能拯救整個地球。就讓這些細菌放出來的危險的屁待在它們該在的地方——即安然待在冰下吧！

47 蛾眼的啟發！ (P. 116)

如果你曾試圖在大太陽底下看清智慧型手機上的內容，你會知道那並不容易。通常需要待在陰暗處才能看清楚螢幕，尤其是小螢幕。如果太陽就在你的頭頂上，你的眼睛接收到的是一陣難受的刺眼眩光，接下來一兩分鐘你什麼都看不到！

然而，由於飛蛾的幫助，這問題如今已迎刃而解。沒錯，就是飛蛾。臺灣和美國的科學家，從這夜行性昆蟲身上汲取靈感，找到了解決正午眩光的辦法。

讓我們在大白天也能看清路邊電視螢幕的科技，其實源自於能讓飛蛾夜間視物的方法。飛蛾複眼上的微觀結構能讓光線進入眼睛，卻不會反射出來。對昆蟲來說，這有雙重好處。牠們能在黑暗中視物，而天敵也不易看到牠們眼睛的反射光。不過，當相似的微小結構被印壓進一片薄而柔韌的薄膜上時，就能遮斷光線，從而避免產生眩光。這表示即使在豔陽下，我們也能清晰看到覆有這層薄膜的螢幕畫面。

仿蛾眼薄膜最初是為了用在太陽能板上而研發，因其具有不會反射光線的特性，故能更有效保存電力。不過如今，該科技已經準備好用於各種新用途。除了智慧型手機的螢幕，玻璃窗、路標、手錶、里程表及燃油表也都可以透過這種便宜的材質改善品質。研究人員聲稱，在天氣晴朗時，仿蛾眼薄膜的可讀性可提高十倍，即使在陽光直射下也能提高五倍。該薄膜還具有自我清潔的功能，汙垢、灰塵和指紋都將不再是問題。

也許仿蛾眼薄膜最棒的一點是，你不必花錢買新摩托車或新手機。它可以像螢幕保護貼一樣，直接黏在舊裝置的表面上。然而，未來這項科技也許會成為製程的一部分，在你要買該產品的時候，就已經直接黏貼在上面了。

所以下次看到飛蛾時，要感謝牠給了我們人類很有用的想法哦！

48 學以色列人戰鬥 (P. 118)

以色列近身格鬥術的故事就像一部好萊塢電影。故事始於成長於絕境中的男人，他的名字叫做伊米‧李確費爾德。伊米是武術家、拳擊手和雜技演員。他也是一名猶太人，而作為猶太人在 1930 年代的捷克斯洛伐克（已解體的歐洲國家）是非常危險的。因為宗教因素，當時的伊米在暴力威脅下，決定要採取應對之策。他與其他的猶太拳擊手聯手，致力於想出保衛他們人民的辦法，其目標是去除武術中的「藝術」的成分。他們想要自創一種實用、有效且便於教學的搏擊之法。這套格鬥技巧就是以色列近身格鬥術。

伊米的故事並沒有到此結束。他於 1940 年納粹入侵之際，逃離捷克斯洛伐克。爾後於 1942 年抵達巴勒斯坦，並開始訓練當地人自衛。他的才能立即得到認可，並受雇訓練軍警部隊。他在 1948 年以色列立國後，成為軍隊的總教練。這個職位一待就是二十多年，而他的成就顯而易見，以色列近身格鬥術如今是以色列國防軍的國技。

以色列近身格鬥術首重實用性。伊米在發展這套格鬥術時，大量借鑑其他的武術。不過，他只採用既有效又容易理解的技巧。因此，以色列近身格鬥術的每個動作在實戰中都是有用的。這套格鬥術教導了如何抵禦刀槍等武器的威脅，如何將家中隨便一樣物品變成武器，並強調迅速出擊，使攻擊者束手就擒。身負以色列近身格鬥技能的人會攻擊人體的脆弱部位，像是眼睛、脖子、臉或膝蓋等。

以色列近身格鬥術也是任何人都可習得的格鬥技。伊米想要發展的是不複雜，且可以簡便教授的格鬥術。故男女老少，不論其年齡與體型，皆可接受訓練。但是，這可不代表訓練會很容易！

49 風靡世界的椰子油 (P. 122)

不論是從報紙或雜誌上，你可能都聽過椰子油。世界各地正興起一股椰子油的健康新風潮。

醫生發現椰子油富含健康的脂肪酸，人體很容易消化吸收。這類脂肪酸變成的熱量較不易轉換成體脂肪，其熱量在運動時也很容易燃燒。不過，椰子油的好處遠遠不止於此！研究顯示，椰子油能多方改善整體健康。舉例來說，椰子油富含天然的飽和脂肪，這些脂肪會增加健康的膽固醇，預防心臟病及高血壓。椰子油也含有豐富的抗氧化劑，有助於減少發炎反應。有些罹患關節炎及其他炎症疾病的患者，表示椰子油可以緩解腫脹與疼痛。椰子油也被認為有助於預防某些類型的癌症。

如果這樣還不夠，椰子油還可改善日常生活。研究顯示，椰子油能改善老年人的記憶功能，促進新陳代謝，讓人更有活力與耐力，恢復肌膚光澤，使看人起來更年輕。也難怪他們把椰子油叫做超級食物──因為它可以創造出超人！

當然，並不是每個人對於椰子油的看法都一致。有些醫生跟科學家並未認可椰子油的益處。例如美國心臟協會認為椰子油是一種飽和脂肪的「問題」來源。也有人說椰子油的好處被誇大了，仍需進行更多的研究來證實。有些記者則認為椰子油的盛行危害到世界各地的農民。

事實上，真相就在這兩者之間。椰子油已被證實對健康有驚人的益處。但是，就像生活中其他事情一樣，東西再好，也要適可而止。

50　高聳的壯麗 (P. 124)

中國廣西壯族自治區的陽朔縣內，有些山峰巖石的形狀相當獨特，可說是世上幾個最有趣的地形樣貌之一。

陽朔位於中國的東南方，自然風光十分如詩如畫。陽朔的山水充滿了名為「喀斯特」的特殊岩石（譯註：溶蝕石灰岩地形）。這些岩石巍然突出地面，就像樹木從地面向上生長。有趣的是，造就這種奇特地形的，不過是兩種十分簡單的成分：水和時間。

要形成陽朔如今獨特的地景，需要很長的一段時間。數百萬年前，桂林曾經是海灣，桂林的山陵當時沉浸在水中。水逐漸侵蝕山陵，將其塑造成柱狀。當水退去後，風雨繼續侵蝕石柱，造就了陽朔獨特的奇景。最終，我們在陽朔縣看到的岩石，是經過幾千萬年的歲月形成的！

陽朔縣內有幾座特別著名的喀斯特溶岩。首先是「九馬畫山」。這座地標是一座面臨灕江的巨岩峭壁。有些人能從溶岩的形態中看到丰姿各異其趣的九匹馬，故因此得名。崖面反射的陽光也很出名，宛若色彩斑斕的彩虹、光彩奪目，遊客為之炫目。顏色會依天氣以及一天的時刻，產生不同的變化。

「象鼻山」是陽朔縣內另一座著名的喀斯特溶岩。象鼻山是座石灰岩的拱門，位於灕江與桃花江的匯流處，拱門看起來像是一頭駐足江邊飲水的大象。拱門之下有一座月牙池，當光線在某種角度下照射時，池子發出的光宛如月亮，因而得名。

雖然陽朔擁有一些世界上最優美的喀斯特溶岩地形，但是世界上還有其他景點也有類似的地形。越南的下龍灣與馬來西亞的姆魯山，是另外兩個喀斯特地形的著名景點，其美景令我們千百年來讚嘆不已。

51　神秘的湯 (P. 126)

抓一把東方哲學、古老儀式、偽科學、迷信，以及北美原住民維靈主義，與一點占星術、超自然能力信仰和自助心理學攪拌一下，煮出來的湯就是新時代運動。

新時代運動是各種不同的靈學、神祕以及魔法派別的大雜燴，它已成為現存宗教之外多數另類信仰的總稱。新時代運動的信仰經常提倡靈性，認為天地萬物以某種有意義的方式連結。然而，它的內容相當廣泛，並且吸收了無數不同的信仰系統，不管其起源或是背景脈絡如何。

新時代運動與科學和主流宗教相反，主要提倡魔法的存在，而不注重科學或神性，此點由新時代運動的治癒理論可見一斑，例如水晶療法。他們認為水晶具有魔力，佩帶在身上能提供保護、療癒的魔力磁場。由於其兼容並蓄的本質，新時代運動甚至納入了一些常見的陰謀論，像是相信幽浮的存在，英國巨石陣的神祕力量等地球不解之謎。

心理學家麥克．蘭岡認為，尋求新時代運動慰藉的人想要追求精神的刺激，卻覺得主流宗教過於複雜或是不願意為宗教而奉獻。此外，由於新時代運動兼容並蓄的本質，每個人都可以有所依從，一旦信其一，要認同其他謬論也就愈來愈容易了。

有些北美原住民對於自己的傳統信仰被明顯的濫用感到被冒犯。他們認為新時代運動利用北美原住民文化當中特有的習俗慣例，單單是為了錢，或是扭曲以符合個人需求。因此，他們將那些宣稱自己實行或精通北美原住民靈性治療，但本身卻非北美原住民的人，稱為「塑膠醫者」。

52　淘金熱 (P. 128)

在加拿大荒野深處中的一座帳篷裡，淘金客約翰嘆了一口氣。現在是1865年，這是他第三次趕上淘金的熱潮。這一次是在加拿大的大灣區，但也有可能是在其他任何地方。畢竟，淘金的故事總是一成不變。有些幸運的人挖到金塊，在你知曉以前，來自世界各地的淘金客便蜂擁而至。他們都抱著相同的夢想而來，但是只有少數人能帶走大筆財富。

他閉上眼睛，聽著落在帳篷上的滂沱雨聲。他想起了他的第一次機會，是1829年的喬治亞淘金熱潮。那時他還小，捲入他父親的「淘金熱」之中。到喬治亞的路途難行，等他們到了目的地時，現場已有數千名其他淘金客。早到的人已經在喬治亞的溪流裡，「淘選」出最容易找到的黃金。淘選是指淘金客以淘金盤在河床上淘洗砂金，這種技術成本低廉又簡單。當約翰跟父親到達喬治亞時，所剩下的都是不容易開採的金礦。只有有錢人才有足夠的資金購買必須的設備，往地底下開採，取得剩下的黃金。

雖然約翰的父親死時一貧如洗，從未發掘出他的第一桶金，約翰還是繼承了他的淘金熱。在1849年的加利福尼亞淘金熱潮期間，包含約翰在內的九萬人跋山涉水來到西部。這是史上最大的淘金熱潮。因為當時還沒有鐵路，橫跨內陸到加州並不容易。因此，約翰一路從美國東岸搭船，繞過南美洲南端。一抵達港口，就立即出發進入山區。由於所有的土地皆為政府公有，所有發現的黃金都屬於淘金客。他們只需證明自己是最早到的，就能宣稱金礦的所有權。不幸的是，約翰並沒有發現金礦，卻在因淘金而興起的舊金山，染上了嚴重的痢疾。

53　打造更環保的未來 (P. 130)

年復一年，地球珍貴的資源日益稀缺，唯一沒少的資源是人類，而人類還需要建材來蓋新房子、新辦公大樓和新學校。解決這個問題的唯一辦法，就是以最少的資源，來獲取最大的利益。這正是永續建築的意義所在。

永續建築的倡導者認為，建築的整個施工過程都可以在無損環境的情況下完成。這麼一來，未來的世代就可以永續使用地球。不過打造綠建築，過程就必須從觀念上落實。

想像一下，某市政府想要興建一棟環保辦公大樓。城市規畫師要做的第一件事，就是選擇一個對環境影響較小的地點。最理想的是選個已經開發過的地點，從而保護樹林以及綠地。

接下來，城市規畫師會轉而關注施工的過程。只有環保建材才能用來蓋辦公大樓，包括木材、鋼材，以及其他從拆除的建物裡回收使用的建材。如果可以的話，這些建材最好都是在當地生產製造、再生或回收取得。環保建材愈接近施工處，浪費在將運送的能源就愈少。

建物的維護成本是下一個需要考量到的要素。城市規劃師會設計出最節能的冷暖氣系統。他們會在屋頂上裝設太陽能板，吸收太陽熱能來供應大樓電力。整棟大樓都會安裝省水的廁所及洗手台。這些節能措施不僅有助於環境保護，長期下來還能省錢。

最後，城市規劃師知道，他們新蓋的辦公大樓總有一天會被拆除。因此，他們使用在建物拆除後還能回收再利用的建材，也會確保這些建材不含任何汙染物，在拆除建物的過程中，也不會釋放任何有害的物質到空氣中。

當這些都完成之後，城市規畫師就能放鬆一下，也許還可以辦個慶祝派對，因為他們已經設計出一棟綠建築，每個施工步驟都具有環保概念——這就是永續建築的金科玉律。

54　隱藏的危機 (P. 132)

貝琪是一位努力減肥，想過健康生活的35歲女性。她每天早上吃一個英式馬芬當早餐。英式馬芬就像其他各式麵包、義大利麵和甜點製品一樣，通常是以精製穀物所製。這些穀物經過大量加工，營養比全穀少。它們與幾種健康問題習習相關，包括心臟病、糖尿病與高膽固醇。

貝琪每天都帶一個三明治當午餐。因為她想要減肥，所以她沒有在三明治裡塗奶油或美乃滋。但是她的三明治總是夾上大量加工並含有鈉的肉品。雖然我們都需要鈉才能存活，但是體內太多的鈉會導致高血壓、水腫和暈眩。

辛苦了一天，慢跑是貝琪下班後最喜歡的放鬆方式。就像每天太陽一定從西邊落下一樣，貝琪每次跑步後會喝一杯提神飲料。她完全沒發現，跑步所帶來的好處已經被她所喝的高果糖玉米糖漿給抵消掉了。高果糖玉米糖漿被用來當做許多食物的增甜劑，從氣泡飲料到早餐的玉米片。許多研究已經將它的攝取，與肥胖、蛀牙和營養不良畫上等號。

貝琪喜歡為她的家人烹煮晚餐。雖然她煮的每一餐通常很營養，但是她習慣用很多的人造鮮奶油。研究顯示，人造鮮奶油中的大量反式脂肪會增加壞膽固醇，降低好膽固醇。壞膽固醇含量高的人較可能罹患心臟疾病、癌症，甚至憂鬱症。

要不是因為她母親在星期天傍晚的一通電話，貝琪可能就一直這樣持續下去。她的母親告訴她，她在一本英文教科書中讀到一篇很棒的文章，裡面強調日常食物中營養的不足。「這篇文章告訴我們一個維持健康的簡單方法，」貝琪的母親解釋：「妳只要吃未經多次加工的新鮮食物就行了！」

55 地球是不是愈來愈暗了？ (P. 136)

1980年代中期，一位名為大村纂的日本研究員得到一項驚人的發現。他的研究數據顯示，過去30年來，太到達地球表面的輻射已經下降了10%。他發現的現象也就是目前科學界所謂的「全球黯化」。

全球黯化是指照射到地球表面的整體陽光減少，日照量的減少意味著熱度的減少。科學家相信，地球大氣層中的某些汙染物質，如碳與硫酸鹽，會導致全球黯化。這些汙染物質所形成的雲層，體積變得更大且更吸水，因此可將更多的陽光反射回太空中。簡單地說，好幾百年來，在大氣中的有害物質可能也一直在冷卻地球。

過去十年間，世界各國政府都限制汙染物質的排放，逆轉了全球黯化的過程。氣候學家觀察轉變的過程，發現全球黯化對全球暖化的影響，遠大於我們從前的想像。

我們可將全球黯化與全球暖化視為是同時發生卻截然不同的兩個過程。全球暖化會讓地球的溫度上升，而全球黯化卻讓地球的溫度冷卻。在全球黯化逐漸消失的同時，全球真正的暖化程度也逐漸顯露。

那麼這是否意味著，為了要對抗全球暖化，我們應該要增加大氣的汙染物質的數量嗎？有些科學家的確認為是的。這項建議並不新奇。在1974年，俄國氣候學家麥克海爾·布迪科建議在大氣中燃燒硫，以製造出霧霾，以保護我們不受地球暖化影響。然而，有些科學家認為，這些汙染物質的增加會造成太多健康問題，例如氣喘及其他呼吸道疾病。

科學家對地球黯化的發現，反映出我們對氣候運作所知甚少。畢竟數十年來，太陽輻射在不知不覺間持續下降。現今針對全球暖化的預測大多未考慮到全球黯化，有鑑於此，全球暖化的速度是否會超越我們的想像變得更快，世界也變得更加炎熱呢？

56 4D列印打造未來 (P. 138)

不久之前，3D列印還是科幻小說的一部分，如今卻實際用在各行各業上──從航太工業到醫學與教育。這項誰都能列印出整個物體的神奇科技，如今已經過時了。不過，印刷的下一場盛事即將來臨。它與3D列印有什麼不同呢？嗯，它不僅用到了第三維度的立體空間，還加上第四維度的影響──時間。

4D列印與列印的材料有關，這種材料會隨著時間的推移，在接觸到不同的外在刺激時（例如溫度、水或氣壓）就會改變形體。為什麼說有用呢？建築工程其實是缺乏效率的行業。組裝家具、蓋房子、鋪設水管都要花很長的時間，而且要是環境改變，或是發生什麼損毀情況，又或是對成品的外觀不滿意時，就必須要重頭開始。建材無法予以調整改變，只會保持相同的形狀。不過，這可不侷限於4D列印的材料。這類物質可從本質上重新設計，想像一下會自動組裝的家具、自我修復的水管，甚至是自行變形的建築，能於自然災害發生時採取相應措施。4D列印還能讓我們在外太空蓋房子，在那樣惡劣的環境下，使用傳統建設工程會非常困難。可以將4D列印的材料想像成機器人，只不過裡面沒有電線，也不需使用電力。誰知道呢，說不定將來列印的材料都有意識思維！

那麼，是誰想出了這種能因應環境變化的材料？就像很多事情一樣，第一個做到的是大自然。DNA（去氧核醣核酸）、RNA（核糖核酸）和蛋白質是孕育生命所需的要素，也存在我們的人體中，它們本質上就是一長串會自我變形的材料。能把自己摺疊起來、進行自我修復、自行複製，而且以微小的能量就能辦到，還沒有錯誤。

其中的訣竅就是將分子的微觀世界變成建築的宏觀世界。當然，說起來容易做起來難。但請放心，一些全球最優秀的材料科學家正致力於開發。很快地，城市不需要人類興建，就會自我建設。

57 廣納百家的語言 (P. 140)

英語是一種不斷地吸收外在影響，逐步演化的語言。數千年前，當說著凱爾特語的英國人住在大不列顛，就開始了英語的演變。西元43年，不列顛島被羅馬帝國征服，生活天翻地覆。這些羅馬士兵不只帶來武器，也帶來了拉丁語。他們是第一批改變英語發展方向的軍隊，但卻不是最後一批。

當羅馬帝國在第五世紀滅亡時便從不列顛撤軍。然而，沒多久他們的位置就被來自日耳曼的入侵部落，像是盎格魯、撒克遜和朱特所取代。這些「盎格魯－撒克遜人」帶來了他們的日耳曼方言。多年來，日耳曼方言與島上原有的凱爾特語，以及羅馬人留下的影響交融混合，古英語就此誕生。到了西元600年，古英語已經和日耳曼所用的方言有所區隔。

西元787年，維京人從丹麥和挪威抵達了。他們在英國北部建立了永久的殖民地。還在11世紀初期時短暫地統治整座島嶼。維京人統治時期創造了更多的文化融合，並且讓古英語與各種斯堪地那維亞語彙接觸，例如代名詞they、them、their便是來自於此。

1066年，諾曼第人征服了英國，這是改變古英語的最後貢獻之一。諾曼第征服者帶來了法語。結果，英語吸收了許多法語單字，像是liberty、continue和journey等等。

中古英語時代從西元1100年持續到1500年。這是個菁英講法語，而農民卻使用英語的年代。也因此，中古英語的文法被簡化了。許多曾存在於古英語的複雜規則因而消失。而在1350年到1500年之間所發生的「母音大推移」，讓母音也跟著被簡化了。

1474年，英語發生最後一次劇烈的變革。是在印刷術第一次被帶入英國時。之後，標準的拼字與文法透過喬叟、米爾頓和莎士比亞的散文傳達給群眾。現代英語亦隨之誕生。

58 漂浮的垃圾場 (P. 142)

你知道嗎？世界上最大的垃圾掩埋場根本就不在陸地上，而是在大太平洋垃圾帶，也就是從日本延伸至美國加州這片海域上漂浮的垃圾。

大太平洋垃圾帶垃圾的來源包括從海上船隻傾倒下來的、從下水道排入大海的，或者是有人丟進海裡的。來自世界各地的垃圾被捲入海流中，最後齊聚一堂。有專家說，大太平洋垃圾帶的面積足有美國德州那麼大；其他人則說有美國的兩倍大。至少大家同聲一氣的是，垃圾帶上的塑膠製品不會在短期內消失。

塑膠是一種堅韌的合成物質，永遠無法進行自然生物分解。仔細想想，這表示我們製造出來的塑膠製品都還在地球的某個地方。至少我們知道那些塑膠製品大多都到哪去了——漂浮在太平洋的中央！

塑膠製品不僅威脅到海洋生態，還危害到人類的健康。塑膠無法進行自然生物分解，陽光卻能將之分解成愈來愈小的碎片。這些塑膠碎片的體積愈小，就愈容易被魚或其他的海洋生物誤食。這表示，你吃的下一條魚有可能已經吞下，在大太平洋垃圾帶上漂浮的樂高積木碎片。

雖然有些組織正試著清除這片垃圾帶上的垃圾，不過這可不容易。首先，我們很難看到那片垃圾帶，所以媒體不會重視這個問題。這些垃圾不是一座巨大的垃圾島。更確切地說，這是一片在水下蔓延的塑膠及其他垃圾碎片。我們很難將這些完全清除。因此，如果我們真的想要清理海洋，應不再使用這麼多的塑膠製品，並且隨時做好資源回收。也許只要我們付出一點努力、多用一些可重複使用的提袋，或許10年後，「大」太平洋垃圾帶就會變成「中」太平洋垃圾帶。

59 唯有源頭活水來 (P. 144)

人類需要乾淨的飲用水才能生存。當我們的供水受到汙染，或是來自不安全水源時，就有罹患疾病的風險。不潔的水中有細菌、寄生蟲這類物質，會導致各種不良的影響。每年有數百萬人的生命遭受水媒疾病的威脅。那些人即使存活下來，也可能要面臨到嚴重的病情以及沉重的經濟負擔。

有些城市鄉鎮在把水輸送給民眾前，會先以過濾及處理系統淨化水源。有些人會先將水煮沸，殺死水中可能含有的病原體後再飲用。有些家庭則仰賴購買已處理過的瓶裝水。但有些人，特別是在開發中國家，仍沒有可信賴的管道取得安全無虞的飲用水。

一家名為弗蘭德森的瑞士公司，決定要研發出能幫助這些人的淨水器。該公司於2005年推出一款名為「淨水吸管」的產品。它的外型像一根吸管，裡面有特殊纖維能以物理方式過濾水。淨水吸管可以在你喝水時，幫你過濾掉99％以上的細菌和寄生蟲。淨水吸管是靠吸力運作，所以不用電力或幫浦。因為淨水吸管以化學製品製成，沒有活動零件，所以安全又耐用。

一根吸管能讓一個人享用一年乾淨的飲用水。每次用完淨水吸管後的清潔工作也很簡單，還能增加使用功能。只要從吸管口吹氣進去，裡面殘留的水就會迴流從底部流出。淨水吸管在過濾了一千公升的水後，就無法再過濾水出來。這樣可以避免在不知情的情況下喝進受到汙染的水。

淨水吸管也曾用於緊急救援及人道援助。每年世界各地都有城鄉因突如其來的天然災害而陷於混亂。颶風和水災會汙染水源，而地震和龍捲風則會造成建物結構的重大損壞。受災影響的城鄉，可能好幾個月甚至更久都沒法喝到乾淨的水。這不僅會導致個人健康的問題，也會導致疾病的爆發。不管在什麼情況下，淨水吸管都能讓任何人在任何時候都享有乾淨飲水。

60　老方法，新世界 (P. 146)

傳統醫學在已經在中國施行近三千年，深植於中國文化的精神及哲學觀點之內。中醫最古老的一部作品是《黃帝內經》，起源於西元前一世紀。它奠定了傳統中醫立基的基本原則，包括陰陽、氣和五行，並且詳細討論針灸的早期方法，即一種將不同長度的細針插入身體不同部位的治療法。

中醫立基的原則是，人體內在系統是由金、木、水、火、土五行元素的平衡所支配。體內五行平衡會影響陰陽整體的均衡，任何的失衡都會讓體內的氣（意即生命能量）阻塞，進而造成疾病以及健康惡化。利用針灸把細針插入某些人體部位，可以刺激氣血，使之運行。其他方法也可以改善氣血運行，例如服用中藥複方以及「拔罐」，即將熱玻璃杯蓋在皮膚上，把血吸入特定區域。

在西方，中醫原本只有華人移民所用，因為他們不適應西方技術，但現已轉變為更受歡迎的另類醫學。已開發國家的七成以上人民都嘗試過另類醫學，由於相信傳統醫療比化學藥物的副作用更少，該產業一直呈現穩定成長。

儘管多數的西方醫師認為針灸和拔罐的功效絕大部分只是心理作用，但很多積極宣傳這些療法的好萊塢藝人已經讓它們愈來愈時尚了。

在2006年，中西醫整合跨出了一大步。一種由中藥材製作的藥物NeuroAiD，經過證實可以幫助中風患者的康復。

世界衛生組織也鼓勵使用通過有效測試的傳統藥物，這意味著，或許未來特定的中醫療法會被西方醫師大量採用。

61　目睹怪異與美麗 (P. 150)

索克拉島位於阿拉伯半島南方約380公里的印度洋上。它是一個只有132公里長的小島，被孤立在大陸之外達七百萬年之久。然而也正因為這樣的孤立，讓索克拉島成為世界上最獨特的地方之一。這個島上多樣化又獨具特色的植物生態，展現出的樣貌，有如科幻小說作家想像中的外星世界。

索克拉島上825種植物中，有超過300種都屬於索克拉島特有。世界上沒有任何其他地方能具備如此奇異、有如異想世界的植物群。以龍血樹（因血紅色汁液而命名）為例，樹枝會發芽成一個傘狀圓頂，葉子形成緊密的蓋子，有如精心除過的草坪，島上幾百棵的龍血樹，像是降落的幽浮艦隊。

另一個更具外星感的植物是沙漠玫瑰，皮革般的植株從岩石中突出，就像幾乎要爆炸的象腿。粉紅色美麗花朵在接近頂端處盛開，外表幾近滑稽可笑，但肥厚的植莖是為了在島上炎熱乾燥的氣候中儲水的完美進化。

鳥類也是出乎意料的變化多端，有些稀有物種在全島四周充滿魚群的海域上繁衍生存。索克拉島還保有超過一千隻瀕臨絕種的埃及禿鷹，是這即將絕滅的物種在世界上最高密度的棲息地。

索克拉人大多是漁夫、農夫和果農。人們鼓勵遊客拍攝島上的非凡美景，但拍攝島上女人卻是一種極度無禮的行為。

即便每天都有班機起降，造訪索克拉島還是有點麻煩，飛機常常超額預訂，這表示行程常有延遲一天以上的情形。過去幾年來島上的交通已經改善很多，但要四處逛還是不方便。另外，在最大城哈迪布之外，唯一的住宿地點是散布在島上的露營營地。不過，有時要親眼見證奇特美妙的美景，一點不方便是值得的。

62 超自然活動 (P. 152)

　　超自然（paranormal）這個字是由兩個部分所組成的：超越（para）和正常（normal）。在希臘文中，para是指「在......之外」或「超越」的意思。超自然是指鬼魂、外星人綁架事件、魔法和讀心術──就是所有現代科學無法解釋的事。所以基本上，超自然的事情我們害怕，卻也同時引起一絲的好奇。

　　舉例來說，1908 年 6 月 30 號，在俄羅斯一個下雪的林地中發生了一場爆炸，其威力甚至是 1945 年轟炸廣島核彈的一千倍以上。這個「通古斯事件」形成了一大圈像火燒過的荒地。而科學家仍然無法解釋這是怎麼發生的。有些人相信這是一顆未發揮威力的彗星。但是這有沒有可能是外星人先進科技的證據呢？

　　還有一個未解的謎團就是天蛾人現象。從 1966 年開始，有一連串的報導描述在美國的西維吉尼亞州出現了一個有翅膀的巨大生物。神祕的是，這些景象在 1967 年銀橋崩塌事件後就恰好停止了，那次災難造成 46 人喪生。有人相信天蛾人就是被派來警告當地鎮民即將降臨的災難。而也有人相信一開始破壞橋樑的也許就是天蛾人。這些揮之不去的問題，讓許多美國人乃將天蛾人的傳說視為懸而未決的超自然神祕事件。

　　那我們又該怎麼解釋那些遠離電燈，突然出現在蠻荒之地的火球呢？這些「鬼火」是鬼魂存在的證據嗎？這些現象中最著名的案例就是在美國密蘇里州黃蜂市附近的鬼火。這個恐怖的白色火光看起來就像在上下飄動。它從 19 世紀後期就經常出現在鎮外的樹林中。有當地人說這是一對印地安戀人，被驅逐家鄉後過世。也有人相信那是一個燈籠，屬於一位數百年前失蹤的礦工。不管那是什麼，人們總是對產生黃蜂市的鬼火臆測紛紛。

63 傾聽你的心聲 (P. 154)

　　智慧型手機已徹底改變我們看待電話的方式。從前手機只是溝通的工具，後來卻演變成電影院、音樂庫、圖書館，如今還成了行動式醫院。

　　許多可檢查病人心率的應用程式已經問世。以前的病人得在身體上靠近心臟的軀幹部位貼上感應貼片，不過現在不需要了。要是使用者感覺胸痛，他們可以把手指放在智慧型手機的相機上，或是把手機放在胸前，就能測量自己的脈搏。配戴智能手錶比用手機還更有效，因為應用程式能隨時監測心率，而非只有在感覺疼痛時才測量。

　　如果出現任何異常徵兆，手機會自動發送簡訊給病人的醫生。專家說，這有助於節省診斷病情的寶貴時間，醫生不必為了觀測病情而費力翻找成堆資料。

　　顯然，這些應用程式是專為心臟疾病患者設計的，能在病患的日常生活中監控心臟活動，是治療心臟病的一大優勢。不過，這些革命性的應用程式也找到了其他的用途。

　　那些沒有嚴重的健康問題，卻又想追蹤生活方式會如何影響健康的人，可以使用這些應用程式進行更全面的健康監測。其他的用途還包括運動員的表現評估、過重者的飲食監控，甚至還可用於安全駕駛系統。

　　從事智慧型手機醫療技術的大衛・阿坦沙說，想像一下，這種儀器「能與相機及其他車上裝置結合，監測駕駛人的飢餓、疲勞以及其他會影響到駕駛能力的問題。」

　　目前，生產這類醫療應用程式蔚為風潮。像 iStethoscope 這種能讓人透過手機麥克風聽到自己心跳，已經是熱門商品。希望將來這種技術能讓醫師救人的速度與效率更勝以往。

64 北京之圍 (P. 156)

　　北京是一座被圍困的城市，不過，圍城的威脅並非來自敵國或叛軍，甚至不是人類，而是戈壁沙漠，並且在這場對戰中逐漸佔上風。

　　戈壁沙漠每年以超過3,300平方公里的速度向外擴展，其東邊正向北京而去。專家憂心北京可能瀕臨沙漠化。雖然很令人震驚，不過這個現象也不是新發現了，而是已經持續了好長一段時間。早在2006年，中國政府就曾宣布，中國的國土面積有27%是沙漠，與1994年的18%相比，有逐年增加的趨勢。換句話說，不斷擴張的沙漠在短短12年便吞噬中國9%的陸地。雖然自2006年以來，沙漠擴張的速度似乎沒那麼劇烈，卻也未曾停止過。

　　說到戈壁沙漠的擴張，成因不勝枚舉。其中最主要的兩個因素是放牧過多，以及大面積的森林砍伐。中國的都市化發展也是成因，使地下水的需求增加，過度抽取地下水讓土壤更容易沙漠化。

　　中國政府決心要贏得這場抵禦沙漠的戰役。為此當局決定，以自然的方式對抗大自然。中國政府計畫築起一道綠色長城，以大面積的樹木為屏障，保護中國的城市不再繼續沙漠化。這項計畫從1978年開始實施，目標在2050年以前，種植從新疆一路蜿蜒至黑龍江，長達4,480公里的樹牆。屆時，他們希望這片森林能覆蓋中國42%的陸地面積。這項充滿雄心壯志的工程也將有助於對抗全球氣候暖化。

　　但是綠色長城就足以挽救北京了嗎？有些專家抱者懷疑的態度。他們反駁種樹雖簡單，長期照護卻難，尤其是當種下的樹木並非原生品種，無法適應當地的環境。如果他們所言無誤，那對北京而言，猛烈的沙塵暴只是微不足道的問題。或許有一天，北京居民醒來後發現，他們的房子已被埋在沙子裡了。

65 食物下毒 (P. 158)

　　沙門氏菌是一種有毒的微小細菌，侵害人類與其他哺乳類動物已有數千年之久。它是怎麼讓我們生病的呢？通常是透過食用受汙染的食物，像是蛋、肉、家禽，甚至是蔬菜水果。沙門氏菌中毒的症狀包括腹瀉、脫水、發燒和嘔吐。有時候，若沙門氏菌由腸子進入血液中，而病人又未接受抗生素治療時，可能造成嚴重的併發症。在某些狀況下，甚至會致死。

　　沙門氏菌並不罕見。相反地，它是美國最常見的食物中毒。美國疾病管制中心（CDC）估計在2011年因為沙門氏菌中毒者有19,336人送醫，有378人死亡。

　　在美國，致命沙門氏菌爆發是重大新聞。每年都有一些備受矚目而導致食品回收的事件發生。光在2011年就爆發了松果、熟雞肝、木瓜、苜蓿芽和火雞堡的沙門氏菌事件。

　　不幸的是，科學家預測未來沙門氏菌的爆發將會更致命。這是因為細菌的抗藥性與日俱增。臨床研究顯示，細菌愈常曝露在特定的抗生素中，抗生素的效用就愈差。亞洲、美洲和歐洲的科學家已經發現某些類型的沙門氏菌，對於大多數抗生素具有高度抗藥性。

　　有些科學家相信，抗藥性是由於大規模的養雞場或「工廠化的農場」過度使用抗生素所致。事實上，世界衛生組織已經連續好幾年針對養殖場中抗生素的使用發布警告。

　　對抗沙門氏菌的戰爭與其他幾項食品安全議題，可以歸納成一個簡單的公式：製造的食物愈多，就愈不安全。舉例來說，一家食品公司想生產更多雞肉以創造更高利潤。但是那麼多雞關在一起容易滋生疾病，為了保持雞隻的健康，公司為牠們注射抗生素。瞧，有抗藥性的沙門氏菌不就爆發了。

　　要真正擊敗沙門氏菌，我們可能需要開始將食品安全，置於食品產業的利潤之前。

66　執行長的運動 (P. 160)

　　高爾夫球是商人的遊戲。大筆的金錢交易都是在高爾夫球場上達成的，去高爾夫球俱樂部打球，就像是說要去開一場商務會議。根據最近的一項調查顯示，高爾夫球與生意是有關聯的，執行長的高爾夫球打得愈好，賺的錢其實比那些分數過高的人還多。

　　分數過高是什麼意思？高爾夫球是少數幾項運動中，低分比高分還要好的運動。球手盡可能以最少的桿數，將球打進球場另一端的球洞裡。為了要讓這場比賽更有趣，球場通常會佈滿障礙物，例如植滿長草的區域（又名為「深草區」）與沙坑（或「沙坑障礙物」）。

　　高爾夫球員使用各式各樣的球桿打球，每一種球桿有其適用的特定區域。例如，「一號木桿」體積重且桿頭大，常用於擊出遠距離的球，而「推桿」則是在進球洞前最後一桿使用。

　　高爾夫球的評分系統中，有許多怪異的名稱。每一個球洞的目標桿數稱之為「標準桿」。在比較好打的球洞裡，標準桿的桿數可能是三桿；在很難打的球洞裡，有可能高達六桿。若是球員球技嫻熟，可能會以低於標準桿的桿數進球。少於標準桿數一桿的稱之為「小鳥」，少於標準桿數二桿的稱之為「老鷹」，多於標準桿數一桿的則稱之為「柏忌」。

　　現代的高爾夫球起源於十五世紀的蘇格蘭（雖然在中國的唐朝也有類似的比賽），貧富皆可打球。不過，到了十九世紀，中產階級的有錢人興起一股逃離都市、一起到鄉間打高爾夫球的風氣。這些入會費高昂，且有正式服裝規定的高爾夫俱樂部，最終成為常態，高爾夫就此成為菁英界的運動。

　　高爾夫球被視為僅限於男性為主、經商人士的運動，並以此聞名，此一印象早已深植人心，就連 golf 這個字也常被開玩笑地稱為「只限男士，女士止步」（Gentlemen Only Ladies Forbidden）的縮寫。

67　沉默的語言危機 (P. 164)

　　現今世界上正在使用中的語言有六千多種，但其中的一千多種被深鎖在已經無法將其傳遞給下一代的老人腦中。如果照現今語言消失的速度，在 2050 年前，50％到 90％的語言將永遠消失。我們身處於一個語言大量滅絕的年代。

　　有些人並不認為這是問題。恰好相反的，這是一種全球進步的指標。他們主張語言愈少，能夠真正彼此溝通的人就愈多。溝通帶來了解，因此世界就會愈和平。

　　但有些人並不那麼確定。韋德·戴維斯教授認為，當語言消失時，其所含的人類遺產也隨之消失。對他而言，語言代表了人類想像力的複雜網絡。如果某種語言從這個網絡中被拔除，某種思維方法也會跟著消失。換句話說，世界上的語言愈少，身為人類的我們就愈缺乏想像力與創造力。

　　要阻止語言滅絕需要很多的努力。聯合國有一張相當長的瀕臨絕種的語言名單。臺灣的邵語和中國的滿語也名列其中。拯救這些語言不只是時間和金錢的問題。最重要的是，政府必須讓人們相信，這些瀕臨滅絕的語言是值得挽救的。

　　好消息是，過去也曾有過成功的案例。在 19 世紀時，由於一位名為艾利澤·本·耶胡達的學者的努力，希伯來語從滅絕的邊緣被救回。他將一個古老的語言改造成可以在日常生活中使用的東西。最後，他的努力有了回報，現在有九百多萬人正在使用希伯來語。

　　我們應該要將世界語言視為人文遺產，語言告訴我們，我們從何而來、信仰哪些神祇、身而為人的意義和我們所處的環境。我們正在揮霍我們的遺產，當它消失時，就永遠不會再回來了。

68　醫生，醫生！(P. 166)

對人類來說，身體會有輕微的酸痛與疼痛是很正常的。我們的身體經常會有輕度的不適症狀，通常我們會予以忽略，因為只是不舒服而已，沒什麼大不了的。但是，若是每一次的小痠痛、每一次的劇痛、每一次無關緊要的微羔，在你的眼裡都是身患絕症的跡象呢？這就是健康焦慮患者（或慮病症患者），永遠都要面對的精神折磨。

慮病症患者會不斷地擔心自己可能罹患了可怕的疾病，並且會檢查自己的身體，一心想要找出症狀來。對健康感到焦慮的患者來說，即使是最無害的症狀，也會導致周而復始的強迫行為，使他們快被煩惱逼瘋。對患者來說，咳嗽絕對是肺癌，頭痛是腦部有腫瘤，胃痛肯定是胃潰瘍。

據統計，就醫的病患中有6%對健康感到焦慮，他們不僅造成自己不必要的困擾，也佔用醫師不必要的時間與醫療資源。

自從網路上的醫療資訊唾手可得後，問題變得更嚴重了。現在，慮病症患者能發現似乎與自己症狀符合的疾病，並且說服自己是罹患該疾病的患者。

值得注意的是，慮病症患者可不是胡亂捏造自己的症狀。他們的症狀或許是真的，但是他們自己過度誇張的自我診斷，往往才是問題。

慮病症通常與強迫症有關。強迫症是一種焦慮的形式，會讓人執著於最微不足道的小事上，結果出現怪異的行為。以開關燈為例，他們會開關十次燈，然後才會離開房間。相同類型的強迫行為被視為是健康焦慮的根源。

醫生在治療疑病症患者時，常遇到一個主要的問題：病人不信任醫師的意見，即使醫師已經再三保證他們根本就沒生病，病人還是很懷疑。醫師通常會將疑病症患者的個案轉介給行為治療師，因為他們更能夠幫助病人面對自己的症狀。

69　死後重生 (P. 168)

如果死亡不是人生真正的終點呢？全球數十億人都這麼認為。有些人期待天堂的永生，有些人則擔心死後會下地獄。還有些人認為，人死後會再回到他們出生的地方，也就是回到這個世界。死後重生的概念被稱為輪迴轉世。幾千年來，輪迴轉世一直是佛教與印度教的一部分。

輪迴轉世也許是信仰的議題，但這並不表示並無其事。多年來有許多疑似輪迴轉世的例子。其中有些事件至今仍未有定論。這些故事是輪迴轉世存在的鐵證嗎？何不自己判斷。

就拿一個名叫萊恩的美國小男孩為例。剛滿四歲的萊恩乞求父母帶他回家。他的爸媽感到很困惑，因為他「已經」在家了。他們問兒子：「你家在哪裡？」萊恩回答說，在好萊塢的一個大房子裡。萊恩的媽媽開始從圖書館借好萊塢方面的書回家。有一天，她給萊恩看一幕電影的場景，萊恩指著其中一名演員說：「那個人就是我！以前的我！」

還有詹姆斯．賴寧哲的奇異故事。詹姆斯跟許多小男孩一樣，從小就很愛飛機。但是他對飛機的了解遠超過他應該知道的，連技術方面的細節都瞭如指掌。有一天，詹姆斯開始做惡夢。夢中的畫面總是一模一樣，他會被一架機身上有紅色太陽的飛機擊落。在惡夢中，他駕駛的那架飛機叫做海盜，而他是從名為納托馬的戰艦上起飛。令人難以置信的是，戰鬥機跟戰艦都是確實存在過的，而且他的夢與在第二次世界大戰中陣亡的飛行員詹姆斯．休斯頓的命運相符。有沒有可能是詹姆斯正在經歷前世的創傷呢？

這樣的故事在世界各地都有成千上百件。輪迴轉世的真相就在那裡，等著任何想要追根究底的人去發掘。

70 非洲英雄 (P. 170)

如果肯亞的旺加里・瑪塔伊有一個獎盃盒放她所得過的國際獎項，那盒子應該跟房子一樣大吧。而這些獎其實都來自一個簡單的概念：植樹的重要性。

她的故事從 1940 年開始，那年她出生在肯亞的一個小村莊。她早年成長在一個富含自然美景與野生動物的地方，這也讓她從小就知道要愛護自然。1960 年，她成為 300 名獲取特別獎學金，得以遠赴美國念書的肯亞人之一。在十年嚴峻的求學過程後，她成為第一位得到博士學位的東非女性。

旺加里・瑪塔伊在 1970 年代活躍於肯亞全國婦女理事會（NCWK）。她在 NCWK 早期的工作經驗，讓她相信環境是改善貧困婦女生活的關鍵。

隨後，她將自己的理論付諸實行。她在 1976 年開始種樹，並在 1977 年推動綠帶運動。到了 1986 年，她所推行的運動擴展至非洲大陸的其他地區。至今，這項運動已經在非洲種植了四千多萬棵的樹。但他們並不以此滿足，未來十年，他們的目標是在全世界植超過十億棵的樹。

雖然瑪塔伊女士的行動思維起源於環境，但後來廣展成了政治事件。肯亞領導菁英因此找她麻煩。在 1982 年和 2001 年間，她遭到鞭打、逮捕、被迫躲藏，甚至一度只能關在自家中。然而，2002 年，民主制度占了上風，瑪塔伊女士獲選進入國會。次年，她被任命為環境與自然資源部副部長。

2004 年，旺加里・瑪塔伊因為推動環保、婦權與政治自由上的努力，而獲頒諾貝爾和平獎。這也創下史上第一次非洲女性獲頒此獎項的紀錄。

當旺加里・瑪塔伊在 2011 年九月因卵巢癌過世，非洲失去了一位最優秀的鬥士。她也許離我們而去了，但她在政治自由上的主張，與對環境的關懷，將隨著綠帶運動永遠留存。

71 來看我玩吧 (P. 172)

只要打電玩就能賺錢，那不是很棒嗎？對許多年輕人來說，這就是夢想。幾年前，很多人也許會對如此荒謬的念頭一笑置之，但世界已經改變了。如今，不僅能以打電玩為業，還有可能藉此過上衣食無憂的生活。這全都是因為電玩遊戲直播的盛行。

電玩遊戲直播說穿了，就是在網路上現場實況，直播玩家進行遊戲的過程。雖然你可能會覺得難以置信，但實際上來看這些實況主（又稱直播主）打電玩的觀眾就有好幾百萬人之多。

那麼，網路直播究竟有何迷人之處，吸引了這麼多人來看別人玩電玩？就像現實生活中的各種娛樂活動一樣，追根究底就是喜歡看熱鬧的人性。直播主的個性、遊戲中的評論、談吐的幽默風趣，以及他們的遊戲技巧等等，都是吸引觀眾的原因。

電玩實況主賺錢的方式不外乎是：直播時直播網站的廣告收益、電玩廠商的贊助、甚至是粉絲的捐贈。根據全球最大的直播平台，即總部設在美國的網站 Twitch 所言，最成功的實況主一年的收入在六位數以上。

當然，只有極少數的頂尖實況主能賺到這麼多錢。在你決定開播自己直播頻道前，要考慮到一些風險。

業餘的實況主待在線上的時間通常很長，幾乎沒有休息的時間，因為他們消失在鏡頭前的時間，意味著他們有可能會失去觀眾。所以，一般胸懷大志的實況主，生活型態都不是最健康的。

實況主也會面臨到網路纏擾的風險。有些觀眾過於迷戀自己喜愛的實況主，因此會想盡辦法和他們成為朋友。這種行為雖然會讓人感到受寵若驚，卻並不總是令人期待。

儘管有這些風險，網路直播仍是許多電玩玩家的熱門消遣。即便死忠粉絲極少，但對許多玩家來說，能夠與全世界分享自己熱衷於電玩的喜悅已足矣。而我們大家，無論是不是玩家，肯定都能感受這股熱情。

72 舞后 (P. 174)

在1970年，76歲的瑪莎‧葛蘭姆跳完她的最後一支舞。對於這位美國傳奇的舞蹈家和編舞家來說，這一年是難以克服的過渡期。葛蘭姆跳了超過半個世紀的舞，到了最後無法繼續跳舞時，得了憂鬱症，沉溺於酗酒，覺得自己因衰老而失去存在的理由。

在葛蘭姆退休息舞前，她曾在白宮為八位總統獻舞，也曾為無數極具影響力的表演編舞。她創辦的瑪莎葛蘭姆舞團，是目前美國歷史最悠久的舞蹈團之一，曾到亞洲、中東和歐洲等地巡迴演出，獲得世界各國的讚譽。

但是，當年老的葛蘭姆看到年輕的舞者取代她的角色，跳著曾經是為她量身訂做的舞時，她傷心欲絕。她說：「我相信人不應該回頭看，也不應該沉溺於懷舊與追憶，可是當你看著舞台上的舞者，就好像看到30年前的自己，而她又跳著你與深愛之人共同創作的舞碼時，你又怎能避免這樣的情緒呢？」

葛蘭姆的現代舞在當時可說是一項創新之舉，她挑戰芭蕾舞的流暢、優雅，以激烈、性感的舞姿對抗傳統舞蹈。她的動作展現出猛烈的激情、內心的騷動與心理的煎熬，全都透過身體將極度的張力與釋放，生動地展現出來。她的核心哲學是讓動作自由。她說：「我的舞不是要好看，而是要有趣。」她從神話故事、民間傳說與歷史中取材，並且常常將對社會的有力評論編織進舞蹈當中。

退休後的酗酒，導致葛蘭姆必須接受醫院的治療，不過她痊癒了，甚至開始寫作，繼續致力於編舞，一直到1991年去世為止。她在現代舞蹈的深遠影響，被拿來與畢卡索之於藝術的影響媲美。這是當時以22歲的高齡，到舞蹈學校註冊時的她，絕對料想不到的。

73 人體力量 (P. 178)

世界上的石油與天然氣已日益稀少，各個企業都忙著找出能夠節能和省錢的創新方案。一家名為Jernhusen的瑞典公司在這方面邁進了一大步。他們提出一種利用能源的方法，這種能源豐富但卻常被忽略──人體散發的熱能。

Jernhusen是一家房地產公司，名下擁有斯德哥爾摩中央車站，這是瑞典最大的車站。每天有超過25萬的通勤人士經過這座車站，有些人會停下來喝杯咖啡、吃點東西，甚至也許是在等下午的火車時打個盹。這些人加起來所散發出的體熱，就能讓車站內暖和舒適，即使室外是瑞典的嚴冬。

Jernhusen的工程師發現這些熱能可以用在其他方面。他們建造了一個創新的暖氣系統，使用斯德哥爾摩中央車站內累積的體熱，加熱一缸缸的水，當水的溫度夠高時，就將水加壓送到一百碼外的街道對面，加熱Jernhusen的另一座辦公大樓。這套系統的安裝費用只有三萬美元，預計每年可省下約三成的能源費用。

瑞典並不是唯一開發這項創新技術的國家。巴黎也施行了類似的方案，將來自地鐵的體熱再度利用，輸送到公共住宅中。美國明尼蘇達州的美國購物商場也是一例，同樣利用體熱作為暖氣系統。事實上，天窗與體熱系統兩者結合的效率太高，有時候商場在冬天時還需要開冷氣，才能維持讓購物者舒適的環境溫度。

雖然體熱系統是一個創新的方法，它還是有些缺點。熱能無法輸送得很遠，因為它容易冷卻。除此之外，氣候比較溫暖，或者傳統能源（石油、天然氣）較便宜的地方，考慮經濟效益，體熱系統並不可行。

74 溝通不良 (P. 180)

　　所以你想學一種新語言，太棒了！但是你必須知道一件事：不是所有的語言都生來平等。有些語言可以讓你在幾週內就和母語人士開心地交流，但有些語言得辛苦學習上一整年，你才有辦法開始抱怨天氣。往下看，你就會知道這是不是你所追求的挑戰。以下列出的都是世界上最困難的語言。

　　首先是阿拉伯文。這個語言難到連最聰明的學生都會做惡夢。阿拉伯文的字母依據單字裡的位置，有四種不同的寫法。現在式動詞時態有13種不同的形式。而全世界流傳的阿拉伯文方言數量，也和一個月的天數一樣多。

　　如果這聽起來對你來說太容易了，那你或許想試試廣東話。你可以先由單調的背誦開始，背完兩萬五千個字。不要忘了，還要精通九種聲調。但至少文法不會是個問題。廣東話中沒有動詞變化、性別或時態。中文文法可說是世界上最簡單的一種文法了。

　　日文是另一個需要花上很多力氣才能精熟的亞洲語言。它幾乎與廣東話相反，發音很簡單，也沒有什麼聲調，但動詞的時態會讓你想拔光自己的頭髮。更慘的是，如果你不想讓人覺得你粗魯無禮，就必須學會另一套新的動詞時態。

　　如果你想學讓舌頭打結的歐語，匈牙利語是個不錯的選擇。匈牙利語的名詞有18種不同的語義格。記下所有的語義格並不是唯一的挑戰。要合宜地說出匈牙利語，你還必須熟悉喉嚨能發出的所有不同聲音。對非母語人士，匈牙利語的發音可說是相當困難。

　　如果以上這些都吸引不了你。還有很多其他的語言都有希望登上世界最難的名單：芬蘭語、波蘭語、愛沙尼亞語、納瓦霍語、巴斯克語和冰島語只是其中的一小部分。只要記住，不管你選擇學習哪種語言，努力不懈才是流暢的關鍵。

75 骷髏會 (P. 182)

　　以鐵門防衛的房間外，有15名新成員緊張不安地等待著入會儀式。密室裡傳來怪聲、哭聲以及尖叫聲。一人進入密室。他看到一群男子身穿長袍，另一群穿著骷髏裝，有個男人打扮成惡魔。他們把他推到一張桌子旁，大喊：「唸出來！」。他唸出神祕的誓言。那些穿著長袍的人抓住他，將他推向該會的雄辯女神Eulogia的畫像，不斷地叫喊著：「Eulogia！Eulogia！」

　　他被趕到外面，那群長袍男子尖叫、哀嚎，驅使他走向一座白色的帳篷。他們大喊著：「劊子手等同死亡」、「魔鬼等同死亡！死神等同死亡！」在帳篷裡，他拿起一根大腿骨。從帳篷裡走出來後，他看見嚇人的景象。有個劊子手站在滿身是假血的男子面前。新入會的成員走向劊子手旁邊的骷髏頭，他跪下來親吻骷髏頭。劊子手作勢割男子的喉嚨。這動作象徵著入會者已從野蠻世界死去，重生進入「兄弟會」。

　　「骷髏會」是耶魯大學最古老的祕密社團，成立已將近二百年，此會有一套祕密的傳統，會員常成為美國最重要的未來領袖。

　　此處所記載令人不安的入會儀式，全是由記者從無數的訪談與祕密錄音中，一片片拼湊而成。除了真正的成員，沒有人確切知道骷髏會內部實際的情況。會員宣誓，緘口保守祕密，不吐露組織內部的運作。

　　雖然骷髏會可能只是怪異的辯論社，在每個星期四與星期日的晚上舉行聚會，但是他們對死亡的迷戀，以及該社團專出美國權力菁英的關係，使得它有別於大學其他的社團。

　　在2004年的美國總統大選中，小布希和他的對手約翰‧克里（兩人皆曾為骷髏會成員）都被問及他們入會期間的事情。布希總統說：「這是祕密。我們不能談這件事。」而當克里被問到，他們兩人都曾經加入骷髏的意義是什麼，他則回答：「沒什麼，因為這是祕密。」

76　冷血動物的滅絕 (P. 184)

　　青蛙、蟾蜍和蠑螈是最早出現在陸地的脊椎動物。這項成就大約在三億五千萬年前出現。從那時開始，兩棲動物就以每250年消失一個物種的速度滅絕。不過那也是在人類的出現，改變地球的自然平衡之前的事情了。

　　近來兩棲動物絕種的速度急遽地增加。從1980年起，已經有超過兩百種兩棲動物永遠地從地球上消失。而情況將會變得更糟。除此之外，還有1,856個物種現正面臨絕種的威脅。這些令人震撼的數字造成了全世界的恐慌，科學家拼命地想了解造成兩棲動物大量滅絕的背後原因。

　　造成兩棲動物大量絕種的原因似乎有好幾個。首先也是最重要的，就是自然棲息地的破壞。當人類砍伐森林，在兩棲動物的棲息地蓋房子時，我們破壞了整個星球的生態。全球暖化也使生態的破壞加劇。為了在其特定的棲息地存活下來，青蛙、蟾蜍和蠑螈都演化出高度特殊的生存方式。全球溫度的微妙變化也破壞了牠們存活的能力。

　　但人類並不是唯一的問題來源。一種名為壺病菌的致命黴菌，毀滅了美洲和澳洲的兩棲動物族群。感染這種黴菌的兩棲動物在數週內就會死亡。科學家連它是從哪裡來的都還不知道，更不用說如何阻止它了。

　　科學家通常將兩棲動物歸類為「生物指標」，表示牠們對環境變化比其他生物要來得敏感。青蛙、蟾蜍和蠑螈就像是一種早期警告系統，能夠告訴我們其他同樣遭受相似環境破壞的物種的狀況。由此可見，既然兩棲動物以驚人速度絕種，那鳥類與哺乳類動物可能也相去不遠。

　　同時，我們也會因為兩棲動物的滅絕，而失去豐富的醫學資源。諾貝爾生物學獎或醫學獎中，大約有10％的研究與兩棲動物相關。這表示，每一個消失的物種，或許有機會治癒一種可怕的疾病。

77　書寫意料之外 (P. 186)

　　以江戶川亂步對恐怖、怪誕事物深刻的理解，以及一身編寫曲折離奇、翻轉情節的才華，他將日本的推理小說，帶向駭人聽聞的新境界。江戶川亂步本名平井太郎，於1923年首次以江戶川亂步為筆名出版了第一篇故事。他的筆名是取自愛倫坡名字的諧音。江戶川亂步藉著將自己荒誕不羈的想像力，與西方推理故事中充滿懸疑的風格相互結合，而獲得成功。

　　例如，江戶川亂步在短篇故事《人間椅子》中，敘述一個容貌醜陋的製椅工匠，因渴望與人接觸，所以在為旅館設計一張豪華的沙發時，他改造了沙發的內部，好讓自己爬進去，藏身其中。這張藏著製椅工匠的沙發就被送到了旅館。旅館裡，顧客坐在他身上，殊不知這張沙發裡面竟藏著一個人。這張沙發最終被賣給了另一戶住著一名年輕女子的人家。這篇故事是以書信的方式進行，透過一位年輕的女作家讀這封信而展開。隨著她繼續往下讀信，故事漸趨明朗，那張她坐著的沙發，下面正隱藏著一個變態的製椅工匠。雖然故事並未到此結束（在讀者翻到最後一頁前，還有個有趣的轉折），卻已經展現了江戶川亂步是如何將讀者內心最根本的驚惶與恐懼操縱自如。

　　另一篇故事《紅房子》聚焦於一群聚在一起，說恐怖故事的男人。有個新加入的成員開始說故事，吐露他是個殺人犯，已經殺了99個人，不過由於他布置得如此巧妙，警方永遠也抓不到他。他以絕對能夠致人於死的謊言或是暗示性的動作，誘騙死者走入死亡的陷阱。他自認為是一位完美的兇手，最後哄騙一個服務生殺死自己，如此一來，他就殺滿一百人了。再一次地，這故事結局也有轉折。重要的是要記住，即使你認為故事已經結束了，江戶川亂步的袖裡總是藏著最後的驚奇。

78　風中的汙泥 (P. 188)

　　印度次大陸的上空籠罩著一大片褐色的雲，它是煙霧、灰塵及其他汙染物的集合，看就像一團髒兮兮的污泥。這是數十年來，化石燃料的濫用與汽車排放廢氣等經年累月的積累。近年來，這個現象已經開始嚴重影響到天氣，以致於千百萬人的生命受到威脅，並有可能造成數十億美元的損失。

一項研究結果顯示，所謂的「亞洲褐雲」直接影響了該地區，導致熱帶氣旋的強度急遽增強，尤其是在印度西岸的阿拉伯海域上方所形成的熱帶氣旋。

現今印度有害化學物質的排放，比 1950 年代還要高出六倍之多。這使空氣中有害微粒的濃度增加，就像一塊會吸收太陽輻射的海綿，影響了陽光所及之處，也使得海平面的溫度上升。結果造成大氣擾動，該地區的垂直風切減弱。垂直風切是指不同高度的風之間，其風速或風向上的巨大變化。強烈的垂直風切是減弱熱帶氣旋形成的要素。因為風切減弱，該地區的氣旋就會增強，增強到一定程度就會在登陸時造成嚴重的問題。

海平面的暖濕空氣會形成氣旋旋轉上升，在這過程中溼冷空氣會取而代之，並釋放出潛熱使溫度上升，最終導致發生狂風暴雨的氣旋式對流加劇。熱帶氣旋必須是垂直地形成，所以如果大氣中的上層氣流風速較快，或與下層氣流的方向相反，那麼垂直風切就會被破壞，氣旋也會消散。

以前，強風朝相反的方向流動（高空垂直風切），就會大幅度減少阿拉伯海域熱帶氣旋形成的頻率。不過，由於褐色雲團會削弱風切的強度，該地區氣旋的強度便會增強。2007 年的氣旋古努是阿拉伯海有史以來最強烈的熱帶氣旋，造成 44 億美元的損失以及 78 人死亡。2010 年的氣旋碧，則造成 47 人死亡。要控制這些風暴，印度就必須處理褐雲形成的原因，可是這件事對發展如此迅速的國家來說，說起來容易可做起來難啊。

79 聘雇的眼淚 (P. 190)

沒有什麼能比失去親愛的人更難以面對的，糾結在驚嚇與悲傷的情緒之中，已無法再去顧及其他事情。但葬禮該怎麼辦呢？依然處在震驚的時候，如何能好好地送走往生者呢？如果你在臺灣，或許該聘用專業的哭喪者（哭孝女，俗稱孝女白琴）了。

專業哭喪者在喪禮上代表家屬哀悼往生者。他們穿著白袍，跪在地上，對著從不相識的對象痛苦地嚎啕大哭。他們的哭喪主要有兩個目的：一代表往生者是好人，而且大家都懷念他；二可以免去家屬在失去親人的悲慟時，還得「行禮如儀」進行喪葬儀式。

在臺灣，哭喪這行業的收入十分豐厚。家屬若要辦一場包含專業哭喪者的送葬，其費用可高達台幣二十萬元以上。你可能會想：「那可是很大的一筆數目，專業哭喪者真是好賺啊！」但這份工作其實比外人看起來的還要難做。你必須要能夠迅速地轉換情緒，從開心立刻變成哀傷，也必須顧及現場觀眾的狀況。專業哭喪者在表達傷痛時得要懂得拿捏分寸。他們要表現出難過與痛苦，但又不能太過誇張或好笑。表演地太過火有可能會對家屬與他們已逝去的親人造成侮辱。

對某些文化來說，聘用專業哭喪者的做法也許很奇怪，在臺灣的新聞中出現專業哭喪者卻也不是什麼奇人異事。然而，這並不是什麼笑話或是騙錢的把戲，這習俗存在數千年之久，並且根植古代文化中。從前的父母會把女兒嫁到遠方，當父親或母親過世時，做女兒的很難回到老家奔喪，於是喪家就近聘請專人替她哭孝。這項習俗不僅中國有，在古希臘、印度與一些非洲國家中也都曾出現雇用專業哭喪者的例子。

80 充滿挑戰的診斷 (P. 194)

我告訴病患我需要填寫一些文件，但事實上我不知道該怎麼處理這個病例。他可能只是罹患了一種典型精神疾病，思覺失調症，但還是有些地方不太對勁。

沒有人能百分之百的確定引發思覺失調症的原因，但我們明確知道哪些因素會增加罹患這種疾病的機率。這個病患的背景中確實隱藏了一些危險性指標。第一，他的姊姊曾被診斷出罹患思覺失調症，這表示他有 6.5% 的機會得病；再者，他有濫用大麻與古柯鹼這類毒品的紀錄，這是另一個助長病發的因素。最後，他今年 20 歲，也是思覺失調症好發的年齡。

可以確定的是，他的症狀並不屬於偏執型思覺失調症。他的腦海中沒有出現任何聲音，也不自認比其他人優越，或是懷疑有人要來抓他。然而，他的確表現出其他精神分裂的症狀。他將自己孤立於朋友之外，不顯露太多的情緒，而且晚上無法入睡。最麻煩的是，他無法有條理地說出句子。他說出來的話變得扭曲，因為腦筋無法有條有理的思考，這可能表示他罹患了混亂型思覺失調症。

他可能是三百二十萬罹患思覺失調症的美國人之一，或只是一個被非法毒品殘害腦袋的憂鬱青年。

在我診斷病患為思覺失調症之前,總是想要百分之百地確診,因為用來治療的抗精神病藥物非常傷身。我上一次開給病患抗精神病藥物時,他得忍受像是暈眩、顫抖和變胖的嚴重副作用,甚至有時候會行動緩慢。另一方面,如果思覺失調症不接受治療的話,可導致嚴重後果。許多病患最後會嘗試用非法毒品來治療自己,而且有超過三分之一的人會在病程中試圖自殺。

我想我會再等等,看他的病情如何發展。我會告訴他一個月後再回來看診。

81 合成的信號干擾器 (P. 196)

人類的內分泌系統是一系列複雜的腺體與路徑,能夠幫助荷爾蒙從身體的一個點移動到另一個點。你可以把這些荷爾蒙想像成一間小小的生物郵局,而它們的作用就是傳遞訊息。舉例來說,當你年輕時,它們會傳達身體該長大了的訊息。而當你變老了,它們開始傳達出不太令人振奮的消息,也就是你的身體該開始萎縮了。內分泌系統負責你的成長、新陳代謝和組織功能,甚至影響你快樂或悲傷的感受。

但是如果有東西開始干擾內分泌系統,那又會怎麼樣呢?這正是全世界的科學家現在正在努力弄清楚的事。他們正在研究阻礙我們體內生物郵政服務的化學物質。這些「內分泌干擾素」是人類創造出來的化學合成製品,它們已經滲透到全世界的自然環境之中。據我們所知,內分泌干擾素對生物有害,也與人類的癌症及其他生殖障礙有關。

雙對氯苯基三氯乙烷,或稱DDT,就是一個典型的化學合成內分泌干擾素。1972年,美國發現DDT會造成鳥類產下軟殼蛋後,下令禁止DDT的使用。DDT也會傷害人類的生殖系統。但現今非洲部分地區仍在使用。

世界衛生組織(WHO)已經發布了幾項報告,概述內分泌干擾素對野生動物所造成的威脅。這些報告顯示,哺乳類、爬蟲類、鳥類和魚類正出現性別不平均、繁殖缺陷與生長障礙的問題。然而,這些並不是決定性的結果。由於目前自然環境中有太多的汙染源,這些研究很難斷定哪些是由內分泌干擾素所造成的,而哪些又不是。

只有在研究室裡進行的研究已證明內分泌干擾素會對人類造成傷害。到目前為止還沒有確切的研究,能確定人類疾病與環境中現存內分泌干擾素的關聯。但是,已經有好幾項研究證實,內分泌干擾素對於居住在自然棲息地的哺乳類動物會產生負面影響。既然人類也是哺乳類動物,難道那不表示我們一樣也有麻煩了嗎?

82 真能預知未來嗎? (P. 198)

有人說諾斯特拉達姆士(1503–1566)曾經預言了法國大革命、希特勒的崛起、紐約911恐怖攻擊事件,以及唐納・川普當選美國總統。有些人則斥為無稽之談。

他最著名的作品《百詩集》(於1555年至1558年間出版)包含了未來的世界史,直到3797年為止。他最著名的預言詩(儘管《百詩集》裡的預言逾千則)大概是以下兩則:「飢餓瘋狂的野獸將會游泳渡河/大部分的戰役將會是對抗 Hister」以及「在45度,天空將會燃燒/大火將會降臨偉大的新城」。

信徒們很快指出 Hister 跟 Hitler 之間的相似處,他們確信諾斯特拉達姆士指的是惡名昭彰的獨裁者希特勒。不過,Hister 是中歐多瑙河的古名,與希特勒一點關係都沒有。第二則預言據說是對911恐怖攻擊事件的描述,北緯45度的「新城」是指紐約。可是事實上,紐約位於北緯40度43分,而「新城」很可能是指不勒斯(又稱拿坡里),因其希臘文 Neapolis 其實就是「新的城市」的意思。

諾斯特拉達姆士的預言最為人詬病的地方在於,這些預言往往只是過去歷史事件的重複,卻被拿來投射未來,假設歷史會重演。他留下的預言沒有註明日期,也沒有特定的順序,所以也很方便解讀。曾有人提出,有名的911恐怖攻擊事件的預言,是1139年那不勒斯侵略事件的重演,因同年附近的維蘇威火山爆發了。

諾斯特拉達姆士籠統的言詞、信徒對其過度的詮釋與斷章取義,皆為諾斯特拉達姆士能預見未來的神祕能力增添神話的色彩。

小布希在2000年當選美國總統後,網路上流傳著一首顯然出自諾斯特拉達姆士的預言詩,這首詩預言了小布希的當選，內容是：「千禧年到來，第十二個月／在無上權利之家／呆頭呆腦的鄉巴佬將會出來／被歡呼為領袖」。這預言還真準！不過後來有人發現，這首詩並不是出自於偉大的預言家，而是網路上博君一笑的惡作劇罷了。

83 打破習慣 (P. 200)

我叫戴夫，我叫戴夫，我叫戴夫。哇，真是抱歉，看來我的症狀又發作了！因為我罹患「強迫性神經官能症」（強迫症），有時我會把同樣的東西寫三次，就像這樣會帶來好運一樣。

五年前，我第一次被診斷出罹患了強迫症。問題的開端是我發現自己有了這一些無法控制的怪習慣，例如說，如果我不將電燈開開關關五次，我就不敢睡覺，而這也是我開始將每一樣東西都連續說寫三次的時候。我向你保證：這樣的習慣讓我很難與別人正常地交談。

醫生說強迫症很普遍。事實上，它被診斷出來的發生率和氣喘相差無幾。他說，這沒什麼好丟臉的。在生活中，我們全都有一些習慣，像是在睡覺前要確定門已經上鎖。患有強迫症的人有些習慣……嗯，這麼說吧，他們的習慣比一般人更奇特一點。

醫生也說強迫症的症狀因人而異，有些強迫症患者偶爾會有揮之不去的念頭，造成暫時的不快或焦慮，但是最後這些想法還是會消失。有些人的強迫症症狀較嚴重，不快的念頭讓他們不時陷入焦躁不安，所以他們會想養成一些習慣，讓自己能安心自在。前一分鐘他們還感到緊張，但下一分鐘他們會在吃午餐前連洗兩個小時的手。

我知道你在想什麼——為什麼我在這篇文章中沒有把每一句都連寫三次？嗯，醫生不只告訴我什麼叫強迫症，也告訴我該如何治療。我接受了兩種治療——儀式療法及暴露療法。這些治療讓我處於引發強迫症習慣的環境下。將它當成是一種抗拒沉迷於「奇特」習慣的練習。到目前為止，這些治療的效果很好，但是還是有努力的空間。還是有努力的……啊哈！被我抓到了！

84 被偷走的光陰 (P. 202)

「把偷走的時間還給我們！」二十世紀時，英國人抗議引進日光節約時間（DST）時，曾提出如此要求。在夏季期間，調整時鐘，將早上的日照時間往晚上挪一小時的想法，歷來頗具爭議性。人們認為此舉可以節省能源、降低犯罪、避免交通意外的發生。而有些人則並不怎麼相信，過去十年的研究結果也顯示利弊參半。

德國於第一次世界大戰期間，首度實施日光節約時間，目的是要節省戰時煤炭的使用。英國隨後跟進，實施自己的夏令時間，不過也造成困擾與混亂，有些機構實施這些改變，有些則乾脆忽略。有位作家以更富詩意的方式表達對夏令時間的不滿，表示不喜歡被迫支持太陽，而不是月亮。

儘管施行的初期頗具爭議，目前超過70個國家實施日光節約時間。美國是在三月第二個星期日的凌晨二點鐘，將時間撥快一個小時，並在十一月第一個星期日，往後調回一個小時。然而，某些州至今仍未實施日光節約時間。從前，有的州即使實施日光節約時間，州內的某些地區仍然拒絕遵守。

原本以為施行日光節約時間，可以降低能源的消耗量，因為日照時間延長，大家晚上比較不會點燈。可是，最近的一項研究顯示，由於夏夜漫漫，大家開冷氣的時間延長，所以家裡冷氣用量的增加抵消了這項優點。

在某些遵守日光節約時間的國家裡，晚上比較明亮，使得交通意外的次數減少。但是，研究也發現，在調整時間後的那個星期，交通事故驟增，或許是因為突然的時間變化，干擾了大家的睡眠模式。

然而，實施日光節約時間確有好處。1999年有一群西岸恐怖分子（實施日光節約時間）將炸彈運到以色列的一個房間（未實施日光節約時間），他們在裝置定時炸彈時，忽略了時間差，使得炸彈比原定計畫提早一小時爆炸，當場炸死了三名恐怖份子，原本會遭受突襲的平民百姓反而逃過一劫。

85　無國界英雄 (P. 204)

1971年，一群法國醫師和記者創建了一個國際組織，其宗旨是不分種族、宗教或政治信仰，為戰爭、天災、疾病的受難者提供緊急醫療救援。組織名為「無國界醫生」，該組織在美國享有高知名度。

「無國界醫生」是由健康產業各層面中的各類專家所組成，該組織在世界一些最貧困與飽受戰爭蹂躪的國家，提供重要的醫療援助。

這些醫師、護士、行政人員與規劃專家活躍於70多國，並且在堅定的道德規範下運作，也就是要他們不歧視、平等對待所有的人。該組織也嚴格維持政治與宗教上的中立，不偏向戰爭中的任何一方。如此一來，該組織便可以不受任何限制，能夠援助最需要救助的人。

「無國界醫生」的主要收入來源是私人捐款，組織也因此而得以保持獨立。來自世界各國的個人捐款者超過570萬人，只有10%的資金是來自政府的捐贈。

「無國界醫生」通常都是第一個抵達危機現場的組織，他們經常置身於天災或人禍造成的重災區，無論是人為或自然災難，有時甚至會目睹十分殘酷、暴力的場面。為了要提供最好的醫療照護，該組織會隨時與當地民眾保持聯繫。正因如此，他們對世界上非常危急的形勢，有其獨特與透徹的觀點。

該組織以此第一手知識，經常大聲疾呼反對人權侵犯、醫療疏忽與暴力，這些都是未獲得媒體足夠關注的議題。

這個和平的組織只有一次呼籲採取軍事干預，也就是在1994年的盧安達屠殺。然而，他們也強力譴責一些非洲與亞洲國家的行為，經常直接與聯合國共事。

由於該組織在世界各地人道主義行動上的優異表現，而於1999年獲頒諾貝爾和平獎。一如往常，獲得的獎金也作為資金，對抗被忽視的疾病。

86　就位！ (P. 206)

「閣下，我要與您決鬥！」在近代早期，這句話響遍了英國上層階級，通常發聲的是一個自覺榮譽受辱的男人。除非辱人的那一方迅速道歉，不然將會有一場決鬥來解決這場恩怨，有時甚至會導致死亡。

現在的擊劍（西洋劍）是一種體育運動，持劍的雙方使用三種不同的劍，進行近距離的格鬥。這其實也是過去歐洲各國習慣的決鬥表現方式。

擊劍運動員站在通常是2公尺寬、14公尺長的長條狀「擊劍劍道」上比賽，中點兩側有兩條運動員就定位的線。擊劍運動員站在準備線後面，向彼此致意，然後裁判會喊「就位！」這是通知擊劍運動員戴上防護面罩、舉劍的信號。比賽開始後，無論何人擊中對方的身體，便可得一分（稱之為「得分」），只要得五分便可贏得比賽。

在中世紀的歐洲，劍術變得多餘，因為穿上盔甲後，需要力量與一把能砍的重兵器，才能劈開對方一身堅硬的鐵甲。然而，槍枝的發達使得盔甲一無所用，擊劍因而在十五世紀再度走紅。由於十六世紀時，研發了既長且輕的護手刺劍，使得劍士強調技巧、速度與技術，更勝於強調力量。之後，從輕劍衍生的劍更輕，劍尖尖銳，側鋒並不那麼鋒利，所以此劍適於戳刺攻擊，而非砍削。

現代擊劍武器包括三種劍：鈍劍、銳劍和軍刀。鈍劍重量輕、彈性佳、劍尖尖銳。銳劍略重，而軍刀是雙刃劍，非常適合削砍跟戳刺。在過去擊劍比賽是由裁判來評分，裁判觀看比賽，若見到有人擊中身體便會大叫得分。然而，這並不可靠，後來便改用現在的電子評分系統。當系統感應到劍擊，燈光就會閃爍，也讓決鬥的藝術真正地現代化了。

87 與幽靈對話 (P. 210)

1848年有一對姊妹，凱特和瑪格麗特・福克斯，說她們可以跟死者對話，宣稱從她們在紐約州海德村的家中可以聽到很大的拍打聲。拜訪她們的人都確認有拍打聲，肯定兩女孩可以跟這個喧鬧的「靈魂」溝通。

在很久之前，就有許多靈媒宣稱自己有跟死者對話的能力。在暗室中，在一小群人的圍繞下，他們試圖聯繫過世的至親。

靈媒可以用很多不同方式來展現靈魂的存在。把鈴鐺和球放在桌子上，當靈媒說話時，球就會開始滾動，或是鈴鐺在沒有觸碰下開始鈴鈴作響。有些靈媒會運用「靈寫板」，那是兩片綁一起的空白黑板，在召喚亡靈後，靈寫板會打開，裡頭寫著留言。然而，許多方法都被揭露只是一般的魔術技巧。

很多的現代降靈會都在大批觀眾面前進行，靈媒會從靈界透露很多個人的訊息。靈媒也常說出有關死者和觀眾一些不可思議的軼事──當然這就證實了他是如假包換地是在跟亡靈對話！

然而，懷疑者堅持靈媒只是使用一種叫做「冷讀術」的語言技巧。也就是製造出有告訴別人資訊的印象，但其實這些資訊大多是觀眾自身所提供的訊息。

例如，靈媒可能會宣稱，他聽到一個名字是P開頭的靈魂在對他說話，而且一直在說5這個數字。就會有觀眾擷取這樣的訊息，接著說：「那一定是我爸爸彼得，他有五個兄弟。」其實字母P和數字5可以用在很多觀眾身上，其實靈媒沒有提供任何細節，只是表面上看起來有。

或許，不令人意外的是，1888當年首先造成靈異現象的瑪格麗特・福克斯坦承，那些神祕的拍打聲，都只是她和妹妹扳動腳趾關節所發出的聲音。

88 神奇的社交數字 (P. 212)

從人類演化之初，我們便一直是社群動物。當人類過著狩獵採集的群體生活後，我們便以複雜的人際關係為基礎，創建起小型的社會，並且發展更廣泛的集體觀念，決定社會世界的規則。

建立與維護這些連繫需要技巧，而社會學家稱此為「社會行為」。社會行為是指考慮他人反應而做出的舉動，並且根據這些反應改變行為。這種以因果關係為依據的行為，導致堅固的社會結構，在這個結構中，人可以把自己的生活安排得更好，設定並達成目標。

然而，過去兩百年來，人們走出原本居住的小鄉村，來到擠滿數百萬人的都會區生活。據估計，到2050年全世界70％的人口都將居住在都市裡。在人類進化史上，我們大部分是過著小型社會的生活，如今又該如何應付這些以都市中心的超級社會的興起呢？

牛津大學的演化人類學教授羅賓・丹巴爾提出，維持有意義的社會互動的人數其實是有限的。丹巴爾表示，人類傾向於形成約150人的自然團體。這個數字大概是傳統狩獵採集部落的人數，以及中世紀村莊的平均規模，也是大家在臉書上會保持聯絡的平均朋友數量。

丹巴爾將150人層層分級為：密友、好友、朋友、泛泛之交。根據丹巴爾的描述，若要算在這150人中，其親密的程度必須是「凌晨三點，你在香港機場的過境貴賓室裡，碰巧看到他們，即使加入他們，你也不會覺得尷尬的朋友」。

近年來，由於工作遷徙、離家上大學，以及網路革命，人們的社交團體更易於跨越國界，甚至是其他大洲。

這引起理論家質疑社區的概念與它的未來，他們擔憂的是，隨著世界愈來愈疏離，缺乏社會互動可能會讓我們在這個擁擠萬分的世界裡，感到非常孤單。

89 最需要教育的地方 (P. 214)

亞當・布勞恩在歷經死亡威脅後，受啟發想要環遊世界，他開始當背包客，來到世界上最貧窮的幾個國家。他的足跡從南非的貧困小鎮，到柬埔寨饑荒的街道。可是直到來到印度，才有了成立「鉛筆的承諾」的想法。有個行乞的小男孩向他伸手，布勞恩並沒有馬上掏錢給他，而是問全世界他最想要的東西是什麼。小男孩回答：「一枝鉛筆」。

從那一刻起，布勞恩不管去哪都會帶上一大堆鉛筆和原子筆，分送給流浪街頭的孩子。他很快意識到，對這些孩子來說，鉛筆這個教育的工具比什麼都還要珍貴。

2008年，在他25歲生日的前夕，布勞恩存了25美元到銀行的儲蓄帳戶裡，希望能成立一個基金，到全球各地貧困的地區蓋小學。然而，他的願望引起了廣大的迴響。

　　在六個月內，他募得了五萬多美元，以及75名準備到寮國蓋學前幼兒園的志工。

　　布勞恩鼓勵在地民眾參與這項計畫，「此次有兩千人捐款，每人所捐的款項都不到一百美元。這就是我們希望在成長過程中開創和發揚的草根運動。」他說。

　　第一所學校建於2009年，成績斐然，只花了三個月及一萬八千美元。這筆費用包括了老師的薪資、蓋學校的建材，以及三年的維護費用。「鉛筆的承諾」其中的一項政策就是，學校所在的社區必須籌募到這項計畫10％的資金。他們可以藉由提供人力與建材，這確保了整個社區都會參與、關懷這項計畫。

　　但是，該組織可不只是一家建設公司，它還培訓師資，長期支援寮國、迦納、瓜地馬拉、尼加拉瓜等國的學校，定期考察測試學生，以確保維持高標準的教學品質。該組織還啟動了一項名為WASH的計畫，務必讓孩子有乾淨的浴室可用，並教他們水與健康方面的知識。

　　截至目前，「鉛筆的承諾」已在世界各地興建了400多所學校，把教育帶到資金短缺，卻求知若渴的地區。

90　韓國決鬥！(P. 216)

　　橫跨五大洲，超過三千萬的練習者，跆拳道已成為世界上最受歡迎的武術之一。但是你知道跆拳道不只是一種武術，而是九種不同派別的韓國武術，而且每一種都有其悠久的歷史嗎？

　　跆拳道起源於西元六世紀。當時韓國半島分為三個王國：新羅、高句麗與百濟。新羅是最小的王國，擔心會被較大的鄰國併吞。鑒於此長期的憂慮，他們組成了一個名為花郎道或「花郎徒」的菁英武士團體。這些花郎道不只開創了近似於現今的跆拳道、著重腳步的徒手格鬥，也建立了一套強調榮譽與服從的倫理規範。最後，「花郎徒」幫助新羅打敗了鄰國，並且在西元918年統一韓國，名為高麗王朝。

　　在高麗王朝統治之下，韓國武術持續茁壯，這時候也出現手搏以及跆拳的早期型態。國王定期舉辦武術競賽，並且命令所有士兵都得接受徒手格鬥的武術訓練，使得這些武術如野火蔓延般廣受歡迎。

　　自1910年起，韓國逐漸受到日本的影響，成為跆拳道歷史上的轉捩點。當時韓國武術被禁止，並鼓勵人們轉而學習日本空手道。因此，韓國武術也融入了一些日式風格與戰術。

　　1945年韓國解放之後，韓國武術又獲得發展茁壯的機會，但此時有九種風格迥異的派別，每一種都有自己的格鬥風格、戰略與哲學。最後，當1959年韓國跆拳道聯盟成立時，這九種派別合而為一。這開啟了教學技巧標準化與簡化的過程，讓國際觀眾能夠更輕易的接觸武術。

　　所以下回你到跆拳道「道場」做些練習時，不要忘了，你正在學習的是超過千年歷史的格鬥智慧總和。

91　兩隻黑猩猩的故事 (P. 218)

　　亞特蘭大大學的研究員發現了黑猩猩不為人知的一面。顯然地，這些人類的遠親可能不如我們所想的那麼自私與殘酷。

　　由於黑猩猩是我們現存的最近親，我們很容易在牠們身上貼標籤，將牠們視為人類所有缺點的起因。所以，沒錯，我們是貪婪的，但是黑猩猩更貪心；我們也會報復，但是我們復仇本能比起黑猩猩在野外的表現根本不算什麼，而且這只是其中一些而已。基本上，當我們想到人類的良善，所想到的是我們的成就，而非與黑猩猩的共通點。

　　通常，各種研究更加深了這些對黑猩猩的負面觀感。黑猩猩的社會常被視為「分裂─融合」的。這表示，在黑猩猩社會中，唯一重要的社會連結只存在於母親與後代之間。如果身旁的黑猩猩有香蕉，黑猩猩社會中的其他成員都會為了拿到香蕉，在背後刺牠一刀。研究員也觀察到，黑猩猩會因為爭奪地盤而大打出手，或者在沒有明顯的原因下殺害對方。

　　但是，亞特蘭大大學做了一個有關黑猩猩行為表現的開創性研究，挑戰這些傳統觀點。研究員進行了一個實驗，將兩隻黑猩猩安置在以金屬網隔開的兩個房間裡。每隻黑猩猩面前都放了一個裝滿不同顏色代幣的籃子。當猩猩拿綠色代幣給研究員時，就可以得到食物做為獎賞。如果拿的是藍色代幣，那兩隻猩猩都可以有獎賞。在這個情況之下，猩猩們都會選擇藍色代幣。牠們選擇幫助其他猩猩，而不是獨自享用。主導這項研究的研究員認為，這證明了黑猩猩會將群體利益置於個人需要之前。換句話說，這表示黑猩猩的行為也可以合乎道德。牠們或許不會每一次都選擇去做有益於群體的事，但是同樣地──人類也不會啊。

92　無路可逃 (P. 220)

小時候，你曾經被困在一個狹小的空間裡嗎？你曾不小心被鎖在黑暗的房間中嗎？或者你曾經掉進很深的水潭中，無路可逃嗎？對於許多人來說，這些可怕的童年經歷並不會隨著時間過去輕易地消失。相反地，這些經歷有時會留下嚴重的後果，我們稱之為「幽閉恐懼症」。

幽閉恐懼症是指對封閉的空間懷有非理性的恐懼。甚至光是想像進入一個狹小的空間，都可能會讓患者十分恐慌。走進電梯、搭地鐵、坐飛機，都會讓患者感到深切恐懼。估計全世界有6%的人口患有幽閉恐懼症，可是卻只有極少數的人會尋求治療。

幽閉恐懼症發生的原因，在於患者的心理將狹小的空間跟童年被困住的恐怖記憶做聯想，然後在每次身處密閉空間時引發歇斯底里的反應。這通常會導致恐慌症發作，患者也許會開始盜汗、感覺暈眩或噁心，並且會開始發抖，有時甚至會昏厥。

對於病情十分嚴重的患者，這種情況可能會對患者的社交生活造成嚴重的問題，通常導致患者刻意避免某些狀況，因為他們擔心會遇到恐慌發作。患者也可能會變得憂鬱，覺得他們的生活被恐懼主宰。他們可能會變得害怕身處於擠滿人的派對房間中，在一些非常極端的情況下，甚至是一扇緊閉的門也會令他們感到害怕。

某一派研究指出，幽閉恐懼症其實是深藏我們所有人內心中的恐懼。在早期人類的身上，感覺到危險的封閉空間其實是一種重要的進化優勢，所以我們現在自然容易出現這種恐懼症。

情境暴露療法一直是治療幽閉恐懼症最有效的療法。這種療法是讓患者逐漸暴露於他們所害怕的事物之中。第一階段療程可能是向病人介紹電梯，說服他們電梯裡面沒什麼可怕的。然後，治療師會逐漸地讓病人處於愈來愈狹小的空間，直到病人即使待在最封閉的空間裡，都能完全自在放鬆。

93　到地心旅行 (P. 222)

你可曾想過人類可以到達地心多深的地方？幾乎每個孩子都曾夢想過在地上挖一個洞，然後從地球的另一端出來。地底究竟有什麼？又會是什麼樣子的呢？嗯，地球並不僅是由石塊和岩石所組成。事實上，它有三個不同的地層，而每一層又各有其不同的物理特性。

首先是外層，它被稱為「地殼」，是由厚實的岩石所組成，同時也被劃分成巨大的地殼板塊。有時候，來自地球深處的能量造成這些板塊移動，而形成地震。地殼平均大約是80公里厚，但在海洋底層也可能只有五公里薄。

地殼下面那一層被稱為「地函」，是由上下兩個部分所組成。整體來說大約有2,900公里厚。堅硬的上層地函和地殼統稱為岩石圈，這個字的英文源自希臘文的「岩石」。內層地函是像蜂蜜一樣打旋流動的液體，由矽、氧、鐵和鎂所構成。

有時，地殼的移動會開出一條通道來，讓內層地函中的高熱熔岩衝出地球表面。這就是火山的形成。我們可以將火山爆發當成是地球在流血。

而在地球的正中心則是地核，地核對科學家來說仍算是謎團，但科學家都公認，地心的密度相當高。專家相信地心是由鐵和鎳所構成。據說它的溫度約莫和太陽表面一樣高。

所以，下一次當你聽到某人想挖個洞，通往世界的另一端時，別忘了告訴他們，他們可能會想帶著急救箱和穿著T恤。下面那裡可是很熱的。

94　人類的第一個字 (P. 226)

語言的起源是一個謎團，數百年來一直困擾著理論學者。早期人類是如何由動物般的吼聲和叫聲，轉變到表達抽象概念和傳達複雜的技巧呢？目前還沒有一個全球一致的結論，這個謎團也被稱為「科學界最難的問題」。

處理這個難題，有兩種主要思考方式。第一種是假設語言是由我們靈長類祖先所使用、預先存在的系統，如求偶呼聲或警告訊號開始逐漸發展。第二種認為語言是突然蹦出來的，起因於大腦重組的隨機突變，因此語言幾乎是在很短的時間內完美形成。

有些科學家認為，語言的基本形式存在於如匠人（180萬年前）之類的早期人類。基本語言介於靈長類溝通的形式和現代語言之間，這種語言可能主要以命令和建議組成，而且也依賴大量的手勢來表達。

黑猩猩的研究中，暗示了語言的發生與社群中的互信有關。黑猩猩使用多元的聲音和呼叫代表不同意義的信號，但牠們也會用信號來欺騙同伴。因此，當一個聲音容易造假時，就常常會被忽略或當成欺騙。只有在社群中的互信足以讓信號表達事情，而非無意的自然或情緒化反應時，語言才能繁茂。

然而，一個尼加拉瓜的現象，使得語言或許是突然發生的理論變得更加可信。1980年，一個聽障學院在尼加拉瓜設立。這所學校著重在讀唇訓練，但孩子們一起玩的時候，卻開始自創簡單的手語。這些孩子的下一代繼續發展這套基本的語言，然後漸漸複雜化。這說明了人類有一種與生俱來的文法構造，可能來自於早期人類腦中的突變，使得人類擁有從無到有、創造複雜語言的非凡能力。

95　惡水 (P. 228)

有個環境危機正在地球的河流、湖泊與海洋中蘊釀。這個危機就是優養化，當過量的硝酸鹽或磷酸鹽被加到水中時，就會產生優養化。

優養化會破壞水中生態系統的整體食物鏈，因為它改變了生物最底層的微妙平衡。簡單的植物，像是在水中茂盛繁殖的藻類，已經經歷優養化。事實上，水藻和浮游植物因生長過快，導致於其他生物無法存活。當水藻成長擴散時，它吸收了水中所有的氧氣，讓較複雜型態的植物無以呼吸。導致魚類和其他水中生物失去了基本食物來源，而活活餓死。

如果這還不夠可怕，科學家也發現優養化正在增加世界海洋的酸性。喬治亞大學最近的研究發現，優養化增加了海洋能自大氣中吸收的二氧化碳量。可以斷定的是，沿海水域的持續優養化將造成幾種蟹類、蝸牛、蛤蜊以及珊瑚的毀滅。

就如同在開放海域中，優養化也很容易出現在淡水系統。調查發現，亞洲有54%的湖泊已經被優養化，而在歐洲與北美洲也各有53%與48%的比例。世界上幾個最大最有名的湖泊也已經優養化，例如美國的伊利湖與中國的太湖。飲用優養化的水具危險性，因此淡水湖的優養化愈嚴重，可以供給全球缺水地區人口的飲用水就愈少。

雖然優養化也會自然產生，但這個危機卻是由人類的行為所直接造成的。農耕尤其被認為是優養化加劇的主要原因。大部分的肥料不是含有硝酸鹽就是磷酸鹽，而這兩種化學物質都會造成優養化。根據某些估計，在1950年到1995年之間地球表面增加了超過六億公噸的磷酸鹽。以這樣的數字來看，不難想見優養化氾濫成災的原因。

96　身為其中之一 (P. 230)

有道是，數大便安全。魚兒聚集成巨群、大批斑馬群體行動，這些動物會融入無數的群體中，以混淆掠食者。這種從眾行為（也可稱羊群行為）明顯有利於整個群體，但實際上卻有著更自私的動機。雖然一群鳥兒可能看起來雄偉且優雅，行動間宛如一體，但事實上每隻鳥兒都在為自己著想，也只會考慮到自己。每隻動物都盡可能靠近群體中心，有效利用其他同伴為活盾牌。當然，在外圍的倒楣鬼不可避免地會被捕食。從眾行為也可見於人類行為，有著同樣自私的動機，以及潛在毀滅性的結果。

股市崩盤是人類從眾行為的結果。陷入恐慌的投資者想搶在別人之前賣出股票，導致一場金融災難，全只因個人心中的恐懼。在瘋狂的購物季時，人們為了買到最後一件庫存商品，在超市蜂擁而上而踩死人。

處在一大群人當中會讓人做出有別於以往的舉動。個人會較不易意識到自己行為所帶來的真實效應，行事取決於原始情緒而非理性，並且會觀看大多數人，以此作為信號來決定如何進行。這種行為被稱之為「暴民心態」，也造成平常人不願為之的暴力與破壞舉動。

最近，有位英國的幻術家做了一項實驗，探討從眾行為的黑暗面。他安排了一個假的電視節目。這個節目要求觀眾投票，決定某位不知情的民眾的遭遇。觀眾可以選擇讓他有好的遭遇，或者壞的遭遇。隨著節目的進行，愈來愈多的觀眾投給他壞的遭遇，結果，這個受害者丟了財產、被通知遭解雇，最後還被綁架。這個實驗是為了要顯示，當人隱匿於群眾時，舉止會有多反常。

97 哈比人 (P. 232)

在超過一萬兩千年前，哈比人存在於世上。體型只有人類三歲孩童的大小，但是哈比人能捕獵一千公斤重的矮象，與像狗一樣大的巨鼠以及殺人蜥蜴一起生活。因為體型小，而被暱稱為「哈比人」的弗洛瑞斯人，曾經居住在印尼的弗洛瑞斯島上，他們或許也是早期人種中最後與現代人（學名為智人）互動的人種。

弗洛瑞斯人可能是直立人的後裔，與現代人類有同樣的祖先。直立人大約於一百萬年前來到弗洛瑞斯。數十萬年以後，直立人被認為可能是受到島嶼侏儒化現象的影響，而演化成體型嬌小的「哈比人」。由於小島上可取得的食物有限，那些只需攝取較低能量的人較容易存活下來。因此，動物傾向於生長成較小的體型。

「哈比人」是2003年考古學家挖掘洞穴時發現的人種。他們發現一具大約一公尺高的女性骨骸，被埋在滿是沉積物的洞穴地板上。一開始，考古學家誤以為那是孩童的骨骸。之後，在洞穴內陸續發現八具骨骸，以及石器跟矮象的骨頭。

弗洛瑞斯人與現代人類不僅在身高上有差別，他們的手臂較長，腳跟牙齒較大，下巴非常短小。不過，他們的大腦比我們的小多了，甚至比一般的黑猩猩都還要小。儘管如此，他們使用複雜的工具、會用火，甚至可能有了語言，這點可以由他們複雜的團體狩獵策略證明。

大多數的證據指出，大約在一萬二千年前，一場火山爆發消滅了許多島上的棲息生物，而弗洛瑞斯人也就此絕跡。距今約一萬一千年前儘管曾經發現現代人類的遺骸，但是在此之前並沒有任何發現，所以還不清楚這兩種人種是否曾經混種。

然而，現今在弗洛瑞斯的居民仍流傳著多起傳說，其中提到小個子、多毛，長得像人類一樣的生物，住在洞穴裡，說著奇怪的原始語言。有人認為這些生物一直到19世紀都還存在，故考古學家們推斷，那些人也許是倖存弗洛瑞斯人的後代，說不定，哈比人至今仍住在印尼某個人煙罕至的森林裡。

98 人類的良善 (P. 234)

我們每天聽到像是「適者生存」、「這是個狗咬狗的世界」這類的話，而這並不能完整的描繪出人類的行為。畢竟，人們有時候還是相當正直的，不是嗎？

為他人的福祉著想稱為利他主義。真正的利他主義是由想要幫助有需求的人的慾望所激發，它的動力並不是來自個人利益、忠誠或責任。把利他主義想像成當你幫助人們減輕痛苦時，體內湧出的那種溫暖模糊不清的感覺。如果你從未有像那種感受，那你可能太遲鈍了。

利他主義並不受限於任何文化或宗教。相反地，它是人類歷史中舉世皆然的道德教義。

佛教提倡愛人，對所有的事物都平等地保有憐憫之心。所以一個佛教徒會像對待他的家人一般，對陌生人伸出援手。這就是利他主義的一例。

伊斯蘭的經書《布哈里聖訓》說：「一個人以愛自己的方式，來愛他的兄弟時，才是真正的信者。」換句話說，如果真的相信上帝，就會以利他的方式來對待旁人。

猶太教將利他主義視為上帝創造萬物的理想目標。猶太教與許多傳統宗教思想一樣，都相信人類的善行在塵世中顯現了上帝的存在。因此，我們之所以善良，是因為每個人心中都有神的存在。

基督教有句眾所皆知的話：你要愛鄰人，像愛自己一樣。這是另一個教導愛人是神性的傳統宗教思想。

不論我們的利他主義是來自宗教或是演化結果，並不重要。重要的是，利他主義是人類獨有的特質，世世代代存在於我們之間，而且看來也不會消失。

如此一來，或許我們該說些像是「善者生存」，或是「這是個狗救落水狗的世界」這類的新說法。

99　射出你的箭！(P. 236)

　　射箭就是張弓拉箭，朝目標射擊，不論那目標是否有生命。射箭的起源也許可追溯到西元前五萬年之久，在非洲發現史前時代的石箭鏃可以支持這項理論。從發明射箭開始，射箭的主要用途在於狩獵和戰爭。成吉思汗的蒙古大軍曾以其威震四方的騎射手征服了亞洲，而許多神話與傳說故事中，神或英雄都是被描述為弓箭手。希臘神話裡半人半神的海克力士、中國神話裡從十個太陽中，射下其中九個的英雄后羿，以及英國民間故事中的英雄羅賓漢，都是赫赫有名的神射手，民間傳說所傳頌的弓箭手可說族繁不及備載。

　　儘管有好的開始，可是在十五、十六世紀快速發展出便於攜帶的槍枝後，弓箭便逐漸失去作為遠射武器的首選。訓練士兵學會用槍的速度也比學會射箭快許多，再加上槍彈能很輕易地刺穿盔甲，使得弓箭很快就過時了。正因為如此，現代的射箭才成為競技的運動項目，而非戰鬥的技能。比賽者對固定距離的目標射箭，然後依其準確度來評分。

　　通常，弓箭手側身面向目標，雙腳微張至兩肩的寬度，以便穩固射手的下盤。然後，將箭搭上弓的過程稱之為「搭箭」。「箭扣」是指箭尾尾端的小槽，剛好能卡住弓弦。之後是舉弓，拉箭的動作要一氣呵成。持弓的左手臂應該要固定伸直，面朝目標方向，而拉弦的右手臂應該要彎曲，手肘與肩膀同高、與箭一致。如果拉弦的手臂太後面，放箭後，箭不會筆直射出。

　　你可能會很訝異地發現，以手拉弓的射箭世界紀錄居然是驚人的1,222.01公尺，超過一公里的距離！以只有木材、弦跟手臂來說還不賴嘛，你不覺得嗎？

100　破案 (P. 238)

　　1247年的中國，宋慈撰寫《洗冤集錄》，書中包含了首份法醫科學的書面資料，法醫科學是用於解決法律問題的科學。書裡講述了一個調查員的故事，他為了解開謀殺疑雲，遠行至一個偏遠村莊。在檢視謀殺案受害者的傷口之後，他在動物的屍體上試驗了許多不同的武器，好確認兇手所使用的武器類型。之後，他請村民帶著他們的鐮刀，到市中心集合。蒼蠅漸漸聚集到其中一柄鐮刀上，因為那鐮刀上仍有大量血液的痕跡。最後鐮刀的主人情緒崩潰，俯首認罪。

　　幾百年過去了。在十九世紀後期的法國，亞歷山卓・拉卡薩涅研究子彈與槍枝的關聯。他的研究奠定了現今彈道指紋比對的基礎，讓調查員知道如何找出發射子彈的槍枝。

　　隨後，在1892年，阿根廷警察約翰・布塞蒂奇以指紋將謀殺案嫌犯定罪，震撼了全世界。最後，布塞蒂奇的指紋鑑定技術傳遍了全世界的警察單位。

　　另一個突破發生於15年後的德國。謀殺瑪格麗特・符爾伯的兇手遭到逮捕，因為調查員採集他鞋子上的泥土樣本，確認他行兇當天的行蹤。

　　1987年，一位名叫柯林・皮區佛克的英國男子，是第一位因DNA指紋分析證據被逮捕定罪的罪犯。調查員相信，若不是DNA指紋鑑定證明另一名17歲少年是無辜的，這名少年可能被誤判殺害了兩條人命。

　　時至今日，全世界的警力運用這些過去累積的突破性發展，並且加以整合，以協助警方辦案，像是美國政府單位建立了龐大的資料庫，包括DNA、指紋、塗料種類、輪胎胎紋、武器與子彈的製造資料等。

　　從只需要徹底洗淨鐮刀的日子到現在，看來，罪犯的日子愈來愈難過了。

Answers

Week 01

Day 1	1	1. a	2. b	3. c	4. b	5. a	6. b
Day 3	3	1. c	2. a	3. d	4. a	5. b	6. b
Day 5	5	1. b	2. d	3. a	4. c	5. c	6. d
Day 2	2	1. a	2. a	3. b	4. d	5. c	6. b
Day 4	4	1. d	2. c	3. c	4. a	5. d	6. b
Day 6	6	1. b	2. b	3. b	4. a	5. b	6. a

Week 02

Day 1	7	1. b	2. c	3. c	4. a	5. d	6. a
Day 3	9	1. d	2. c	3. a	4. c	5. a	6. c
Day 5	11	1. b	2. b	3. d	4. a	5. a	6. c
Day 2	8	1. b	2. a	3. d	4. a	5. b	6. c
Day 4	10	1. d	2. b	3. c	4. a	5. b	6. c
Day 6	12	1. d	2. a	3. c	4. b	5. b	6. c

Week 03

Day 1	13	1. c	2. a	3. b	4. d	5. a	6. d
Day 3	15	1. a	2. c	3. d	4. b	5. a	6. c
Day 5	17	1. c	2. b	3. b	4. a	5. b	6. d
Day 2	14	1. b	2. d	3. a	4. c	5. c	6. a
Day 4	16	1. c	2. b	3. d	4. c	5. a	6. a
Day 6	18	1. a	2. a	3. d	4. b	5. a	6. c

Week 04

Day 1	19	1. b	2. a	3. b	4. b	5. a	6. c
Day 3	21	1. a	2. b	3. d	4. a	5. c	6. b
Day 5	23	1. b	2. a	3. d	4. c	5. c	6. b
Day 2	20	1. d	2. b	3. a	4. c	5. b	6. d
Day 4	22	1. b	2. d	3. c	4. a	5. c	6. a
Day 6	24	1. d	2. b	3. c	4. b	5. d	6. b

Week 05

Day 1	25	1. b	2. c	3. c	4. a	5. b	6. a
Day 3	27	1. c	2. c	3. b	4. d	5. a	6. b
Day 5	29	1. c	2. d	3. b	4. d	5. c	6. b
Day 2	26	1. b	2. c	3. d	4. a	5. c	6. b
Day 4	28	1. b	2. c	3. d	4. a	5. a	6. c
Day 6	30	1. a	2. b	3. a	4. c	5. d	6. d

Week 06

Day 1	31	1. c	2. a	3. d	4. a	5. d	6. b
Day 3	33	1. b	2. c	3. c	4. b	5. b	6. b
Day 5	35	1. b	2. c	3. d	4. a	5. a	6. d
Day 2	32	1. d	2. b	3. b	4. c	5. d	6. a
Day 4	34	1. a	2. b	3. d	4. a	5. b	6. a
Day 6	36	1. c	2. b	3. d	4. a	5. b	6. d

Week 07

Day 1	37	1. c	2. b	3. b	4. a	5. a	6. c	Day 2	38	1. b	2. b	3. c	4. b	5. a	6. d
Day 3	39	1. b	2. d	3. c	4. a	5. d	6. b	Day 4	40	1. b	2. b	3. d	4. c	5. b	6. a
Day 5	41	1. d	2. d	3. b	4. d	5. a	6. c	Day 6	42	1. b	2. d	3. b	4. b	5. c	6. a

Week 08

Day 1	43	1. b	2. c	3. a	4. a	5. c	6. c	Day 2	44	1. c	2. a	3. d	4. b	5. b	6. d
Day 3	45	1. a	2. c	3. a	4. b	5. d	6. b	Day 4	46	1. b	2. a	3. c	4. c	5. a	6. a
Day 5	47	1. c	2. a	3. b	4. b	5. c	6. d	Day 6	48	1. b	2. b	3. c	4. b	5. a	6. c

Week 09

Day 1	49	1. d	2. a	3. c	4. a	5. b	6. c	Day 2	50	1. b	2. b	3. d	4. b	5. a	6. a
Day 3	51	1. a	2. b	3. d	4. b	5. a	6. d	Day 4	52	1. a	2. c	3. d	4. b	5. b	6. b
Day 5	53	1. b	2. a	3. b	4. b	5. c	6. a	Day 6	54	1. a	2. a	3. d	4. a	5. a	6. b

Week 10

Day 1	55	1. a	2. b	3. b	4. a	5. c	6. a	Day 2	56	1. b	2. a	3. d	4. c	5. a	6. a
Day 3	57	1. c	2. a	3. d	4. a	5. c	6. d	Day 4	58	1. a	2. d	3. b	4. a	5. d	6. a
Day 5	59	1. c	2. b	3. d	4. a	5. b	6. c	Day 6	60	1. c	2. d	3. a	4. d	5. c	6. b

Week 11

Day 1	61	1. b	2. a	3. c	4. d	5. a	6. b	Day 2	62	1. b	2. c	3. c	4. a	5. b	6. b
Day 3	63	1. c	2. b	3. d	4. b	5. c	6. c	Day 4	64	1. c	2. a	3. c	4. a	5. a	6. b
Day 5	65	1. b	2. c	3. d	4. a	5. a	6. b	Day 6	66	1. b	2. d	3. a	4. c	5. b	6. d

Week 12

Day 1	67	1. b	2. b	3. d	4. a	5. b	6. c	Day 2	68	1. c	2. a	3. b	4. a	5. b	6. d
Day 3	69	1. c	2. a	3. b	4. b	5. a	6. a	Day 4	70	1. a	2. c	3. c	4. c	5. a	6. d
Day 5	71	1. c	2. b	3. d	4. b	5. a	6. d	Day 6	72	1. c	2. b	3. c	4. d	5. b	6. b

ANSWERS

Week 13

Day 1	73	1. b	2. c	3. c	4. a	5. b	6. b	Day 2	74	1. a	2. c	3. c	4. b	5. b	6. b
Day 3	75	1. c	2. a	3. a	4. d	5. b	6. c	Day 4	76	1. d	2. c	3. d	4. a	5. b	6. b
Day 5	77	1. d	2. a	3. b	4. d	5. a	6. c	Day 6	78	1. d	2. b	3. c	4. a	5. b	6. d
Day 7	79	1. b	2. c	3. d	4. a	5. a	6. b								

Week 14

Day 1	80	1. a	2. c	3. d	4. b	5. a	6. b	Day 2	81	1. a	2. a	3. d	4. b	5. b	6. b
Day 3	82	1. c	2. a	3. b	4. d	5. a	6. d	Day 4	83	1. b	2. a	3. d	4. b	5. b	6. d
Day 5	84	1. a	2. d	3. b	4. c	5. b	6. d	Day 6	85	1. d	2. d	3. b	4. a	5. b	6. a
Day 7	86	1. a	2. d	3. c	4. a	5. b	6. d								

Week 15

Day 1	87	1. b	2. d	3. b	4. a	5. c	6. b	Day 2	88	1. b	2. a	3. d	4. a	5. d	6. c
Day 3	89	1. b	2. d	3. a	4. c	5. b	6. d	Day 4	90	1. b	2. b	3. d	4. b	5. a	6. b
Day 5	91	1. c	2. b	3. c	4. a	5. a	6. a	Day 6	92	1. b	2. d	3. c	4. b	5. a	6. c
Day 7	93	1. a	2. b	3. d	4. c	5. a	6. a								

Week 16

Day 1	94	1. c	2. a	3. b	4. a	5. b	6. d	Day 2	95	1. a	2. c	3. c	4. a	5. a	6. a
Day 3	96	1. b	2. b	3. c	4. d	5. a	6. d	Day 4	97	1. c	2. d	3. b	4. a	5. c	6. d
Day 5	98	1. a	2. b	3. d	4. a	5. b	6. a	Day 6	99	1. b	2. d	3. a	4. c	5. b	6. d
Day 7	100	1. b	2. c	3. d	4. a	5. b	6. b								

焦點英語閱讀 三版
六招打造核心素養閱讀力 3

作　　者	Owain Mckimm／Zachary Fillingham／Laura Phelps／Richard Luhrs
協力作者	Evan Gioia (Units 6, 11, 13, 21, 40, 47)／Maddie Smith (Units 10, 59)
譯　　者	黃詩韻／林育珊／邱佳皇
審　　訂	Helen Yeh／Treva Adams
企劃編輯	葉俞均
編　　輯	王婷葦／柯宜芝
主　　編	丁宥暄
校　　對	申文怡／陳慧莉
內文排版	陳瀅竹／林書玉
封面設計	林書玉
圖　　片	Shutterstock
製程管理	洪巧玲
出 版 者	寂天文化事業股份有限公司
發 行 人	黃朝萍
電　　話	+886-(0)2-2365-9739
傳　　真	+886-(0)2-2365-9835
網　　址	www.icosmos.com.tw
讀者服務	onlineservice@icosmos.com.tw
出版日期	2024 年 8 月 三版三刷（寂天雲 Mebook 電子書 APP 版）

Copyright © 2017 by COSMOS CULTURE LTD.
版權所有　請勿翻印

郵撥帳號 1998620-0 寂天文化事業股份有限公司
訂書金額未滿 1000 元，請外加運費 100 元。
〔若有破損，請寄回更換，謝謝。〕

國家圖書館出版品預行編目 (CIP) 資料

焦點英語閱讀. 3, 六招打造素養閱讀力 (寂天雲 Mebook 互動學習 APP 版)/ Michelle Witte 等作；黃詩韻, 林育珊, 邱佳皇譯.
 -- 三版. -- [臺北市]：寂天文化, 2024.08 印刷
　面；　公分
ISBN 978-626-300-273-9 (16K 平裝)

1.CST: 英語 2.CST: 讀本

805.18　　　　　　　　　　　　　　　　1130110

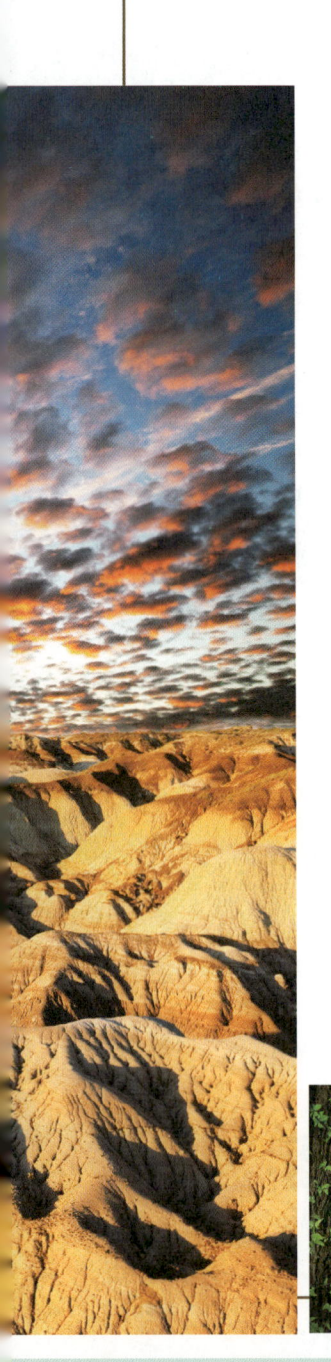